PRAISE FOR ROBERT ELLIS

Murder Season

"*Murder Season*: a terrific sick-soul-of-LA thriller. Before you can say *Chinatown* we are immersed in a tale of mind-boggling corruption where virtually every character in the book—with the exception of Lena—has a hidden agenda. Ellis is a master plotter. Along the way we meet wonderful characters."

—*Connecticut Post*, Hearst Media News Group

"Within the space of a few books, Ellis has demonstrated that rare ability to skillfully navigate his readers through a complex plot filled with interesting, dangerous, and surprising characters."

—Bookreporter.com

"Best Mystery/Crime Novels of 2011."

—*Deadly Pleasures Mystery Magazine*

"Top Twelve Books of 2011."

—*Miami Examiner*

The Lost Witness

"Scorchin⋯⋯⋯⋯⋯⋯⋯⋯⋯⋯⋯⋯ appears to be. Ellis succe⋯⋯⋯⋯⋯⋯⋯⋯⋯⋯ulling surprise after surp⋯⋯⋯⋯⋯⋯⋯⋯⋯⋯plunging down a mounta⋯⋯⋯⋯⋯⋯⋯⋯⋯⋯, starred review

"Ellis serves up a killer crime tale with riveting characters and relentless twists."

—*Booklist*, starred review

"Ellis piles on the Hollywood atmosphere and procedural detail, and the end revelation is expertly timed and genuinely shocking."

—The *Guardian* (UK)

"*The Lost Witness* is a tough thriller that makes Ellis a name to watch."

—The *Evening Telegraph* (UK)

"*The Lost Witness* is another gripping story by a writer who knows the seamy LA underworld well."

—*Toronto Sun*

City of Fire

"Los Angeles, under a cloud of acrid smoke . . . Robert Ellis's *City of Fire* is a gripping, spooky crime novel."

—The *New York Times* Hot List Pick

"*City of Fire* is my kind of crime novel. Gritty, tight and assured. Riding with Detective Lena Gamble through the hills of Los Angeles is something I could get used to. She's tough, smart, and most of all, she's real."

—Michael Connelly

"*City of Fire* by Robert Ellis is a no-holds-barred barn burner of a thriller that blends Los Angeles–style crime fiction à la Michael Connelly with pulse-pounding Dean Koontzian psychological suspense. Like Connelly's gritty Bosch saga, *City of Fire* features a tough but deeply flawed protagonist, a tantalizingly complex plot, fully realized—and realistic—characters, and most of all, a palpable intensity. And if that weren't enough, the bombshell plot twist at the novel's conclusion makes this an absolute must-read for thriller aficionados."

—*Chicago Tribune*

"Robert Ellis's brisk, complex *City of Fire* is hot stuff. Ellis excels at vivid writing and the expert plotting keeps the reader off-kilter. Ellis takes the police procedural and makes it a tale of personal corruption and desire, where right and wrong overlap. Here, the answers aren't easy as Lena wonders about 'blowback . . . what the truth could do to a soul.' LA, which is written about so often, seems fresh in the hands of an original storyteller such as Ellis."

—Best Mysteries of 2007, Oline H. Cogdill,
South Florida Sun-Sentinel

"*City of Fire* begins like a roller coaster, building tension, anxiety and fear. Then it plunges at full speed, spiraling and twisting through scenes that will have hearts pounding and fingers flying through the pages. But there is no smooth braking to a stop in this book. It careens to the end and then flies off the rail with a shocking twist that will leave readers stunned. Robert Ellis is a master of suspense."

—*Mystery Scene*

ALSO BY ROBERT ELLIS

Murder Season
The Lost Witness
City of Fire
The Dead Room
Access to Power

CITY OF ECHOES

CITY OF ECHOES

ROBERT ELLIS

THOMAS & MERCER

Published by Thomas & Mercer, Seattle

www.apub.com

Amazon, the Amazon logo, and Thomas & Mercer are trademarks of Amazon.com, Inc., or its affiliates.

ISBN-13: 9781477827727
ISBN-10: 1477827722

Cover design by Marc Cohen

Library of Congress Control Number: 2014959519

Printed in the United States of America

This novel is dedicated to my friend Denny Donahue

"The power to guess the unseen from the seen, to trace the implications of things, to judge the whole piece by the pattern, the condition of feeling life in general so completely that you are well on your way to knowing any particular corner of it—this cluster of gifts may almost be said to constitute experience."

—*Henry James*

CHAPTER 1

Matthew Trevor Jones shivered as he walked down the sidewalk and entered the restaurant. He could feel a cool breeze sweep across the back of his neck, the door snapping shut behind him. When the cold air finally dissipated, he started toward the bar, searching for a familiar face but not finding one.

It was Tuesday night, and he could smell corned beef and cabbage, fifty-dollar steaks with twice-baked potatoes, and that long list of other scents and fragrances that usually accompany a crowded dining room. He could feel his body warming up to it all, the tension of the day beginning to fade and die out.

The moment was exceedingly pleasant.

When his friend had suggested that they meet at Musso & Frank to celebrate his promotion to Hollywood Homicide, Matt thought about the pricey menu, but only for a second or two. He was excited about his new job as a homicide detective—stoked to be working in Hollywood in spite of the commute he would be facing every day between here and his house on the Westside. But even more, Musso & Frank was the oldest grill in LA, and he loved everything about the place: the waitstaff storming in and out of the kitchen, the sound of loud chatter, of laughter, forks and knives and plates being gathered and stacked—that thunderous din that somehow seemed so soothing as it struck the wood-paneled walls and laughed out loud, refusing to be dampened or quieted or shut down. He knew that he had just entered a restaurant on Hollywood Boulevard, but everything about the place smacked of New York. Everything about it reminded him of train rides into the city as a teenager and the modest home in New Jersey where he had been raised by his aunt. Everything about it brought back memories of his aunt and their life together. At least the good ones.

The front door swung open.

Matt turned and watched a young couple enter, the woman smiling at the maître d' as she smoothed back her blond hair. Even though he didn't recognize her, Matt guessed that she might be an actress. People were eyeing her from their tables as if she was, and no one looked away as she strolled down the aisle with her friend toward an open table that seemed more private than the rest. From the sleepy look in the young woman's eyes, the glint, the joy, the easy way she carried her body—and from where Matt stood, it was a better than decent body—he could tell she liked attention.

He watched her take her seat before turning away to check the time. It was early. Hughes wouldn't show for another twenty minutes, maybe even a half hour. Spotting an empty stool at the bar, Matt sat down and ordered a beer, then noticed his cell phone vibrating in his pocket. He pulled it out and checked the touch screen, hoping that it might be Hughes. Instead, he found the name of his new supervisor, Lieutenant Bob Grace, blinking on the display. They had met for the first time earlier in the day. Grace had given Matt a tour of the Hollywood station, shown him where his desk would be in the morning, and introduced him to his new partner, Denny Cabrera, who only had fifteen minutes because he was on his way to court.

Matt took in a nervous breath and exhaled as he stepped away from the bar to take the call.

"Sounds like you're celebrating," Grace said.

"Not yet."

"So everything's cool? You're still good?"

Matt could hear the worry in his supervisor's voice. It seemed obvious that Grace wanted to know if he had been drinking. But even more, it seemed clear that he needed to know he could trust Matt's answer.

"Everything's good," Matt said. "I just got here, Lieutenant. What's up? What can I do?"

Grace cleared his throat. "You were supposed to start tomorrow, Jones. I know that's how we left it. But I'm in deep shit, and I need you tonight."

"What's happened?"

"Somebody's been murdered in Hollywood. That's all I know. That's all it takes."

Matt glanced at the blonde seated with her friend, both caught up in the good mood of the room and laughing like they didn't have a care in the world.

"Where?" he asked.

"Between Yucca and Hollywood on North Cherokee. You can't miss it. You'll see why it's so fucked up when you get there."

"I'm still in Hollywood," Matt said. "I'm only a block away."

"That's even better. Listen, Jones, I realize I'm throwing you into the fire on this one, but it can't be helped. We've had a bad week. You and Cabrera are all I've got left tonight."

All I've got left . . .

Matt understood what Grace meant and didn't take it as a slight. Cabrera was almost as green as Matt, with just three months under his belt working in Hollywood. Between the economy and the budget cutbacks that had come out of Washington and Sacramento, cops had been pulled off the street, and crime had become a burgeoning industry. Both detectives had been fast-tracked to Homicide.

"Don't worry about it," he said to Grace. "Where's Cabrera?"

"He just walked out of the squad room. He'll be there in five minutes. So will the coroner's investigator and the crime lab. They were shutting down another crime scene when the call came in. They're coming from Melrose. Everybody's close by."

"Then I better get going."

"Listen, Jones. This is your first . . ."

Grace stopped talking. Even through the loud din, Matt could sense his supervisor's concern fermenting in the break.

"My first what?" Matt said, feigning naïveté.

Grace remained quiet. When he finally spoke, his voice had changed.

"You know what I'm saying, Matt. Just take it easy. If you've got any questions, call me, no matter what time it is, okay?"

"Okay. We'll touch base later."

"Thanks," Grace said. "And I'll make this up to you. I promise. Now keep your eyes open and be safe."

Matt ended the call. As he hurried out the front door, he sent a quick text message to Hughes. All it said was: *Dinner off. Call me.* His fingers were trembling. He felt that cold breeze working the back of his neck again. Halfway across the sidewalk, he realized that he'd just stepped out of the warmth and into the wind.

CHAPTER 2

You'll see why it's so fucked up when you get there . . .

Matt kept replaying the words in his head. He should have asked Grace what the hell he meant, but his head had been spinning through most of the conversation. By the time he thought about it, he was already out the door hustling over to his car, parked at the curb. Now his stomach was churning and he couldn't seem to catch his breath.

He popped open the trunk, pulled a hooded sweatshirt over his head, and got into his windbreaker. Starting down the sidewalk, he tried to keep a measured pace, which was difficult because he could see the flashing lights from the first-response units beating against the side of a building on North Cherokee Avenue. He lowered his gaze, passing a souvenir shop on the corner. Inside the store he could see a middle-aged couple standing before the window display filled with hundreds of fake Oscar statuettes. Ordinarily, the sight of tourists picking out their Oscar would have given him a lift, but tonight no longer seemed very ordinary.

You'll see why it's so fucked up when you get there . . .

The truth was that Matt didn't understand why he felt so anxious, no matter what his supervisor may have had in mind. It was something about being on a homicide investigation. Some odd combination of excitement and terror that didn't make any sense but kept following him, just as it did a few years back when he left his uniform behind and started working narcotics.

He turned the corner and gazed up the tree-lined street. It looked like the murder had occurred in the middle of the block in what appeared to be a near-empty parking lot. Four patrol units had barricaded the street with their cars. While two cops were stringing crime-scene tape from tree to tree, another five were asking onlookers to back down and move to the corner on Hollywood Boulevard.

You'll see why it's so fucked up when you get there . . .

It seemed more than odd that so many cops had arrived on foot this quickly. The number of bicycles parked on the sidewalk didn't fit either. But as Matt cleared the trees and glanced across the street, he caught the sign in the storefront and knew in an instant why Grace had been so rattled.

It was an LAPD community station.

The murder had been committed in a parking lot directly across the street and within fifty yards of the station's glass doors. The only barrier between the two locations was a wrought-iron fence about six feet high and a hedge bordering the parking lot. Matt read the sign painted beneath the LAPD logo on the storefront window.

Because We Care.

If you couldn't find a safe spot outside a police station in Los Angeles, where could you?

He tried to let the thought go, but still, this was the City of Angels, and the answer had a certain sting to it. One that he knew would make the late-night news and embarrass the department.

He turned away and spotted a cop with a clipboard standing by the entrance to the parking lot. Digging his badge out of his pocket, he signed in, then ducked beneath the yellow crime-scene tape. A photographer was already on scene, ripping off rapid-fire shots of a black SUV, the white-hot light from his flash unit pulsating all over the vehicle and what was obviously ground zero. The truck from the Scientific Investigation Division was already here as well. Large blue tarps were being stretched across the perimeter to block the scene from the television cameras that were beginning to assemble on the corner.

When Matt heard someone call out his name, he turned back and saw his new partner hurrying toward him.

"You think it's him?" Cabrera said with his eyes locked on the SUV.

Matt shrugged. "Who?"

"The stickup guy. The three-piece bandit. You think he finally shot somebody?"

"It's a little soon, isn't it?"

"I'm just saying . . ."

Matt gave him a look. "I know exactly what you're saying. We just got here, Cabrera. Who the hell knows?"

It was a bad exchange for a first exchange with a new partner, and Matt knew it. He turned back to the SUV, his heart pounding in his chest as he stepped around the shell casings littering the asphalt. There was something unusual about them but it didn't cut through, the condition of the SUV too mesmerizing. It looked like every window in the vehicle had been shot out. Three rounds had pierced the driver's-side door. Still, he couldn't see who was inside the car. When he finally got close enough to ease his head through the window, he got the view he had been looking for in all its harshness, then flinched before he could catch himself.

What was left of the victim appeared to be stretched across the front seats on its back. In spite of the multiple gunshot wounds to the face, chest, and shoulders, in spite of the blood splashed all over the body and interior of the car, in spite of the blanket of shattered glass the corpse was wearing from head to toe, Matt's best guess was that the victim underneath was male. Still, it was only a guess.

He felt Cabrera move in beside him and thought he heard his partner sigh as he got his look and took the blow.

"I'm sorry," Matt said in a low voice.

Cabrera glanced at him, then back at the dead body. "Sorry for what?"

"What I did back there. What I said."

"Forget it," Cabrera said.

Matt nodded, his eyes fixed on the corpse. "You think it's a man or a woman?"

"I've got no idea. These shitheads don't take time to aim anymore. They watch too much TV. They fly sideways. They pull the trigger and spray, then it's done and run."

Matt didn't say anything, watching the photographer frame his camera from the passenger-side window. As the man burst through another series of rapid-fire shots, the corpse appeared to be vibrating in the light. Matt found the simulated animation of the body extraordinarily unnerving. For a half second he thought it might really be moving. That everything he was seeing had been staged for his benefit as some kind of sick initiation by the department.

Welcome to Hollywood Homicide. The dead body in the shot-up SUV was just about to sit up and say boo.

He wished for it, hoped for it, but knew that it was only a fantasy.

Cabrera gave him a nudge and pointed to the victim's left arm. "Maybe it really was a holdup."

Matt didn't get it until he tilted his head to the right and spotted the gunshot wound on the inside of the victim's left forearm. He understood that he was staring at an entrance wound, and that whoever this was had most likely been holding their arms up at the time of the shooting. But even more, it was a big wound. Way too big to have been made by a 9 mm pistol. He remembered those shell casings on the pavement. At a glance they had appeared longer than most. But just as he turned to look, he noticed a pair of cops standing off to the side and realized that they were waiting for him.

"You guys get here first?" he said.

They nodded at him and stepped out of the shadows, the older of the two introducing himself as Hank Andrews, with his partner, Travis Green.

Matt moved closer to shake hands. "You run the plates?"

Andrews nodded. "A GM dealership over at the auto mall on Brand. They're closed. We're trying to track down the manager, but he's not answering his cell."

"How'd you get his cell number?"

"Glendale PD gave us his home number. He's got a live-in girlfriend. She doesn't know where he is. She's worried about him."

"Did she give you a description?"

Andrews nodded again.

"Does it match?"

The cop fought off a grimace. "You looked inside that window just the same as we did, Detective. Who could tell?"

A cell phone began chirping from the SUV.

Matt rushed back to the driver's-side window and gazed inside with Cabrera. The phone was set in the ashtray, blinking on and off and lighting up the dash. Matt turned to the photographer in the passenger-side window as he dug a pair of vinyl gloves out of his pocket and slipped them on.

"You got a shot of the phone?" he said.

The photographer pulled his eye away from the camera and nodded. "From every angle. Go ahead, pal. Take the call."

The phone stopped chirping and went dark. Matt glanced back at Cabrera, then reached inside and carefully lifted it up and out of the SUV. He could feel the weight of everyone's gaze on him as he flipped it over and slid the lock open with his thumb.

The phone lit up, indicating that the caller had left a message. A long moment passed as Matt gazed at the display and noticed that the usual banter that makes up a crime scene had been overwhelmed by a wave of absolute silence. His eyes made a second sweep across the display; then he clicked through to the next screen. The murder victim had just received a text message. It was short and to the point. All it said was: *Dinner off. Call me.*

CHAPTER 3

Matthew Trevor Jones. Matthew Trevor Jones. I'm jonesing for Jones. Ya hear that, Jones? Everybody here's jonesing for Jones. Now cut the shit and wake the fuck up. We got your ass, ya know what I'm sayin', Jones? We got your sorry ass outta that desert shithole and brought it the fuck back to—

The dream had a roll to it. Movement, but no definition. Matt wasn't really sure what had happened.

He could see a blanket draped over his body and feel the rails of a rescue stretcher below his waist. An EMT was leaning against the open rear door of an ambulance but had turned away to wave at someone just as their eyes met. When Matt thought he heard the rotors from a chopper, he looked toward the sound, but all he saw was a bus lumbering through an intersection on a busy street.

A busy street in the US.

He filled his lungs with air and, as he exhaled, tried to break through the fog. He could see a parking attendant's shack on the other side of the lot, a billboard, and the rear entrance to a restaurant called Musso & Frank, but nothing about the place registered. Squinting at the bright work lights mounted on stands to his right, he noticed that they were pointed at a black SUV. A handful of people were here—some wearing police uniforms, others dressed in street clothes—yet every one of them seemed infatuated by that SUV.

He turned back to the ambulance. A man with a badge clipped . to his leather jacket had joined the EMT, and it looked like they were whispering.

Something about the cop's face seemed familiar, but as he sized him up, he couldn't find the memory. He was dressed casually and wore a heavy sweater beneath his jacket. Matt guessed that he stood just short of six feet tall and was about thirty years old. His black wiry hair was cropped so close to his skull that it looked more like a three-day beard against his dark complexion. When he finally stopped whispering to the EMT and turned to him, Matt noticed that his eyes were glazed. It seemed more than obvious that he was deeply troubled about something.

Matt heaved his body forward and struggled to sit up. Both men rushed over, but he pushed them away, rubbing his fingers back and forth over his eyes and forehead. He could hear the cop jabbering in his ear through the haze.

Matt, are you okay? You blacked out, man. Are you okay, Matt? Are you okay?

The wind picked up. A cup of piping hot coffee came out of nowhere. Matt took a short first sip, then another, until he looked up at the cop's chiseled face and something changed. Maybe it was what he still saw in his eyes, the spark and worry reflecting back at him. Maybe it was something else. Either way, Matt could feel himself breaking the surface hard. He could feel the push of reality, no longer scrambled, in all its starkness.

Something horrible had happened tonight.

Something worse than that.

Matt searched for his voice, the words coming out low and rough. "Tell me what happened? How long have I been out?"

Cabrera leaned closer, resting his hand on his shoulder. "You blacked out, man. You were standing over there by the SUV. You were looking at something on the cell phone. Then all of a sudden you went down like you took one on the chin."

"Where's the phone?"

"It broke when it hit the ground. SID says they can recover whatever was on it, but they'll have to do it in the lab."

Dinner off. Call me.

Matt shook his head at the memory. "Is the body still here?"

Cabrera gave him a look and nodded. "They're bagging it up right now."

"Give me a hand. I need to see it."

"You sure?"

"Yeah, Denny. I'm sure."

Matt reached out for Cabrera's arm, holding on until he found his balance. After a few moments they made their way over to the SUV and watched as the investigator from the coroner's office gave the nod. Then the corpse was hoisted out of the vehicle and into a blue body bag set atop another stretcher. Matt could hear shards of broken glass raining onto the pavement as the body was moved. He could smell the blood, the meat. When someone tried to zip up the bag, he grabbed their hand and pushed it away.

He needed to take a look at the murder victim. A long last look, no matter how deep it cut.

Cabrera switched on his flashlight, shining it on the corpse. "It's like this, Matt. We haven't been able to reach the manager at that GM dealership in Glendale. But the victim's a male and, according to Gainer here, about the right age. The driver's-side window was down, like he was talking to somebody. His wallet's missing, and we haven't found a watch or any jewelry. Glendale PD has agreed to pick up his girlfriend and bring her down to the coroner's office for a possible ID."

Matt glanced at the investigator from the coroner's office and nodded. He had met Ed Gainer a year ago when a drug deal ended in a shoot-out on Main Street in Venice. The shooting had occurred on a Sunday afternoon, when both the streets and beach were wall-to-wall people. Innocent people mixed with gang trash. Gainer's calm demeanor had rubbed off on everyone as they searched for the wounded and covered ten people who were dead.

Matt turned back to the corpse in the body bag, trying to see through the coating of blood and shattered glass. The lines of the victim's face and nose. Zeroing in on the left hand, he began searching for a wedding band that Cabrera had already told him would not be there. The joint in the victim's fourth finger appeared broken, as if the ring had been yanked off with force. He looked back at the gunshot wound on the inside of the victim's left forearm, calculating the odds of pulling into a parking lot and meeting the three-piece bandit on the night the robber decided to become the world's next killer.

"You find a weapon?" he said, still thinking it through.

Cabrera shook his head. "On the victim? No. Why?"

"What about the shell casings on the ground? They stood out. They seemed long."

"Ten-millimeter Auto rounds. Fifteen of them."

Another memory surfaced. Matt had been reading a brochure about a Glock 20 just a few days ago. The pistol fired 10 mm Auto cartridges and had a magazine capacity of fifteen rounds. The manufacturer had described the semiautomatic as the perfect weapon to deliver a safe and accurate finishing shot when hunting big game, the 10 mm Auto rounds providing maximum ballistic performance and maximum penetrative power. The ultimate force.

The kill after the stickup had been made with a Glock 20, a virtual cannon. One shot would have been enough. This asshole had used all fifteen.

Matt gripped the stretcher to steady himself as it sunk in, his voice barely audible. "You need to call Glendale PD, Denny. Tell them to turn around. They can take the live-in girlfriend home."

Cabrera looked back in confusion. "What are you talking about?"

"This isn't her boyfriend."

"How could you possibly tell?"

Matt turned to the victim's face, still trying to see through the horror and form a clear picture, still trying to look back in time.

"Because I know him," he said finally. "We were meeting here for dinner tonight."

"You know who this is? The guy drives a black SUV?"

Matt shook his head. "He drives a silver Escalade. This must be a loaner."

"A loaner? How can you be sure? Look at him, Matt. How could anyone be sure?"

Matt tightened his grip on the stretcher and met his partner's eyes. "His phone, Denny. The knockout punch. The text on his phone came from me. He's a cop. He's a detective from North Hollywood. We were friends. His name's Kevin Hughes. He wore a watch and a gold wedding band. He carried a wallet and a gun. And now the asshole who did this to him has everything, including his ID and an LAPD badge."

Cabrera switched off the flashlight. A long moment passed, and no one moved. Somehow Matt had managed to say what he needed to say.

He took a last look at his friend, buried in the darkness of that body bag. Then he turned and walked away, hoping he wouldn't trip or fall down as he heard someone zip up the bag. He could feel a certain weight on his back again. A prickling sensation between his shoulder blades. Either everyone was staring at him, or it was the mix of juice and terror and now despair, that odd combination that felt so hideous tonight. So rotten. He wiped his eyes and brushed his fingers over his cheeks—he didn't want to lose it in front of everyone. As he tried to pull himself together, he saw a man leaning against the fence. It was Hughes's partner, Frankie Lane, staring at him as if the world had just stopped spinning and tumbled through a black hole. Frankie was supposed to have joined them for a couple of beers, maybe stay for dinner if he could.

Their eyes met. Matt nodded slowly, almost imperceptibly, then watched Frankie wilt onto the fence.

Welcome to Hollywood Homicide.

CHAPTER 4

It wasn't very big, but it was beautiful: a two-story Mediterranean off West Kenneth Road in Glendale. The grounds were heavily landscaped, the gardens, stepping down the hill to a small pool and spa in the backyard, more than just lush. Over the rear wall was a picture-perfect view of both Glendale and downtown Los Angeles, a view that had become lost in the trees and forgotten by the original owner, who sold the house cheap before his bank could steal it away and foreclose.

Matt couldn't see any of this because it was 3:00 a.m. and he was still sitting in his car. He'd been parked across the street for the better part of an hour, sipping coffee and chewing nicotine gum while trying to decide how to go about the impossible task of walking up to that house and ringing the doorbell.

Matt had never made a next-of-kin notification before, yet he had a feeling that this one wouldn't require many words. He was wearing the news on his face. On his person. One look and Hughes's wife, Laura, would know.

During the course of the night, any doubt as to the identity of the murder victim had been lifted. By 10:00 p.m. the manager from the GM dealership had been located at a bar in Eagle Rock. By 10:30 they had the name of the customer who had been given the black SUV as a loaner while his Escalade was being serviced. An hour later a tech from SID called from the lab to say he had brought the cell phone back to life.

Matt glanced at his watch. Seconds had ticked by, not minutes, and it was still 3:00 a.m.

He took another sip of coffee and looked back at the house. Except for a small table lamp burning in the foyer by the front door, every window in the place was dark, peaceful, and at rest.

Hughes had been more than a friend to him. More, even, than a mentor. After their tour of duty in Afghanistan, it had been Hughes who convinced Matt to write off his troubles by leaving the East Coast and moving to Los Angeles. It had been Hughes who took him under his wing and brought him into the department. Matt's aunt had died six months before he enlisted. He could remember Hughes telling him that there was no longer a good reason to live in New Jersey. It was time to begin what he called *the forgetting process*. LA was a city of distraction that ran 24/7. Any bad dreams he might still be carrying from his childhood, any losses, any monkeys still clinging to his back would be wiped out by the bright sunlight and what they'd just been through overseas.

Matt got out of the car, his jaw muscles twitching. He took a step toward the house and then another, struggling to dampen his mind. He could hear a small pack of coyotes yipping and howling further up the hill as he reached the walkway. The kitelike sound of the wind blowing through the palm trees in the dark sky above. As he climbed the front steps, he took a quick glimpse through the window and saw a note on the table by the lamp. The note had been left for Hughes by his wife, and seeing it felt like a flock of blackbirds had just flown through his soul.

He turned away, staring at the illuminated doorbell for a long time. Then he finally pressed the button and listened to the chimes invading the serenity of the house. A lamp on the second floor switched on, its light spilling onto the front lawn. Looking through the window again, he waited to see Laura walk down the staircase. When several minutes passed and nothing happened, he rang the bell again and moved closer to the window so that she would be able to see his face from the landing.

More time passed, nervous beats in the center of his chest followed by quick breaths. The hallway on the second floor remained dark. Matt thought it over. It was the dead of night. She wasn't going to answer the door.

He pulled out his phone, found Hughes's home number, and hit Call. Laura picked up on the first ring and sounded frightened.

"There's someone at the front door," she said. "There's someone trying to get into the house."

Matt paused a moment. What came next was inevitable.

"It's not a burglar," he said. "It's me, Laura. I just rang your doorbell."

"What are you doing here? Where's Kevin? Why isn't he answering his cell phone?"

Inevitable.

"Come downstairs and open the door, Laura. We need to talk."

Inevitable.

He could hear the change. The sudden short gasp. The quick flash of dread.

"Oh, God. Oh my God."

He slipped the phone into his pocket and took a step back. He tried to keep cool, but he could hear her shrieking through the door as she raced downstairs and fumbled with the locks. When the door finally opened, their eyes met, but only briefly before she pulled him inside and buried her head in his chest. Her cries came from a place where nothing was left. Deep and dark and all the way through. She kept repeating words that were difficult to understand. Eventually, Matt realized that she was begging him to say that Kevin wasn't really dead. That the man she loved could be brought back.

He led her into the kitchen. After hitting the light switch with his elbow, he guided her over to the breakfast table and eased her into a chair. When she looked up at him, she seemed so helpless, so wounded, that he couldn't hold the gaze.

"What happened, Matt? Tell me. You were meeting for dinner. Your new job. It was supposed to be a celebration."

"You want a drink? A cup of coffee?"

She shook her head and wiped her cheeks, her soft voice breaking up. "Tell me what happened to Kevin. Tell me what happened."

Matt spotted a box of tissues on the counter by the sink. As he reached for it, he noticed a pregnancy test kit on the windowsill and thought he might lose it.

"I don't know, Laura," he said. "We think he was shot during a holdup."

She cocked her head, as if she didn't understand. "For money?"

Her voice was so faint. Matt nodded and sat down beside her, watching her struggle to put it together.

"But Kevin never carried a lot of cash," she said.

"Is there anyone I can call? Anyone who could come over and be with you?"

"He never carried a lot of cash," she repeated quietly.

Her dirty blond hair was tangled from sleep, her deep blue eyes wet as rain. She was wearing a T-shirt and a pair of cotton pajama bottoms with images of flowers and rainbows and pots of gold. Matt thought about that test kit on the windowsill and wondered if she was pregnant. He wished he hadn't seen it.

"Do you know who did it?" she managed.

"We think so," he said in a gentle voice. "But he's never shot anyone before."

"Someone saw him?"

Matt shook his head. "It's early. We're still working on it."

Laura closed her eyes and started weeping again. After several moments she began to speak as if she were alone in the room.

"I was so worried about him . . . so worried . . . while he was away . . . I waited and worried . . . I watched the news every night and had nightmares that he wasn't gonna come home . . . that I'd never see him again . . . when I woke up, I felt guilty for having them, but I couldn't make them stop." She opened her eyes, still looking inward. "And then he comes home . . . Kevin comes back to me, and it happens here . . . it happens here . . . for his money . . . his cash . . ."

Her voice died off. Matt didn't say anything. He couldn't find the words. He couldn't get past the image of his friend buried in the dark hole of that body bag. He couldn't turn off the memory or wrestle it to the ground. The blood. The shattered glass. A bag of human flesh with no form.

He felt his cell phone in his pocket. He wasn't sure how long it had been vibrating. After a while he pulled it out, glanced at the name on the display without really seeing it, but took the call.

"What is it?" he said quietly.

"What's wrong with your voice, Jones?"

It was his supervisor, Lieutenant Bob Grace. Matt sat up and tried to pull himself together, but together still seemed a long way off tonight.

"I'm in the middle of something," he said. "I didn't know it was you."

Grace hesitated for a moment. "Where are you?"

"At the house with his wife."

"Why is it taking so long?"

Matt walked over to the sink and gazed out the window at the gardens and pool. "What is it? Why did you call me?"

"You need to wrap it up, Matt. You need to come back in as soon as you can."

He turned to check on Laura. She was still inside herself and didn't appear to notice that he was even on the phone. Her lips were quivering. She was talking to herself again, only this time in utter silence. He thought she might need a doctor.

Matt turned back to the window and lowered his voice. "Did something happen, Lieutenant?"

"We'll talk about it when you get here. I'm waiting with Cabrera in my office. Do your best for her, but get back here as soon as you can."

Matt started to say something, then stopped when he heard the phone click and realized that Grace had hung up.

CHAPTER 5

He'd left her in ruin . . . but with the promise that he would come back as soon as he could. He had been straight with her—in all likelihood he wouldn't return for a while. He could remember her giving him the nod, like she'd heard him. She had found his eyes and met them like she understood. Still, he had felt uneasy about leaving her alone because he wasn't sure. In the end he'd called her neighbor, a woman Laura told him she liked and was becoming a friend.

Matt made the turn onto Pacific Avenue, gunning it down the hill toward the 134 Freeway. He spotted a cop hiding in the lot at the Jack in the Box, so he slowed down until he passed the next traffic light, then clicked through the six-speed manual transmission and rocketed up the ramp. The transition to the Golden State Freeway was just ahead. At 4:00 a.m. traffic would be light and he could circle Griffith Park and reach the Hollywood station in less than fifteen minutes. He was driving a metallic gray Honda coupe. The car was fast but light, and at ninety miles an hour he could feel the wind beating against the windshield and trying to crash through.

He took a deep breath and exhaled slowly, settling into the seat and wondering why Cabrera and Grace were waiting for him. Over the five hours that Matt had remained at the crime scene, no one had come forward. Not even the parking attendant could shed any light on what had happened. It was a cold night, the old man had told them. He went inside the restaurant for a cup of coffee and was away from his booth for ten to fifteen minutes.

But maybe something had turned up when the patrol units canvassed the neighborhood. The Las Palmas Hotel cut into the north end of the parking lot. Across the street on the next block stood a new apartment building, and Matt had counted twenty-five units with windows and balconies.

Before Matt left to give Laura the news, he and Cabrera had received word that a man fitting the description of the three-piece bandit had botched a holdup five blocks away about an hour before Hughes was killed. It didn't feel like much of a long shot that the robber had become frustrated and moved to the lot behind Musso & Frank. When he spotted Hughes in the SUV, he tried again.

Matt glided off the freeway and blew through the first red light on Los Feliz Boulevard. As he raced up the hill, rain began pelting the windshield, and he could feel his tires slipping on the asphalt. He glanced at the speedometer—a cool fifty—then looked back at the road. Water was already beginning to stream along the curb. He tightened his grip on the wheel and eased into the left lane instead of slowing down.

Matt had transferred from the Pacific Division but was well aware of the string of holdups that had been occurring in Hollywood and along the Strip. The flyer that patrol units were passing out tonight had been posted at every station in Los Angeles County for the last six months. With each new holdup, victims were interviewed and reinterviewed, the flyer updated, and the composite sketch refined.

A white male in his midtwenties, average in height and build, wearing shades and a hooded sweatshirt was too common to make an impression on anyone in LA. But the shirt and tie underneath, the gray flannel slacks, and the gun he was holding did. Even more, one of his first victims happened to be a gun enthusiast and was able to identify the pistol as a Glock 20. In spite of the heavy firepower, the young man's demeanor hadn't appeared overly threatening. According to most witnesses, he was soft-spoken and polite, the holdups conducted quickly, oftentimes while victims were distracted and just getting out of their cars. Months earlier, when the LAPD began passing out flyers in concert with the Sheriff's Department in West Hollywood, a reporter from the *Los Angeles Times* read the description of what sounded like a young urban professional and gave the robber a nickname that stuck: the three-piece bandit.

Matt didn't like the nickname because he thought it softened the blow. No one who conducted their business at gunpoint could be considered soft-spoken or polite.

The rain picked up in a hard wave and sounded like stones hammering the roof of the car. Matt slowed some as he hit the light at Franklin, then floored it down Western. Once he made the right onto Sunset, he thought about the gun. The Glock 20. It had been mentioned in the flyer and on TV, along with advice to the public on how to act if they were ever confronted by the man.

If you must reach for something or move in any way, tell the robber what to expect so that he won't be startled. A suspicious move may trigger a violent reaction, endangering your life and others. Follow the robber's commands, but do not volunteer to help. The longer the robbery takes, the more nervous the robber may become, escalating the chances of a violent outcome.

Matt wondered how Hughes had handled himself. His gut told him that Hughes knew the drill and would have complied. That there was no reason to fire the gun. No reason for the man in the suit to become a killer. Any response from Hughes would have occurred after the holdup, when the robber backed off and tried to get away.

Matt drove down Wilcox and pulled into the lot behind the station. As he ran through the cold rain, all he could think about was Cabrera. He hoped his new partner had lucked out. He hoped Cabrera had snagged them a witness, or even better, a lead.

CHAPTER 6

He found them in Grace's office and, from the sullen looks on their faces, knew that something had happened and that it probably wasn't good.

Grace closed the door and moved over to his desk. Cabrera stood against the wall with his arms folded over his chest. Matt picked up on those dark eyes again. They were burning with worry the same way they had burned earlier in the night when Matt came to and saw him standing with the EMT by the ambulance.

He crossed the room, rolling a chair out of the way, and leaned against a filing cabinet. The two men seemed anxious yet subdued. As he thought it through, he guessed that the Robbery-Homicide Division had stepped in and taken the case away from them. Though they wouldn't have needed to explain, RHD's reasoning would have been plain enough. Hughes had been a cop, and the story was about to move from the Metro Section of the *Times* to the front page.

"Take a seat," Grace said in an easy voice.

Matt refused with a shake of his head, staring back at the man and bracing himself for the disappointment. The overhead lights were out, the office lit by only a desk lamp and what filtered in from the squad room through the glass wall. He could hear the rain beating against the windows, the wind gusting outside. Hughes had been his friend and he owed him. He didn't just want this case. It was more than that. Hughes's murder cut to the bone.

"What is it?" Matt said. "What's happened?"

Grace glanced at Cabrera, then back at Matt. He was a tall, lanky man in his midfifties with gray hair and a gaunt face, but still in good shape. His eyes matched the color of his hair, his gaze clear and sharp. Matt had liked him the moment they met and shook hands.

"Tell me," Matt said.

Grace pushed a laptop aside and sat down on the edge of his desk. When he finally spoke, his voice was quiet but steady.

"Cabrera told me what happened at the crime scene, Jones. He thinks it's too personal. He thinks you can't handle the job."

Everything slowed down, the words digging through Matt's gut until they reached the core and started feeding on it. He was no longer looking at Grace. His eyes were pinned on Cabrera now. He could feel the rage exploding through his body, the tightness in his chest.

"It's my case," he said.

Grace cleared his throat. "What's that, Jones? I didn't hear you."

Matt kept his eyes pinned on Cabrera. "It's my fucking case."

"I'll decide whose case it is," Grace said. "I'm in charge here. Now take a seat and cool down."

Matt didn't move. "Fuck you."

Grace turned sharply. "What did you say to me, Detective?"

"Nothing. I was talking to my new partner."

Grace looked him over. "The way you're acting, Jones, I think Cabrera might be right. You and Hughes go way back. You've got a history, too much history—and after tonight, there's too much at stake."

Matt wasn't listening, still focused on Cabrera, still unable to dial back his anger. His voice was deep and dark and barely audible.

"You know what it means to partner up, right, Cabrera? It's about trust and watching the other guy's back. It's about knowing when to take and when to give back. It's about an understanding. Two becoming one."

Grace reached out for Matt's shoulder. Matt shook him off.

"I want to hear him say it," Matt said. "Go ahead and say it, Cabrera. I'm not up to the job."

Cabrera looked him over for a while, then took a step closer, shaking his head as if he wanted this to end quickly. "I'll say it, Jones. Look at you. You're a mess. You can't handle this case. You're too close. Too deep in. You're not ready to—"

It happened before anyone had time to even blink. Matt charged forward, seizing Cabrera by the neck and face and slamming the back of his head against the wall. Cabrera let out a groan and tried to break Matt's grip. When he couldn't, Matt knocked him back again, holding him still and watching panic well up in his eyes. He could hear Grace shouting. He could feel his supervisor struggling to pull him away. Matt tightened his grip on Cabrera's forehead, staring at him eyeball to eyeball, seething.

"It's my case," he said. "It's my case."

"Let go of him, Jones. Jesus Christ. Knock it off and let go."

"My case," Matt said through clenched teeth.

He gave Cabrera a final shove before releasing his hold on him. Once Cabrera regained his composure, he took a step toward Matt, but Grace pushed him out of the office and managed to get the door closed.

CHAPTER 7

"Take a seat, Jones. And that's a goddamn order."

Matt watched Grace move in behind his desk and sit down. Through the glass wall he could see Cabrera in the squad room, pacing and muttering and rubbing the back of his head. After several moments, Matt rolled a chair over to Grace's desk and finally joined him.

"What the fuck is your problem, Jones? Your supervisor on the Westside told me you were smart. I need this like I need—it's not even your first fucking day."

"It's my case," he said quietly.

"It's your case," Grace repeated. "You keep saying that, and I keep telling you that we'll talk about it later."

He shook his head at Matt, then reached for his laptop and opened the lid. Once the computer woke up, he plugged in a portable drive and clicked open a short list of files.

"They finished canvassing the neighborhood about a half hour before I called you. No one saw anything, Jones."

"What about the hotel?"

"The windows on that side of the building face the parking lot. On the other side you can almost see the Hollywood sign. Not many people want a room with a view of the parking lot. And even if they get stuck with one, most people keep the blinds closed. Besides, the place is famous. They shot the movie *Pretty Woman* there. Everybody wants the room Julia Roberts stayed in, and that's in the front. Cabrera said that the guys who made the sweep spoke with everyone who was checked in. No one saw anything until after the last shot was fired."

"Then what?"

"Then nothing, Jones. All they saw was a parking lot and a handful of cops who showed up too late."

Matt thought about the apartments across the street. The twenty-five windows and balconies he'd counted before he left to notify Laura.

"What about that new apartment building?" he said.

"It just opened. They've only rented a couple of units. No one saw anything."

Grace's eyes kept dancing back to that list of files on his laptop. There was something odd about it. Matt settled deeper into the chair, watching his supervisor and wondering if he had missed something. Why did Grace, a seasoned pro, still seem so anxious? Matt didn't know him very well but trusted his read.

"You're leaving something out," he said. "Something important. What is it?"

Grace appeared surprised by the question but seemed to come to some sort of decision. After a quick glance at Cabrera, still pacing in the squad room, he opened a file on his computer and motioned Matt closer. Almost instantly Matt understood why both men had doubts about his ability to work the case. It was video from a security camera. Matt guessed from the angle that the lens was positioned over the entrance of the apartment building across the street. In spite of the distance, in spite of the darkness, he could see them in the background. The hooded sweatshirt. The outstretched hand grasping something shiny that had to be the pistol. Hughes sitting behind the wheel in the black SUV.

Matt dug into his pocket for a piece of nicotine gum, gave it a few hurried bites to release the drug, then parked it against his cheek. Leaning over the desk, he moved closer to the screen. After several minutes Grace pointed at the time code burned into the image and running along the bottom edge of the frame. His supervisor didn't need to say anything. Matt knew that the robbery was taking too much time. There was too much talking. Too much back and forth. Hughes wasn't complying.

And then it happened. A single flash from the end of the gun. A single shot just past the four-minute mark and Hughes wasn't moving anymore.

Matt stared at the screen. He could feel the sweat percolating on his forehead. The shallow and uneven rhythm of his breathing.

The robbery itself took no more than twenty seconds, with everything stolen tossed into what looked like a small backpack or grocery bag. Matt watched the killer slam the door shut and back away. Then the muzzle flashed for another fifteen seconds before going dark. After that the killer fled toward the northwest corner of the lot and vanished. Thirty seconds later, Hank Andrews and Travis Green entered the lot with their guns drawn. A group of five more cops from the community station stepped in behind them. But in the end it didn't matter. They were entering the lot from the other side and moving forward the way they were trained to approach an active crime scene—smart and cautious buys everybody another day. By the time they reached the SUV and saw Hughes's body, the three-piece bandit, the cop killer in the hooded sweatshirt, was long gone.

Matt noticed the sound of the rain beating against the windows again. He listened to it for a while. When he finally looked up from the blank screen, he caught Grace staring at him. His supervisor had been studying his reaction to the video. He had been measuring Matt while he watched his best friend being gunned down with heat.

"You're all I've got, Jones. Robbery-Homicide doesn't want this one. I checked. Their plate's already full. It's the same story here in Hollywood. Budget cutbacks, early retirement—days are only twenty-four hours long and my guys have all the meat they can eat right now. The autopsy's set for seven. Your partner thinks you're in a jam. You're in the middle of a personal crisis. Your best buddy got himself murdered last night. Your pal. Your bro. I get it, Jones. Believe me, I get it. Your new partner thinks that you can't handle the load. But before I put you out on the street, I need to know that he's wrong. I need some sign that he's wrong. Some sign that you can eat fire and not get burned. I need to get the shithead who did this off the fucking street, and I need to do it in a hurry. He's killing people now."

Some sign that you can eat fire and not get burned.

Matt played back the words in his mind, with just the sound of the storm outside filling the room. After several moments he met his supervisor's eyes and held the gaze as he climbed out of the chair and leaned over the desk.

"Here's the sign, Lieutenant. Here's the signal. You ready?"

Grace nodded without saying anything.

"It's my case."

CHAPTER 8

Matt figured that the waitress knew something was up the moment she got a look at their faces and grabbed a couple of menus. Now, as she set down their plates and topped off their coffees, her eyes went straight to Cabrera and stayed there.

The anger still showing on his face was plain enough.

They were sitting in a booth at the Denny's restaurant on the corner of Sunset and Gower. They hadn't spoken to each other since the meeting in Grace's office went south except to come to an understanding. The autopsy was due to begin in just over an hour. Matt didn't want to watch a medical examiner cut open his best friend's dead body and catalog the parts. Cabrera agreed that it was over the top and said that Matt should wait upstairs. Then he suggested that they get something to eat before heading downtown, because neither one of them would be hungry after leaving the coroner's office, no matter where they had been in the building. Since becoming a homicide detective last July, Cabrera had attended two autopsies. Death permeated every inch of the place, he had told Matt. Both times it followed him out to his car.

The pact they'd reached had been accomplished with less than six sentences. At no point during the exchange did Cabrera meet Matt's eyes or even look in his direction. Not a word had been spoken since.

Matt took a sip of coffee and watched Cabrera dig into his bacon and eggs French-toast special. Cabrera was still doing his best to ignore him, and it looked like it was costing him. When the food hit his mouth, he would turn and gaze out the window at the strip mall on the other side of the parking lot. After he swallowed, he'd grunt or mutter something undecipherable, launching his eyes on a low path back to his plate.

Matt finally looked away. It was a partnership with some rough edges, but he couldn't worry about it right now. He'd already pushed aside Cabrera's betrayal and all of the anger that came with it, because he knew that he had to.

The security video he'd seen of the holdup and murder was almost useless. He had watched it a second time when Grace left the room to talk to Cabrera. The lens was too far away—almost an entire block away—the camera recording nothing more than a ghostlike figure holding something shiny that flashed, before running off and disappearing into the night. While digital enhancement had come a long way, Matt didn't need a tech from SID to tell him that giving detail to glowing shapes and shiny objects in images this degraded only happens in the world of make-believe or a shitty TV show.

He heard Cabrera drop his fork on his plate and saw the waitress walking over with their checks. Cabrera had made it a point to order separately. As she reached their booth, her eyes flicked back and forth between them.

"You guys really need to keep it down over here," she said. "You're disturbing our other customers."

It looked like Cabrera didn't think it was funny. His brown cheeks turned a purplish red and he grabbed his check and stormed off. The waitress turned to Matt and shrugged. Matt didn't react either. Instead, he left a tip and ordered a cup of coffee with one sugar to go. It was 6:00 a.m. It had been a long night.

CHAPTER 9

The rain had stopped, the sun burning bright in a vibrant-blue mid-October sky. In spite of the cool air, steam was rising up from the freeways, casting the Library Tower and most of downtown in a milky glow. Matt sat on the steps outside the administration building at the coroner's office, trying to keep his mind off what was going on in the basement of the building next door.

It wasn't easy. It had been two hours, and Cabrera was still there.

On the drive over, Matt had decided against even entering the lobby. Instead, he bought a copy of the *Times* from the box on the corner and used the break to work on gaining some degree of emotional distance. The story about the three-piece bandit's first murder was sketchy, didn't include the identity of the victim or any photographs, and remained in the Metro Section of the paper. But the journalist had managed to get to Grace before his deadline and the article included confirmation that a security camera had recorded the holdup and murder, and that the victim was an off-duty police officer.

Matt heard a door open and turned. When he saw Cabrera exiting the building next door, he got up and started walking toward the metallic green Crown Victoria on this end of the lot. He hit the clicker and heard the alarm chirp. As he opened the driver's-side door, Cabrera stopped and leaned on the roof from the other side, gazing back at him. Something was different. The anger he had been showing on his face had waned. His eyes were glassy, and he appeared quiet and dazed.

"How'd it go?" Matt said.

Cabrera thought it over, fighting off a yawn. "All through-and-throughs except for one slug."

"What kind of shape is it in?"

"Okay, but not great. It's the one that got him in the arm. It passed through, nicked a rib, and ended up in his chest."

It was a lucky break, and Matt knew it. Because of the velocity and power of the bullets, he hadn't expected them to find any slugs in the body, much less one intact. Last night, as the SUV was loaded onto a car carrier bound for the crime lab's garage, Matt had been warned by a criminalist that the likelihood of finding an undamaged slug anywhere in the vehicle was nil. Now Martin Orth, the SID supervisor shepherding their case through the system, would have something to examine and possibly work with.

Matt's phone started vibrating, and he fished it out of his pocket. It was Hughes's partner, Frankie Lane. As he took the call, Cabrera turned away to check out the view.

"How you holding up?" Lane said in a raspy voice.

"The autopsy's over. It's done."

"You watched them cut up Hughes?"

"No. My partner did."

"You see today's paper?"

Matt glanced at Cabrera, still gazing at the city with his back turned. "Yeah, I saw it."

"The three-piece bandit, or whatever the fuck they're calling the piece of shit. You got video, Matt?"

"Nothing that would ID the guy. Just what he did."

Lane coughed. When he spoke, his voice had an urgency to it. An edge.

"I'll bet," he said. "Listen, Matt, we need to talk. This morning, man. Not this afternoon."

"Where are you?"

"At my desk, or outside catching a smoke."

"You started again?"

"Yeah," he said. "Last night. See ya soon."

Matt heard the line click and switched off his phone. Cabrera turned and gave him a look without saying anything. When a light breeze swept by, Matt picked up on the harsh odor from the autopsy room that had saturated Cabrera's clothing and followed him to the car. But only for a split second or two. He was really thinking about Frankie Lane, the things he'd said and the way he'd said them. Lane didn't sound like he was grieving. He sounded nervous.

"What is it, Jones? Who called?"

"Hughes's partner," he said. "Frankie Lane. He says we need to talk."

CHAPTER 10

It took almost an hour to make the short drive out to the North Hollywood station, the 170 Freeway inching along at under thirty-five miles an hour, due largely to the growing number of potholes. When they finally arrived, Lane was waiting for them by the entrance. He was smoking a cigarette and talking to his supervisor, Lieutenant Howard McKensie. Both men appeared exhausted and unshaven, and Matt guessed that neither one of them had gone home last night. Matt had met McKensie many times over the past couple of years, knew how much he thought of Hughes, and was surprised when the lieutenant vanished into the building with nothing more than a halfhearted wave.

It left a bad taste in his mouth, like downing a shot of vinegar. McKensie knew better than most that he and Hughes served together and had been close friends.

Matt tried to let it go as he watched Lane get rid of his cigarette and approach the car with a small backpack slung over his shoulder. When Lane bent down to shake hands, his eyes flicked over to Cabrera, then bounced back.

"Who's he?" Lane said.

Matt shrugged. "Denny Cabrera. Frankie Lane."

Lane pulled his hand away. "Why didn't you come alone?"

"Was I supposed to?"

Lane couldn't seem to find the words and nodded finally.

"What's wrong, Frankie? What is it? And what's wrong with McKensie?"

Lane stepped back and appeared to be overwhelmed by the barrage of questions. The situation. His hands were trembling, his fingers stained from nicotine. After a long moment he came to some sort of decision.

"Okay, Matt, okay," he said. "As long as I don't have to worry about the guy, you can bring him along. What's your name? Cabrera? Denny Cabrera? Do I need to worry about you, Cabrera?"

Matt glanced over at his partner, then turned back to Lane. Something was going on. Something heavy. On a good day Lane appeared emaciated, his ultra-pale skin set against his frizzy black hair, giving his thin face the look of someone who had spent forty-five years living in darkness. But this wasn't a good day, and as Matt watched him still measuring Cabrera, he thought he could see the Grim Reaper moving in behind his back.

"Do I need to worry about you?" Lane repeated.

Cabrera shook his head back and forth in a wide arc, his eyes locked on Lane's. Matt recognized the look on his partner's face from both his time in Afghanistan and as a patrol officer on the streets in Los Angeles. It was the look you gave someone as you eased your hand toward your sidearm, popped the strap, and switched off the safety.

"No need to worry about me," Cabrera said. "We're all friends here."

Lane nodded and turned back to Matt. "Bring him along then."

"Bring him along where, Frankie?"

"We're taking a short drive. I want to show you something. It's just down the street."

Matt and Cabrera traded quick looks as Lane climbed into the backseat.

"Make a right out of the lot," Lane said. "When you hit Tujunga, make another right. After a couple blocks you'll see North Hollywood Park. I'll tell you when to pull over, Matt. I'll tell you when. I can trust you, right, Cabrera? No need to worry about you. Everything's cool. Everybody's safe. No need to worry about either one of you guys. My partner's dead, but that was last night, and today everything's cool."

Matt was staring into the rearview mirror as he pulled out onto Burbank Boulevard. He could see Lane fidgeting in the backseat, checking the windows both left and right, turning around and peering out the rear window to see if they were being followed. His movements were short and jerky and frantic, his eyes wild like the eyes of a man trapped inside a straitjacket.

CHAPTER 11

Matt gave Lane a hard look as the man blazed across the lawn. Had he not known better, Matt would have said that Lane had spent the night snorting blow, peaked and hit bottom, and was now struggling to shed the paranoia and climb back out of his high.

Had he not known better.

Still, as he and Cabrera followed Lane's frenetic path through the trees to the far side of the park, he had no confidence in the man. He could see it on Cabrera's face as well. It felt like they were placating Frankie, and unfortunately they didn't have that kind of time.

Matt fought off the urge to check his watch and looked around to get his bearings. They were south of the library and blocks away from the recreational center. There was nothing here, just acres of trees and grass as the park widened, then began to narrow, following the course of the Hollywood Freeway on its western border. Although paths cut through the lawns, Matt didn't see a single bench or picnic table. Even with the sound of the freeway in full bloom, he was struck by how remote and secluded it felt here. How far away it seemed despite the park's footprint and the strong smell of diesel exhaust and spent gasoline permeating the air.

Matt turned back, crossing another path onto the lawn. As they hiked beneath a series of large oak trees, he looked ahead and began to understand where Lane might be leading them. He could see the flowers and battery-powered candles and notes and photographs set on the grass before the tree on the very end. It was a memorial, sacred ground—someone had died here.

Lane slowed to a stop as they reached the tree, and Matt followed his gaze to a photograph stapled to the bark.

It was a young woman, a brunette with bangs and gray eyes smiling directly at the camera. She had a certain way about her, a certain look that vaguely reminded him of a friend's younger sister back in Jersey. Maybe it was her bangs or just the clean feel of her smile.

"You know her?" Lane asked.

The memory faded, and Matt nodded. He had seen photographs and images of the murder victim on the late-night news. Her name was Faith Novakoff, and until two weeks ago she had been a freshman in college living in a dormitory in Exposition Park. The LAPD had held a short press conference, releasing only the most basic information about her murder: Novakoff, who had just turned eighteen, was last seen walking out of the Tap Room, a popular bar on Ventura Boulevard in Sherman Oaks. She had gone missing for a week before her body was found.

That's all Matt remembered—a single press conference, a single night on the news. He turned to check on Cabrera, caught him staring at Lane as if the North Hollywood detective needed to do a psycho stint with the department shrinks in Chinatown, then turned back.

"Where's this going, Frankie?" Matt said in an edgy voice.

Lane lit another smoke without answering the question, then knelt down and unzipped his backpack. After a quick peek through the trees, he reached into the pack and dug out two three-ring binders. Two murder books.

"You guys remember Millie Brown?" he said. "It was a big case. Lots of media attention. She was raped and murdered eighteen months ago. Your supervisor, Bob Grace, was the lead investigator before his promotion."

Cabrera stepped forward, losing his patience. "Who doesn't remember? They got the guy. Ron Harris. He was the girl's teacher. They had him solid. Rock solid. Enough of the guy's DNA to repopulate the planet. Harris couldn't face the music and did himself in after opening statements. What's this gotta do with the price of coffee? Nothing, because it's bullshit. I'm sorry you lost your partner, man. But we've got work to do. Not sit here and waste time doing group therapy."

Matt watched Cabrera step away and attempt to pull himself together. Then he turned back to Lane and found him still kneeling on the ground, still fidgeting and checking his back. He knew that people experienced grief in different ways. Because Lane had been Hughes's partner, because Matt knew Lane himself, he felt like he owed him something. He owed him, but not right now. Not today with Cabrera around and their murder case circling the drain.

"Denny's right, Frankie. We're looking for the bandit. We don't have time for this. We need to get out of here."

Lane shrugged and took a hit on his smoke, as if he hadn't heard what either one of them just said. He stood up and started leafing through one of the murder books. Matt could see Millie Brown's name printed on the spine.

"Brown was murdered eighteen months ago," Lane said. "It took a year to bring Ron Harris to trial. Your partner's right. Harris couldn't take it and killed himself after the first day. In all that time the department never released a single detail about how Millie Brown was murdered or the condition her body was in when they found her. Because Harris hung himself, nothing was made public in court. These are photographs from the girl's crime scene. Take a look."

Lane found the page he was looking for and passed the binder over to Matt.

"How'd you get this, Frankie?"

"Grace gave it to me and Hughes ten days ago. Now take a look."

"Why would Grace give you guys his murder book?"

Lane's eyes shifted. "Take a look."

Matt finally gave in, lifting the murder book closer. There were four photographs set in a plastic sleeve. Four photographs of a nude Millie Brown stretched out on her stomach on the ground. Matt couldn't be certain from just four photos, but the wounds appeared to be confined to the girl's face. Harris had posed her body to maximize the shock for whoever found her. Her arms and legs were spread open. Her wrists and ankles had been tied to stakes driven into the ground. Although it was difficult to see with all the blood, it looked like what was left of the girl's face was resting on a pane of mirrored glass about the size of a sheet of copy paper.

As Matt examined the images, memories began to surface about the girl's murder and the horrific cloud it had cast over the city. The story had been impossible to escape, particularly in the six weeks leading up to the trial. Millie Brown had been a senior in high school and the daughter of Congressman Jack Brown. A popular girl of uncommon beauty with natural blond hair, refined features, and friends and family who loved her. A girl with a bright future who had been raped and murdered and had met a particularly gruesome end that was never described in any detail. Ron Harris was married with two young children, denied any involvement in Brown's death, but claimed to have had "a secret but consensual affair" with the girl, his student, over the last three months of her life. His claim had come late and only after Grace and his partner, Leo Rodriguez, plus a second team of detectives confronted him with overwhelming evidence of his guilt.

The public was expecting another big-city murder trial, as well as the media circus that went with it. The kind of trial LA seemed to have made its own over the past few decades. The public needed it for closure. The breadth and weight of the crime demanded it. Public opinion polls were crystal clear: most of the angels living in the City of Angels wanted to see Ron Harris burn. But Harris had other ideas, and after the first day of trial, after the prosecution had presented its opening statement, he returned to his cell and denied the public the revenge they sought and the justice they needed. Harris had a plan, a way out, tying a bedsheet around his neck and leaping into the void.

Coward that he was.

Matt's mind surfaced. He noticed that Cabrera had moved in behind him and was gazing over his shoulder at the photographs. He wasn't sure how long his partner had been there and paused a moment to give him more time. He could see Lane just a few feet away holding his place in the second murder book with his finger. Lane was staring back at them, waiting and trying to keep still, without much success.

"Okay, Frankie," Matt said after a while. "We've had our look."

Lane opened the second murder book and traded it for the first. The place he had been holding turned out to be another set of four crime-scene photographs slipped into a plastic sleeve. Matt studied each image with great care, adjusting the binder so that Cabrera would have a better view. Like Millie Brown, Faith Novakoff had been stripped of her clothing and staked to the ground with her nose and forehead resting on a mirror. Like Brown, the only wounds on her body appeared to be confined to her face, which was unrecognizable because of the profuse bleeding.

Matt looked up from the binder at Lane. "What were they shot with?"

"They weren't shot, Matt. They were slashed."

A moment passed. "Just their faces?"

Lane met his eyes, then nodded and took a deep pull on his smoke. "With a box cutter. A razor blade."

Matt returned to the photographs, ignoring the chill wriggling up his spine. The heavy bleeding indicated that both victims had been alive when they were slashed. Death hadn't been easy for either one of them, nor would it have been quick. He looked back at Lane.

"You said nothing was ever made public, Frankie. Who made the connection?"

"The photographer here at the crime scene. A criminalist and an SID supervisor out at the crime lab. All three had worked the Millie Brown case. After that, Hughes and I requested the same medical examiner. Art Madina performed the autopsy. He saw it, too."

"But Harris is dead," Matt said.

Lane shrugged. "Copycat."

"What did Grace say?"

"The same thing."

Cabrera grimaced. "How?"

"We're living in the age of the Internet," Lane said. "It's been eighteen months since Brown was murdered. The dam could've sprung a hundred leaks. I think that's the way Grace put it."

"The way he put it," Cabrera said, shaking his head. "What's this gotta do with what we've gotta do?"

Lane took another pull on his smoke, remaining quiet for several moments as he wrestled with something in his head. When he finally spoke, his voice had a frenzied shake to it.

"I don't think Hughes was killed by some yuppie asshole fuck with a piece," he said. "I think he was gunned down by the same freak who did Faith Novakoff right here under this tree . . . and I think I'm fucking next."

It hung there, over their heads and caught in the canopy of the oak tree. Matt filled his lungs with air and exhaled slowly, his mind going. He didn't want the wave of doubt and absurdity that he was feeling in his gut to resonate in his voice.

"Do you have anything to back up what you're saying, Frankie? Anything at all that connects anything to anything else?"

Lane seemed to be drowning in a pool of self-doubt, his eyes wagging back and forth across the ground. "Maybe we stumbled onto something. Maybe we hit it blind." He glanced at Matt and shook his head, then turned back to the memorial and stared at the picture of Faith Novakoff stapled to the tree. "Maybe we hit a nerve. Something crazy we never saw coming. All I know is that there's no way that asshole in the papers shot Hughes during a holdup. Hughes was too smart for that. He would've seen the prick coming. I can feel it, man. It has to be connected to Novakoff's murder. Something I can't see that's fucking everything up. My partner's gone, for Christ's sake. Nothing's gonna bring him back."

Lane turned away to hide his face. Matt could tell that he was weeping. As he reached out for Lane's shoulder, he was thinking about the way Hughes's wife had taken it, and feeling like he'd just been cut in half again.

CHAPTER 12

The sight of Lane turning his face, the sound of the detective weeping on the very spot where Faith Novakoff had been found raped and murdered and staked to the ground—

Lane had forced him to take both murder books, hoping that he would read them and see things the way he did. Even as Matt sat in the passenger seat for the ride back to Hollywood, paging through the crime-scene photos and listening to Cabrera's nonstop criticism of everything that had happened over the past hour—berating Lane and discounting his skills as a detective, accusing the man of being mentally unstable and emotionally wasted, a fool and a moron, an imbecile and a coward—he couldn't shake the sights and sounds of Lane's paranoia and obvious breakdown.

He found it unnerving and even now kept quiet and ignored Cabrera as best he could for the rest of the drive. What troubled him most was that Lane's fall seemed so out of character. It didn't fit with the person he'd known as Hughes's partner—the beers, the talks, the trips to Dodger Stadium, the meals the three of them had shared. It didn't fit with any of the things Hughes had told him about Lane on his own. Hughes had liked Lane and admired him and said that he had learned more from Lane than from anyone he'd ever worked with. That once you got used to his idiosyncrasies, he was a great guy and an even better detective. The kind of guy you'd want close by if the ground opened up and your world fell in.

Cabrera pulled into the lot behind the station and found a spot close to the building. Matt grabbed the murder books and followed his partner through the rear entrance, passing the holding cells and entering the detective bureau. When Cabrera headed for his cubicle—what they used to call the homicide table when they had real desks—Matt glanced at his own but kept moving. There were two detectives standing beside the coffeemaker just this side of Grace's office.

"Is he in?" Matt said.

They gave him a measured look. One of them said, "I don't think so," before they walked off.

The door was open. Matt didn't see Grace inside, but his laptop was in plain view. Even better, the portable drive was still sitting right beside it. He walked in and pulled a chair up to the desk. The computer was already awake. After plugging in the portable drive, he waited a beat for the computer to recognize the device, then opened a window and found the video file. Before leaving for breakfast and the autopsy, Matt had e-mailed a copy of the file to Henry Rollins, a forensic analyst from the Photography Unit whom he had worked with many times while assigned to narcotics. He'd sent a copy to himself as well but at the moment didn't want to take the time to boot up his computer, log on to the network, and download the file.

He needed reassurance more quickly than that.

He needed something to break the spell Lane had cast over their investigation of Hughes's murder. No matter how ridiculous the assertions Lane made might seem, Matt needed to see the video one more time to feel it.

He clicked open the file and watched as the clip began playing on the screen. He could see Hughes's silhouette in the SUV. He could make out the figure of a man in a hooded sweatshirt standing by the driver's-side door with his gun up and ready.

"Who the hell are you?"

Matt turned to the door and saw the two detectives he'd passed in the hall staring back at him. Both appeared to be in their forties but shared little else in form other than the heavy look in their eyes. The big round one on the left had dark hair, olive skin, and a goatee. The short one on the right looked thin and gaunt, with gray hair and pockmarked cheeks.

"Matt Jones," he said. "Who the hell are you?"

A moment passed, but then their eyes flushed with recognition.

"The new guy?" the big one said.

Matt nodded. The two detectives walked into the room with outstretched hands. The big one did most of the talking, introducing himself as Joey Orlando and then pointing to his partner at the homicide table, Edward Plank. Plank seemed preoccupied with the video playing on the laptop. Once Orlando noticed, he looked back at Matt and seemed uncomfortable as well.

"You caught a tough break," he said. "The toughest. Anything we can do, anything at all, just ask."

Plank nodded but kept his eyes on the screen. When Matt turned to the laptop, the gun was flashing, and Plank was shaking his head in disbelief.

"Anything at all," Plank said in a low voice.

Grace walked in and tossed a FedEx envelope on his desk. Matt watched as his eyes went from the video clip on the laptop to the spines of the murder books Lane had given him to read.

"You guys meet?" Grace said.

Orlando nodded. "Just now."

"Good," Grace said. "I think you're gonna like it here, Jones. Orlando and Plank are two of the best." He turned to Orlando. "I need to talk to Jones. How 'bout you two guys giving us a minute?"

"Sure," Orlando said. "Good meeting you, Jones."

Matt nodded back just as Grace began closing the door. "Same here," he said.

CHAPTER 13

Grace pushed the laptop aside as he sat down, the surveillance video still rolling in a loop on automatic replay.

"Cabrera told me that Lane was a wreck. He thinks that whoever killed Faith Novakoff murdered his partner. Now the killer's out to get him. It sounds to me like Lane hit the wall and needs help."

Matt didn't say anything. He was troubled by Cabrera's "private" talks with Grace. This time it seemed innocent enough. Still, there was a theme to it, a rhythm, and he didn't like it.

Grace glanced at the binder with Millie Brown's name on the spine. "He and Hughes stopped by about a week and a half ago. They showed me pictures from the Novakoff crime scene. They wanted to hear how things went with the Brown investigation."

"What did you say?"

"That I felt sorry for them, Jones. That I was glad it was their case and not mine."

Matt slipped a piece of nicotine gum between his cheek and gum, wishing it was a Marlboro.

"You called it a copycat," he said.

Grace nodded. "Harris hung himself. He's dead. And we had him by the short hairs. There was too much evidence. Too many people coming forward. Every move we made pointed in the same direction. That's why he hung himself. He listened to the deputy DA's opening statement and knew that there was no way out, Jones. He listened and he did the math. In one day everything added up to zero. Ron Harris was an asshole."

"But Frankie said nothing was ever made public about the murder. How could anyone duplicate it?"

Grace leaned back in his chair, his eyes losing their edge as he gazed into the past. "Millie was found in one of those picnic areas off the parking lot at the Hollywood Bowl. A couple with two young children. They'd taken their lunch up there and they found her. Me and my partner got the call. Me and Leo." He paused for a moment, staring through the window. "You saw the pictures," he said in a quieter voice. "She'd been dead for more than twelve hours. Everyone who was there, including me, will live with that memory for the rest of their lives. Leo had nightmares for months."

"But how could anyone duplicate it now?" Matt said.

"People talk, Jones. The way the girl was staked to the ground. The wounds to her face. She was young and beautiful and the daughter of a congressman. She came from a decent family. A wealthy family. We kept the details out for a lot of reasons, but you remember the rumors. They may have been roughed in, but they were close. Too close. The couple finally talked to one of the tabloids—and who wouldn't? They were paid a lot of money. Other than what the deputy DA said in his opening statement, I don't know about our side. It's been eighteen months. You can't keep a secret like that forever. At this point I'm not sure there's even a reason to. That's what I told Lane and your friend Hughes."

As Matt thought it through, memories began to surface. He remembered the chatter that some of the rag sheets and gossip TV shows were spewing out at the time. He could remember looking at the crime-scene photos on the ride back to the station and thinking to himself that somehow the way Millie Brown and Faith Novakoff had been murdered seemed familiar to him. It was a strange feeling—spooky—and he waited for it to pass.

He watched Grace glance at the surveillance video on the laptop. The killer was racing across the parking lot toward the camera, then veering to the left and out of view. After what seemed like an eternity but only amounted to thirty seconds in real time, the first responders, Hank Andrews and Travis Green, began to enter the lot from the other side. Grace shook his head at them and turned away, like he couldn't watch.

"What about the mirror?" Matt said. "Why do you think Harris placed the girl's face on a sheet of glass? It has to mean something, right?"

Grace shrugged but didn't answer.

"You just told me that her body was found at lunchtime. That means she was killed in the middle of the night."

Grace nodded. "Within an hour or two of midnight either way."

"So maybe the mirror was meant for whoever found her the next day."

"Or maybe," Grace said, "Harris was just trying to make it look as far from what it really was as he could. The guy was wrapped too tight. He killed Millie because she wanted out of the relationship and was threatening him with exposure. He may have called whatever the fuck he was doing to her consensual. He may have called it a secret affair. But he was the only one who did, and he waited until he was cornered to do it. Every one of her friends knew exactly what was going on. Harris killed Millie Brown because he had a lot to lose. His job, his wife, his two kids. He tried to make it look like it was done by some freak. He used a box cutter on her face. He made her pay. He made it hurt. And in the end we realized that the killer really was a freak. It was the girl's science teacher, and we got him."

CHAPTER 14

Matt tossed the murder books onto the counter and sat down at his cubicle. He could hear the sound of muffled voices, but because the partitions were six feet high he couldn't tell who was in the room. Just Cabrera, whom he could see was seated right beside him, talking to someone on the phone.

His workstation came with a small fluorescent light, a hanging coatrack, and double set of plastic file holders. An official LAPD calendar, along with a list of department phone numbers, was tacked to the partition above the phone. As he looked the cubicle over, he wondered who might have invented it and what kind of person they were. Someone in the sciences, he guessed, like Ron Harris. Someone who worked with lab rats. Someone with a long list of issues.

He shook it off and unlocked his cell phone, skimming through his list of new e-mails. When he didn't see a reply from Henry Rollins, he picked up his desk phone and entered his number from memory. He was surprised that he hadn't heard anything from Rollins after e-mailing the surveillance video more than six hours ago. The phone rang seven times before the SID analyst finally picked up.

"It's Matt Jones, Henry. How's it going with my video?"

"Do I really need to say it?"

Matt leaned back in his chair. "No, you don't have to say it. I thought it was a lost cause when I sent it over. I just wanted you to take a look. Just in case. So what, three seconds in and you bailed out?"

"No, I'm still on it," he said. "Let's see what happens."

"You're saying there's a chance?"

"No question I can clean up these images," he said. "Maybe a little. Maybe more than that."

Matt was stunned but didn't want to get his hopes up. Lane had tainted his perspective more than he realized. Although Frankie couldn't make a single connection between Hughes's murder and the death of Faith Novakoff, Matt couldn't draw a line in ink from Hughes's murder to the three-piece bandit either. They didn't have a single witness or a single lead. Just fifteen shell casings from a Glock 20 and a slug that would take time to analyze and carried no guarantees.

"That video's all we've got," he said, hoping he didn't sound too desperate. "How much time do you think you'll need?"

Rollins laughed. "I know it's all we've got. We just finished reviewing the street cams. We went through every image within ten blocks of the crime scene. Your shooter isn't there. He entered the parking lot the same way he left it."

From the north, Matt thought, because the killer was smart enough to know that there weren't any cameras north of Hollywood Boulevard until you reached Franklin Avenue. By the time he made it to Franklin, he would have been behind the wheel, his car indistinguishable from any other car immersed in a sea of traffic.

"What do you think?" Matt said. "How much time?"

"Let's see what happens over the next couple days."

Matt had been thinking that it would be a matter of hours, not days. Still, he thanked Rollins and hoped for the best. As he hung up the phone, he turned and found Cabrera staring at him. He must have been listening.

"We've got a shot?" Cabrera asked with raised eyebrows.

Matt nodded. "Maybe."

"Well, you're having better luck than I am. I just got off the phone with Orth at the crime lab. Everything's backed up. They're not even gonna get started on the SUV until late tomorrow."

"I thought we were at the top of the list."

Cabrera shrugged. "Orth says that is the top of the list. If we were on the bottom, it could take six months."

"What about the slug?"

"Same thing. Late tomorrow."

"Because we're at the top of the list."

"Right," Cabrera said. "We're first in line."

Matt glanced at Cabrera's laptop and could see that he was working on the chronological record and had begun to put together a murder book. A blue binder with Hughes's name on it was leaning against a stack of files.

Matt listened to the din of muffled voices for a moment, then turned back to Cabrera. "Does Leo Rodriguez still work here?"

"Grace's old partner?"

"Yeah."

"I've never met him. I think he retired after Grace's promotion. If he didn't, then he's probably downtown at Robbery-Homicide. It would've happened before I got here. Why?"

"Grace was talking about the two of them seeing Millie Brown's body staked to the ground."

Cabrera waited a moment, mulling something over, then looked back. "For the record, Jones, I'm sorry I lost it out there with Lane."

Matt didn't say anything.

Cabrera loosened his collar. "I talked it over with Grace. He said the same thing happened to him and Rodriguez."

"And what's that?"

"What you were just talking about. Millie Brown. The way they found her. He said it really shook them up. Frankie has to deal with Novakoff's murder, and now his partner's dead, too. No wonder he's not thinking right."

Matt didn't like the tone of Cabrera's voice. It sounded like he was trying to placate him. It sounded like bullshit. He shot his new partner a touch-and-go look. He could feel the anger stirring in his gut but kept his mouth shut. When Cabrera turned back to his computer, Matt got up and walked out of the room.

CHAPTER 15

No wonder he wasn't thinking right . . .

Matt pulled out of the lot in his Honda, drove up Wilcox, and made a right on Franklin. After a few minutes he picked up Los Feliz, heading east toward the Golden State Freeway. Fifteen minutes later he was in Glendale, making the climb into the hills. When he saw Hughes's house just ahead, he pulled up to the walkway and parked.

He wasn't sure if he was here because he felt like he needed to check in on Laura or because he needed a break from Cabrera. Either way, the short drive seemed like a good idea.

He walked up to the house and rang the doorbell. Feeling a chill in the air—the steady breeze—he zipped up his sweatshirt and waited. When Laura didn't come to the door, he checked the window before starting around the house. He saw Laura's car in front of the garage. Hughes's silver Escalade had been returned from the dealership and was parked off to the side. Matt stared at it for a while, felt his chest tighten, then stepped into the side yard.

He could hear Laura's voice as he eased around the corner and looked down the hill at the pool. She was with the woman who lived next door. The woman Matt had met when she came over last night. They had pushed two chaise lounges together. They were drinking coffee, sharing a blanket in the cool air, and talking in soft voices.

He couldn't tell what they were saying. All he knew was that Laura needed it right now, and he didn't want to interrupt or intrude. After several moments he backed out and returned to his car.

He shivered and climbed in behind the wheel. He fought off a yawn as he headed back toward the freeway. The coffeehouse on Pacific Avenue looked too busy to deal with. When he spotted the Jack in the Box, he pulled into the drive-thru lane and ordered a large coffee with two sugars. The paper cup was hot to the touch and warmed his hands. Removing the top, he took a first sip and felt his stomach begin to glow.

The caffeine seemed to revive him, and he started driving. He felt the sudden need to keep moving and wondered if he was running away from something. Seeing Hughes's SUV parked in the drive must have been the trigger. He had thoughts in his head. A steady stream rolling just beneath the surface. His past, his present, his future.

No wonder he wasn't thinking right . . .

He had no idea where he was going. Still, he could see himself. He could see himself from behind, almost as if he were driving the car in his rearview mirror. A metallic silver Nissan. Almost as if he were the man driving the Nissan.

He could see himself.

He was parking his car and getting out with his cup of coffee. He was pushing another piece of nicotine gum against his cheek and wishing for a Marlboro again. He was walking into the park. He was hiking down the long row of oak trees in the muted light just before sunset.

And then he stopped.

There were two girls, eighteen or nineteen years old, straightening up the memorial for Faith Novakoff. They had brought fresh flowers and a pack of fresh batteries for the faux candles.

Matt knelt down in the grass and took a sip of coffee as he gazed at them.

He felt so uneasy about so much. The fact that his father had walked out and abandoned him and his mother when he was only a boy. The fact that his mother had died a year later of breast cancer. Because his father still didn't want him, Matt went to live with his aunt, whom he didn't know very well but grew to love.

So uneasy about so much.

Lane's wild story. Cabrera working on the chronological record and, right or wrong, going with the flow like the man worked for a fucking bank.

Matt ran his fingers through the grass and tried to focus.

Why did he have this bad feeling in his gut? This horrific sense that he was staring at the void and about to be tossed in?

He heard something and his mind snapped back. The two girls were screaming. He looked for the source, then back at the girls, and realized that they were staring at *him*. When he stood up, their bodies shuddered in terror and they fled across the lawn. He watched and listened. They were too far away to say anything. The shrieking seemed to lessen some as they reached the street, but it didn't stop.

No wonder he wasn't thinking right . . .

CHAPTER 16

Matt climbed out of the car, then heard someone call out his name and checked the lot. It was Cabrera, hustling over to their unmarked Crown Vic. Grace was right behind him, scrambling out of the station with Orlando and Plank and a handful of cops in uniforms.

Grace pulled the cops aside. "We go with our lights on. You lead the way. You guys take the rear, and we'll ride in the middle. Four cars. We stop for nothing. We're in a hurry, but we're not racing. And stay together."

Grace hopped into the backseat, riding with Orlando and Plank. Matt slid into the passenger seat as Cabrera started the car and found his place in the middle of the caravan.

"What is it?" Matt said.

Cabrera's eyes were big and wide and shiny. "A guy working on the tower at the top of Mount Lee heard a girl scream. He called nine-one-one. First responders just called back with confirmation. They found her body on a trail just below the Hollywood sign."

"Why all this?"

Cabrera shook his head back and forth, gave him a look, almost as if he couldn't speak.

"What's going on, Cabrera?"

"She's like the others," he said finally.

Matt took it in hard and grimaced. It felt like all the air in his lungs had made a rush for the exit in a single instant. He settled back into the passenger seat, considering what had just happened.

Another murder like the others.

The drive up Beachwood Canyon to the Hollywood sign was more difficult than expected. More of a winding, mazelike journey past homes strewn through the steep hills and wrapped around every curve. It was a dark night. The air still had a bite to it, and the wind had picked up, as if January had arrived three months early. When they gained elevation, Matt could see the carpet of lights from homes on the Westside vanishing as the marine layer swept through the basin like an ocean wave over sand.

The caravan finally reached the communication tower and parking area within the fence at the top of Mount Lee. Matt pulled two flashlights out of the glove box and tossed one over to Cabrera as they got out. Grace led the way down the hill. He was moving fast, too fast for the steep terrain and unsure footing. As they passed the Hollywood sign, Matt gazed at the unlit letters in the darkness. They stood three stories high and were set a hundred yards across the mountaintop, and he found the close-up view surprising, even bewildering. He could remember reading somewhere that it was rigged with alarms and surveillance cameras linked to the LAPD. But when they reached the trail in the dry brush and he spotted a pair of first responders waving flashlights at them fifty yards down the way, he realized that the crime scene was too far away for the killer to have tripped an alarm or camera.

Cabrera gave him a nudge as they approached. "There she is," he whispered.

Matt looked ahead and could see her form in the darkness. His stomach was churning and he wasn't sure why. While serving overseas, he had seen more dead bodies than he could count. Many of the corpses had been found in similar terrain. Most of them had been armed men, but every once in a while he'd come upon a woman or a child who had been executed or wounded and left to die alone under a hot sun in the rocks and sand.

But this time it was different.

He could feel it. The work of a madman.

Ignoring the others, he knelt down before the girl's nude body and switched on his flashlight. Her wrists and ankles had been bound and staked to the ground, her face mutilated and placed on a sheet of mirrored glass—just like the others. But what struck Matt most about the way the body had been left were the variety of different scents in the air. Her blond hair was rich with the fragrance of shampoo. He could smell the soap on her clear skin. Freshly applied deodorant. When he examined her nails, both her toes and fingers appeared to have just been polished.

A tremor quaked through his body from somewhere deep inside. It seemed so odd. So singular. So familiar.

"What is it?" Grace said. "What do you see?"

Matt stood up and turned, sensing that something was wrong by the sound of Grace's voice. His supervisor appeared nervous and afraid and looked like he was struggling to keep cool and hide it.

"The killer cleaned her up, Lieutenant."

"The copycat. How so, Jones?"

"He gave her a bath, did her hair, and painted her nails before he staked her down in the dirt and cut up her face."

A moment passed. Long and dark and exceedingly still.

Grace didn't say anything, and Matt didn't think he was looking at the girl's body anymore. He was too caught up in whatever was on his mind. Matt backed out of the way, unlocked his phone, and found Howard Benson's number in his contacts list. Benson worked in the Missing Persons Unit. Anyone involved in narcotics spent a lot of time working with Missing Persons, and he and Benson knew each other well. Benson picked up on the first ring.

"Are you still in the office?" Matt said.

"I've been trying to get out of here for the past two hours. How can I help?"

Matt turned back to the body. "A young woman, eighteen to twenty, about five ten, blond hair, on the slender side but with a belly, maybe a student."

"That could be anybody, Matt. What color are her eyes?"

Matt knelt down again and panned his flashlight across the victim's face, straining to see through the blood. The mutilation was hideous, her skin puffy, her features so deformed that it looked like she was wearing a mask made of pulp. It was an image that he knew he'd walk with for the rest of his life.

"I can't see her eyes," he said.

"What about a tattoo? A small heart-shaped tattoo just below her left hip bone. There's a birthmark beside it."

"You've got someone in mind?"

"A girl went missing five days ago. Another student. She had blond hair and lived in a dorm in Westwood."

Matt pulled the phone away. Orlando and Plank were on the left side of the body, and he asked them about the tattoo and birthmark. Orlando slipped on a pair of gloves. The investigator from the coroner's office wasn't here yet, nor was anyone from SID, including the photographer. Touching or moving the body in any way would compromise the investigation and possibly take down a trial. But Orlando had other ideas. The soil beneath the corpse was loose and sandy. Matt watched as the detective scooped away the debris and Plank shined his flashlight on the girl's hip.

"It's there," Orlando said. "A heart-shaped tattoo just below her left hip. And there's a small birthmark right beside it."

Matt brought the phone back to his ear. Benson must have heard Orlando's confirmation.

"I'd call her a Jane Doe for now, Matt. But her name's probably Brooke Anderson. I'll give her parents a heads-up and make sure her dental records are at the coroner's office in time for the autopsy."

"Thanks."

"How do you like working homicide?"

Matt winced. "It's got its moments," he said.

He switched off his phone and returned it to his pocket. Grace still appeared extraordinarily concerned. He had his phone out and was taking pictures of the victim with the built-in camera. It was a violation on pretty much every level. Matt watched Cabrera pick up on it and give him a look. Orlando and Plank seemed to notice as well but were visibly overwhelmed by the victim's plight and still dealing with it. When Matt heard the chatter from a handful of SID techs and saw their flashlights moving down the slope, he turned back to Grace and watched him slip the phone into his pocket.

Why?

He let the question pass. Then he parked a fresh piece of nicotine gum against his cheek and forced himself to take another look at the girl's face. After a few minutes he moved deeper down the trail for some fresh air and turned back to watch from a distance.

What was he seeing?

What the killer wanted him to see.

Why the display? Why the complexity? Why was he torturing his victims with such a hideous death?

But even more, why did it seem so familiar?

Matt sensed something in the center of his back and turned to face the mountain. The darkness. He wondered if someone was out there. It felt like there was. He panned his flashlight off the trail and through the brush. In Afghanistan this same feeling was usually followed by a shot from a sniper.

He switched off his flashlight and moved another fifty yards down the trail, letting his eyes adjust to the darkness. The dead of night. He quieted his body and listened. He didn't see anyone, but the sensation was stronger now. He could almost feel it in his bones. The killer was watching them. He was hiding in the darkness. He felt close.

CHAPTER 17

It was late. Almost midnight.

Matt grabbed the murder books Lane had given him and walked out of the station to his car. Cabrera had already left.

It had taken five hours to process the crime scene, much of the time spent working beneath a tarp, with news choppers hovering above. Still, the media got their money shot when the girl's body was bagged, strapped to a stretcher, and hauled up the mountain to an emergency vehicle waiting behind the fence. It was more than a money shot. It took five men almost fifteen minutes to reach the top. Two patrol units had stayed behind and would remain at the crime scene overnight. In the morning, Orlando and Plank would return with an SID photographer and a handful of criminalists for a more thorough look in daylight.

Matt tossed the murder books onto the passenger seat and climbed in. As he jammed his key into the ignition, the rear door to the station burst open and he spotted Grace hustling down the walkway. He was talking to someone on the phone. The conversation appeared heated, and he seemed way too distracted to notice Matt. Too animated. Too everything to be righteous.

Grace fumbled with his keys but got himself together and pulled out of the lot with his tires screeching. Matt waited a beat, then made the turn onto Wilcox and started following.

Grace was heading north toward the Valley, the rich fog of the marine layer fading away with each block until it finally vanished. And he was moving fast, running red lights all the way up Cahuenga Boulevard and down the hill on Barham toward the Warner Bros. lot. Matt gave himself a safe cushion, keeping his eye on the car from fifty yards back. There was enough traffic to remain concealed, but not enough to lose sight of the car. The conditions were perfect. When Grace made a left onto Lakeside Drive, Matt closed the distance by half and followed him into the neighborhood. It looked like Grace was working his way around the gates and private roads of a nearby golf club. When he made a hard right onto Toluca Lake Avenue, Matt pulled to a stop and killed the headlights.

He could see Grace making a U-turn and parking in front of a house five or six doors down on the left. The house was recessed from the street. He could see his supervisor hurrying toward the building and slipping out of view.

Matt noted the time and waited. After a few minutes he idled forward and pulled to a stop in front of the house.

It was clear to Matt that Grace didn't live here. He had parked at the curb, not in front of the garage, which was attached to the house. But even more telling, the homes on this side of the street were set on the lake and way out of any cop's price range. Most of them were outright mansions. The rest were big enough to probably qualify as mini-mansions. This one came with a wooden security gate, a six-foot wall, and a terra-cotta roof. From what Matt could see through the trees, every window in the place was lighted. Grace had gone without sleep for almost forty-eight hours, just as Cabrera and Matt had. So why a meeting at midnight? Why had he photographed the murder victim with his own camera when

SID would have given him a complete set of images as soon as they were downloaded and entered into evidence?

Matt opened the lock on his phone, called Central Dispatch, and identified himself to the woman who answered. After double-checking the house number, he gave her the address. Within a minute or two the dispatcher was back on the line.

"George Baylor," she said. "White male. Fifty-five years old. Five foot eleven inches tall, one hundred and eighty-five pounds. Blue eyes. Light brown hair. He's an MD. He's a doctor."

The name seemed familiar—but everything seemed familiar.

"What have you got on him?"

"Nothing," the dispatcher said. "He's clean. I can e-mail you the picture off his driver's license if you like."

"Thanks."

Matt gave the dispatcher his e-mail address and got off the line. When his phone beeped a minute or so later, he checked his e-mail and gazed at the photograph of Baylor. He had hoped that seeing his face would jog his memory, but it didn't. All he saw was a guy in his midfifties managing to pull off a smile at the DMV.

Matt got out of the car, weighing the risks as he walked underneath the trees and approached the left side of the wall. Because it was so late, because of Grace's odd behavior, Matt's best guess was that his supervisor wouldn't be here if he only intended to stay for ten minutes. Still, if Matt guessed wrong, if he was seen on the property, he wouldn't be able to explain himself. Things would get tricky, or maybe worse.

If he was seen . . .

He gazed over the wall at the two-story Mediterranean. The side yard between Baylor's house and his neighbor's amounted to less than thirty feet but included a twenty-foot-high privacy hedge, running from here all the way down to the lake. Although he could hear a dog barking in the distance, he didn't see any signs that Baylor owned one. No burned grass or land mines—the landscaping meticulous.

Matt took a deep breath and exhaled slowly. Then he pulled himself up over the wall and dropped down on the other side. Moving quickly through the side yard, he ducked as he passed a formal living room, then slowed and finally stopped when he spotted movement in the next set of windows. Baylor had installed shutters, and the slats were open. Matt stepped away from the light reflecting out of the room, found a place in the darkness, and became very still.

It was Baylor's study, and the two men were sitting before a desktop computer downloading files from Grace's cell phone. A few moments later Matt had confirmation that his guess was right when images of Jane Doe's dead body began to appear on Baylor's oversized computer display.

Why did Grace believe that Baylor needed to see these pictures tonight? What part of this couldn't wait until morning? If the case against Ron Harris was so airtight that Harris hung himself rather than roll the dice in court, why did Grace still appear so agitated?

It didn't make any sense. There had to be a missing piece.

Matt turned and looked into the backyard as he thought it over. The place felt more like a resort than a home. He could see a terrace by the water that included an outdoor fireplace, a pool and spa, a lounging area, and a barbecue pit. It looked like another set of steps led to a lower-level terrace for sunbathing and access to the dock. Even better, there was a boat tied to the dock.

Here, Matt thought, in the middle of LA.

He turned back and looked through the window. Grace and Baylor were still at it, enlarging images of the girl's corpse and talking it over as they examined each one. It looked like it was going to be another long night for everyone. Matt glanced at his watch, then headed back through the yard and climbed over the wall. When he was certain that no one was on the sidewalk, he stepped out from beneath the trees, slipped into his car, and drove off. Somehow he needed to stay up long enough to make a pass through Millie Brown's murder book. He needed to know how Grace and Rodriguez had come to their conclusions before he went to sleep. Home was on the other side of town. Fighting off a yawn, he hoped that the traffic wouldn't be too bad. It usually didn't slow down until 2:00 a.m., but maybe he'd be lucky tonight.

He reached the 134 Freeway and started up the ramp, feeling like maybe he really had lucked out. But after the first mile, he wasn't so sure. That car was in his rearview mirror again. The man in the silver Nissan.

CHAPTER 18

Matt walked into the house, flipped on the lights, and opened the front curtains. He'd seen the man in the silver Nissan twice in a single day. He didn't believe in coincidence. At the same time, the guy had been easy to shake. So easy that Matt didn't know what to make of it.

Willing to wait and see what might happen next, he filed it away, grabbed a beer out of the fridge, and sat down at the kitchen table with the Millie Brown murder book. He took a few moments to clear his mind of all that had happened since he got the call two days ago and realized that his best friend was dead, gone. In spite of his exhaustion, he wanted a clean read on the Brown case before he closed his eyes. A take without bias or any thought of Cabrera or Frankie Lane or even what his imagination, his instincts, were trying to tell him right now.

He lived just north of the Palisades in the hills overlooking Potrero Canyon Park, Santa Monica, and the Pacific Ocean. He couldn't really tell what style the architect would have called his house. At times Matt thought the place looked like a ranch, other times modern, but most days it looked just like what it probably was—a run-down box with a carport attached. It was the dark spot in the neighborhood. The house everyone had hoped would be knocked down when the old woman who had lived here finally died.

But Matt had been lucky enough to know her grandson, Kevin Hughes. And when the real estate bubble burst, Matt had steady work as a patrol officer and could afford the lowered mortgage rate.

He liked the place because he could see the ocean from the living room and kitchen, even his bedroom. He liked watching the deer and coyotes that lived in the park and often climbed the hill at night to sleep in the grass behind his house. But more important, he liked the place because it was made of wood. He had ridden out two earthquakes since moving in. The house creaked and swayed but moved with the hill and didn't fall down.

His mind surfaced and he checked the front window. The marine layer was as thick as a steam room, but he could still see most of the street. The Nissan hadn't followed him home. He pushed a fresh piece of nicotine gum against his cheek, thought about that Marlboro again, and knew that he was ready.

He opened the murder book, read through the preliminary reports, then flipped to the chronological record and dug in. From what he could tell, Grace and Rodriguez shared equal time contributing to the murder book. And while Rodriguez was a decent writer, Grace seemed even better, his descriptions so well composed that they might have been pulled out of a crime novel.

But what struck Matt most was the tone he could hear coming from both detectives.

It seemed more than clear that finding Millie Brown's body staked to the ground with her face slashed had changed them. That getting their hands on the killer had become more than a mission. That anything or anyone that got in the way of their success would be confronted and convinced otherwise, using whatever means necessary. That included the crime lab. They spent every favor and were first in line every time. They enlisted Orlando and Plank and used them to assist, until Ron Harris was singled out and arrested.

Curiously, Harris wasn't their first suspect. A man working for the construction company that Millie's father had hired to remodel their home looked good for the murder from the very beginning.

Matt's eyes lingered on his name. Jamie Taladyne.

Five years ago Taladyne had been accused of sexually assaulting a young woman while remodeling a dormitory at one of the schools on the Westside. Even worse, he had been convicted but ended up serving only two years of a ten-year sentence due to overcrowding.

Matt hadn't been aware of a second suspect and flipped through the sections of the binder until he found a photograph of Taladyne and a transcript from his initial interview with Grace and Rodriguez. Taladyne was twenty-nine years old, of medium build, with light brown hair and striking, almost hypnotic sky-blue eyes. He had contact with Millie on a daily basis. According to an entry made by Rodriguez, Taladyne's coworkers often saw them talking together. After the murder, a carpenter came forward claiming that Taladyne had admitted he was infatuated with the girl and couldn't get her out of his mind. During the interview, Taladyne claimed that she had often flirted with him and teased him. That on one occasion she had removed her clothing and put on a bathing suit with her bedroom door open because she knew that he could see her as he cut drywall in the room across the hall. Taladyne denied his coworker's claim of infatuation but said he liked the girl just the same. He had no reason to hurt her. He was at home that night alone, and probably at that hour, in bed getting some sleep. When asked if he would take a polygraph, Taladyne agreed without a moment's hesitation. When he passed the test, Grace and Rodriguez cut him loose.

Matt checked the window again as he took a sip of beer and thought it over. Jamie Taladyne seemed like a perfect fit but had found a way to pass a polygraph. Within a week of the murder he'd been dropped as a suspect.

Matt paged ahead and found the coroner's report, skimming through it quickly. Damage to Millie Brown's vagina seemed to suggest that she had been raped, but no semen had been found anywhere on her body. No pubic hairs from the killer were found, nor were there any scratches, abrasions, or bite marks that might indicate a struggle. Matt grabbed the second murder book, opened it to the coroner's report, and found the same conclusions. Faith Novakoff had been raped as well, yet her body showed only minor signs of the assault, and her killer had left nothing behind.

It seemed strange, but Matt let it go.

Pushing the second binder aside, he returned to the first and continued reading. Ron Harris came later in the investigation because finding him required interviews with people who knew Millie, a review of her text messages and e-mails, and DNA analysis of unwashed clothing found in her laundry hamper.

Millie Brown had been more than sexually active. Semen samples had been taken from two pairs of jeans, three bras and T-shirts, and five pairs of panties—what amounted to a week's worth of clothing. DNA analysis pointed to a single individual and did not match the samples taken from Jamie Taladyne. After Grace and Rodriguez sifted through the evidence and spoke with Millie's best friend, they realized it was more than likely that the semen had come from her science teacher in high school, Ron Harris.

Matt could tell that something changed when Grace and Rodriguez realized that their primary murder suspect was the victim's teacher. Someone who had broken what amounted to a sacred trust. Although they had enough to pick up Harris over the weekend, they waited until Monday, maximizing the shock value by pulling him out of his classroom in a pair of handcuffs. Grace made a note that when he looked back at the school from the car, every window was awash with the faces of teachers and students, every one of them peeking out from the shadows, frightened and stunned—a trust broken forever.

From that moment on, the investigation moved in a straight line and at high speed. Grace and Rodriguez sweated Harris out for fifteen hours in the box, often letting Orlando and Plank fill in for them when they needed a break. They offered food and coffee to Harris, bagging up everything the man touched and rushing it out to the crime lab for DNA analysis. They listened to his denials that Millie wanted out of the relationship and was threatening him with exposure. They listened to his numerous claims that he had no involvement with Millie on any personal level and that whomever they had been speaking with had lied to them. When Grace presented Harris with copies of the e-mails and text messages he had written to Millie—overwhelming evidence that SID had downloaded from the girl's computer and cell phone—Harris left himself open to the endgame and agreed to a polygraph.

It was a mistake, Grace noted in his report. The same one so many guilty people make when they're trying to convince detectives that they're innocent. Harris failed the polygraph and was held overnight.

By the following afternoon, preliminary results were in from the lab. Harris's DNA matched the DNA from the semen found on Millie's clothing. Within two hours Grace and Rodriguez, along with Orlando and Plank and a team of SID criminalists, had a warrant and were searching Harris's house.

They knew exactly what to look for because Dr. George Baylor, working side by side with Dr. Art Madina, one of the most talented medical examiners in the coroner's office, told them what to look for.

Millie Brown had been murdered with a razor blade.

And they found it in Ron Harris's toolbox in his garage. A razor blade set inside a box cutter.

A moment passed. A moment long enough to revive those hideous images of Jane Doe's cut-up face. Matt gulped down half the bottle of beer, trying to shake them off and hoping that he wouldn't dream tonight.

Baylor was part of the original team, most likely a hired professional whom the district attorney's office relied on to back up the county's findings and testify in court. But that only upped the ante and made the list of questions bigger than it should have been.

Grace and Rodriguez had Ron Harris so locked in, the man took his own life.

Matt got up and started pacing. His imagination was still trying to skip ahead. Every answer to every question pointed down a road that ended a mile or two back. Either way, no matter how you cut it there was a madman out there. Some sick fuck from another planet.

He glanced at the clock on the stove. It was one thirty in the morning. He was new at this. He needed someone to talk to. He thought about his dad.

CHAPTER 19

Frankie's service picked up after seven rings. Matt listened to the outgoing message. When he heard the beep, he paused a moment, wondering if he shouldn't just forget it.

"It's me, Frankie," he said finally. "Sorry about the late-night call, but I know why you lost it this morning. We need to talk. Call me back when you can."

He switched off the phone. One thirty in the morning. He needed to talk to someone. He found Cabrera's cell number and punched Call. Cabrera picked up after a single ring.

"What the fuck?"

Matt ignored the attitude. He could tell from the sound of Cabrera's voice that he'd been awake, even though he was probably in bed and lying down.

"In the Millie Brown case there was a second suspect, Jamie Taladyne. Grace and Rodriguez dropped him from the list when they found Ron Harris."

"You called me after going forty-eight straight to tell me this?"

Matt opened the slider and stepped out onto the rear deck, trying to choose the right words. There was no view of Santa Monica or Venice Beach tonight. Just the park at the bottom of the hill buried in an eerie fog.

"You saw what Grace was like tonight," he said. "Something's wrong."

"Something's wrong?" Cabrera pulled the phone away and muttered a few unrecognizable words in frustration. "Harris was doing the girl," he said. "She wanted out and had his perverted ass up against the fucking wall. He smoked her and tried to make it look like it was done by some sick fuck. The science and everything else worked like a compass, Jones. All his shit pointed north. Taladyne was never on the map."

"How come you know so much about it, Denny?"

"Because you left the murder book behind when you split this afternoon, and thanks to the lab putting us on hold, we've got nothing to go on with our own case."

Matt leaned against the rail, gazing at his neighbor's house and lowering his voice. "You seem so sure this isn't our case. Grace took those pictures of the girl's body. You want to know why?"

"I don't think so, Jones. I don't think I do."

"He had a meeting tonight with a doctor by the name of George Baylor. Baylor would have been a witness for the prosecution if Harris had lived long enough to go to trial. Grace wanted him to see the pictures. It was so important to him that he couldn't wait until morning. He drove over to Baylor's house in the middle of the night."

A long moment passed. When Cabrera eventually spoke, the anger and frustration in his voice had been transformed into genuine concern.

"How did you come by information like that?" he said. "Better yet, don't tell me, Matt. You need to listen to me, man. You're talking crazy and you're gonna get yourself in trouble. You're gonna get yourself fired."

Matt shook his head. "Something's wrong, Denny. We need to find Taladyne. We need to talk to him and see what's up."

"Listen to me, man. You're not listening." Cabrera paused, as if thinking it over, then came back. "I won't let you take me down with you, Jones. Do you understand? It's not gonna happen. Do you have any idea where I came from? My father was a day laborer who stood outside the fence at the Home Depot on San Fernando Road and hoped to make a buck any way he could. My mother cleaned rooms at a Motel 6 in Sun Valley. They busted their butts for me. They're the two greatest people I've ever met or even heard of. I'm not just the first kid from my neighborhood to graduate from college. I was the first kid to make it all the way through high school. I like my job, man, and I don't wanna lose it. I wanna make it a career."

Matt didn't know what to say. He understood where Cabrera was coming from. Although he didn't agree, he understood and could accept his partner's reasoning for everything he had just said. But halfway through, Matt had been looking past his house and noticed a red LED light blinking from the street. As he strained to see through the fog, he noticed the outline of a car, the red light coming from something like a GPS device mounted on the dashboard.

It was the car in his rearview mirror. The silver Nissan.

"I've gotta go," he said.

Cabrera was incensed. "Were you listening to me? Did you hear anything I just said?"

"I heard everything, Denny. I understand—believe me, I do. But right now I've gotta go."

He switched off his phone, then looked back at the Nissan and felt his body rock with anger. The car was parked underneath the trees on the other side of the street and could have been there for the past hour. Even worse, the guy behind the wheel had a picture-perfect view of the front entrance to his house and the door off the carport.

It felt like an insult. A personal violation. It was after one thirty in the fucking morning.

Matt rushed into the living room. As he began to draw the Smith & Wesson .45 holstered on his belt, he stopped when he noticed the baseball bat leaning against the closet door. He grabbed it, then headed back onto the deck and rushed down the steps. He was following a coyote trail below the ridge and around the house next door. As the path began to rise up the slope, he slowed down, and then stopped when he reached the street.

He could see the silver Nissan idling in the fog. He was close, just twenty-five yards away. Although he was standing behind the car, it looked like the man inside was talking to someone on his cell phone. It looked like the man was distracted, oblivious to his surroundings.

Matt studied the shadows cast by the streetlight blowing through the tree branches and thought he spotted a seam of darkness in the fog that matched the car's natural blind spots. As he stepped into the seam and started moving forward, he knew that he was invisible. He knew that if the man checked any mirror in the car, all he would see was fog.

Matt noted the license plate number, committing it to memory, then eased his way to within two feet of the driver's-side door. He could hear the man talking to someone on the phone. Although he couldn't make out what he was saying through the glass or over the sound of the engine, he could tell by the tone that it was a business conversation and guessed that the subject matter had something to do with him.

Matt felt another wave of anger wash through his body and tried to bury it. Inching closer, he became still, invisible, and looked the man over with great care. He was in his early forties, on the chunky side, with a receding hairline. A white male with a face so soft and plain that it would be difficult to pick him out of a crowd, much less a lineup. Matt noted the suit jacket hanging from the passenger seat, the striped tie that had been pulled away from the open collar, the glow of a cigarette between the man's fat fingers, the spent cup of coffee and the .38 revolver resting on the console between the bucket seats.

Nothing about the guy or the car he was sitting in felt like law enforcement. Nothing about anything Matt was staring at had the feel of being legitimate or righteous.

Not at this hour.

Not in front of his house.

He raised the bat over his head and stepped up to the window. When the man turned, his eyes lit up and he shrieked and hit the gas. Matt swung the bat but only managed to get a piece of the rear fender. The man in the silver Nissan had been fast. Too fast. Matt watched him take the bend hard and vanish around the corner, the fog wafting in his wake like smoke from a grass fire. Like trouble.

CHAPTER 20

It didn't feel much like sleep, but Matt had grown used to it. Every night overseas had gone exactly the same way, not just for him but for everyone he had been with. They didn't really sleep or dream, because no one could get to a place safe enough to let go. Instead, they spent four or five hours suspended in what they called the *blur*.

After his return home, it had taken Matt three years to get a decent night's rest. But now that feeling was back.

He could see Jane Doe's face in the darkness. The slashes. The blood. The deformity that somehow reminded him of a clown's face, swollen and all ripped up.

He could see Grace standing over her corpse, his entire being riddled with fear and anguish.

He could see a man he imagined was Cabrera's father huddled with other men outside a Home Depot, hoping every car that pulled out of the lot might mean a few hours' work.

But in the end the blur always returned to the same image. The same memory. His oldest memory.

He could see his father walking out the front door, tossing a suitcase in the car and driving off. He could hear his mother weeping, the tears flowing down her cheeks. He could feel her hugging him and telling him that everything would be okay.

It had taken him many years to figure out who his father really was. When his mother had been alive, Matt was too young to wonder. When his aunt took him in, the subject never came up, until one day, at twelve years old, Matt opened the business section of the *New York Times*. Money had always been tight and he knew that his father had been a deadbeat dad who bailed on child support, didn't remember a single birthday, and never helped out. His image of his father was of an indigent, a bum who slept in public places, wore tattered clothing, and rarely bathed. A loser with empty pockets who walked out on his obligations and left his wife and son out on a limb to fend for themselves. A man who, when his wife died of cancer, couldn't be reached and refused to take back and raise his son. So when Matt opened the newspaper and learned that he shared his father's name, when he saw his picture below the headline and read the caption *M. Trevor Jones, chairman, president, and CEO of PSF Bank of New York*, one of the five largest banks in the United States, when the old image died and the new one slapped him across the face, Matt turned to his aunt and asked her why she hadn't said anything.

Because I promised your mother that I would never bad-mouth your father in front of you, and unfortunately I'm not capable of keeping that promise, Matty. I don't care for your father very much. I don't think he's a good man.

In many ways it had been a relief.

For years Matt had blamed himself for his father walking out on them. Now, at the grand old age of twelve, he realized that it was the other way around. There was something fundamentally wrong with his father. Something bent and broken. But even more important to Matt, all of the anger that he had been harboring for all these years, all of the rage and hatred he had felt for the man, all of it in a single moment burned up and vanished before his eyes. What remained was curiosity, the same kind of curiosity he'd felt when his aunt had taken him to the Bronx Zoo and he got his first look at a rattlesnake.

Over the years Matt's interest in his father only grew. Although he agreed with his aunt, he kept his thoughts to himself because he didn't want to upset her. He began reading the business section of the paper every day. He knew the year that his father began serving on the board of directors of the Federal Reserve Bank of New York. When *Time* magazine added his father to the list of the world's one hundred most influential people, he bought a copy, read it late at night with a flashlight, and hid it under his bed. He scoured the Internet and knew the terms of his father's forty-million-dollar pay package for the year. Even more, he knew that his father was the highest paid CEO of any bank in the country.

His curiosity had nothing to do with his father's wealth. It was all about the hypocrisy and what appeared to be a radioactive form of greed. It was all about a man who walked down Wall Street thinking that he was a king but emanated darkness and all things evil. It was all about the memory that came to Matt when he couldn't sleep and floated in the blur—his father walking out the front door with his suitcase and driving away. Forever away.

It was all about a single question.

Why?

Matt thought that he deserved an answer. And after his return from Afghanistan to New Jersey, he called his father at his office in New York City. When the woman who answered the phone claimed that Mr. Jones didn't have a son by the name of Matthew Trevor Jones and hung up on him, Matt laughed at her bitchy attitude, went on the Internet, and found a home address. As it turned out, his destitute asshole father—dear old Dad— lived in Greenwich, Connecticut, off Indian Field Road. From the satellite photos Matt pulled off the search engine on his computer, the man was slumming it in a palatial mansion on Long Island Sound. A large yacht, more than seventy feet long, was anchored just offshore.

Matt chewed it over for several days, then decided to make what amounted to an hour's drive north into Connecticut. Dizzy with curiosity, he had no real plan and no guarantee that his father would even be home. The road was desolate, the walls and gates sparse. As he neared the water and his father's mansion came into view, he pulled over and got out of the car. He was beginning to feel nervous and wondered if confronting the man might be a bad idea. Maybe he should have written his father a letter or made a second attempt to reach him on the phone.

He looked past the ten-foot wall and through the gate. Although there was an entrance for show on the side of the house, he could tell that the place faced the sound. He could also tell at a glance that this was no mini-mansion. Instead, the building was big and loud and had the appearance of being way overdone. But what struck Matt most about the place was how cold it felt—more like a hotel than a home, more public than private, almost institutional but almost Vegas as well.

How could anyone build something so cheap and tasteless on such a magnificent piece of land?

A woman in a chef's uniform walked outside and lit a cigarette. Matt saw her and stepped back but wasn't sure that he'd been quick enough. Easing forward, he peeked through the gate. Her back was turned. She'd missed him. She didn't know that he was here.

He glanced back at his car, debating whether or not he should leave. He could remember seeing a dirt road on the satellite photos that wandered through the woods encircling the house and provided public access to the water. It took a few moments to find it. Tall reeds and dune grass covered the entrance. By all appearances, the way had been deliberately obscured by the people living on Indian Field Road, who didn't want strangers around.

Matt parted the reeds, climbed over the gate, and started down the road. It was a summer evening, about an hour before sunset. He could see the rear of the mansion over the wall and, through the thick foliage, six cars parked in a lot that could easily fit ten more. As he passed what he thought was the kitchen door, he looked for the woman smoking the cigarette, but she must have gone back inside.

He kept moving, thinking. As he started around the bend, he began to hear voices coming from the other side of the wall. After another twenty-five yards, they became more clear and he stopped. They were close. Too close to be seen over a ten-foot wall. Matt took a step forward, his eyes dancing from tree to tree until he found the right one. All he needed was another five, maybe six, feet.

He grabbed hold of the first branch and started climbing. Once he had the height, he found a space within the leaves and inched his head upward until his eyes finally rose above the wall. There were three people sitting on the other side of the pool on the main terrace. It was a safe bet that the woman was his father's second wife. The two men looked to be about five years younger than Matt and no doubt were their sons. They were drinking wine and eating hors d'oeuvres, served by a young Hispanic man dressed in a tux. The woman had bleached blond hair and was wearing too much jewelry. Matt guessed that her looks had faded ten years ago, and no amount of plastic surgery could bring them back or even soften the severity he saw in her face. The two sons were dressed like boys, with matching blue blazers and tapered tan slacks to go along with their soft faces, their long hair and bangs.

Matt turned away, thinking about his mother. He had been so young when she died. He had felt so blue and so lonely—scared to death that he might end up in a state-run home or on the street.

His eyes found their way across the water to his father's yacht. From here it looked more like a ship, and Matt thought it probably required a crew to operate. But what really caught his eye was the name of the yacht printed across its stern.

Greedy Bastard, Greenwich, Connecticut.

Matt shook it off and turned back to the house. They were laughing about something. And then, after a few moments and as if on cue, it finally happened.

All three of them turned as a man exited the house and strode across the terrace with a glass of wine in his hand. Matt wouldn't have needed an introduction, because he saw that same face every day in the mirror when he shaved. That same face, less twenty-five years.

It was his father, his deadbeat dad, slumming it on the sound.

M. Trevor Jones.

Matt couldn't take his eyes off him. Every line on his face, every gray hair on his head, but even more, the sound of his father's voice—Matt drank it in, like swilling a gallon or two of gasoline that had been sweetened with honey.

The sound of his father's voice.

It was almost as if he'd fallen into the river of what used to be. He could remember hugging his father when he came home from work at night. He could remember the smell of his skin. The memory seemed so clear and vivid.

But after fifteen or twenty minutes passed, after studying the man and trying to measure him, something happened that Matt didn't understand at first. He was gazing at these four people sipping wine on their terrace and snacking on whatever their butler was serving on his silver tray. He was gazing at what amounted to his own family, but the spell had faded and all the honey was gone.

He couldn't help thinking how ridiculous they seemed.

Maybe it was the way his father looked at his wife, the phony smiles and the forced laughs that they shared. Maybe it was all the gold jewelry the woman was wearing, or the way the two boy-men were dressed up to look like twins. Freaks.

It felt perverted and corrupt. It felt dirty.

No matter what it was, Matt realized that he no longer needed to meet his father. That he no longer needed his father to tell him why he had abandoned him. Matt had just answered the question for himself. He could see it before his eyes. He could see it in who they were.

No matter what the hardship, his father walking out on him and his mom had been a gift. A blessing in disguise. A lucky break in the sense that he was out of their lives forever and had no influence over them.

Matt heard a phone begin ringing and panicked. It was his cell.

He scrambled to dig it out of his pocket and shut off the sound but slipped from the tree and began falling. Butterflies swarmed his stomach as he dropped through the air. When he finally landed, he found himself sprawled out on the couch with his .45 in his right hand and the phone in his left. He dropped the gun and tried to pull himself together as he checked the time. 6:00 a.m. He brought the phone to his ear without looking at the caller ID. It turned out to be Laura Hughes, and she sounded upset.

"Matt," she said in a shaky voice. "Oh, God, Matt. Someone broke into the house last night."

Matt reached for his .45 and got to his feet. His mind cleared.

"I'm on my way," he said.

CHAPTER 21

The intruder had entered the house through a window on the second floor that opened into Hughes's study and, like the master bedroom, overlooked the pool and backyard. He had used a glass cutter, making a round hole just big enough to reach inside and open the latch. A long piece of clear tape had been attached so that the glass could be removed without making any sound.

Matt looked at it still taped to the roof over the first-floor porch, then turned to Laura. She was watching from the hallway and seemed more than nervous.

"There aren't any alarms on the second floor?" he asked.

She shook her head. "Just downstairs."

She was still dressed for bed. She was wearing another T-shirt and that pair of pajama bottoms with pictures of flowers and rainbows and pots of gold. She had added a robe, which she kept tugging on and pulling across her chest.

"Everything was okay with Kevin, right, Laura? He didn't seem quiet or preoccupied? He wasn't worried about something or someone? He didn't mention anything going on at work?"

Those blue eyes of hers got bigger and were right on him. She seemed surprised by his questions. She seemed confused and nervous about them. When she spoke, her voice was low pitched and scratchy.

"I thought you said it was a holdup."

Matt nodded. "I did," he said. "But it might be more than that."

"More than that?"

"Did you see anyone hanging around yesterday? Maybe sitting in their car looking at your house."

"I didn't see anyone, but I wasn't looking. You're scaring me, Matt. You think this has something to do with Kevin's death?"

"I didn't say that. Everything's gonna be fine. Trust me. It's okay."

He hadn't said it, but deep inside he knew that there was no other explanation for the break-in and that it wouldn't take long for Laura to figure it out on her own. He looked away from her just as a ray of sunlight struck the carpet. He could see shoe prints in the pile. The impressions were fresh and distinct and led out of the study and down the hall.

"When was the last time you vacuumed?"

Her eyes dropped to the carpet. "A few days ago. Why?"

Matt shrugged. "Just curious," he said. "I need to go through Kevin's desk. It's gonna take a while. You might as well shower and get dressed."

She gave him a look. "When was the last time you had something to eat, Matt?"

"I don't remember."

"Then I'll go downstairs, make a pot of coffee, and fix you some eggs."

He watched her walk off but waited until he heard her reach the first floor and step into the kitchen. Fishing his cell phone out of his pocket, he switched on the flashlight and followed the shoe prints down the hall. Whoever the prints belonged to had made a round trip that began in the study. When he followed them into the master bedroom, when they stopped at the end of the bed, he felt his heart sink. Based on the compression of the carpet pile, the intruder had spent more than a few minutes watching Laura sleep.

Matt tried to keep his emotions in check, following the prints from the end of the bed to a chair by the window. Laura had tossed her jeans over the arm. A bra and a pair of panties the color of raspberries were laid out on top. As he looked back at the bed, he tried not to think about what had happened here last night, or what could have happened. He tried not to give the pictures that were playing in his head any definition.

If he hadn't noticed the footprints, he would have thought that this was over. Whoever broke into the house took what they wanted and split.

If he hadn't noticed the footprints, it *could* have been over.

He took a deep breath, considering his options. He needed to make two phone calls. First to Grace so that they could work things out with Glendale PD and get SID out here. But even more important, Matt knew with complete certainty that the threat to Laura was directly related to her husband's murder on LAPD soil. He needed to bring Metro Division into the mix. He needed a protection detail, two teams, twenty-four hours a day.

He checked his watch. It was still early. No one would be at the station for another twenty minutes, which was okay by him because he wanted the place to himself for a while.

He switched off the flashlight on his cell phone and returned to Hughes's study. While he waited for the laptop to boot up, he dug a pair of vinyl gloves out of his jacket pocket, slipped them on, and began searching through the desk. It looked like Hughes had kept files on every one of his cases. As Matt opened a folder and skimmed through the copy, he realized that his friend had been keeping a record of his personal thoughts: things he'd learned from Lane, the mistakes they'd made, and the steps they'd taken that finally led them to an arrest. But even more, he could tell from the tone of his friend's notes how much he loved being a detective.

Matt returned the hanger file to the drawer, searching the tabs for Faith Novakoff's name. He found the file off the rails and pushed to the bottom of the drawer. When he opened it, the folder was empty. He moved over to the window for a closer look in better light. The bottom of the hanger file had been bent into a square in order to accommodate what Matt judged was a stack of paper at least an inch thick. Matt had no doubt that Hughes would have kept notes on what was obviously his biggest case as a homicide detective. And he had no doubt that his notes had been stolen last night.

He moved back to the desk and sat down, pulling the laptop closer. He was looking for the word-processing program that came with Hughes's office software. Every other program was here—spreadsheets, accounting, business presentations—everything but the word processor, the program Hughes would have used to type his notes. Matt checked the trash folder on the start screen and found it empty.

It occurred to him that Hughes might have shared his notes with Lane. Opening his e-mail program, he clicked the Sent folder and began skimming through the list of messages. While he didn't see anything written to Lane, there appeared to be hundreds of e-mails sent to a single address that Matt didn't recognize by name. After checking the dates, he realized that they went back more than five years and included his time with Hughes when they were in Afghanistan.

Matt picked one at random and opened it. As he began reading, he became embarrassed. It was a love letter that Hughes had written to Laura, and below that, her reply to a previous love letter. He knew that he should stop reading and close the window, but something about the words drew him in. He guessed that his weakness came from the vacuum in his own life. All the personal things that he'd been dealing with, all the people he'd pushed away or put on hold.

He heard Laura coming up the stairs and finally closed the window. He could smell bacon in the air, fresh-brewed coffee.

He turned and watched her step through the doorway. She still looked frightened. But even more, he was struck by her gentleness and grace and overwhelmed by a feeling that he'd just violated her trust. He felt like he needed to make things up to her for reading something so personal, something he had no right to look at.

"The TV was on in the kitchen," she said. "The three-piece bandit just sent text messages to the stations claiming that he had nothing to do with Kevin's death."

Matt took it in as he gazed at her. "You know what that means, Laura. Nothing."

"I know," she said in a quieter voice. "That's what anyone would say. It's a murder. It's the killing of a police officer. He's claiming that he didn't do it." She looked at the hole in the window for a moment, then turned back. "I'm just trying to understand what's really going on."

He could feel her eyes homed in on his face. He could see her wheels turning. She was picking up on his guilt, and he needed to chill. Reaching into his pocket, he pulled out a piece of nicotine gum but decided not to open it.

"Where did Kevin keep his guns?" he said.

"In a locked rack in the bedroom closet. I already checked. They're all there."

"Your parents still live outside Philadelphia, right?"

She nodded without saying anything.

"Would you have any interest in visiting them?"

She shook her head back and forth. "I'm not going anywhere until you get the guy who shot Kevin."

Matt nodded, then told her about his plan to call in Metro and set up a protection detail. Although he didn't mention the impressions he'd found in the carpet, the idea that she needed cops guarding her seemed to underline the weight of her situation and frighten her even more. After pulling herself together, she agreed on one condition.

"I want you to stay here, Matt. I know you're working a case. I know you don't have time to hang around and hold my hand. But you'll need to take a break somewhere, so it might as well be here. I need you right now."

Matt's eyes drifted across the carpet and up to her face. He owed her. But even more, he hoped the guy who had stood at the foot of her bed would come back tonight. He felt like he owed him something, too.

CHAPTER 22

Matt made a right off Franklin Avenue onto Beachwood Drive, heading for the horse ranch just below the peak of the mountain. As he started to make the climb, he found Cabrera's cell number on his list of most-recent calls.

He had already spoken with Metro, and the first team from the protection detail had arrived at Hughes's house before he'd left. Matt was much less worried about Laura's safety now. It seemed to him that their presence had an immediate calming effect on her as well. To his credit, Grace was on board even before Metro showed up. Details had been worked out with Glendale PD, and they agreed that because the threat to Laura originated from an LAPD case, Hollywood would run the investigation. Matt was just glad things had gone smoothly and had stayed while SID criminalists spent a couple of hours scouring the house and yard.

Hughes's laptop computer had been taken down to the lab. Analysis of the fingerprints SID lifted in the study, along with the hair and fiber samples they collected, would take time. Most likely those samples belonged to Hughes and his wife and would lead to nowhere. But they'd walked away with one fact. The burglar wore a

size eleven hiking shoe. According to the criminalist who discovered the print in the garden below the roof and open window, the
cast SID poured was so perfect that it revealed the wear and deg-
radation of the tread. Not only would they be able to identify the
manufacturer, if and when they had a suspect and located the shoe
they would be able to lock it in with nearly the same probability as
a fingerprint.

Cabrera picked up after five rings without saying hello.

"I need you to do me a favor, Cabrera."

"What kind of favor?"

His partner's voice sounded dead. The guy was still pissed off.
Matt grimaced. "I want you to run a plate for me."

"Why can't you do it yourself?"

"Because I've had a busy morning. Didn't you talk to Grace?"

"He's not here. Orlando and Plank aren't here either."

"Will you run the plate for me or not?"

Cabrera hesitated. Matt couldn't believe it.

"Okay, okay," he said finally. "Give me the fucking number."

Matt recited it from memory, then told Cabrera that the plate
went with a silver Nissan. He gave him the model of the car and
said he believed it was less than two years old.

"What's this about?" Cabrera said.

Matt paused to think it over before he spoke. "I'm guessing
you don't want to know," he said.

"You're probably right, Jones."

Cabrera hung up on him. Matt shrugged it off, the road steep-
ening as he passed the Beachwood Market and Café halfway up.
He couldn't worry about Cabrera. He needed to keep pushing,
keep driving forward. There wasn't enough time to look back.

Beachwood Drive eventually came to an end, and he found
a place to park at the horse ranch. As he grabbed his phone and
got out, he glanced at the face before slipping it into his pocket
and realized that he'd missed a call. It was from Frankie, and he'd

left a message. Matt located the fire road that snaked around the mountain and started hiking west toward the Hollywood sign as he listened to the message. Lane had been brief, and he could hear road noise in the background.

"Got your message, Matt. Thanks for understanding why I was such a wreck yesterday. I'm following up what may or may not be a couple of decent leads this morning. Laura told me what happened and said you're staying at the house. That's good news. Let's talk later in the day and trade notes."

Frankie sounded better. But even more, he was back in the game, working on a couple of leads while everyone else was immersed in a world of hunches, best guesses, and dead ends.

Matt took a deep breath and tried to let go of the frustration. As he hiked around a bend, he stopped to look at the Hollywood sign, then located the spot on the trail where Jane Doe's body had been found. He was more than two hundred yards away. Still, it wasn't difficult to find, because the daylight crew from SID was working the crime scene. Even from a distance, their blue jackets with LAPD/SID printed across the back more than stood out in the rough terrain. Matt searched for Orlando and Plank and spotted them climbing up the slope by the sign. Grace was with them, and it looked like all three were heading back to their cars.

As he watched them struggle up the mountain, he opened another piece of nicotine gum and bit into it to release the drug. After a minute or two, he could feel the nicotine smoothing the edge of his morning away. In spite of the good feeling, he hated it. Both he and Hughes had started smoking cigarettes and become addicted while overseas. Of the choices they were given, cigarettes seemed less harmful than the meds command was trying to push on everybody to help them relax at night and then wake up in the morning. There were too many suicides and too many rumors about the drugs. He could remember one day when the CEO of the pharmaceutical company that was providing those drugs came to Afghanistan for what was supposed to be a two-day tour. Matt saw him and couldn't believe his thug-like appearance. They never did find out who took a shot at the man, just that it had come from an American soldier with a rifle. After that, no one from any corporation profiting from the war ever showed up for a tour. It was understood by everyone at every level of command that the first shot had been a warning—a blowback pitch by a very talented marksman—and that the next shot would be a *money shot* and knock the asshole down.

The wind picked up, jogging Matt's mind to the surface. He looked back at the mountain just as Orlando and Plank followed Grace over the rim. Once they disappeared, he let his eyes drift down the slope until they came to rest on the SID techs examining the trail. He remembered that feeling he'd had last night, the sense that someone had been hiding out here and watching them. It was the reason he'd parked at the top of Beachwood Drive and hiked in from the east. Eyeing the trail, he had a better than decent view but knew that he was still too far off. He needed to close the distance by at least half.

Matt zipped up his sweatshirt and started walking. He glanced at the SID techs, then let his eyes wander through the harsh landscape as he hiked around another sharp bend. He was looking for a place where he might feel safe. A hiding place with an up-close-and-personal view. A place that a sniper might call *home*.

The face of the mountain steepened to his right, and as the fire road straightened out, he was struck by an explosion of color on the eastern side of the slope. Moving off the path and up the mountain, he realized that they were poppies the size of his palm. Vibrant yellows and reds, brilliant oranges and blues, the flowers carpeted the entire ridge as they swayed back and forth in the wind. It seemed so strange, so peculiar. This was late October, not April, and the poppies were in full bloom. It seemed like nature had lost its way and no longer knew what day it was.

He scanned the mountains, searching for another patch of color, another aberration, another sign of spring in the hostile landscape. When all he saw was gray, he climbed further up the ridge until he reached the top. And that's when he found it. A boulder that had rolled down from the mountain peak until it reached the ridge and what was a bird's-eye view of the crime scene.

He was less than a hundred yards away, and two or three stories above the spot where the girl's body had been found. A grove of bushes on the other side of the boulder provided a perfect blind. When Matt noticed that several branches had been bent back or broken and tossed to the side—branches that were high and would have obscured the view—he could feel it in his gut. The killer had been here last night. The madman had been watching.

Matt checked the ground, looking for further confirmation. The soil was loose and dusty, so finding a footprint seemed unlikely. But he noticed something shiny caught in the leaves of a bush with thorns. A small piece of paper—or was it foil? Digging into his pocket for a vinyl glove, he slipped it on and plucked the piece of trash out of the leaves.

It was a small wrapper from a Fifth Avenue candy bar.

The wrapper didn't mean anything on its own. Hundreds of people hiked these trails every day. If he had headed east, he would have picked up the trail to Mount Hollywood and the two-acre garden overlooking Griffith Observatory and the entire LA basin known as Dante's View. Still, he dropped the wrapper into his shirt pocket and made a mental note to collect samples of the branches that had been tossed to the ground. Living skin cells containing DNA could easily have been transferred to the twigs, particularly if it had taken any effort to break them off.

He turned back and gazed down at the crime scene. He thought about the way Jane Doe had been left to die alone in the darkness. The things the killer had done to her.

Why did everything seem so familiar? So close to home?

Matt didn't think that it was something he'd seen in real life or even at a movie theater. It had to be déjà vu. The thoughts, the feelings, the pictures in his head had to be an illusion of some kind. Even so, it made him anxious. He wished that he'd had the chance to interview the man who heard Jane Doe scream and called it in, but Grace had spoken with him alone.

He thought it over one more time.

There was the very real possibility that the killer had been here last night, sitting on this boulder and watching them process the crime scene. The feeling might have been coming from his gut, but he thought that he could count on it. And the breadth of the view, the trimmed-out blind, seemed to back that up. The killer liked to watch his victims being discovered. He liked to see what happened after they were dead. It was part of the kick. Part of his sickness. Part of the ritual—

It suddenly dawned on Matt why all of this seemed so familiar. It wasn't something he'd seen. It was something he'd read.

CHAPTER 23

The killer was making some sort of demented statement. The way each young woman had been bathed and then soiled and staked to the ground, the wounds to their faces, the spilling of blood onto sheets of mirrored glass. Matt had been thinking about it ever since he knelt down before Jane Doe. The idea that her murder resembled the ritual slaughter of an animal. That something about it originated in stories from the Old Testament, from Homer or even Hesiod. That the killings of all three students were part of a religious ritual performed by a modern-day freak.

But it had been the trail to Mount Hollywood that triggered the memory. The idea of a garden planted on top of the mountain by an actor, Dante Orgolini, in the 1960s. The majestic view the garden offered of Los Angeles, from downtown all the way west to the Santa Monica Bay and the Pacific Ocean.

Dante's View.

Just the thought of it had given birth to a memory.

Matt had read *The Divine Comedy* in Mr. Peterson's English class as a sophomore in high school. An illustrated hardcover edition was on one of his bookshelves beside his desk in the den.

Although the drive home would cost him the rest of his morning, he had to return at some point to pack a bag for his stay at Laura's. In terms of traffic, late morning was by far the best time of the day.

He found the book buried in a stack of oversized art books on the bottom shelf, then crossed the room to sit in his reading chair by the window. As if on automatic pilot, he checked the street for the silver Nissan. He'd checked once or twice this morning from his car but hadn't seen the man and guessed that he was getting some rest after a long night.

He glanced back at the book, feeling the weight of the epic poem and its meaning in his hands.

It was all about greed. All about the predatory desire for wealth, status, and power. The seven Ps carved into Virgil's forehead, each one removed by an angel as he passed through the seven terraces of the seven deadly sins. Matt turned to part two in the poem, *Purgatorio*, and began skimming through it as quickly as he could. He already knew what he was looking for. When he came to the passage, he read through it and stopped to think it over.

The penitents were bound and laid facedown on the ground for spending too much time pursuing material possessions. Too much time thinking earthly thoughts. Too much time chasing money and screwing everybody they could to get more. Too much time ignoring what little humanity they might possess in favor of the animal living beneath their soiled flesh . . .

A long moment passed. He noticed that his hands were trembling slightly. His fingers. The churning in his stomach was back. The dread.

He was staring at his first real piece of the puzzle, and everything about it felt dark and twisted and out of control. But even more, he knew in his gut that a critical error must have been made in the Millie Brown murder case. Grace wanted to believe that they were chasing a copycat. But Matt could see it now. Killers this vicious only come in ones.

CHAPTER 24

Matt saw them talking in the conference room. Cabrera was sitting in a chair at the table. Orlando and Plank stood over him with their hands on their hips. Everyone in the room looked agitated and pissed off.

When Matt opened the door, all three immediately stopped talking. In spite of the obvious bad vibes, he walked in and joined them at the table. The silence had a certain weight about it. After a while Orlando turned and gave him a hard look up and down.

"What are you holding in your hand?" he said.

Matt tossed two evidence bags onto the table. The first contained the wrapper from the Fifth Avenue candy bar. The second was filled with sections from the branches he suspected the killer might have touched. When he explained what they were, the anger and suspicion showing on Orlando's face only seemed to intensify. Joey Orlando was a big man. A powerful man. And Edward Plank, no matter how much smaller in size, stood right beside him, scooping up the evidence bags and stuffing them into his pockets.

Orlando took a step forward and then another, until he was standing in Matt's face. It looked like his goatee needed a trim. He was wearing a red tie, and Matt noticed a salsa stain on his shirt just above the pocket.

"You need to stand down, Jones. Way down. You need to work your own case." He glanced over at Cabrera, then turned back. "And by the way," he said, "the bullshit you're trying to sell that says there's something wrong with the case we made against Ron Harris—that's not gonna go over very well around here. We don't need dumb guys working at the homicide table, Jones. Mind your own fucking business and work your own shit and we'll get along just fine. Keep sticking your nose in my shit, and nothing's gonna work for anybody. Got it?"

Matt held the man's gaze, which wasn't easy. "Are you speaking for yourself, Orlando? Or is this coming from Grace?"

The big man seemed stunned that Matt had the audacity to say anything that wasn't a direct reply.

"I just asked you a question, Jones. Do you understand what I'm saying or not?"

Matt paused to think it over, knowing that it would piss off Orlando. Pissing off Orlando seemed like the way of the future.

"I got it, Joey," he said finally. "I got it good."

"Then get the fuck out of my way."

Orlando pushed him aside with a meaty hand and stomped out of the room. Plank followed him out, sporting a mean little sneer between those pockmarked cheeks. When Cabrera stood up and tried to make it to the door, Matt grabbed him and pushed him back into the chair.

"Who else have you told?" Matt said.

Cabrera shrugged. "I don't know what you're talking about."

He tried to get up, but Matt had him by the shoulders and pushed him down again. "You told those guys what we talked about last night, Cabrera. You broke a trust. As backstabbers go, you're pretty fucking good at it, man. Now I want to know who else you've talked to. Did you tell Grace? Are you pimping for him? Tell me the truth, you shithead. I can tell when people lie. Who are you talking to?"

"You need to fuck off, Jones. And by the way, we're partners. I don't take orders from you."

Matt gritted his teeth and pushed harder. "Who did you talk to?"

"No one, you jerk. Why would I? They might think I'm as crazy as you are. Now step back and get out of my face."

"We need to find Jamie Taladyne."

"Everybody around here's looking for Jamie Taladyne."

"Orlando said that?"

Cabrera nodded. "You need to listen to what he just told you, Jones. There was a message to it. Keep your ass out of his shit."

Matt stepped back, leaning against the plate-glass window, his mind going at a hundred miles an hour. He had what felt like confirmation now. Something was wrong with the case against Ron Harris. Something big enough that Orlando felt the need to take him on even though two witnesses were in the room. It was the classic move of a bully, someone who expected his victim to stand down and stay down.

Cabrera leaned back in his chair, eyeing Matt for a few minutes with a counterfeit smile on his face.

"Like it or not, we're partners, Jones. It's like you said the other night in Grace's office. It's about trust and watching the other guy's back. It's about knowing when to take and when to give back. It's about an understanding. How did you put it? I remember now. It's about two becoming one."

Cabrera's insincerity—the words he used—settled into the room like nerve gas. Matt wanted to tell the prick to eat shit. Instead, he tried to reel in his emotions and asked about the license plate.

Cabrera laughed at him. "You said it was supposed to match up to a silver Nissan. According to the wife of the man who owns the car, that plate number goes with a Lincoln that's parked in the long-term lot over at Burbank airport."

Matt gave him a hard look. "Did you check to see if it's still there?"

Cabrera shrugged without a reply.

"Thanks for doing me the favor, Denny. I appreciate the effort."

"The way you say it, doesn't sound like you mean it, Jones."

Matt didn't reply. Fearing that he might strike the man, that he might hurt him, he took a deep breath and walked out of the room. Their partnership still had some kinks to it. The dynamic duo still had a ways to go . . .

CHAPTER 25

Matt read the sign on the door. It turned out that Dr. George Baylor was a plastic surgeon with an office in a medical building a block away from the Los Angeles County + USC Medical Center and the coroner's office. He wasn't sure why Baylor being a plastic surgeon surprised him, but it did.

He tried to open the door but found it locked. When he noticed the buzzer, he pressed the button and reached for his ID. He guessed that the office was closed for lunch and just hoped that Baylor ate in.

After two or three minutes, the door popped open and a middle-aged woman with a young face and gray hair peeked out. Matt raised his ID and held it against his chest.

"I'm trying to reach Dr. Baylor," he said. "It's important."

"Would he know what it's about?"

"Yes."

Her eyes went to his name on the ID, then flicked up to his face. "Let me see if he's in."

She pulled the door shut and turned the lock. She obviously knew whether Baylor was in or not, but Matt didn't mind, because she seemed nice. After waiting another few minutes, the door opened to reveal Dr. Baylor himself.

"Come in," he said with a broad smile. "Please, come in."

Baylor shook his hand, then led him through the empty lobby and into his office. After offering him a chair, the doctor walked over to his desk and sat down.

"How can I help you?" he said.

Matt wasn't sure how to put it without admitting that he'd followed Grace over to the doctor's house last night. He stalled for a moment, weighing the risks as he took in the office. Baylor's various degrees and credentials were neatly framed on the far wall. Behind the desk stood a credenza and shelves filled with books and periodicals. To his left was a view of downtown LA so spectacular, Matt had no doubt that it was a major factor in the rent.

He cleared his throat and looked back at Baylor. "I guess the best way to put it is to come right out and ask."

"Ask what?"

"You met with my supervisor last night, Lieutenant Grace. He showed you a series of photographs he took with his cell phone of a young woman who was murdered up by the Hollywood sign. I need to know what you spoke about. I need to know why my supervisor thought those pictures were so important for you to see that it couldn't wait until morning."

Baylor was measuring him. The smile was still there, but he was measuring him.

He reached across the desk. "Let me see your ID," he said in an even but still pleasant voice.

Matt passed it across the desk and watched Baylor roll his chair closer to the lamp on the credenza. He was dressed in a crisp white shirt, a blue silk tie that almost matched the color of his eyes, and a pair of gray slacks that were well tailored and probably handmade. And while his brown hair had lightened from the sun and appeared spiked, his grooming was meticulous. Matt could sense a certain energy, a certain enthusiasm, radiating from the man's being. He never would have guessed that he was fifty-five. Baylor looked and seemed ten years younger.

"Matthew Trevor Jones," Baylor said, thinking it over. "I know that name, but I don't know you. Tell me how I know that name?"

Dr. Baylor's smile was back. There was a gentleness to the man. A certain kindness in his demeanor, his presence, even if it felt like he might be playing him.

"I don't know," Matt said. "Jones is a pretty common name."

He laughed. "It is. But not when you add a Matthew Trevor to it. Matthew Trevor Jones. See what I mean?"

Matt nodded.

"What's your father's name?"

Matt gave the doctor a long look. "Exactly what you think it is, Doctor."

"And your father is exactly *who* I think he is, isn't he? I read something about him in the business section of the *Times* a few days ago. I remember seeing his picture. You look just like him."

Matt had never spoken about his father with anyone other than Hughes. Dr. Baylor's questions made him feel uncomfortable. All he could manage was another uneasy nod.

Baylor leaned forward, returning Matt's ID. "What's he think of you being a homicide detective way out here in Los Angeles?"

"My guess is that he doesn't know."

"Ah," Dr. Baylor said. "Of course."

Something changed after that. The warmth and kindness showing on Baylor's face moved into his eyes. If the doctor had been playing him, the game was over.

"So you want to know why Bob Grace came to my house last night," he said. "Why? It seems like such a trivial detail."

"There's the chance that two cases that seem unrelated might not be, Doctor."

"Other than the girl, which case are you talking about?"

"A detective from North Hollywood was shot the other night. He was killed."

"If it's that important, why didn't you just ask Grace?"

Matt couldn't answer the question. He was on dangerous ground just being here. He had no doubt that Baylor would call Grace as soon as he left.

Baylor studied him for a moment, then shrugged. "Grace wants me to attend Jane Doe's autopsy and compare the results with the murders of Faith Novakoff and Millie Brown. The autopsy was originally scheduled for this morning but got pushed back to this afternoon. The delay has something to do with Jane Doe's dental records."

"So Grace brought the pictures over just in case you needed to be convinced?"

"Something like that, but I didn't need to be convinced. He's worried."

"He thinks maybe Ron Harris wasn't good for Millie Brown's murder? He thinks maybe they got it wrong?"

Baylor's eyes narrowed and that smile was back, all the curiosity. "He didn't say that, Matthew. The evidence against Harris was overwhelming. He thinks it's a copycat. He wants to find Jamie Taladyne and speak with him. But that's not what's on your mind, is it? You're thinking somehow something went wrong. Something catastrophic. That's why you took the chance and came here instead of talking to Grace. What is it?"

Matt got up and walked over to the window as he thought it through. After a few moments, Baylor joined him and leaned against the sill.

"What is it?" he repeated.

"Have you ever read *The Divine Comedy*, Doctor?"

The expression on Baylor's face froze like he'd been stunned by the question. Matt could see his wheels turning, almost as if the doctor had a memory so extraordinary that he might have been reading the epic poem in his mind as they stood there. After several moments, Dr. Baylor's face lit up, as if he'd just experienced a revelation of some kind. When he finally surfaced and looked back at Matt, there was something new in his eyes and he appeared genuinely impressed.

"The seven terraces of the seven deadly sins," he said in a quiet voice. "But we're only concerned about one of them, aren't we? They were bound and laid facedown. When did you see it? When did you figure it out?"

"About two hours ago," he said in a low voice. "I don't think we're looking for a copycat, Doctor."

"But why young women? If it's about greed, why kill a girl who's still in school? They're innocents."

"I haven't gotten that far yet."

"But there's an answer, isn't there? There would have to be."

Matt gave Dr. Baylor a look. "May I ask you a question?"

"Anything."

"Why did Grace want your help? Is it about the wounds to their faces?"

Baylor nodded. "I'm a reconstructive surgeon. So, yes, I became involved because of what was done to Millie Brown's face."

"You mean because she was slashed."

"She wasn't slashed. I don't know what happened to Faith Novakoff just yet. But from the pictures of Jane Doe I saw last night, I don't think she was slashed either."

"But their faces were cut. They were mutilated. They looked swollen and deformed."

Baylor walked over to his bookcase. "The wounds they received actually have a name. Nothing about them was haphazard. Nothing about them was random."

The doctor found the book he was looking for and leafed through it as he returned to the window. After a few moments, he laid the book down on the windowsill and pointed to a photograph.

It was a young woman's face, and while she hadn't been killed, Matt found the photograph extremely difficult to look at. Dr. Baylor pointed to the girl's wounds.

"You see it, Matthew? She's been cut from the edges of her mouth to her ears on both sides. The scars the cuts left extend across her entire face in what looks like a hideous smile. Something out of a horror movie. The Joker maybe, but even more grotesque. The cut originated in Glasgow, Scotland, and was named the 'Glasgow smile.' When it became popular in Chelsea, people called it the 'Chelsea grin.'"

"Became popular?"

Dr. Baylor nodded again. "Gangs hoping to send a message to other gangs."

An image of Jane Doe's face surfaced in Matt's mind. The torrent of blood masking the wound in real life but also hiding the wounds in the crime-scene photos Matt had seen in the two murder books. He thought about what the last ten minutes of Jane Doe's life must have been like. He thought about the kind of man who could do something like this to a girl, a woman, or any living thing.

Not a copy, but the One.

He looked back at the photograph of the girl in the book. "You're a plastic surgeon. Could you make those scars go away?"

Baylor shook his head. "No one could. Not even an undertaker."

"But how do you think she survived?"

The doctor eyed the photograph for a moment, then met Matt's gaze and lowered his voice. "She didn't scream," he said. "When they want to kill someone, they make the cut with a box cutter or a piece of broken glass and then start kicking the victim until he or she screams. The act of screaming rips the wounds apart, and the victim bleeds to death."

Matt looked away and took a deep breath. It was almost as if Baylor had given him another piece of the puzzle, too horrific in size and scope to comprehend. Too hot to touch. He closed his eyes for a moment, trying to get rid of Jane Doe's image in his head. When he opened them, the image was still there and seemed even more gruesome, even more grim.

CHAPTER 26

He needed a cigarette. A Marlboro. He stood by his car, trying to slow down his heart rate. When he popped another piece of nicotine gum into his mouth, he could feel a stomachache coming on.

The déjà vu was back. Hard.

He could see Jane Doe's face. He could smell the shampoo in her hair and the scent of her clean skin. But now everything was even more real because the image came with a soundtrack. Now he could hear the girl screaming.

He climbed into the car, found a news station on the radio, and started heading back to Hollywood. In need of a major distraction, he tried to focus on what the reporter was saying.

Something about something being something, or was it nothing?

It didn't work. He could see Jane Doe's murder going down so clearly that he might have been standing right beside her. He could see her nude body staked to the ground, her full breasts in the gravel and dirt. He could see a shadowy figure making the cuts on both sides of the girl's face. And then that scream. The full-blown sound of terror. He could hear it. He could see it. The wounds bursting open and the river of blood flowing down onto a sheet of mirrored glass.

He shivered. He could feel a tremor working its way through his body from somewhere deep inside his core. When the quake passed, the car felt ice cold, and he turned on the heat.

The rest of the drive back to Hollywood was lost in a heavy fog. Pulling into the lot behind the station, he wasn't really sure of the route he'd taken or how much time he'd used.

He walked into the squad room and didn't see anyone he recognized. When he checked the homicide workstations, no one was around. He found Cabrera still sitting in the conference room. He had his laptop with him and what looked like a new tablet. Two murder books were open, along with several file folders and what remained of his lunch.

Matt opened the door and walked in. When Cabrera looked up, he could tell that the anger in the man had faded again. Mr. Hyde had become Dr. Jekyll on the merry-go-round.

"What's going on?" Matt said.

Cabrera pushed his coffee mug aside. "I called Burbank PD and asked them to check on that Lincoln over at the airport."

"Why are you doing me favors?"

"It wasn't a favor."

"Okay," Matt said. "What did Burbank find out?"

"The Lincoln's there, but someone ripped off the plates."

Matt knew that this wasn't good news. It meant that the man in the silver Nissan was up to something and didn't want to be found when he was through. His first impression of the man had been the true one. Trouble.

"What's this got to do with our case, Jones?"

"I don't know. Somebody's following me."

"Who?"

"A guy."

"When did it start?"

"I'm not sure. I made him last night on the way home."

Matt glanced at the door. He'd driven from Baylor's office back to the station without checking his rearview mirror. It was a sloppy move. A dangerous move.

"I've got some news, Jones."

"What kind of news?"

"Taladyne news."

Matt turned back to Cabrera but didn't say anything. Their eyes met.

"Jamie Taladyne went off the grid the day after Ron Harris hung himself in his cell."

"How far off?"

"All the way off. He cashed out his bank account, got rid of his cell phone, cable TV, everything. None of his credit cards have been used in six months. Jamie Taladyne is either hiding out or he's dead."

"Did anyone talk to his parole officer?"

"It's a woman. She said she hasn't heard from him since Harris died."

"Who'd you get this from, your pal Joey?"

"He and Plank split before you did, Jones."

Matt's cell phone started ringing in his pocket. When he checked the caller ID, he saw the name of Hughes's supervisor, Lieutenant Howard McKensie, on the LCD screen. He switched on the phone, but all he heard was a faint voice lost in digital noise and static.

"Are you there, Jones? Are you there?"

"I'm here, Lieutenant, but it's a bad connection."

"Frankie's been in a car accident."

Matt felt the blood draining from his head and sat down. "Is he okay?"

The digital noise returned. Cabrera looked at Matt and rolled his chair closer. After several seconds, McKensie's voice broke through again.

"I'm just south of Mint Canyon."

"Is Frankie okay, Lieutenant?"

"You need to be here, Jones. Placerita Canyon Road off Route 14. You need to hurry."

McKensie's voice faded into the static and Matt lost the call. A long moment passed. When Matt spoke, his voice was just above a whisper.

"Frankie's been in an accident."

Cabrera nodded, digging his keys out of his pocket. "I'll drive," he said.

CHAPTER 27

The smoke from the wildfire came and went with the breeze, the road blocked by two deputy sheriffs. When Matt and Cabrera showed them their IDs, they were asked to pull off to the side and walk the rest of the way. The blaze was 90 percent contained, but more trucks were on the way.

Listening to the distant sirens, Matt climbed out of the car with Cabrera and started walking. The road was a narrow two-lane, the slope to his right a ten-story drop to the bottom of the canyon. Up ahead he could see the fire engines through the smoke. A group of maybe ten people were gazing down the hill with great interest. As he and Cabrera got closer, he spotted Lieutenant McKensie standing with an old man in the middle of the pack. The old man was unshaven and dressed in a flannel shirt and a pair of blue jeans. McKensie must have sensed their arrival because he turned. When Matt got a look at his face, he knew that Frankie was dead.

"He went over the cliff," McKensie said in a raspy voice. "They're searching for a second body."

Matt traded looks with Cabrera, then took a step closer and gazed over the edge. What was left of Frankie's burned-up car was a long way down. Frankie would have known it was over the moment he skidded off the road. The car must have exploded when it hit the bottom—everything within a fifty-yard radius of the vehicle was scorched and blackened. Matt could see four men strapping something onto a stretcher. When they gave it a lift and started up the slope, he realized that it was Frankie. Like the terrain, Frankie looked charred and broken and all burned up.

Matt turned away, thinking about him but also about Hughes. As he pulled himself together and turned back to watch, he felt someone give his arm a tug. It was Cabrera, waving him away from the group.

"What is it?" Matt said.

Cabrera narrowed his eyes and lowered his voice to a whisper. "There aren't any skid marks, Jones."

A moment passed, the darkness getting darker in the middle of a sunny afternoon.

"See for yourself," Cabrera went on. "There aren't any skid marks anywhere on this road. Frankie went over the edge and never hit the brakes."

Matt took a step back and examined the asphalt. It was an old road, the blacktop faded after years of bright sunlight to a neutral gray. If Frankie had hit the brakes, the skid marks would have stood out like fresh paint.

Matt turned back to the slope, thinking about the message Frankie had left on his cell phone. *I'm following up on what may or may not be a couple of decent leads*, he'd said. *A couple of decent leads.*

Why Mint Canyon?

It took the four men about an hour to carry Frankie up the slope. Matt watched as they rolled his blackened corpse into a body bag under the direction of a local coroner, who seemed worried that the body might fall apart. Once the bag was zipped up, he noticed two of the four men talking to McKensie. They were deputy sheriffs, and they were saying that there wasn't a second body. When Matt noticed the old man shaking his head, he traded looks with Cabrera and took a step closer.

"Why are you shaking your head?" Matt said. "What makes you think two people were in that car?"

"Because I saw them. Two fellas, not one."

"Where?"

The old man glanced at McKensie, then turned back. "It's like I was telling him. I've got a gas station next exit up on Route 14. The guy driving this car pulls in for a fill-up, so I turn on the pump. A minute later, I look out the window and see him talking to two other guys like they're best friends."

"What kind of car were they driving?"

The old man nodded. "It was a Ford. A dark gray sedan."

"Did they buy any gas?" Matt asked. "Did they come inside and use a credit card?"

"No. They watched this guy fill his tank, and that's pretty much it. When he was done, one of them decided to ride with him, and the other guy followed them out. That's why I said there's gotta be another body down there."

The deputy sheriff shrugged. "We're bringing more people in, but we didn't see anyone and we were working a wide path. Even if he'd been thrown out of the car halfway down, we would've found him."

Matt turned back to the old man. "Do you remember what these two guys looked like? Not the guy who bought gas. The other two."

"Sure," he said. "The one that got in the car was a big guy with dark hair—had a belly like mine. I'm pretty sure he had a goatee and a bright red tie, too. The one that followed them out looked kind of skinny. He was a little guy with gray hair. Something was wrong with his face. His cheeks were all messed up."

"You sure that's what they looked like?"

Matt could feel the shadow passing over his soul before the old man even nodded. He turned and saw Cabrera staring at him. His partner looked frightened. In spite of the cool breeze, beads of sweat were dripping down his forehead. Lieutenant McKensie must have noticed, and turned to Matt.

"What is it, Jones?" he said. "Do you know these guys?"

Matt's eyes were still locked on Cabrera's. He didn't know what to say, or who was safe enough to say it to, so he lied. He told McKensie that nothing about the old man's description rang a bell. Cabrera backed him up, but his voice was a little shaky and he had trouble catching his breath. In the end it didn't really matter. From the exasperated look on McKensie's face, Matt didn't think he bought what either one of them was saying.

CHAPTER 28

Matt walked out of the old man's gas station with a pack of Marlboros and lit up. The cigarette tasted like shit and smelled even worse, and all of a sudden he remembered two of the five reasons why he'd quit. He shook them off before the other three surfaced and took another drag, deeper this time. As he climbed in behind the wheel, he looked over at Cabrera staring out the windshield with glazed eyes and a blank expression on his face.

"Mind if I smoke?" he said.

Cabrera shook his head without a reply. Then Matt started the car, cracking the window open as he pulled into the street with the tires screeching.

They were about thirty miles north of Los Angeles. At this hour the freeways would be parking lots. Matt expected that the trip back to Hollywood would take an hour and a half, maybe two. Cabrera never spoke as they rolled south. Every once in a while, Matt would check on him, and every time he did he saw the same thing.

Cabrera's eyes were turned inward. The man was deep inside himself. So deep that Matt wondered if he was lost.

Matt left him alone, wrestling with his own demons and trying to concentrate on the stop-and-go traffic. By the time they finally reached the station, the sun had set and he could feel the dread following them into the parking lot. He found an open space on the far side, switched off the headlights, and killed the engine. Orlando and Plank's gray Crown Vic was parked in the next aisle. When he noticed it sitting in the darkness, the feeling of impending doom seemed to become even more vivid.

"We're here, Cabrera. We're back at the station."

Cabrera didn't say anything and didn't move. After several moments passed, Matt tapped him on the shoulder.

"You okay?"

Cabrera nodded. "I owe you an apology," he said in a quiet voice.

"Forget it."

"I'll never forget it, Jones. Never. These guys killed Hughes and you know it. Today they murdered Frankie. He told us they would, remember? He said he thought that maybe he and Hughes touched a nerve. He didn't know who. He just knew that they touched it. The night you called, the night Grace was taking all those pictures of Jane Doe's dead body, I finally got it. I got it, but I didn't wanna say I got it. I wanted to feel safe. I wanted to live the dream. The illusion. The fantasy. I was hoping everything would switch back to normal. And now everything's all fucked up. Forever fucked up. We're where Frankie was, the city's next two dead guys. We're fucking next."

Matt lit another cigarette and pointed through the windshield. "Keep cool," he said. "They're coming out."

Orlando and Plank had just walked out the rear door and were heading across the lot to their car. They were walking with purpose, like they were in a hurry. Matt kept still as they passed by, but it didn't seem to matter. Orlando turned just as he pulled the driver's-side door open. He was staring at them, his face showing nothing but contempt.

Matt kept his eyes locked on Orlando and spoke under his breath. "What kind of cop would murder two of his own?"

Cabrera took a deep breath and exhaled. "I need to show you something."

After another beat, Matt finally broke the stare-down session with Orlando and turned to Cabrera. "Show me what?"

Cabrera's eyes were still focused on Orlando. "Look," he said. "He thinks it's a joke. They're laughing at us."

Matt turned and watched them drive by, with Plank staring back at them. When they pulled out of the lot, he looked back at Cabrera and noticed that he was returning his gun to his holster. His fingers were trembling slightly and appeared sweaty. Matt looked back at Cabrera's face and tried to get a read on him, but nothing clicked.

"Let's go," Cabrera said. "I want you to see something."

They got out of the car and entered the building. As they walked into the squad room, Cabrera grabbed his laptop from a drawer at his workstation and pointed to the conference room.

"Better close the door," he said.

The computer had only been sleeping. Once Cabrera opened the lid and typed in his password, they were up and already on the Web. He pulled the mouse closer and clicked on a bookmark that brought them to the *Los Angeles Times*. After double-checking that the door was closed, he looked up at Matt.

"I was running that credit check on Taladyne this morning," he said. "While I waited for the reports, I had some time to kill and stumbled onto this."

Matt sat down beside him, eyeing the screen carefully as he rolled his chair closer. Cabrera passed over the mouse. It was an article with a catchy headline dated ten days after Ron Harris committed suicide in his jail cell.

LAPD Detective Dies in Freak Accident

It was the story of Grace's former partner, Leo Rodriguez. It was short and to the point, and Matt wasn't sure how he'd missed it, except to say that he must have been working a narcotics case and off the grid. According to the Santa Monica Police Department, Rodriguez's body had been found in the alley behind a metered parking garage at Santa Monica Boulevard and Second Street. His car had been located on the roof and had two hours left on the meter. When investigators saw that the safety rail had given way, they came to a quick conclusion: Rodriguez had fallen to his death eight stories down by accident. He was survived by his wife, Sally Rodriguez, and had no children.

Matt could feel his stomach going again. He got to his feet and started pacing beside the plate-glass windows. Grace's office was dark, but there were a number of people in the squad room. He could see Cabrera closing the window on his computer and deleting the bookmark. Matt thought that getting rid of the bookmark was probably a good idea.

"It happened three months before I got here," Cabrera said. "By then it would have been old news, I guess. No one talked about him. I just assumed that when Grace made lieutenant, his partner either retired or got bumped up to Robbery-Homicide. After they arrested Harris, both of them were heroes."

Matt stopped pacing and leaned against the wall. "We're in a fucked-up place, Denny. But we need to keep things straight. The way I see it, one of three things could've happened."

"Just three?"

Matt nodded. "Just three, the first being that Santa Monica called it the way it really was. A freak accident. Rodriguez steps over to the rail for a look at the view, the rail breaks, and he falls. Accidents happen every day. It was good enough that everybody signed off on it."

"Everybody did. What's next?"

"Rodriguez jumped. He jumped, but he didn't want it to look like he jumped, so his wife would get more money. He fed the meter, broke the rail, and did a swan dive eight stories down onto the asphalt."

Cabrera had a look going and was shaking his head. "But after today we both know that it didn't happen that way. Leo Rodriguez didn't fall and he didn't jump. He was pushed."

A beat went by, and then another. They were in perfect sync.

"We should talk to his wife," Matt said.

Cabrera picked up the phone. "I'll get her address."

CHAPTER 29

Sally Rodriguez lived on a quiet street in South Pasadena a block from the library. She had blond hair and aqua-blue eyes and a smile that came from her mouth but seemed to live in those eyes of hers. Matt guessed that she was close to fifty and, from her figure, that she took care of herself.

After giving their IDs a cautious look, she welcomed them into the house and offered them coffee from a fresh pot. Matt gladly accepted, taking a seat with Cabrera at the kitchen table and watching her set down three mugs.

"So what is it you want to know about Leo?"

Matt glanced over at Cabrera, who nodded at him. They had talked about it on the drive from Hollywood. They didn't want to overwhelm her, nor did they want to stir the pot. Matt would start the conversation. If necessary, Cabrera would follow up.

"Did your husband ever talk about his cases, Sally?"

"Of course."

"Do you remember the Millie Brown investigation? She was murdered about a year and a half ago."

She gave him an odd look as she sat down. "You know I knew that's why you were here."

A moment passed.

"Why's that?" Matt said finally.

"Because that's the one case that really got to Leo. Seeing what happened to that girl really got underneath his skin. He'd worked a lot of murder cases, but that one changed him."

Matt added half a teaspoon of sugar to his coffee and took a short first sip. Admittedly, he was starving, but still, it might have been the best cup of hot java he'd ever tasted.

"I think both my partner and I can understand how your husband felt. We're working a very similar case right now."

"I'm so sorry," she said. "For both of you."

Cabrera remained silent but nodded at the woman in appreciation.

"Thank you," Matt said. "But I'm curious. You said working the Millie Brown case changed your husband. How?"

She shook her head. Matt could tell from the expression on her face that she was looking into the past and that the memories of her husband were good ones, but still painful. Still too close.

"Leo and his partner wanted to solve the case so badly. They were so desperate to get the guy. They couldn't stop talking about it. They couldn't let it go at night. Bob Grace practically moved in. We had a house in Santa Monica at the time. I moved here after Leo's accident. He loved the water. I did, too, but I needed something different."

"But what about Leo? How did he change?"

She paused a moment, still looking into the past. "It happened after Ron Harris committed suicide. I could tell that Leo was upset about something. He'd lost his appetite and couldn't get to sleep at night. He was jumpy. He stopped laughing, and he seemed sad. Not on the outside. I mean on the inside."

"Did he say what was troubling him?"

She shook her head and lowered her voice. "He wouldn't talk about it. He told me that if he said anything to me, I wouldn't be safe."

Another moment passed. Matt traded a quick look with Cabrera, then turned back to Sally Rodriguez. Her eyes were on him, and he could see that she was frightened.

"Are you okay?" he said.

She nodded, but he didn't believe her.

"Do you have any idea what your husband meant by that?"

"No," she said. "But it had to be bad. It was the first time that he kept anything from me."

"Did he bring work home with him? Did he keep files? Is there any chance you brought them with you when you moved?"

"Leo kept a home office," she said. "But losing him—I don't know, I really leaned on Bob. He was more than just Leo's partner. He was a good friend and a wonderful man. He spent two days helping me go through Leo's things. We cleaned out Leo's office and threw everything away."

Matt gazed at Cabrera on the other side of the table. Leo Rodriguez didn't fall to his death and he didn't jump. He was pushed off the roof by his own partner, Bob Grace. That wonderful guy who went through Leo's things after his death and threw everything out.

CHAPTER 30

Matt checked the rearview mirror and was relieved when he didn't see anyone following them. The list of possibilities seemed to be getting longer. They were on the road after making a short stop at Tommy's World Famous Hamburgers on North Hill Avenue in Pasadena. Matt had just finished a double cheeseburger with fries and a cup of hot coffee. He hadn't eaten anything since Laura made him breakfast, which seemed like three or four days ago. Cabrera had inhaled two chili dogs and was sipping a cup of coffee as well.

"Now we know," Cabrera said.

"Know what?"

"Grace, Orlando, and Plank. Now we know that they murdered Rodriguez just the same way they did Hughes and Frankie Lane. Something about Harris hanging himself in his cell must have meant something to Rodriguez."

Matt gave him a look. "Or pushed him close enough to the edge that they were afraid he'd talk."

The thought had a certain weight about it. The idea that Rodriguez might have lost his life for wanting to come forward. Matt let it go, then made a U-turn and pulled up to the curb in front of Dr. Baylor's house on Toluca Lake Avenue. He had called Baylor from Tommy's, so there would be no need to climb over the wall tonight.

Cabrera followed him out of the car. "You gotta feel something for Rodriguez's wife. If she ever finds out what really happened—"

"You mean *when*, don't you? We're gonna solve this case, Denny. We're gonna see this through."

Matt rang the buzzer at the gate, then heard the lock release and saw Baylor open the front door. The doctor waited for them on the porch, then introduced himself to Cabrera and shook hands. As they entered the house and Baylor led them down the hall and into his study, Matt noticed that the doctor's demeanor had changed. That expression of youthful amusement and curiosity that seemed to linger on Baylor's face this afternoon had completely vanished. Now Baylor seemed edgy and distracted. He looked tired, almost bleary-eyed.

Matt watched him pour himself a glass of water. "How did the autopsy go, Doctor?"

"Not very well," he said. "Please, both of you, have a seat. Would you like something to drink? Something stronger than mineral water?"

Matt shook his head and remained standing. "What do you mean, not well? Who did the autopsy?"

"Art Madina. I didn't mean it that way."

Cabrera cleared his throat. "Is everything all right, Doctor?"

Baylor nodded. As he walked over to the couch, Matt couldn't help but take in the room. The ornate moldings, the built-in bookshelves, the twenty-foot ceilings, the gas fire burning beneath an elegant mantel, the thick walls and wide-planked floors, the imported carpets that appeared so tasteful, the large canvases that reminded Matt of Jamie Wyeth or maybe his father, Andrew, the oversized windows that opened to the lighted pool and spa on the terrace and the lake beyond. Baylor's home was something of an architectural wonder in its sheer simplicity and understatement. And Matt's first impression the other night had been entirely wrong. Baylor's house didn't feel like a resort. The place was too comfortable for that. It felt too much like home.

"There's been a development," Baylor said.

Matt turned and found the doctor eyeing him carefully. "What happened?"

"What you figured out on your own." Baylor took another sip of water and lowered his voice. "After the autopsy we compared the results from all three victims. Madina and I agree. It's more than likely that all three were murdered by the same man. The wounds to the face. There's no pause, no hesitation—just a clean cut, as if he does this sort of thing every day. By the way, the dental records match. Jane Doe is Brooke Anderson. She grew up in the Midwest. Her mother runs an insurance company. Madina spoke with her over the phone. She's on her way out to claim the body."

She had a name. A family who loved her. A presence that seemed closer now. No one said anything for several moments, everything grim. Matt took a seat in the chair beside the couch, thinking about the girl's mother and the horror she couldn't possibly see coming when she got a look at her daughter's face.

Baylor stood up and walked over to the fireplace. "There's more," he said. "Madina found a puncture wound on her arm. We think that she was sedated with something, and that's why there aren't any signs of a struggle from the rape. It would have to be a drug with a short enough life that it wasn't picked up in the tox screen. Something that would only last long enough for the killer to prepare her body, move her to Hollywood Hills, and make the cuts to her face. No marks were found on Brown or Novakoff, but that doesn't mean that they weren't there. In all probability, they were there but missed."

Matt was still seeing Brooke Anderson's ruined face. Still seeing her mother standing over her daughter's corpse as the medical examiner unzipped the body bag. He remembered reading in Millie Brown's murder book that Jamie Taladyne cut drywall. He thought about the blade used to slash the girl's face.

He snapped out of it. After trading quick looks with Cabrera, he turned back to the doctor.

"I'm assuming that you've talked to Grace."

Baylor nodded.

"How did he take it?"

"Not very well. All of a sudden he's got a lot to lose."

CHAPTER 31

A lot to lose . . .

Matt backed the Crown Vic into a space at the rear of the lot and killed the headlights. As he looked up and down the rows, he didn't see Orlando and Plank's car, and let himself settle into the bucket seat. The station appeared quiet. He was thinking about Laura Hughes and not letting her down. It was after nine and he would have to get up early in the morning. Brooke Anderson's mother would be arriving at the coroner's office at 8:00 a.m. to identify and claim her daughter's body. Apparently, she was coming alone. The medical examiner had asked Baylor to attend, and Baylor had asked both Matt and Cabrera to join them. For whatever reason, Matt agreed.

"Do you need to go inside for anything?" he said in a quiet voice.

Cabrera looked back at him in the darkness, nervous. "It's not safe here."

"I know, but what are we gonna do? We can't disappear."

"It's not safe."

Matt nodded because he understood. Last night he had fought off the urge to connect the dots. He had pulled off a clean read of Millie Brown's murder book without bias or any thought of Cabrera or Frankie or even what his imagination, his gut instincts, were trying to tell him early on. But as they drove back from Toluca Lake, Matt had managed to sift through the evidence in his mind and reach the only conclusion he deemed possible.

"What about Baylor?" Cabrera asked.

Matt lowered the window and lit a cigarette. "We didn't say anything. He has no idea what we're thinking. All we did is get his take on the girl's autopsy."

Cabrera shook his head. "But he knows. I could see it in his eyes."

"What does he know?"

"He's smart enough to know that something's wrong and we're working it. He's smart enough to know that all of a sudden there are two sides to this thing, and he could get hurt. I'll bet he never told Grace that you stopped by his office. And that's probably why he wants us to be there for the girl's ID. He wants to know what we know. He wants to keep close. I could see it, Matt. He's scared. Who wouldn't be?"

Matt took a deep pull on his cigarette and blew the smoke out the window. "It's still a work in progress, but here's how I see it, Denny. Here's my take. You ready?"

Cabrera nodded.

"Okay," Matt said. "Okay, then here it is. Millie Brown was murdered and left in a picnic area at the Hollywood Bowl. Grace and Rodriguez were on call that day. I'm giving them the bene-fit of the doubt. They were good cops, good detectives with good records, and their hearts were in the right place. But when they got a look at the girl's body, when they saw how fucked up she was, how deranged the killer must have been, it shook them up so bad that Rodriguez's wife told us it changed who he fucking was. Grace said the same thing. The murder changed them, and they got all jacked up. They decided that they were gonna get this guy no matter what. Jamie Taladyne worked construction and was cutting drywall at the girl's house. He was standing right in front of them. He'd been convicted of a sexual assault. He had the history and did time. Even better, he had contact with Millie, and the girl was teasing him and coming on to him and showing off her brand-new body. No doubt about it, Jamie Taladyne was wrestling with his demons. He had everything it takes to be good for that girl's murder."

"He had it," Cabrera said. "So how did he get past a polygraph?"

"Do psychopaths have a conscience? Do they feel remorse? It doesn't matter anymore. Somehow he passed the test, and Grace and Rodriguez did the same thing any one of us would have done. They cut him loose."

Cabrera reached for the pack of Marlboros on the console and lit one. Matt noticed that his fingers were quivering as he held the lighter.

"You smoke?" Matt said.

Cabrera took a shallow drag on the cigarette and started coughing. "Never in my life."

"Why start now?"

He waved the smoke away from his face and set the lighter down. "Because the way things are going, I could be murdered in my sleep tonight. Fuck it. We're the city's next two dead guys, remember?"

Matt tried to shrug it off but couldn't. "What did you do with the murder books?"

"Tossed them in the backseat before we drove out to Pasadena."

Matt turned and saw the binders on the floor. As he grabbed Millie Brown's murder book, he asked Cabrera to pull a flashlight out of the glove box. Paging through the chronological record, he found the point when Ron Harris's name first came up and the high school teacher evolved into a genuine person of interest. He passed the binder over to Cabrera, then ditched his spent cigarette out the window and lit another.

Fuck it.

"Okay," he said. "Grace and Rodriguez will do anything to find the girl's killer. Orlando and Plank are on board, and I'm giving them a mulligan, too. They were good detectives with good records, and their hearts were in the right place. But then everything changes. Grace and Rodriguez find out that Harris is doing Millie. The idea of a high school teacher fucking his student makes them sick."

"Harris was a pervert. He was in a position of trust."

"And it worked like a magnet. All of a sudden he's got a target on his back and they're locked in. They've heard from one of Millie's friends that she wanted out and was threatening him with exposure, so now they've got motive."

Cabrera puffed on his cigarette without inhaling. "They bring him in. They sweat him out. Two teams. Grace and Rodriguez, then Orlando and Plank."

Matt nodded, his eyes on a cop walking into the station. "They've already found semen in the girl's underwear from her laundry hamper. Like you said, enough to repopulate the planet. They're feeding Harris, giving him coffee, taking everything he touches out to the lab. They've already been through Millie's computer. They've found the e-mails he wrote to her and the e-mails she sent back. All the text messages on her cell phone. They know for a fact that he's lying to them."

Cabrera took another puff on his cigarette. "They wear the piece of shit down until he finally breaks. He's tired and he wants it to end. He can't see straight. He can't think straight. He agrees to take a polygraph and he fails. They've got him."

"He fails because in the back of his mind he thinks he's a criminal for fucking one of his students. He fails for the wrong reason, but Grace and Rodriguez think they've finally got confirmation for the murder. They think he's good for it. They *know* he's good for it. It all seems so fucking clear. They've got him, Denny. But they still need to seal the deal."

Cabrera rolled down the window and got rid of his cigarette. "What are you talking about?"

"They swore to themselves that they were gonna get the guy who cut Millie Brown's face up. They swore to themselves that they were gonna make the freak who killed her pay."

Cabrera turned and gazed out the windshield as he chewed it over. Several moments passed before he turned back. "The box cutter," he said, still thinking it through. "You're saying that they planted it."

Matt watched a cop exit the building and drive off in a patrol car, then took another long pull on his smoke. "Check the record. I'll bet they didn't get a warrant to search Harris's house until they made the DNA match. They could've gone in earlier. They had more than enough to convince a judge that this guy was bogus, but they needed to transfer his DNA to the box cutter. They needed the lab to make the match."

Cabrera panned the flashlight over the murder book and started reading. After a few moments, he stopped and looked at Matt.

"They planted it," he said in amazement. "That's probably what set Rodriguez off. He was part of it and couldn't handle it. He wanted to talk."

"It's the only explanation that works," Matt said. "They wanted insurance to make up for the horror of the crime, the weight of the depravity. Baylor and the medical examiner had already told them what to look for."

"They knew what to look for, so they knew what to buy."

"That's it," Matt said. "They had all the DNA samples they needed from both the girl and Harris. It would've been easy."

"They needed insurance," Cabrera said. "They sweetened the pie."

A long moment passed, and then another, swollen and bruised and all beat up.

Matt was thinking about Ron Harris. The man deserved a lot of things, but he didn't deserve to die the way he did. An innocent man, married with young children, stood accused of the horrific murder of his student. But Millie Brown was more than a student to him, and in the end he obviously meant more to her than anyone involved would ever admit. Matt could see it. Harris sitting through his first day in court, listening to the deputy DA lay out their case and knowing in his gut that he had no chance to clear his name. Harris knowing that he was innocent, knowing that the box cutter had been planted, knowing that he would burn. Harris feeling the panic, the terror, seeing his wife seated behind him, his parents, everything slipping away. But then there would have been all those angels from the City of Angels sitting there, too. All those faces in the gallery, all those people who wanted to see him dead. The spark of evil in their eyes. The spark of revenge and the will of the mob. Everyone watching convinced beyond a shadow of a doubt that he'd cut up Millie Brown's face and watched her bleed to death. They didn't need the deputy DA to present the evidence. They already knew.

Matt pulled out of it and tried to clear his mind. Cabrera switched off the flashlight.

"Jamie Taladyne went off the grid the day after Harris killed himself, Matt."

"You said that."

"But he's been loose for months. He's out there somewhere. He's free and he can't help himself. He's killing again."

Matt rubbed his forehead as he thought it over. "You understand what's at stake, right, Denny? We agree on what's going on?"

Cabrera closed the murder book. "It couldn't be more clear. Grace, Orlando, and Plank fucked up hard. They've murdered three cops to protect their secret."

"They're looking for a way out," Matt said. "That's all that matters now. They need Harris to take the fall for Millie Brown's murder no matter what really happened because they planted the murder weapon. They're cornered because of that box cutter and the fact that they're directly responsible for an innocent man taking his own life. Everyone Taladyne's killed since Brown—Faith Novakoff, Brooke Anderson, there could be more—every murder since, Grace has to play like the killer's a copycat. If Grace can't sell it, if Orlando and Plank screw it up, they know they're dead. They know they'll get the needle."

"And we're in a world of shit," Cabrera whispered.

It hung there in the darkness of the car. Their new reality in all its harshness. Matt glanced at his Honda halfway up the row of cars and grabbed the murder books. Cabrera checked the lot for his SUV, then reached for the door handle.

"You gonna sleep tonight, Denny?"

Cabrera opened the door. "I don't know yet. Give me a smoke for the drive home."

CHAPTER 32

Matt couldn't tell if it was the silver Nissan behind him. All he could see was a pair of headlights through the glare. He'd picked them up as he drove east on Sunset and made a left onto Western. Now they were following him on Los Feliz as he approached the freeway entrance, two cars back, the driver laying low.

Matt circled down the ramp and eased the car onto the Golden State Freeway with his eyes flicking between the speedometer and the rearview mirror. On a good night the average speed of freeway traffic in Southern California was somewhere between seventy-five and eighty-five miles an hour. Anyone doing the speed limit—anyone driving at fifty-five—more than stood out. Matt set the cruise control at a lethargic fifty miles an hour, hung in the right lane, and watched the driver barrel down the entrance ramp, then suddenly let up on the gas.

He got a good look as the car coasted beneath a streetlight. The man in the silver Nissan was back.

Matt tightened his grip on the wheel, mulling it over. The Glendale exit was less than a mile away. Laura's house was another mile up the hill just north of the freeway. He needed to deal with this guy, and he needed to do it in a hurry. He checked the mirror again. The follower was still back there, rolling at a listless fifty miles an hour.

Matt checked the cruise control, watching the traffic pass by hard and fast and ignoring anyone who hit their horn. He could see the interchange just ahead. When he reached the 134 Freeway, he took the first exit, gliding down the ramp and side street, and making a right at the light onto San Fernando Road.

The silver Nissan was still in his rearview mirror, five cars back and hiding in the right lane. Matt wondered if the man might not be delusional, still not realizing that he had been spotted. He smiled as he lifted his .45 out of its holster and rested it on the console. Powering up the Honda, he swerved through the next layer of traffic in a sudden burst, then slowed down again as he shifted lanes. On the other side of the train tracks to his left was an industrial area. Block after block of warehouses and light manufacturing plants until the roads converged on DreamWorks and Walt Disney Animation Studios to the west. At this hour the entire area would be a ghost town until you reached the studios.

He saw the light ahead and caught it just as it turned yellow, making an easy left onto Flower Street. Once he rolled over the train tracks, the traffic vanished and he was on his own. He checked the mirror again and saw the Nissan make the turn as well, then brake and begin following at a calculated distance.

But no matter what the distance, there was no place to hide here. The man in the silver Nissan had no cover. It was the reason Matt had chosen the exit on San Fernando Road. It was the perfect place to draw the man out and confront him.

He slowed down to an even thirty-five miles an hour. He made a turn at the corner, and then another, watching the Nissan cruise a hundred yards back. Matt pushed forward, leading his follower deeper into the industrial landscape and making turn after turn, until it felt like he was lost in a maze. When he spotted a street that looked particularly dark and desolate a block or two past Glendale Water & Power, he made a quick right, pulled into the shadows halfway down, and skidded to a stop.

Matt ripped open the door, climbed out with his .45, and leaned over the hood.

But the silver Nissan never made the last turn.

He waited five minutes, listening to the power lines hum overhead with his pistol pointed at the end of the road. When it felt like a sure thing, he got into the car and worked his way back to San Fernando Road.

He drove slowly, searching for the silver Nissan. He had that feeling again, the one in the center of his back that told him he was being watched. But as he stopped at each intersection, the streets were empty, his follower apparently gone.

The drive to Laura's house took less than ten minutes. He kept an eye out for the Nissan and told himself that the feeling still digging into his back was just a case of nerves. Still, as he reached the neighborhood, he drove around the block just to make sure. When he spotted a gray Crown Vic hidden in the shadows across the street, he thought his heart might break out of his chest.

He made another trip around the block, coasting past Laura's driveway. That morning, the protection detail out of Metro had parked their black Chevy Suburban in front of the garage. But now it was gone. He didn't see it in the drive or anywhere on the street.

Matt pulled down to the next house and fished out his cell phone. His contact at Metro, Jerry Tanaka, picked up after five long rings. From the background noise, it sounded like the call had been forwarded and Tanaka was in a bar.

"Where's my protection detail?" he said through clenched teeth. "Where the fuck are they, Tanaka?"

"Take it easy, Jones. They're at the house. What's your problem?"

"They're not at the house. They're nowhere, man."

"Hold on for a second," Tanaka said.

"I don't have a second."

"Hold on anyway."

The phone clicked and he heard an irritating stream of digital noise in the void. He was nervous. The wait was excruciating, but he knew that he couldn't get out of the car. He couldn't take the chance that his voice might carry. After three or four minutes—maybe it was five or six—Tanaka came back on.

"They're on a break," he said.

"A break? Are you insane?"

"I just got off the phone with them. They said you told them that they could take an hour's break."

"Who told them?"

"Matt Jones from Hollywood Homicide," Tanaka said.

"Are these the same guys who showed up this morning?"

"No. They're the second shift."

"When did I tell them that they could split?"

"About ten minutes ago."

A beat went by. Matt felt the anger bloom all over his body and burst through his skin.

"Listen, Tanaka. That wasn't me. You're blowing it. You're in a fucking bar thinking that the day's all over, only it's just getting started. You're fucking up. Now bring them back and bring them back fast."

"I'll do what I can, Jones."

"A woman's life is at stake, Tanaka. Fuck you."

Matt slipped the phone into his pocket, drew his .45, rocked back the slide, and hustled down the street in silence. As he reached the driveway, he could feel the outrage overwhelming his senses. He started around the house, as slowly as he could manage. He stopped and listened. There was someone in the yard, someone standing at the top of the steps leading down to the backyard and pool. Matt moved around the corner for a better look.

It was Joey Orlando. Cop killer.

All of a sudden Matt was glad that he hadn't wasted time confronting the man in the silver Nissan. He raised the .45, moving forward in silence. He had been trained to move in silence. He was good at it. He stopped three feet short of Orlando's back and listened to the detective breathing. He looked him over from head to toe and felt repulsed by his entire presence. Orlando was watching Laura in the window as he stood hidden in the darkness. Even worse, it was a close-up view from the side. She was in the kitchen, rinsing dishes in the sink and looking out the back window at the lighted pool. She was wearing a black T-shirt that rose above her midriff and a pair of jeans that rode well below her hips. Her hair was pulled back, and from the color of her full lips, it looked like she was wearing makeup. She looked good. She looked better than good.

"Enjoying the view, Joey?" he whispered in a hoarse voice.

Orlando flinched, then caught himself and froze, thinking it over. "Yeah, Jones," he said finally. "It's a pretty good view tonight."

"Where's Plank?"

"What's it to you?"

Matt jabbed the .45 into his back. "Where's Plank?" he repeated.

Orlando shrugged. "Home, I guess."

Matt stepped around Orlando with the gun aimed at his chest. He could feel his pulse slowing as the adrenaline backed off. He was all business now as he watched Orlando eye the .45. After a few beats, the big man with the goatee and the salsa stain on his shirt seemed to ignore the drawn weapon and finally met Matt's gaze.

"You were overseas, Jones. How many people did you kill?"

"What are you doing here, Joey?"

"I drove out to your place thinking you'd be home." He glanced at Laura, then looked back and flashed a dirty smile. "It's pretty clear why you're not."

Matt ignored the innuendo. "What do you want?" he said.

Orlando shot him a knowing look and lowered his voice. "Too bad what happened to Frankie Lane this afternoon. I heard he drove off a mountain and got himself all burned up. I heard he was a nice guy, but now he's just a piece of meat. I wanted to make sure I expressed my condolences, Jones."

A long moment passed with Matt staring at Orlando and Orlando staring back. A warning that didn't appear to be veiled or spoken in code.

"You got it right, Orlando. Frankie was okay. You ever meet him?"

"No," Orlando said, smiling through a yawn. "I never fucking did. It's getting late, Jones. See ya tomorrow at the office. Maybe we'll go out and grab a cup of coffee. Just the two of us."

Orlando was a motherfucker.

Matt watched him turn and walk off, keeping an eye on him until he got into the Crown Vic and finally vanished down the street.

He slipped his .45 into the holster, then took a deep breath and exhaled.

He might have been all business, but he could feel the weight of the moment preying on him as well. He checked his watch, wondering how much more time it would take the protection detail to get here. He no longer had any confidence in them. He turned and looked at Laura in the window. Her T-shirt and jeans. The makeup that she was wearing tonight. He lit a cigarette and looked at her again. Then he turned away.

CHAPTER 33

It had taken twenty minutes for the protection detail to return. When they finally arrived, Matt kept himself together but told them exactly what had happened and made sure they understood that they had been played. Although both officers appeared to be professionals, neither one of them understood the potential downside, because Matt couldn't tell them how lethal Orlando was or what kind of cop he had become. From the expressions on their faces—*what gives?*—Matt guessed that they thought he was either paranoid or making a big deal about nothing. After all, Orlando was an LAPD detective whom Matt worked with.

By the time he got his overnight bag out of the car and Laura opened the front door, he was exhausted and just wanted to hit the sheets and get some sleep.

"You don't look so good," she said. "Have you eaten anything since breakfast?"

"A couple hours ago. I'm just tired."

"You want something to drink?"

"Maybe a beer that I could take upstairs."

She seemed disappointed that he didn't want to stay up for a while and talk, but Matt ignored it. He followed her into the kitchen. As she pulled a Corona out of the fridge, he spotted the glass of white wine on the counter. He watched her take a sip, then noticed the look she gave him as she switched off the lights.

She still wanted to talk.

Matt followed her upstairs and down the hall to the bedroom directly across from the master bedroom. She walked in, set her wineglass on the side table, and started turning down the bed.

"You don't need to do that, Laura."

"I know, but I want to. Let me get you some fresh towels."

She stepped into the bathroom, pulled a set of towels from the closet, and hung them on the rack beside the shower. She checked the room, then walked out and reached for her wineglass. When she sat down on the bed, Matt took a swig of beer and pulled the chair over.

"Are you okay?" he said.

She nodded but didn't say anything. Her eyes were on him. Her wheels were turning again.

"How'd your day go?" he asked.

She shrugged, her voice throaty and just above a whisper. "I'd rather hear about yours."

He didn't want to tell her about Frankie. He wanted to hold off until later, maybe in the morning after she got a decent night's sleep. But even more, he didn't want to tell her about anything for the very same reasons Leo Rodriguez had held back on his wife, Sally. If Laura knew what was really going on, she'd be even less safe than she already was.

He saw her eyes drift down to the pack of Marlboros in his shirt pocket.

"I thought you and Kevin stopped smoking together," she said.

"We did."

"So what happened?"

He shrugged and tilted his head.

"You don't want to tell me, do you?" she said.

"Tell you what?"

"What happened to you today. You don't want to tell me because you think that I can't handle it. Something happened. Something horrible. I can tell, Matt. You're smoking again, and I can see it in your face. In your eyes. It's like you've aged ten years in the last fifteen hours."

Matt took another pull on the Corona. "It's been a long couple of days, that's all. I need some sleep, and you do, too."

Her eyes were still on him, measuring him. After a moment she got up from the bed.

"Do you think the burglar will come back tonight?" she said.

Matt finally understood, flashing a warm smile at her as he got up from the chair. "I think he already took everything he was looking for. If he does come back, the guys outside will take care of it. They're the best we've got."

She stepped into his arms and rested her head against his chest. Matt could feel her pressing her body against his. He could feel her body relaxing in his arms. She was still frightened.

"Thanks for staying with me," she whispered. "You don't know how much it means."

"Everything's gonna be okay, Laura. I promise. You're safe here."

"I miss him," she said. "I don't think I can make it."

"We'll get through this," he said quietly.

She tightened her hold on him, then gave him a look with those eyes of hers. A moment passed before she let go.

"You're a good man," she said.

He watched her pick up her glass and cross the hall. Just before closing the door, she turned and wished him a good night.

Matt started to close his own door but looked down the hall toward the study and had second thoughts. After tonight, after the events of the day, it seemed more than plausible that Orlando had been the one who had broken into the house last night, stolen Hughes's files on the Faith Novakoff murder case, and walked into Laura's bedroom while she slept.

More than plausible, but not definitive. There were too many question marks. Too many black holes. He thought about what Cabrera had said, and it didn't help.

They could be murdered in their sleep tonight.

Matt placed his .45 on the bedside table, switched off the lights, and stepped out of his clothes. As he got into bed, he looked across the hall at the crack of light beneath Laura's bedroom door and tried to quiet his mind. After several moments he became aware of the sound of rushing water. The two bathrooms must have shared a wall because he could hear Laura in the shower. He thought about her magnetism and the spell she seemed to cast over every-one she met. Her blond hair, her full lips and soft skin, the curves and smooth lines of her body. He could smell the light scent of her perfume on his face. He could still smell her hair from just moments ago when she rested her head on his chest. He could feel her body pressing against him and relaxing. He could see her in the shower. The warm, soapy water cascading all over her naked—

Matt switched on the lamp and tried to get rid of the images in his head. He remembered the guilt he'd felt when he read her love letters earlier in the day. He tried to concentrate on that feeling and build on it. Tried to remember that Laura was his best friend's wife. Tried to remember that she'd just lost her husband and was particularly vulnerable right now. Tried to keep in mind that she might even be pregnant. But after fifteen minutes, the shower was still going, the wall was too thin, and all of a sudden Matt was wide awake and reaching for the murder books he'd tossed in his overnight bag . . .

CHAPTER 34

Matt eased open her bedroom door after a second light tap but didn't find her sleeping. It was six thirty in the morning. When he didn't see her clothes on the chair, he called her name and listened for her in the house.

Nothing. Just the strange sound of the wind whistling outside.

He walked over to the windows facing the backyard. He could see the wind pushing and pulling at a large oak tree that was being held together by steel wires. When he looked down the steps at the pool, he spotted Laura cutting back a bougainvillea that was creeping up a small tree. She had a windbreaker on and a pair of rubber boots that rose to her knees. A large mug of coffee was set on the stone wall. He looked up at the sky. It seemed too dark for this time of day and too cold, like maybe it might even rain; like maybe it was January instead of October; like maybe the whole world had come undone and was out of order.

Matt turned back to Laura and watched her for a few moments. The feelings he had experienced last night, the wild thoughts and fantasies, were gone. As he tossed it over, he wondered if what had happened last night hadn't been a result of his extreme need for sleep. As he tossed it over, he wondered if his unbridled thoughts hadn't been born from the paranoia and outrage he was feeling. Last night had been a crossroads. Matt knew that as a police officer, a homicide detective, he could no longer trust his own.

Sleep had finally come about an hour after Laura turned off the shower. Matt had opened Millie Brown's murder book and reread every entry that mentioned Jamie Taladyne and his past. When sleep arrived, it was dreamless, which he appreciated and took as a good sign.

He walked back into the guest room, showered and shaved and got dressed in some fresh clothes. When he entered the kitchen, he could see the two officers from Metro standing in the driveway, drinking coffee and waiting for the next team to arrive. They seemed like good guys, but he still wondered if he could trust them after what happened last night. In the end, did he really have any choice?

He pulled on his sweatshirt and grabbed his jacket, then walked outside and down the steps to the pool. Laura was still working on that bougainvillea. She looked tired, but at least she was in her element. Before all this, Laura had been a landscape designer and worked at a nursery on Orange Grove in Pasadena. Before all this.

"You're up early," she said.

"You are, too. How'd you sleep?"

She gave him a look and shrugged. "You want breakfast?"

"I'll get a sandwich on the way in, but I need to talk to you about something."

Her eyes came back to him and stayed there. He could tell that she was bracing herself for the bad news that she sensed had happened yesterday. Matt watched her set down the clippers. He couldn't let it go any longer.

"You're gonna tell me what happened yesterday, aren't you?" she said.

Her voice was soft and throaty again. She seemed so defenseless.

"It's about Frankie, isn't it?" she went on. "It's about Frankie, and he's hurt."

She sat down on the stone wall. Matt joined her.

"He's dead, Laura. His car went off the road in Mint Canyon yesterday, and I don't think it was an accident."

Their eyes met, and she reached for his hand. A long moment passed.

"How did you know it was Frankie?" he whispered.

"I called him after lunch and left a message. He never called back. That's not Frankie. When I saw your face last night, I knew something had happened. When you didn't want to talk about it, I knew that it probably wasn't good."

"Are you still locked into staying here? Is there any chance that you'd reconsider and visit your parents in Philly?"

"I have to go back to work, Matt. Next week."

"I bet they'd give you more time off if they knew what was going on."

"But there's Kevin's funeral. They're releasing his body the day after tomorrow."

His phone started vibrating in his pocket. Digging it out, he saw Cabrera's name and stepped away from the wall. He had sent Cabrera a text message before he showered, asking him to call back as soon as he could.

"What's up?" Cabrera said.

Matt glanced at Laura, then turned away and spoke in a low voice. "I think we need to talk to the girl Taladyne raped in her dormitory."

"That was five years ago, Matt. She would've graduated. She's probably long gone by now."

"I don't think so. Grace and Rodriguez interviewed her when Taladyne was a suspect in Millie Brown's murder. Her contact info is in the murder book. It says she was living in Playa del Rey. She was at the beach, and it wasn't that long ago. She could still be there."

"What about meeting Baylor at the coroner's office for the ID?"

"I'll take care of that if you'll check out the girl and see if you can set something up."

"When?"

"This morning. Any time she's free. I'll text you her contact info and meet you out there as soon as I can."

"Sounds good," Cabrera said. "What's her name?"

"Leah Reynolds. And just so you know, I ran into Orlando last night."

It sounded like the phone went dead. Matt checked the signal, then the power, which was low. He had forgotten to charge the battery last night.

"Are you there, Denny? You there?"

"I'm here," Cabrera said. "You ran into Orlando. What happened?"

"Nothing good. We'll talk later. Be careful."

Matt slipped the phone into his pocket and turned back to Laura. She had been watching him. When he started walking toward her to say good-bye, her eyes stayed on his face. He thought about that pregnancy test kit he'd seen on the kitchen counter the other night. She had that look going—the same one he'd seen in so many women carrying a child. She seemed so fragile, so vulnerable, so gentle, so possibly pregnant. Or was he just projecting his emotions onto her being? Was she just a blank canvas that he couldn't help filling in? Either way, he promised himself that he'd be there for her.

CHAPTER 35

His paranoia had returned, following him from the parking lot into the lobby at the coroner's office. The cops in their uniforms were obvious, but so were the cops in plainclothes. Every glance his way sharpened the edge. Every long look made him wonder if they might not be tied to the enemy in some way.

Grace, Orlando, and Plank.

It was like being overseas. He could no longer tell who was who. If he wanted to stay alive, he could no longer trust anyone at face value. If he wanted to stay alive, he couldn't take anything for granted anymore.

A woman sitting behind the front desk directed him to the conference room down the hall on the right. When he gazed through the doorway and didn't see anyone from Hollywood Homicide, he stepped inside and found Art Madina sitting at the head of the table. Baylor was seated with a middle-aged woman who had to be Brooke Anderson's mother but bore no physical resemblance. A video monitor was mounted to the wall, the screen switched on but blank.

Matt nodded at Baylor as he took a seat on the other side of the table. It sounded like Madina was trying to prepare the woman for the horror she was about to face. The medical examiner had hoped that they could conduct the identification using a video camera, but it seemed like the woman was insisting on seeing her daughter in the flesh.

Matt winced as he listened, trying to bury the memory of Brooke Anderson's disfigured face with no success. He wondered if he should speak up and tell her about his experiences as a soldier in the desert. He wondered if he should tell her that while she'd never forget seeing her daughter's corpse, a video image had the chance of dimming over time. An image provided emotional distance, no matter how slight, and had the chance of becoming unreal and fading into the background. Seeing her daughter with her own eyes would have the opposite effect. The experience would become radioactive. The moment would remain in sharp focus, haunting her until the day she died.

As it turned out, Matt didn't need to interrupt. Madina had switched gears and was making the case for him. Still, as Matt looked her over, he didn't think she'd change her mind.

There was something about her. Something about the way her face had been stained by her grief.

She was a meaty woman in a small frame, with plain features that seemed masculine and institutionalized. Her black suit appeared well tailored, her light brown hair so even and unnatural in color that Matt guessed that it had been dyed for the trip. He checked her hands. They didn't look particularly rough or worn, but her fingers were too short and fat for the ring she was wearing. Instead of appearing elegant, what was most likely a very expensive piece of jewelry looked cheap and out of place.

He remembered Baylor telling him that she was the CEO of an insurance company in the Midwest. He looked back at her ring, then at her face, her person, as he thought it over. Anyone in her position had to be used to dealing with crises on a daily basis. She was probably used to getting her own way as well. Today, he thought sadly, it would cost her.

"I'm sorry, Dr. Madina," he could hear her saying in a surprisingly gentle voice. "Everything you and Dr. Baylor just said makes a great deal of sense to me. I think you're both probably very good at your jobs, and you know better than I do how things like this work. But I need to see my daughter. I need to see her one last time."

A beat went by, impregnated by darkness. Then Madina glanced at Baylor, switched off the video monitor with the remote, and everyone rose from the table.

"Mrs. Anderson," Baylor said. "This is Matt Jones, one of the detectives assigned to your daughter's case."

Although what the doctor had just said wasn't exactly accurate, Matt ignored it and shook the woman's hand. She nodded slightly but was too upset to hold the gaze or say anything. When he glanced back at Baylor, something was going on with him as well. Fear? Nerves? Compassion? He seemed overwhelmingly concerned for Brooke Anderson's mother. And as Matt followed them out the door, he watched him take her arm and support her.

The elevator was at the other end of the hall. They walked in silence. A death march. When Matt's phone began vibrating in his pocket, he pulled it out and slid the lock open. Cabrera had sent a text message: *Contact info still good. We're on for 10.* Matt checked his watch and sent a one-word reply. Although he would be facing rush-hour traffic, most people would be headed downtown. He thought he could make it on time.

The elevator doors opened. As he stepped inside with the others, he immediately became aware of the harsh odors emanating from the morgue and operating room in the basement. He could see it registering across Mrs. Anderson's face as well. He noted her grip on Dr. Baylor's arm. She was squeezing it as if holding on for dear life. When the doors opened in the basement, the smell of rotting flesh became even stronger, and the woman's face turned grim and lost all of its color.

Matt wished that he had spoken up. He wished he could have convinced her that nothing good could come from this. He was with Baylor. He got it. He understood. Brooke Anderson's mother. They were walking in her shoes now.

"This way, please," Madina said.

They followed him past the operating room and down the hall to the very end, the sound of an ME's electric skull saw cutting against the sound of their shoes beating against the tiled floor. They stood in silence as Madina unlocked a door and swung it open.

Brooke Anderson was here, lying beneath a sheet on a stainless steel gurney.

A long moment passed before they entered the room, like driving by the last exit before hitting a toll road. When Madina closed the door, Matt became aware of the bright fluorescent lights vibrating and humming. The white walls and the white sheet. It was a small room, almost the same size as the elevator, and Matt could smell Brooke Anderson's corpse through the sheet. He remembered kneeling beside her nude body in Hollywood Hills that night, the smell of her soap and shampoo wafting in the cool fresh air.

But all of that was gone now. The only thing left was the stench.

He looked up and saw the girl's mother leaning against Baylor's chest with her arms up and ready to block the view. Both of them looked terrified, their eyes big and wild and pinned to the white sheet.

And then Madina lifted the cover away, and their faces froze as if someone had crept into the room and taken a snapshot.

Matt followed their gaze down to Brooke Anderson's face and took the hit. Time hadn't been very kind to the victim. The

Glasgow smile. The Chelsea grin. The cuts between her ears and lips were even more exaggerated, more distressing, more hideous than before. Matt wasn't sure if there was a God or not, but that was the first thing that entered his mind. As he stared at the girl's wounds, he wondered what God would do if he did exist. Would he fix her face? Or would she be forced to pass through the heavens like this for the rest of eternity? Would it depend on who she had been? Would it depend on how she had acted throughout the course of her short life? Would it depend on anything at all? But even more, could anyone or anything, even a god, really fix this?

He heard the girl's mother let out a yelp and looked at her. The snapshot had become unglued, the mother cringing and shaking and weeping as Baylor held her from behind. She couldn't stop looking at her daughter's face. She was moving her lips, but nothing was coming out. Matt watched Baylor trying to comfort her but knew that they were five minutes too late. They had used the elevator to reach the basement. They had opened the door at the end of the hall and lifted the sheet away.

They had looked at her.

The girl's mother struggled to take a breath. Her chest heaved. She was drowning in it. She was ruined.

CHAPTER 36

The twenty-mile drive between the coroner's office and Playa del Rey took just over an hour. Matt didn't mind. The sun had burned off the marine layer, the sky a bright blue. In spite of the cool air, the windows were down, the wind beating against his face.

He needed it.

He cruised down Pershing Drive and made the turn toward the ocean. Every house on the quiet street came equipped with a million-dollar view of the beach. If you could get past how close each house stood to the next, how tight the lots were packed, how surreal it all seemed, every one of them had the look and feel of having been made in paradise. When he spotted Leah Reynolds's house three doors down, he realized that it was no exception. He noted the large windows, the wraparound decks off each floor, a central chimney that housed three flues, and what appeared to be an enclosed terrace for a small pool and spa. But even more, he could smell the ocean in the air, the salt water. And when he pulled in behind Cabrera's SUV and switched off the engine, he could hear the waves crashing on the beach without the sound of a freeway in the background.

He thought about his run-down house in the hills overlooking Potrero Canyon Park and smiled a little. He hadn't smiled in four days, and he needed that, too.

Cabrera got out of his car and walked over. Matt disconnected the charger and checked the battery on his phone as he switched off the ringer. The power icon indicated only a slight charge. It wouldn't be enough to get through the morning.

"How'd it go with Brooke Anderson's mother?"

Matt gave him a look and got out of the car. "We're in a bad place, Denny. I caught Orlando peeping on Hughes's wife last night. I think he's the one who broke into the house the night before. He stole the files Hughes was keeping on Faith Novakoff's murder, then went into the bedroom for a look at his wife. I think there's a good chance he's a perv."

"You think he suspects what we know?"

Matt shrugged. "Probably not that they planted evidence on Harris or murdered three cops. Probably none of the details. We wouldn't be here if he did. But he knows something's up. And he knows it's not good."

"How? Why?"

"Because my .45 was aimed at his chest."

Cabrera let it sink in, then shook his head.

Matt looked up at the house. It was a good guess that the young woman with light brown hair watching them from the deck was Leah Reynolds. She waved at them with a tentative expression on her face, then walked into the house. A moment later she opened the front door.

Matt led the way up the steps. He pulled out his ID, but Reynolds didn't do much more than glance at it before showing them into the living room. As she found a place on the couch, he looked her over and wondered, just as he always did, how anyone could hurt her. How anyone could deliberately hurt anyone at all.

Reynolds was a gentle-looking woman with an angular face, freckled cheeks, and brown eyes that weren't much darker than her tanned skin. She was wearing jeans and a T-shirt, her bare feet and legs folded beneath her body. When she offered them coffee, both Matt and Cabrera thanked her but declined.

"Nice neighborhood," Matt said.

She smiled at him. "I'm lucky to live here."

"Are we gonna get you in trouble with your boss?" Cabrera asked. "Are you gonna be late for work?"

She shook her head. "Not at all. I'm not working right now."

Matt understood what Cabrera was getting at because he had thought the same thing. He looked around the room. The tiled floors, the fireplace, the modern furniture, the oversized windows facing the ocean. Reynolds had money.

"Who lives here with you?" he said.

He must have touched a nerve because she looked down at the floor and lowered her voice. She was thinking about something.

"No one," she said. "I really haven't been able to . . . you know . . . be with anyone for a long time."

Matt knew that it didn't matter that five years had passed since the woman had been raped by Jamie Taladyne. Rape usually carried a life sentence for its victims. Usually, but not every time. There were always the lucky ones.

"I'm sorry," he said. "We can't thank you enough for talking to us. And I apologize for both me and my partner for any bad memories that might resurface."

She nodded but seemed to become more timid. "Did he do it to someone else? Your partner told me on the phone that you were working on something similar."

"It's possible," Matt said. "For now we're just trying to get a sense of who Taladyne is and where he might have moved to. Things have come up that weren't covered when you met with Detectives Grace and Rodriguez a while back. We'd like to hear what happened to you in your own words. Taladyne served two years in prison. I realize that's not nearly enough time. But we were wondering if you'd seen him since his release. We were wondering if he ever tried to contact you."

She shook her head. Her eyes had lost their focus and reach.

"My counselor said that he might, but he never did. After the trial, I never saw him again."

"What about phone calls? Frequent hang-ups?"

"My number's unlisted."

Matt glanced at Cabrera, then turned back to Reynolds. "Why don't you tell us what happened?"

She paused a moment to compose herself. When she finally spoke, Matt had to lean forward to hear her.

"I was going to school in Westwood," she said. "I had a single room in a dorm that was being renovated. I saw him every day. He was nice to me. He seemed like a good guy. Jamie always had a smile. I used to talk to him. Once or twice we went out for coffee. I kind of liked him. Then one night I came back to my room after dinner and he was waiting for me. He tied me to the bed. He took off my clothes. He cut them off with a box cutter. A razor blade. And then he raped me. He didn't stop until the next morning."

Matt traded looks with Cabrera again. As difficult as it was to listen to, Reynold's story seemed to mirror the events leading up to Millie Brown's murder.

His phone started vibrating and he reached into his pocket. When he saw Lieutenant McKensie's name blinking on the face, he looked back at Reynolds.

"I'm sorry but I have to take this." Matt turned to Cabrera. "It's Frankie's supervisor. It's McKensie."

Cabrera's eyes widened a little. Matt got up, opened the slider, and stepped onto the deck as he punched in the call. McKensie didn't sound very happy.

"We need to meet, and we need to meet right now, Jones."

Matt hesitated, feeling another wave of paranoia sweep over him. "Why can't we talk over the phone?" he said. "What do you want?"

"In case you haven't noticed, I lost two homicide detectives this week. My office, Jones. Not later. Now. Or I swear I'll nail your sorry fucking ass to the cross."

The call ended, but not with a hang-up. Instead, it sounded more like McKensie had thrown the phone against the wall. It sounded like he was in a real bad mood.

CHAPTER 37

Matt pulled into the visitor's lot at the North Hollywood station and found a place to park where he could keep an eye on the front entrance. Releasing his seat belt, he pried the lid off a cup of coffee that he'd picked up at the 7-Eleven next door and took a quick sip. The coffee was strong and piping hot and tasted like it had just been brewed. He took another sip through the steam, trying to force himself to relax and stay focused.

Cops were walking in and out of the building. Patrol units were passing through the lot and making the turn onto Burbank Boulevard. Few looked his way, and those who did didn't seem very interested. Everything appeared casual enough. Through his windshield, everything he saw looked ordinary and true.

Matt didn't know what to make of it.

He wondered if all the paranoia and dread wasn't blowback from the war. While he had never experienced any issues in the past, he wondered if seeing Brooke Anderson's body, or even the anticipation of seeing her body, had triggered something so deep inside he couldn't find it or even name it.

He thought about his father. Or maybe it was just the idea of having a father. Someone he could talk to, and—

He tried to clear his mind.

He was disappointed that he couldn't stay with Cabrera and see the interview through with Leah Reynolds. Still, they had talked it over before he'd left, and he felt confident that he and Cabrera were on the same page.

Unlike Millie Brown, Reynolds was alive and had seen Taladyne every day before the rape. They had talked, and as she said, they had something going on. It didn't matter how casual it might have been. Matt knew that there was still the chance that Taladyne had spoken about himself—the things he liked to do and the places he liked to go. Still a chance that he might have said something that could point them to where he had been hiding since Ron Harris hung himself in his jail cell. But just as important to Matt were questions he knew that Grace and Rodriguez couldn't possibly have covered, given the fact that they had been investigating a single murder. Did Taladyne ever mention that he had a problem with people who had money? Did he ever talk about greed or religion? Did Reynolds sense that he was bitter or angry? Did he ever say anything about hating something or someone for whatever reason? Did Taladyne ever talk about seeking revenge?

Matt took a last sip of coffee and got out of the car. As he walked toward the entrance, he could feel the butterflies working his stomach. He thought that he might be shaking, but when he checked his hands they looked steady.

He entered the lobby, his ID out and ready for the desk sergeant. They must have been expecting him, because a cop escorted him directly to McKensie's office and asked if he'd like anything while he waited. McKensie was in a meeting that should have ended fifteen minutes ago, the cop said. Matt thanked him but declined and sat down facing the glass walls and door. When the man vanished around the corner, he got up and moved straight to the lieutenant's desk. There were two files on top, and Matt could read both Hughes's and Frankie's names on the tabs. A black-and-white snapshot of the two detectives was leaning against a framed photograph of McKensie's wife and children. Matt checked the hall, then flipped open the file with Frankie's name on it and took a quick glimpse inside. A preliminary report of the *accident* in Mint Canyon had been drafted and sent over by the Sheriff's Department. Matt heard footsteps in the hallway, saw McKensie turn the corner, then closed the file and rushed back to his seat.

McKensie must not have noticed, because he entered the room without saying anything or even acknowledging Matt's presence. Kicking the door shut with his foot, he tossed a file folder on his desk and sat down.

"What is it, Lieutenant? What do you want with me?"

McKensie didn't respond, and Matt looked him over. Even though his hair had turned white, Matt knew from Hughes that McKensie was only in his midfifties. His skin was tanned and heavily lined, and he had the look and gravelly voice of a man who drank more nights than he should. His eyes were a brilliant green, with heat and fire in them, his body thirty to forty pounds over-weight but hard and tough, like a street fighter's. As Matt sat there trying to interpret McKensie's silence, his dead stare, he thought about getting up and making a run for it. He wondered how far he'd get down the hall.

"You asked me to come here, Lieutenant. I'm here."

A moment passed, and then another, before McKensie spoke in an exceedingly quiet voice.

"I hate you," he said.

Matt froze. The man's eyes were drilling him, and he appeared to be seething. He was sipping something from a coffee mug that Matt didn't think was coffee. The weight of the air in the small room turned heavy and felt oppressive.

"I really hate you," he went on.

"You're not my commanding officer. Am I supposed to care?"

"I told you that I needed to see you. That it was important, Jones. It took you two fucking hours to get here."

Matt shrugged. "I was in Playa del Rey."

"Doing what? Getting laid after a long breakfast?"

Matt got up. "Listen, Lieutenant, I don't know what's going on, and I don't have time to figure it out."

He started toward the door.

McKensie lowered the mug and leaned forward. "Sit down, tough guy. I've got something to say to you, and I'm not finished. If you walk out now, you won't make it to the lobby. I'll have you arrested. I swear to God I will. I'll have you locked up, and I won't tell anybody about it for twenty-four hours."

Matt stopped as he reached the door, wondering if McKensie was crazy enough to do it. He turned and gazed at the man sitting behind his desk. The fierce, wide-open eyes, the face cut in stone, the clenched teeth, his hands balled up into fists. The answer was undoubtedly yes, he would spend the next twenty-four hours in jail, and no one would know. Matt grimaced, then returned to the chair.

"That's better, Jones. Take a seat. Pull yourself together." McKensie took another sip from his mug, then met Matt's gaze. "I gave you a call," he said finally, "because I got a heads-up from the Sheriff's Department this morning."

"Okay," Matt said. "You got a heads-up. What is it?"

McKensie opened the file that he had walked in with, leafed through several sheets of paper until he found the one he was looking for, then slid it across his desk. It was an e-mail from the Sheriff's Department that included a driver's license and a blowup of a young man's face printed on a single sheet of copy paper. Matt had no idea what it meant and looked back at McKensie.

The lieutenant nodded. "The three-piece bandit was killed last night, Jones. He tried to rob an off-duty deputy sheriff in a parking lot in West Hollywood, and it didn't pan out."

Matt took a deep breath. "Who is he?"

"He's been identified as Sean Hudson, a twenty-five-year-old kid who had been out of work for more than a year. He had a wife and a newborn son. The Sheriff's Department has his piece, a Glock 20, but the mag was empty. They finished searching his apartment three hours ago. No ammunition was found, and a preliminary examination of the pistol indicates that it's never been fired. Hudson's wife claims that he never bought any ammo, because he didn't want to hurt anyone. That means that the kid was telling the truth when he released those text messages to the media. He couldn't have killed Hughes. The Sheriff's Department will be holding a press conference sometime this afternoon, or before that if the story leaks. The kid didn't kill Hughes, but you and your partner knew that a long time ago—just like you know that Frankie Lane didn't die in a fucking car accident."

A long moment passed, the entire office charged with electricity. Matt's hand automatically went for the pack of cigarettes in his pocket. McKensie shot him another hard look.

"This building's a smoke-free environment, Jones."

It didn't matter anymore. He lit a cigarette and took a deep pull, then watched McKensie grab the pack out of his hand and light one, too. McKensie leaned closer, waving the smoke away from his eyes in a lazy arc.

"Here's my problem, Jones. Here's what keeps me up at night. When Hughes got all shot up, why didn't his case go downtown with his fucking body? A cop gets knocked off, the best and brightest usually take over and all the troops rally. When two cops get knocked off, the rally gets even bigger. I've lost two of my best, you hear what I'm saying? Downtown isn't investigating these cases.

You are. Matt Jones. Just bumped up from busting thirteen-year-olds for selling weed in the school yard. It's bullshit, and it stinks."

Matt listened and took it, but held on and didn't say anything. Sliding the wastebasket closer, he flicked the ash from his smoke into the can and took another pull. McKensie was still staring at him with those green eyes of his. Still breathing fire.

"What the fuck is wrong with this picture, Jones? What the fuck is up with Bob Grace? I never liked that guy. I never liked anybody who liked that guy. I always thought Bob Grace was a piece of shit. This has something to do with the Faith Novakoff murder and that girl you guys found up by the Hollywood sign the other night. And guess what, Jones? This morning's e-mail from Missing Persons included someone new. Another coed. Nobody's seen her for seventy-two hours."

McKensie flashed a brutal grin, took a last drag on his smoke, and ground it out on the tiled floor with his heel. Then he pulled another e-mail from his file and slid it across the desk. Matt looked at the girl's face, her dark hair and dark eyes, her round cheeks. She could have been someone's sister or cousin, smiling from across the dinner table at Thanksgiving.

"You're not saying much, Jones, so I'm gonna make a wild guess that whatever's on your mind is pretty fucking bad."

Matt remained quiet. Another girl had gone missing. Another victim. He scanned through the e-mail. Anna Marie Genet. A freshman at a private college on the Westside. She had just turned eighteen. She looked so normal. So innocent and young.

McKensie leaned even closer and lowered his voice. "Who were the two guys that met up with Frankie at the gas station, Jones?"

"I can't really say, Lieutenant."

"But Frankie was murdered, right?"

Matt nodded. "I think so."

"By the two men at the gas station. The two men driving a Ford sedan. They knew Frankie, and Frankie knew them."

Matt took another look at the photo of the girl, then turned back. "Yeah," he said. "There's a good chance they knew each other."

McKensie's eyes were on him, hard. After a while he cocked his head, as if a new thought had just surfaced in his mind.

"Are you in danger, son? Is that why you won't talk to me? You and your partner think you're next?"

Matt hesitated, but only briefly. Still, he could tell from the expression on McKensie's face that his eyes had given him away.

A moment passed. Then another. Was it light, or was it darkness?

"What did you find at Frankie's apartment?" Matt said finally.

McKensie shook his head and shrugged as he considered the question. "Nothing," he said. "Nothing out of the ordinary."

"What about his files on the Faith Novakoff case?"

"He must have had everything with him in the car. They burned up in the fire."

Matt shook his head. "Nothing burned up in the fire except Frankie, Lieutenant."

Another stretch of silence passed as Frankie's death settled into the small glass room. Matt got rid of his smoke, glanced at the files on the desk, then looked back at McKensie.

"Any chance I could get into Frankie's place for another look?"

CHAPTER 38

Matt had never been to Frankie's apartment before. When McKensie told him that it was only a ten-minute drive from the station, he decided to ride with the lieutenant and grabbed his cell phone charger out of the car. Not much was said along the way, and Matt spent most of the time worrying about Cabrera. Before they had left the station, before the battery on his phone died, Matt had tried to check in. When Cabrera didn't answer, Matt sent him a text message and waited for a reply, until his phone finally lost power and shut down. He remembered his confrontation with Orlando last night, then thought about his partner, alone in Playa del Rey with Reynolds.

He never should have left him behind. They should've backed out together and rescheduled the interview with the young woman for later in the day.

Matt glanced at McKensie, then looked out the window. They were heading west on Riverside Drive, about three or four blocks from Laurel Canyon Boulevard. McKensie pointed at a two-story apartment building on the other side of the street, made a U-turn, and parked at the curb. He left the engine running and rolled down the windows. The winds had shifted, the Valley warming in the bright sunlight. McKensie settled into his seat, like he had something he wanted to say.

Matt gazed at the apartment building while he waited. He was surprised by its sterile appearance and wasn't sure why. The place must have been built thirty-five years ago, yet it still had a modern feel about it—large glass windows, vaulted ceilings, and clean lines. He looked through the grove of palm trees at the entrance. It seemed quiet and tranquil, the building well maintained. For whatever reason, he couldn't see Frankie living here.

"It stays with me," McKensie said finally.

Matt turned. McKensie was staring at him again.

"What stays with you?"

"Everything you just said to me in my office, son. And everything you didn't. It stays with me, Jones. I wanted you to know that. I want you to be able to count on it."

Matt nodded but didn't say anything. He still wasn't sure that he could trust the lieutenant. As he played it through in his mind, there was the chance that McKensie really was clean and had put it together on his own. *Frankie was a cop. Cops know cops. The two men who killed Frankie drove a Ford sedan. Lots of cops drive Ford sedans. There's a problem, and it's in Hollywood. There's a problem, and it has something to do with the investigation of a serial killer.*

But no matter what McKensie had just said, there was still the chance that he didn't hate Grace but went way back with him. There was still the chance that they were friends. Still the chance that McKensie was trying to bullshit Matt into saying how much he knew and play him for a fool.

As a soldier in Afghanistan, Matt had learned all too quickly that if he didn't see the chance, if he didn't see every risk and possibility all at once, he would've come home early. He would've come home in a box.

At the same time, Matt knew that he couldn't afford to let himself stand still. He needed to get inside Lane's apartment, and taking the risk by getting McKensie to open the door seemed like the only way.

McKensie grabbed his file folders off the dash, and they got out of the car. Entering the lobby, Matt watched the lieutenant fish a key ring out of a small manila envelope. There were only two keys—both marked with tags, both shiny and new—and Matt guessed that the keys in the ignition of Frankie's car had melted in the fire and couldn't be recovered. The thought faded as McKensie swung open the door. Once they were inside, the lieutenant pointed at the staircase across from the elevator.

"Second floor," he said. "Number twenty-six, halfway down on the right."

Skylights led the way through the narrow hallway. An eerie silence followed in their wake. When they finally reached the door, McKensie inserted the key and gave it a turn, but the dead bolt slid only halfway and stopped. He passed his files over to Matt, made sure he had the right key, and gave it another try. The dead bolt began to turn, then froze up again. Frankie's door wouldn't budge.

"There's something wrong with the lock," he said.

"Was there anything wrong with it before?"

"I don't know. By the time I got here, the guys were already inside."

The door across the way snapped open and a hard light flooded the hallway. Matt turned and saw a middle-aged man standing in the threshold, his face shadowed from the glare.

"You're back," the man said.

McKensie glanced at him, still straining to turn the key. "That's right, Mr. Kay. We're back."

"Someone came out this morning to fix that."

McKensie let go of the key. "Someone came out to fix what?"

The man let out a faint smile. "The lock."

"Was he wearing a uniform?" Matt asked.

"No, sir. Slacks and a tie, and he had a helper. Looks like the helper wasn't much help."

Matt didn't need to ask the next question but did. "Do you remember what they looked like?"

"You bet I do. They looked like a cartoon, only they weren't that funny. One was big and round with dark hair and a goatee. His helper was a short, skinny guy with gray hair. There was something wrong with his skin. His cheeks. They were working on the lock when I went out for breakfast. They didn't seem very happy to see me, or maybe they were just in a hurry."

Matt traded a hard look with McKensie, wondering if Orlando and Plank were still inside the apartment. Wondering if McKensie really was in on it. Wondering whether he had swallowed the bait and just walked into a trap. He gave McKensie another look but couldn't get a read on him. Handing over the files, Matt fished a pair of vinyl gloves out of his pocket and started turning the key back and forth on his own. Nothing worked until he pulled the door closer and gave the handle a hard lift. When he felt the deadbolt finally release, he tossed the key over to McKensie and told the man standing in the harsh light to get back inside his apartment and lock the door. Then he drew his .45, ripped back the slide, and gritted his teeth.

CHAPTER 39

Matt eased the door open with his foot, his pistol up and ready. It was an open floor plan, the living room giving way to a kitchen and an elevated dining area. On the right he could see a powder room, the door open, the room clear. He noted the hallway, saw another off the dining area to his left, and guessed that they met somewhere behind the kitchen.

He closed the front door as quietly as he could. Then, with his eyes rocking back and forth between McKensie and both hallways, he took a moment to listen. The apartment was exceedingly still. Just the sound of light traffic on Riverside Drive bleeding through the windows.

He turned back to McKensie and couldn't help noticing the lieutenant's gun. It was a .38 revolver that looked particularly old and menacing. From the intense, even bruising expression on McKensie's face, Matt guessed that both the man and the gun had killed—

He pushed the thought away. "What's back there?" he whispered.

"A bedroom and a den," the lieutenant said. "Two bathrooms, attached."

Matt nodded, pointing McKensie toward the hallway entrance on the other side of the dining area. He watched him head off, then crossed the living room and started down the hallway on the right. He moved quickly, silently, until he reached the corner and saw McKensie entering the master bedroom. Matt hustled down to the den, peeking inside and finally entering the room. He checked behind the door, glanced at the corners, still pushing forward, still eyeing everything in big gulps. He slid open the closet door and found a small filing cabinet and some clothing. Nothing he saw seemed out of place. When he checked the bath, the room was clear.

He stepped back into the hall. McKensie was just exiting Frankie's bedroom and turned his way.

"Nobody's here except for the ghosts, Jones."

Matt nodded but stepped into the bedroom for a look on his own. When he was satisfied that they were alone, when McKensie finally holstered his .38, he did the same.

Ghosts.

He had noticed them as well. That odd feeling of emptiness that overwhelms a space when someone dies and everyone knows that they're never coming back. The hollowness was so pervasive that he could almost taste it.

But then he thought about his partner. He thought about Cabrera, and all the ghosts flew away.

He reached inside his pocket for his phone and charger. As he stepped into the kitchen, he spotted an outlet by the stove. Once he had power, he switched on the ringer and turned up the volume so that he could hear it from anywhere in the apartment. When the face lit up and he saw that he had two voice messages, he felt an instant wave of relief.

But the relief lasted no more than a few seconds. Then the dread was back. That churning in his gut.

Both messages had been left by Lieutenant Grace.

He paused a moment to check on McKensie. He could see him over by the window, talking to someone on his cell. It sounded like he was on the line with SID and that he wanted Frankie's apartment to be treated as a crime scene.

Matt looked back at his phone, wondering if the two calls from Grace had anything to do with why Cabrera couldn't be reached. He clicked Play and listened to the first message. Grace wanted to know where he was. He claimed to have good news, but the tone of his voice sounded way too friendly to be righteous. The second message mirrored the first, with Grace's voice even more silky and smooth.

Where are you, Matt? You need to come in. Same with Denny. We need to talk. There's a joint press conference between us and the Sheriff's Department. It's set for 5:00 p.m., downtown at police headquarters. It's your case, and I expect you and your partner to be there. Both you guys need to come in.

Then what? Matt thought. *A ride in the trunk of your car?* If Grace knew that the three-piece bandit had been gunned down last night by a deputy sheriff, why didn't he just say it? Why the lure?

Matt opened his recent call list, found Cabrera's number, and hit Call. After three rings he could feel his chest tightening. After the next four, he was listening to Cabrera's outgoing message and shaking his head. He left another short message and laid the phone down on the counter to charge. Then he took a closer look at Frankie's apartment.

There were no visible signs that anyone had been here, and he wondered if Orlando and Plank had managed to get past what appeared to be a door that was out of alignment. He thought about the earthquake that rolled through LA this past summer. He knew that picking a dead bolt could be done in less than five minutes. But picking a lock with the dead bolt jammed into a doorframe would have taken time and patience. Even more, Orlando and Plank had been seen by Frankie's neighbor. Their physical appearance stood out to the point where the neighbor even made fun of them. They looked like characters in a cartoon, he'd said. Both of them could be identified, and they were smart enough to know it.

Matt took a last look at the living room—the muted green paint with white trim, the art on the walls, the carpets laid over hardwood floors, the furnishings. The apartment didn't match the building's bland exterior. Frankie's personality was everywhere.

He let a moment pass before checking on McKensie again. The lieutenant was still staring out the window with his back turned. Still talking to someone on the phone, and everything about it sounded legitimate.

Matt gave his vinyl gloves a tug, snapping them over his wrists as he walked down the hall into the den. The walls were the same color as the living room, only five shades darker and five times more soothing. The room had a certain feel about it. The writing table and laptop computer, a reading chair by the window, a couch and a coffee table, the extra-wide venetian blinds concealing a pool and spa one floor below, the built-in bookshelves. From the titles, it looked like Frankie was a history buff.

Lincoln and Kennedy, Kennedy and King—four assassinations, four murders, and a homicide detective with skill and talent on his own time. There must have been seventy-five books here.

Matt turned and noticed a poster framed behind glass and hanging beside the doorway. It was from Roman Polanski's *Chinatown*, and it had been signed by both Polanski and Jack Nicholson, but also by the screenwriter, Robert Towne.

He glanced at the writing table, noted only two top drawers, then opened the closet and began searching through the filing cabinet. After a few minutes he realized that Frankie didn't bring his work home with him. Every file Matt opened was personal: bank statements, tech manuals, insurance policies, but nothing about Faith Novakoff's murder or any other murder he had investigated. And the drawers were packed full. There wouldn't have been room for any additional files.

He moved to the desk and opened the first drawer. Pens, a stapler, a couple of notepads. He opened the second. Bills, a checkbook, and a calculator—the same things he would have found in his own desk drawers.

Matt switched on the laptop. While he waited for it to boot, he stepped into the bathroom for a look around. Something had caught his eye when he cleared the room, but he hadn't lingered on it. Now, as his eyes swept across the counter, he spotted it by the sink. It was a hair curler, lying beside a tube of lipstick and an electric toothbrush. Several moisturizers were on a small shelf beside the mirror. Inside the shower he found a body wash made for women, along with shampoos, rinses, shaving cream, and a razor blade. Behind the door a sheer robe hung from the hook, along with a negligee.

He hadn't been aware that Frankie had a girlfriend and was surprised that Hughes had never mentioned it. Of course, Hughes had never mentioned that he and Frankie were working the Faith Novakoff murder case either.

His eyes moved back to the tube of lipstick on the counter. He wondered if the Sheriff's Department had notified her about Frankie's death. He wondered how she'd taken the news.

Matt pushed the thought aside and returned to the laptop computer on the writing table. Opening the root directory, he sifted through Frankie's data files: letters, photographs, an accounting program, and what looked like thousands of music files. Like the folders he'd found in the closet, every document Matt opened on the laptop was personal. He checked the trash folder, sorting through it by date. There were hundreds of files here—so many in fact that Matt guessed they dated back to the day Frankie bought the computer. Matt paged down to the most recent files, chewing it over and realizing that it didn't make any sense.

Orlando and Plank had come here for a reason, just as someone, presumably Orlando, had broken into Hughes's house for a reason. So why hadn't they emptied the trash folder and deleted Frankie's data files? On Hughes's computer, the deletions had been more than obvious. How could they be sure something wouldn't be found on Frankie's computer that didn't point to them? The more Matt tossed it over, the less sense it made.

He picked up the house phone and noticed that the caller ID list hadn't been deleted either. Even more surprising, Orlando's name popped up from a call made the day before Frankie died.

Matt looked up and watched McKensie enter the room and sit on the arm of the couch.

"SID will be here within the hour, Jones. Two patrol units are on their way now. I've got a meeting in twenty-five minutes that I can't get out of. What do you want to do?"

"Who's Frankie's girlfriend, Lieutenant?"

He shrugged. "We think that her name is Jenna Marconi, but she hasn't returned our phone calls. When we drove out to her house this morning, her neighbor told us that she's been in Seattle the last couple of days, visiting her parents. They spoke yesterday and she said she'd be home tomorrow."

"What do you mean, you think she's his girlfriend?"

"Frankie never told anybody that he was seeing someone. He died less than twenty-four hours ago. I know what you saw in the bathroom when you cleared it. We went through the place last night, and we're still trying to figure it out. All we have are these."

McKensie opened one of the files he'd been carrying and placed it on the writing table. He flipped through several sheets of paper until he came to a list of telephone calls made from Frankie's cell. Then he pointed to a number that had been highlighted with a yellow marker.

"Frankie called her six times," he said. "Six times over the past week. The number's registered to Marconi. Last Thursday night, Frankie followed it up with a call to this number. Rosalita's Garden Café. We checked. It was a takeout order for two delivered to Marconi's address."

"So she hasn't been told that he's dead."

"We won't release his name until we've cleared this up—if that's what you're asking, Jones."

"Any idea what she looks like?"

McKensie nodded. A blowup of the photo from her driver's license was underneath the list of phone numbers. She had light brown hair and dark brown eyes, and even though it seemed like the photo had been snapped at a bad moment, she looked more than just attractive. According to her license, she had just celebrated her thirty-fifth birthday.

Matt turned back to the list of phone numbers, sliding the sheet of paper closer. McKensie had jotted down the woman's address in Echo Park beside her telephone number, and Matt committed both to memory. As he continued skimming through the list, his eyes stopped on another entry highlighted in yellow. He didn't recognize the area code but remembered seeing the same number as he went through Frankie's caller ID on the house line.

"What's this?" he asked.

"The reason Frankie was driving to Mint Canyon. It's a Ford dealership."

Matt became very still. "A what?"

"A Ford dealership. Frankie made an appointment with the manager."

"Did you talk to him?"

"Yes, I did."

"And what did he say?"

McKensie shook his head as he thought it over. "Nothing," he said finally. "Frankie made the appointment but never identified himself as a police officer. I talked to the manager myself last night. He told me that he thought Frankie wanted to buy a car."

"Why would Frankie drive up to Mint Canyon to buy a car? It doesn't make any sense. He left me a message and said that he was working a couple of decent leads."

"Maybe he was, Jones. Maybe he was working a couple of decent leads. But Frankie didn't tell the guy what he wanted, and then he stopped for gas. Frankie never made it to the meeting."

Matt met McKensie's hard gaze and thought that his eyes looked glassy.

CHAPTER 40

A Ford dealership in Mint Canyon . . .

The idea that Frankie made an appointment with the manager because he wanted to buy a new car was so ludicrous that it made Matt angry. He wanted to hit something. Kick it. Smash it. Break it open with his bare hands. It didn't help that he had spent the last three hours with a pair of criminalists from SID scouring Frankie's apartment for fingerprints and still hadn't heard from Cabrera.

It was after seven, and he'd skipped out on the press conference without another call from Grace. Just as odd, after a week of cold weather, the sun had gone down and the air remained hot and dusty and dead. He wiped the sweat from his brow as he tossed it over. Should he drive back to Playa del Rey? Or should he head north for Mint Canyon and interview the manager on his own? He had only one choice, because at this time of night either trip would mean spending hours in stop-and-go traffic.

He popped open the lid on another cup of coffee from the 7-Eleven beside the North Hollywood station. After a couple of sips, he lit a cigarette and climbed into his car. Frankie's apartment had offered them a vast array of fingerprints. Although it would take a while before the lab could process them all, the samples they'd lifted from the apartment, particularly the front door and den, were ultraclean. Both criminalists had told Matt that there was no evidence the place had been wiped down or disturbed in any way.

No evidence, other than Frankie's neighbor, that Orlando and Plank had been there. No evidence at all that they had made it inside.

He grabbed the murder book off the backseat and leafed through the pages until he found Leah Reynolds's phone number at the beach. He entered it into his cell and waited. After seven rings her voice mail picked up. He left a brief message, then pulled out of the lot onto Burbank Boulevard. An entrance ramp to the Hollywood Freeway was just down the street.

Mint Canyon could wait until morning. But Jenna Marconi's place in Echo Park was on the way to Playa del Rey. He thought he should stop by and talk to her neighbor. He wanted to see if she knew why Marconi wasn't returning McKensie's phone calls. Because Frankie was a cop, news of his death would have spread through the Sheriff's Department and the LAPD before his charred body made it to the morgue. Keeping his name on ice for another day seemed like a long shot, and there was no way Matt would let the woman hear about Frankie's death on her own. He'd seen how Laura had taken the news. He couldn't let it happen to Jenna Marconi, no matter how long they might have been together or how close or far apart they were. If she kept a negligee at Frankie's place, she deserved to hear about his fate from a friend.

Traffic heading into town wasn't as heavy as he expected, and he made the fifteen-mile drive to Echo Park in thirty-five minutes. Once he exited the freeway onto surface streets, he headed north on Alvarado just west of the lake, made a right on Sunset, and then a left on Quintero. Marconi's home was at the end of the street on the corner.

Matt pulled over and gazed at the house for a moment. The lights were on. While they may have been on timers, he thought that he could see the shadow of someone thrown against the drawn curtains. He looked up and down the street, wondering if he had the right address. From the variety of homes, their condition, and their size, it appeared to be a neighborhood in transition a stone's throw from Dodger Stadium. But under the cover of darkness, he couldn't tell if the people who lived here were on their way up or falling down.

He dug his phone out of his pocket, found Laura's number, and hit Call. When she picked up, he lit a cigarette, switched off the air conditioner, and lowered the window.

"It's me, Laura. It's Matt."

"Is everything okay?"

"Everything's good, but I'm gonna be late."

"I thought you might be," she said. "Did you see the press conference? Were you there?"

Matt remained quiet, thinking it over and wondering how Grace, Orlando, and Plank were going to explain Kevin's murder after the Sheriff's Department found the three-piece bandit's Glock 20 and determined that it had never been fired. As of today they no longer had a reasonable theory for the robbery and killing. As of today they'd lost their fall guy, their scapegoat, their chump, their dupe, or anyone else who could've taken the ride for their murder spree.

"Did anyone call you, Laura?"

"No," she said in a quiet voice.

"What did they say at the press conference? Did anyone mention Kevin's name?"

"They did. And they said that the robber had been shot last night in West Hollywood."

"What did they say about Kevin?"

She paused. When she finally spoke, Matt could hear the emotion in her voice. The anguish.

"That it would take time to sort things out," she said. "That it would take more time."

Her voice faded from a throaty whisper into a silence with weight to it. An open wound.

Matt took a pull on his smoke and exhaled, his eyes still riveted to the house. He saw the shadow move across the curtain. This time he was sure of it. And Matt's memory was tack sharp. The house number matched the address that McKensie had jotted down in his file. He could see it. Jenna Marconi had made the trip from Seattle one day early and was home.

"Are you okay, Laura?"

"I've been thinking," she whispered.

"Okay," he said. "Tell me."

"The way Kevin was murdered, and then Frankie. This was never about the guy they shot last night, was it? The man the news calls the three-piece bandit never had anything to do with Kevin or Frankie."

"No," he said. "I don't think he did."

"This is about that girl they found in the park, isn't it?"

"It's complicated, Laura. I'd rather talk about it when we're sitting in the same room."

"That's okay, Matt. I get it. I already know the answer."

He waited a moment. He could hear her breathing over the phone. He could picture her sitting at the kitchen table with a glass of wine. She knew too much. Even though it had only been a guess on her part, a hunch, she could be in danger now. He wished that she had gone to Philadelphia.

"I've got a question for you," he said in a lower voice.

"What?"

"It's about Frankie. It's easy."

"Ask me anything," she said.

"Was he seeing anyone?"

She didn't say anything at first, and Matt sensed that the question surprised her.

"Frankie never spoke about it," she said finally. "But Kevin thought that he was. He didn't want to press him. Frankie was shy and liked his privacy. We invited him over for dinner a few weeks ago. We were hoping that he'd bring her along, but he showed up alone."

"So the name Jenna Marconi means nothing to you?"

"Is that her name?"

"Yeah."

"Is there something about her that Frankie might have been embarrassed about?"

"I thought the same thing," he said. "But no, at least not on the outside. She's thirty-five and she's a knockout."

"Maybe it's just too new."

He hadn't thought about that. He checked his watch.

"Maybe," he said. "Maybe he wasn't ready. Listen, I'm sorry but I've gotta go. Are you gonna be okay?"

"Until around midnight, I guess."

Her voice was back. She was hanging in there. She was tough.

"I'll see you then," he said. "We'll talk if you want."

Laura said good-bye and Matt slipped the phone back into his pocket while trying to clear his mind. It wasn't easy, especially here and now. He climbed out of the car, got rid of his cigarette, and crossed the street. As he approached the front door, memories of Frankie rushed through his mind and he thought about how he would deliver the bad news. The words he would use. His tone of voice. Two death notifications inside a week. Two dead guys who were part of his own life. Maybe she'd be like Laura—take one look at his face and know.

He found the doorbell, heard the ring, and felt his heart beating as he waited. The shadow cast on the drawn curtain started forward but then hesitated and froze. Matt didn't get it and rang the doorbell again. When Marconi's shadow remained still, he leaned forward and spoke through the door.

"Jenna, it's Matt Jones. I'm a friend of Frankie's. I need to talk to you. It's important."

He listened for several moments but couldn't hear any movement from inside the house. When he glanced back at the window, Marconi's shadow was gone.

He didn't understand why she was doing this. Was it possible that she already knew and wanted to be left alone?

He stepped away from the door, taking another look at the house. The driveway was gated and included a warning that guard dogs were on the property. Matt peered over the gate into the backyard. The entire place was fenced in, but he saw no signs of a dog. Just lawn furniture, a grill, and a late-model Chevy sedan parked before the garage. Thinking it over, he realized that if she really owned a dog, he would have heard it bark when he rang the doorbell.

He started down the sidewalk, slowing as he reached the corner. The curtains were open on this side of the house, as were the windows, and he could see the light from a television flickering in a darkened room. He tried to look inside, but the ground on the adjoining street sloped too far downward. The wood-paneled fence was higher here as well and matched the angle of the hill.

He started down Macbeth Street. After passing a row of bushes, he noticed a small gate in the gloom. At first glance he thought it opened to the property next door. But as he moved closer, he realized that this was his way into the backyard. Even better, he didn't see a lock. The gate was attached to the fence by a simple latch.

Without hesitating, Matt swung open the gate and stepped into the yard. He paused a moment, glancing at the moon overhead and studying the way the shafts of light from the open windows cut into the night and fell onto the lawn. Once he found the lanes of darkness, he was invisible and started forward in utter silence. He could see Marconi in the living room window as he approached. He could see her—

Matt knelt down before the window, the adrenaline bursting through his veins in a rush that made him dizzy. His eyes flicked around the dingy room, stopped on the TV, then jetted back to the couch. He tried to focus. Tried to keep cool.

It wasn't Jenna Marconi lowering the sound and dropping the remote on the coffee table.

It was the killer, Jamie Taladyne, in the flesh.

CHAPTER 41

The front door crashed open and Joey Orlando burst into the living room with his shoulder lowered. Matt backed out of the window light as he watched Taladyne jump to his feet in terror. But then everything slowed down when Plank followed his partner into the house with a shotgun, and Bob Grace, the cop who had murdered his own partner and scammed the man's wife, sauntered into the living room looking fresh and mean in a dark gray suit.

Orlando grabbed Taladyne, smashed him in the face, and pushed his crumpled body back onto the couch. After cuffing him around the front, he pulled out a pistol and pointed it at the man. Not the 9 mm semiautomatic holstered to his belt but a snub-nosed revolver that he'd fished out of his pocket.

A throw-down gun, and Orlando just happened to be wearing a pair of leather gloves. Trouble in Echo Park tonight.

Matt checked the yard behind him, then turned back and gazed through the open window, his mind reeling. Frankie had found Taladyne but hadn't made an arrest. He'd even bought him dinner last Thursday night.

Why?

Orlando pressed the gun against Taladyne's head as Grace switched on a lamp and sat down on the coffee table directly before the man. Curiously, on Grace's nod, Plank handed over the shotgun and hurried out of the house.

"Jamie Taladyne," Grace said with a smile and in a smooth voice brimming with confidence and danger. "Great seeing you again. How long's it been, Jamie?"

Taladyne remained quiet and edgy and looked confused. From his view through the window, Matt couldn't tell if he was seeing fear in the man's sky-blue eyes or complete madness. All the same, he couldn't have weighed more than a hundred and seventy-five pounds. In spite of his knack for killing women, and even without the handcuffs and drawn guns, Taladyne was no match for anyone in the room.

"How long's it been, Jamie?" Grace repeated. "A year and a half since you walked away from Millie Brown's murder free and clear?"

Orlando smacked him across the face. "Answer the man."

Taladyne grimaced as he shook off the blow. "It's been a while," he said in a low, raspy voice.

Matt watched Grace take in the room. The place was a dump. It seemed obvious to Matt that money was a real issue here. As he glanced at the walls in need of fresh paint, the dilapidated furniture, the grime that seemed to coat every surface, he thought about the way the victims had been left. He thought about seeing Brooke Anderson staked to the ground and the predatory desire of the killer for money and power and a way out of this hole. Dante's epic poem and the seven Ps carved into Virgil's forehead, each one removed by an angel as he passed through the seven terraces of the seven deadly sins. He thought about the victim's faces, each one carved and ruined and seemingly beyond an angel's grace. He was staring at Taladyne and still wondering how it all fit. Still thinking

about the questions Dr. Baylor had raised in his office the other
day.

If these murders are about greed, why are the victims so young?

His mind surfaced. He could hear Grace's ether-like voice
wafting in the air again.

"Do you live here alone, Jamie?"

"This is my sister's place."

"Where is she?"

Taladyne paused a moment, reluctant. "Visiting our parents,"
he said.

"Where?"

"The North Pole, you asshole. What's it to you?"

Orlando smashed him in the face again.

"Where?" Grace repeated.

"Seattle."

Plank walked back into the house carrying a cardboard box.
Grace glanced his way, then turned to Taladyne.

"Which bedroom is yours?"

"The one on the right. Why?"

Grace didn't answer but nodded at Plank, who vanished down
the hall with the box. After a few moments a light came on in a
room at the other end of the house. Whatever they were up to had
been planned and required props. Matt was more than curious
but couldn't pull himself away from the view through the window.
Grace had just pushed the muzzle of the shotgun into Taladyne's
chest. And that smile of his was back, along with those hollow gray
eyes that matched the color of his hair.

"Tell me, Jamie. When you moved in to live with your sister, did you call the police and let them know that you're a sex
offender?"

"Yeah, sure. You guys were my first call."

"Do you think that what you did is funny?"

Taladyne just looked at him.

"You're a real ladies' man, Jamie. You've got a gift. All the same, I can't believe that a loser like you beat a polygraph."

Taladyne stewed in silence, tugging on the short chain between the handcuffs.

Grace laughed, then leaned closer and lowered his voice. "For the record, that works for me. There's no way in this world that you killed Millie Brown, because the murder weapon was found in Ron Harris's house. For the record, Ron Harris killed the girl and we got our man. But between friends like you and me, Jamie—man-to-man so to speak—we both know what really happened to Millie Brown. It's our secret what you did to her. Secrets are best kept between friends, don't you think?"

The room fell silent. Heavy. Corrosive. Dead.

"Why are you doing this?" Taladyne whispered in a shaky voice. "If you're here to arrest me, why don't you just get it over with?"

Orlando struck him again. Harder this time.

Grace sat and watched, his gaunt face showing patience, his eyes smoldering above those high cheekbones. "We're not here to make an arrest, Jamie. And there's no good cop, bad cop tonight. Everybody here is all in. You murdered Brown, but you didn't murder Brown. That's the irony. Ron Harris killed the girl, because the newspapers said he did, and we still have to account for that murder weapon winding up in the man's house. But now the story has new life and a new direction. Now it's all about you becoming infatuated with both the girl and Harris and what everybody thinks he did to her. You knew Millie. You talked to her. She got off on teasing you and tried to seduce you. A girl who looked like that. A beautiful girl. So after her murder, after you were released as a suspect, you read the papers and watched the news of Harris's arrest with a peculiar kind of interest. You waited anxiously for his trial. The people who found the girl's body ended up talking to one of the tabloids and described the condition she had been left in. You didn't have much to go on, but after doing a little research on the Internet, you figured it out and started dreaming about committing a murder just like Millie Brown's. I'll bet you dug it so much that it got you hard. It was already in your blood, Jamie. You'd spent a night with Leah Reynolds. She was young and hot, and you couldn't get her out of your sick fucking mind. You tied her up and cut off her clothes with a box cutter. A razor blade. You fucked her over and over and over again. You rode her like an animal all night long. It was already in your blood, Jamie. You were a natural. You were ready to take the next step. So when you saw Faith Novakoff walk out of that bar in the Valley, that's all it took. You knew exactly what you wanted and what you needed. You knew exactly what you were gonna do to that girl's face, and you succeeded. You pulled it off. She ended up looking exactly like Millie Brown."

"I didn't," he said, stammering. "I wasn't even here."

Taladyne jumped to his feet, but Orlando grabbed him by the neck and yanked him back down. Moments passed. Another vicious beating, with blood dripping out of his nose, then more of that hard-core silence.

"Are you saying that you've got an alibi?" Grace said, measuring the man.

Taladyne nodded, the sweat dripping down his face. "I told Detective Lane everything."

"You told him what?"

"Two weeks ago," he said. "Two weeks ago I was up in Mint Canyon. The night the girl got killed I'd checked into a Motel 6. I had a job interview early the next morning."

"A job interview where?"

"At a car lot. I'm good with tools, and I like cars. I really needed a job. I still do."

"How'd you pay for the room?"

"Cash. My sister gave it to me."

"Did you use your real name?"

Taladyne paused again, then shook his head. "That name's no good anymore. People remember it from the news and my trial."

"Did you see anyone that night? Did you talk to anyone?"

Taladyne remained silent. Matt felt a wave of dread roll over his spine as he thought it over. A job interview at a Ford dealership. Frankie had been trying to verify Taladyne's alibi but never made it. Even worse, Taladyne couldn't answer Grace's question. He'd hesitated.

Matt looked back at the man with the striking blue eyes and realized that he was going to die tonight.

He could tell from the look on Grace's face that he didn't believe anything he'd just heard. But even more, there was no way Grace could let Taladyne walk out of the room. There was no way Grace could let any doubt be cast on his arrest of Ron Harris. Too many people were dead. Too many people had been murdered. Enough to fill a graveyard.

Grace laughed like an executioner who enjoys listening to a tall tale every once in a while. "How'd you make out in the interview?" he asked.

Taladyne didn't reply, his eyes burning.

"I thought so," Grace said. "Why don't you just admit what you did? Why don't you just say it?"

Taladyne leaned back and switched off.

"You're blaming us, Jamie? We didn't make you—you did. Let's hear what you've got for two nights ago when the girl was killed up by the Hollywood sign."

Taladyne pursed his lips and shook his head. Orlando hit him with a vicious chop to the stomach.

The man buckled over and let out a gasp, struggling to catch his breath. When Grace gave him a second poke with the muzzle of the shotgun, it looked like Taladyne could see his fate. He started to sob, his hands trembling as he covered his bloody face.

"Come on, Jamie. Answer the question. Where were you two nights ago? Admit it. Say it so we can all go home."

Taladyne's eyes rocked back and forth, as if he'd just spotted the finish line. "Here," he said after a while. "I was here."

"That's the best you can do? Where was your sister?"

Taladyne shivered, his gaze losing its focus and dropping to the floor. "In Seattle," he whispered. "I was alone."

Grace traded a dark look with Orlando, who fished a black hood out of his pocket and pulled it over Taladyne's head. Taladyne whimpered in fear and started shaking.

"Please," he said. "Please. Why don't you just arrest me?"

Orlando punched Taladyne in the face with his gloved fists. Then Grace prodded him with the shotgun again.

"Admit it, Jamie. Say it."

"Please. I want to go back to prison. I'll do it. I'll go back."

Orlando smashed him in the face again. Taladyne couldn't see the punches coming and made a feeble attempt to protect himself by bobbing his head and blocking his face with his cuffed hands.

Grace leaned closer. "Admit it, Jamie. Say it."

Orlando beat him again. Then again and again, until the man tumbled off the couch onto the floor.

"Okay, okay, okay. Please stop. Please. I'll say it. I'll say it."

Grace nodded at Orlando, who pulled Taladyne up and yanked the hood off of his head. His face was a mess.

"Admit it," Grace said. "Say it, and make sure you're telling the truth. I need to believe you."

Taladyne looked terrified, his entire body shuddering. "I did it," he said quickly. "I did it."

"Did what?"

"Cut them. Killed them. Left them there to die. Now take me back to prison. I belong in jail."

A moment passed. Then, to Taladyne's horror, Orlando removed his jacket, rolled up his sleeves, and grabbed the .38

revolver he'd set down on the table. A grin spread across Grace's face, like he could read Taladyne's mind and enjoyed it. As Matt watched, he thought about the things Lieutenant McKensie had said to him in his office earlier in the day.

I never liked that guy. I never liked anybody who liked that guy. I always thought Bob Grace was a piece of shit.

McKensie's take didn't even begin to cover it.

Matt moved closer to the window screen, drawing his .45 and gently pulling back the slide to chamber the first of eight rounds. He wasn't sure why, really. He was just as outmatched as Taladyne. If he made a move, if he did anything at all, Taladyne would be the first one to die. Either Orlando would shoot him in the head with the revolver, or Grace would get him in the chest with the shotgun. Either way, Taladyne was circling the drain, and Matt couldn't do anything but watch.

The next few minutes seemed to unfold in slow motion, just like the images he had in his head of an unconscious Frankie driving his car off the cliff with his eyes closed. He watched Grace get up and step away from the couch. Then Orlando pushed Taladyne's forehead back, jammed the revolver into his mouth, and kept repeating the words "Fuck you, you sick motherfucker" through clenched teeth. Taladyne was weeping now, the tremors quaking through his entire body at a more frantic pace. He reached up and clasped Orlando's gloved hand with both of his own, almost as if in prayer. He tried to pull the gun out of his mouth. He tried to yank the thing out with his fingers still quivering, any strength he might have had eaten away by the terror. And Matt could tell that this was exactly what Orlando wanted: Taladyne's hands close enough to the gun to be painted with blood spatter.

CHAPTER 42

Orlando pulled the trigger. The sound of the single shot in the small room was deafening.

Taladyne's head snapped back, his body wilting onto the couch. But then, after the house had absorbed the echo from the gunshot, Jamie Taladyne's body started moving again. His eyes were wide open and fixed in a grotesque thousand-yard stare, his body twisting and convulsing, with blood spewing everywhere. Orlando didn't seem to know what to do and started to panic. He tried holding him still with his knee. He grabbed his chest and pushed down. All Matt could hear were the springs from the cushions clinking as Taladyne bounced up and down, his shoes banging against the table and skidding on the hardwood floor. Grace stepped closer to watch. The horror seemed to go on forever, the corpse staring back at them from the other side. Matt looked at Orlando and knew that he was scared shitless. On and on and on, Taladyne's bones rattled in the dark and dingy room. On and on, until Grace had seen enough and gave Taladyne a vicious kick in the head with his heel.

And then it was over. Then Taladyne's body quieted and finally came to rest. Orlando didn't seem to trust it at first but eventually let go of the corpse, his chest heaving. Grace took a step back, still staring at Taladyne's ruined face while chewing a piece of gum.

"We need to get out of here," he said in a quiet voice. "Now pull yourself together and make it look right."

"What about a note?"

"We don't need one. He was broke. Find his checkbook and a stack of bills."

Orlando nodded anxiously. "The piece of shit couldn't even die right."

Grace gave him a look, then started down the hall toward Taladyne's bedroom. Backing into the darkness, Matt rushed to the other end of the house with his gun still drawn. When he reached the lighted window, he lowered his body and peered over the sill. Plank had spread the contents of the cardboard box across Taladyne's bed. They were clippings from newspaper articles, and he was taping them to the wall above a small desk. Matt guessed that there were more than a hundred pictures of Ron Harris and Millie Brown, Faith Novakoff and Brooke Anderson. Even from across the room he could read the headlines, which announced Harris's suicide and Taladyne's arrest and eventual release as a suspect.

When you added them all up, the press clippings taped to a wall in a run-down house told the story of a man obsessed with a killer and his victim. When you added them up, they told the story of a convicted rapist who had done time, a *nobody* who wanted to be a *somebody*. They told the story of a man watching a killer, studying a killer, and finally becoming a killer in his own right. A man who blamed the LAPD for his plight. A man who had lived in hiding and became a copycat.

When you added it all up, this was just the way Grace needed the story to be told. Just the way he'd framed it out for Taladyne a few minutes ago. The day wasn't even over and he had his scape-goat, his chump, a new dupe wrapped and ready to go.

Matt watched him enter the room and gaze at the wall. A certain glow was showing on his face.

"I've got a few more to put up," Plank said.

Grace lowered the shotgun to the floor and leaned it against the wall. "I think we're good, Edward. I think that's enough. Put the rest in one of his desk drawers. He's a collector, you know what I mean? He saves things. He collects."

Plank shrugged, then gathered the remaining press clippings. When Orlando walked in, Grace unlocked his phone, appeared to sort through two or three windows, and held out the screen.

"Here's his cell number," he said. "Now call Jones and tell him that we've got a lead on Taladyne. Give him the address."

Orlando dug into his pocket for his phone. "You're gonna let him find Taladyne?"

"We're gonna let him find everything and call it in. We're gonna let him close the case. He'll be the city's next hero, his first case, and we got our man. We'll be in the clear."

"But what about Taladyne's sister? What's she gonna say about this?"

Plank dumped the remaining press clippings into the top desk drawer and grabbed the shotgun. "She's gonna say the same thing any sister would say when they find out their brother's a mad dog fuck killer. He was a good man. I never saw any of this crap. He didn't do it."

Grace smiled again. "And she can say it all she wants."

Orlando nodded, entering the number and lifting the phone to his ear.

And then time stopped.

Life stopped.

Everything started spinning into the black, and on this night, it couldn't be written off as a dream.

Matt's cell phone was ringing.

He could see their faces through the window. They were staring at him, their eyes big and wild and panicky. He could see Plank raising the shotgun just as he started to turn away and lost his footing. He could hear the blast as his body tumbled down the hill. The sound of glass shattering and gunshots from the semiautomatic that he'd seen holstered to Orlando's belt.

Everything was rushing by in a jumbled blur—until the moment the world went chemical.

He could feel the sudden pain cutting into his upper chest and left shoulder. The agony mixed with terror and disbelief as he rolled to the bottom of the hill, slammed against a tree, and came to a stop.

He'd been hit.

CHAPTER 43

He'd been shot . . .

Hard. Deep. Blood all over his shirt and shimmering in the moonlight on the lawn. A 9 mm round that felt like it was still buried in his shoulder.

If it had been a .45, the roll down the hill would have been endless.

He tried to pull himself together. He'd fucked up. He should have done something to help Taladyne, no matter who he was. You're either true or you're false. You're either real or you're not. Taladyne was going to die no matter what—

Matt winced at the back and forth playing in his head. He'd witnessed a murder. He should have done something.

The gun was still in his hand. Orlando had just taken another shot, which hit the tree. As if on automatic pilot, Matt scrambled to his knees, gritted his teeth, and started shooting. The .45 sounded like a cannon. He pulled the trigger five times in four seconds, watching all three men lunge out of the way as the rounds ripped through the walls and into what was left of the bedroom window.

Orlando peeked over the sill and took another shot. Matt put two more rounds in the wall just below the window frame.

And then it became quiet. No one returned fire. No one peeked over the sill.

Matt glanced back at his wound and spun toward the gate. Ejecting the mag with one round chambered, he slammed his last eight into the gun handle. He knew that he didn't have the means or the time to get locked into a firefight. He knew that the odds of three against one didn't work out in the real world. Even worse, he could feel the blood oozing out of the hole in his shoulder, the pain beginning to burn through the shock like a white-hot branding iron.

He covered the wound with his hand and stumbled through the gate onto the sidewalk. As he tried to canter up the hill, he could feel the weakness in his legs but thought that it might be more about fear than his loss of blood.

He wasn't dizzy. His mind remained clear.

But then he reached the corner and heard Grace's voice. Darting into the shadows behind the row of bushes, he parted the branches ever so slightly. They were running across the street. They'd found his car, his ride, his way out.

All three of them. Orlando hadn't been wounded.

He tried not to panic. Tried to keep cool. He could hear Grace saying something about the new deal and that everything was still good—maybe even better. He could see Orlando handing Plank a couple of spent cigarette butts from the ashtray and that cup of coffee Matt had bought at the 7-Eleven, then pulling the floor mat out of his car and rushing back into the house. He could see Orlando shaking out the mat in the living room while Plank dropped a cigarette butt on the sidewalk and another by the front door. Even better, he placed Matt's coffee cup on a table beside Taladyne's corpse. It didn't take much for Matt to realize what they were up to. It was all about putting Matt at the crime scene. It was all about letting SID discover the evidence on their own—hair and fiber and a DNA trail so focused that it would stop on the head of a dime.

When Grace started talking to someone on his cell phone, Matt didn't need to hang around to know that the picture had just been repainted and that once it dried, nothing about Taladyne's death would look like a suicide.

Shots fired in Echo Park. One man dead and believed to be Jamie Taladyne, the primary suspect in the murders of Faith Novakoff, Brooke Anderson, and LAPD detectives Kevin Hughes and Frankie Lane, from the North Hollywood Division. Homicide detective Matt Jones exchanged gunfire with his supervising officer and two detectives from the Hollywood Division as he fled the house. Jones is known to have been friends with both Hughes and Lane and may have carried out the execution-style murder of Taladyne as an act of revenge. Jones should be considered armed and extremely dangerous.

Matt bolted to the end of Macbeth Street and made a left. The exertion caught up to him, his loss of blood quickening. His eyes flicked from house to house in the neighborhood. When he spotted an old Toyota pickup parked in the driveway before a house with its first-floor lights out, he pushed his hand against the wound and sprinted across the lawn.

The windows were up, the doors locked.

He turned and looked at the freestanding garage. The door on the side was cracked open and he could hear the sound of a clothes dryer tumbling in the background. Eyeing the house for a moment, he turned back and stepped into the garage, searching for a rag or cloth or anything he could use to slow down the bleeding. He spotted a sink in the gloom and saw the washer and dryer against the far wall. Inside the dryer he found a load of wet bras and panties.

He let out a groan, then caught himself as he noticed the laundry basket on the washer filled with clean white towels. Tossing the underwear back into the dryer, he carried the basket over to the sink. The tap water was ice cold, and he wiped the sweat from his face before ripping away his shirt and dabbing the wound. The pain came from a place he'd never been before or ever even imagined could exist. Sharp, biting, two miles past the last exit on the way to doom. He clamped his jaws down and muscled through it, grateful that he didn't pass out or vomit.

As he took a moment to pull himself together, he glanced about the garage, looking for anything that might help him short-circuit the ignition and hot-wire the Toyota pickup outside. He saw a small toolbox on the shelf and grabbed a hammer, a couple of screwdrivers, and a pair of pliers. When his eyes landed on the toilet bowl plunger by the sink, under any other circumstances he would have laughed out loud at the memory of what life had been like as a sixteen-year-old growing up in Jersey. He would have thought about his aunt and how hard she'd worked to take care of him and keep him on the right path.

Still, Matt didn't need a key or a coat hanger or even a set of auto jigglers to break into a car.

He grabbed the plunger, holding the bulb under the tap water. Then he hurried out to the pickup, sealed the plunger over the door lock, and gave it a hard push.

The locks blew open, and he was in.

But the house lights had popped on as well, and an old man was opening the front door.

"Who's out here?" he was shouting. "What are you doing to my truck?"

Matt watched the old man start down the walkway. He looked ornery and maybe even a little crazy. Despite his age, it didn't seem like he was going to back off.

Matt reached for his badge and pulled out his .45. "Get back in your house," he said. "I'm a police officer. Now go inside and get me the keys."

The old man appeared stunned that Matt had asked him for his keys. He looked unsure, his eyes moving from the .45 to the hole in Matt's shoulder, then over to the badge. When the old man didn't move, Matt grabbed him by the shirt and pushed him toward the house.

The old man grunted and groaned. "I've seen badges like that on the Internet. Stop pushing me. You're getting blood all over me."

Matt shut it all out, unable to worry about what he was doing. He shoved the old man into the house with as much force as he could muster and spotted several sets of keys on a rack by the door. On the second-floor landing he could see a young woman shielding a boy and girl, who Matt guessed were seventeen or eighteen.

"I'm a police officer," he repeated. "No one's in danger here. I need your pickup, simple as that."

The boy let out a muffled "Yeah, right," while the old man grabbed the phone and dialed 911. Matt ignored it and rushed outside. Gathering up the towels, he climbed into the Toyota and turned the key. He wished that the pickup hadn't been red and so easy to spot but shrugged it off as he backed into the street. The old man had pressed his face against the living room window, his eyes crazed, screaming into the phone. Matt looked away, shifting into drive and speeding off.

He could hear the sirens already approaching the neighborhood and thought about Grace's phone call. The Hollywood Freeway was no more than a mile off. When he reached Sunset Boulevard, he felt a sense of relief in spite of the blood seeping through the towel and dripping onto the seat, in spite of the flashing lights in his rearview mirror and the sound of sirens in the night. They were heading for Taladyne's house. It would probably take them another five minutes before they made the connection between Grace's call and the old man's.

His cell phone started ringing. As he dug it out of his pocket, it crossed his mind that Grace was sick enough to call and wish him luck. But when he slid the lock open and glanced at the caller ID, it was better than that.

It was his partner who had become lost. It was Cabrera.

CHAPTER 44

"I'm hit," Matt said.

"How bad?"

"I don't know. Upper left shoulder. They killed Taladyne, Denny. They planted the murder weapon on Ron Harris so Taladyne goes down for everything else, like he's a copycat. I heard it. I saw it. Now everything we talked about is real."

"Taladyne gets a pass for killing Millie Brown but goes down for Novakoff, Anderson, and maybe even this fourth girl, who's still missing, Anna Marie Genet. Grace sets him up for killing Hughes and Lane, but it sounds like you're taking the fall for Taladyne. It's on the radio, Matt. Not a police radio. KNX picked it up off a scanner. Grace wants the world to know. They're saying you executed the man. There's no way they can let you tell your side of the story. No way Grace is gonna let you talk."

Matt spotted the entrance to the Hollywood Freeway just ahead. He tried to get a grip on himself as he made the turn and vanished into the sea of traffic heading north. The sirens were beginning to fade into the distance now. His mind still seemed

clear, just that swirling feeling in his stomach; just the blood dripping onto the seat like sand through an hourglass.

"Where have you been?" Matt said.

"I turned off my phone. I'm sorry. I'm just leaving Leah
Reynolds's place. Grace kept calling and leaving messages about
the press conference. I didn't want to fuck things up, so I turned
it off."

"Fuck what up?"

"Are you ready?"

"Ready for what?"

"Taladyne," Cabrera said. "He didn't rape her."

A long, dark moment passed. Just the sound of the freeway in
the background. Some kid in a Subaru with straight pipes whizzing by in the night. It felt like the pickup was floating a foot or two
above the road. The lights through the windshield were beginning
to glow like neon. He thought about Taladyne's alibi. He hoped that
he'd been lying and that it didn't exist. He hoped that Taladyne's
story about a job in Mint Canyon wasn't true. That at the very least
Taladyne died for the murders he committed.

"He didn't rape her, Matt. He didn't do it. The whole thing was
bullshit. The whole thing was about money. Reynolds made it all
up."

The house on a beach called paradise, he thought. The home
of a young woman who didn't live with anyone and didn't have a
job. He'd had a feeling that something was wrong as he looked at
her sitting on the couch with her legs folded beneath her body.
He'd had a feeling but couldn't see it for what it was. He misread
the signs. He'd been confused by her apparent gentleness and the
shadow cast by what he thought had been done to her. He'd seen
Reynolds as a victim.

"She admitted it?" he said.

"I sort of think she's wanted to talk about it for a long time. It
took a while to draw it out of her. It took all day."

"What did she say?"

"That she and Taladyne had a thing going, just friends until one night it turned into more than that. She dug the guy. Taladyne saw it as a one-night stand. You can guess what happened after that. She got pissed off and made it look the way it looked. At first it was a joke. She just wanted to scare him and get back at him. But when Taladyne was arrested, things got out of control. It happened in her dormitory, so her lawyer sued the university, and now all of a sudden there was a lot of cash on the table. A college kid from nowhere staring at a five-million-dollar settlement. She licked her lips and said *show me the money.*"

It settled in like a cloud of poison gas. Everything snowballing into chaos. Matt checked the rearview mirror. He could feel his body slowing down. Darkness edging in—along with the idea that Grace had made yet another catastrophic mistake.

Matt pulled out of it. "Frankie found Taladyne," he said. "That's why he was in Mint Canyon. Taladyne claimed that he had an alibi for the night Novakoff was murdered. A job interview the next morning at a Ford dealership. He checked into a Motel 6 on the night of the murder. He used an alias and paid the bill in cash."

"You sure about that?"

Matt nodded, then remembered that he was on the phone. "McKensie knows that Frankie made an appointment with the manager, but neither one of them knows why, because he didn't show up."

"You want me to call McKensie?"

"He's got the guy's number. They've talked. I'm sure he'd remember if he'd met Taladyne."

"What about your status, man? And what about McKensie? After tonight everything's upside down. We're in the wind. We're roadkill. Both of us."

Matt paused a moment. He needed to get to Laura's but just remembered that the protection detail from Metro Division was still at the house and probably waiting for him. He pulled the towel away from his chest and glanced at the wound as he chewed it over. A memory surfaced from earlier in the day. The things McKensie had said to him outside Frankie's apartment.

"Call him, Denny. Tell him everything. If he wants to meet, don't do it. If he checks out Taladyne's alibi and calls you back, then we know we can trust him."

"Where are you gonna be?"

"Hughes's house," he said. "And one more thing. Tell him Jenna Marconi is a dead end. Frankie was seeing someone else. Marconi turned out to be Taladyne's sister."

"Frankie's girlfriend already came forward, Matt. It was on the radio. They released Frankie's name after they talked to her."

"Who is she?"

"A neighbor," he said. "She lives in the building next door. They hooked up a couple of months ago."

CHAPTER 45

They were standing beneath a lamppost in the yard beside the garage, drinking coffee. Just the two of them. The same two cops who had been duped by Orlando and left Laura alone while they went on break.

Matt was twenty feet away, standing in the gloom and using every ounce of his being to breathe silently and remain invisible. They seemed so relaxed that he guessed no one could have imagined his stupidity in showing up at one of the most likely places in his address book.

They were three or four years younger than him, strong and in good shape. The one on the right was wearing a gold wedding band.

Matt watched and listened. He'd parked two blocks away and entered the property through the neighbor's backyard, then climbed the steps up from the pool. He knew that he had lost a considerable amount of blood. He also knew that if he died tonight, he would die a murderer, and all of the lies and killings Grace, Orlando, and Plank had committed would stand forever.

Matt raised his gun, the muzzle poking through the shadows and breaking into the light. Both cops looked his way and froze. Matt knew that they still couldn't see him. Just the muzzle. Just the nose of his .45.

"I don't want to hurt you," he said in a low voice. "But I think you should know that I'm wounded and I'll do anything it takes to defend myself. Anything it takes to survive. And I mean *anything*."

He stepped out of the darkness and stood before them. He could see fear washing over their faces as they looked him over. He could almost read their minds—wounded animals are unpredictable and dangerous. With great care they lowered their coffee cups to the ground and raised their hands in the air. The one with the wedding band was shaking.

"Take it easy, Jones," he said. "Backup's on the way. You don't stand a chance."

Matt took another step closer. "Turn around and lean against the garage."

A moment passed, brief but poignant. Then he watched them turn their backs and lean forward at a forty-five-degree angle. They knew the drill. Matt moved in behind them, trying to remain focused and make sure that his search was thorough. He took their pistols, two 9 mm Berettas, and stuffed them inside his belt. He pulled their handcuffs and then their keys to the black Chevy Suburban in the drive. When he was through, he stepped back and tossed a pair of handcuffs at the cop wearing the wedding band.

"Cuff your partner," he said.

The cop seemed reluctant and hesitated.

Matt shook his head slowly and waved the .45 at him. "It's not worth it, man. It's not even close to being worth it. Cuff him, or you're gonna die."

His partner shot him a nervous look and turned with his hands already behind his back. Once he was cuffed, Matt tossed the second set over.

"Now cuff your left wrist and stick your arm through his."

The cop shook his head and muttered something but did as he was told. Then Matt stepped closer, cuffing his right wrist so that their arms were interlocked behind their backs. After they settled down, he pushed them over to the Suburban and opened the back door.

"Get in," he said.

It was awkward, but both men managed to climb into the backseat. Matt could see the one with the wedding band staring at the pair of Berettas stuffed inside his belt.

"You're a dirty cop, Jones."

"Yeah," Matt said. "Dirty as the day is long."

He slammed the door shut and walked around the garage to the kitchen. He could see Laura through the windows. She was sitting at the table with a cup of coffee, her eyes glued to a live news broadcast on television. The city was in lockdown, the manhunt underway.

Matt pushed the door open and walked in.

CHAPTER 46

Her face lost its color. He could see her rising from the chair. He could see her rushing toward him and guiding his body to the floor as his legs gave way and he collapsed.

He kept his eyes on her.

He could feel everything beginning to fade, everything beginning to darken, like the world was hooked up to a dimmer switch. He hoped that he wasn't closing in on the end. He hoped that all he needed was some rest, a minute or two to gather his strength.

"I can't stop the bleeding," he whispered.

She said something, but it wasn't cutting through. She got to her feet and ripped open a cabinet. Inside he could see a first aid kit set beside that pregnancy test kit he'd noticed the other night. He tried to think about her being pregnant, but his mind had lost its focus and couldn't stand still for very long. She tossed the kit on the floor, grabbed an ice pack out of the freezer, then rinsed a pair of clean kitchen towels under hot tap water. When she returned, he looked into her eyes, eyes the color of dusk and rain, and felt a sense of relief.

She looked so gentle. So feminine.

He watched her wipe his bare chest down. He watched her wrap the ice pack in a clean towel and press it over the wound. After a while he began to relax some and became aware of her body. Her leg on top of his leg. Her bare shoulders. Her breath on his face.

"Hold this," she said.

He heard it. At least he thought he did.

She placed his hand on the ice pack and got back to her feet. He couldn't imagine what she was doing. And if he died, he wanted to die with that feeling that her body was touching his body. That her face was the last thing he might see.

He didn't want to die over here by the door. He didn't want to be alone.

He heard the microwave start up and turned. After a minute or so, she pulled out a tall glass of tea and added ten to twelve teaspoons of sugar, along with some ice. Then she was back, wrapping her arm around his head and supporting him.

"Drink it," she said. "It's not hot. Just drink it, fast as you can."

He couldn't taste anything but the sugar. And Laura smiled at him when he finished the glass. Then she lifted the ice pack away and covered the wound with gauze. When his blood continued to wick through the pad, she added another and pushed down with her hand.

Her leg was on top of his again, and he could feel her breasts resting on his stomach. He looked down at her top. It was parted and he could see her bra and cleavage. When he looked up, he found her gazing back at him. His eyes drifted down to her lips and chin and then back up to her cheeks and dirty blond hair. He could smell her skin. The soap she bathed with, the shampoo in her hair. He could smell her being.

He met her eyes again and saw the laughter in them, the kindness. He took in a deep, slow whiff, holding her in his lungs and savoring the variety of different fragrances as they passed through his nose.

So clean. So pleasant.

She moved her head closer and looked into his eyes. It was a different kind of look this time. A new look. He could feel the electricity beginning to arc through his body again. His heart pounding in his chest. And then she moved even closer, until something unexpected happened.

She kissed him.

Deep and slow, her tongue in his mouth. She kissed him. It only lasted for ten or fifteen seconds. Only a short time passed before she lifted her head up and gazed into his eyes with that smile of hers.

"How do you feel?" she whispered.

"Better."

"We need to get you to a doctor. The bleeding's not gonna stop."

"We can't go to a hospital."

"I know," she said.

"Dr. Baylor."

"Who's he?"

"Someone I'm working with. He lives close by. Five, ten minutes."

"Can we trust him?"

Matt thought it over. He wasn't sure.

"He's all we've got," he said.

She nodded and helped him to his feet. He felt okay. Actually, he felt better than okay. His balance was back. His mind had cleared some. He watched Laura grab the keys to her SUV and followed her out the door. But just a few steps later he heard a car pulling up to the house.

Matt waved Laura back, easing through the side yard and peeking around the garage. A man was getting out of a dark gray sedan. When he turned, Matt spotted the shotgun and got a look at his face.

It was Edward Plank, and he was alone.

They must have been covering their bases. They must have split up. Grace's interest wasn't in making an arrest, he kept reminding himself. It was all about making another hit in an almost endless line of hits. All about keeping their secret and filling up the graveyard.

Matt exchanged his .45 for the pair of Berettas, racking the slides back on both semiautomatics. He could see the two cops from the protection detail following Plank's progress up the street and onto the lawn before the garage. Once he was within earshot, both of them started shouting. Plank looked up, spotted Matt on the corner, and fired two heavy blasts with the shotgun. The shells blew a hole through the garage door and took out the lamppost.

But that didn't mean that Plank was invisible.

The man was out in the open, and tonight wasn't going to be his night.

Matt fired both Berettas. The first two rounds punched through Plank's chest and knocked him on his back. As he squirmed on the grass, panic-stricken and struggling to reach his shotgun, Matt kept pressing forward with both guns exploding. Plank tried to block the shots with his arms and hands but lost the battle, his body bouncing off the lawn from the barrage. Matt gritted his teeth, still shooting and showing no mercy. One round after the next until he was standing directly over Plank's corpse and firing into the dead man's body. One round after the next for what Plank had done to Hughes and Lane, and how about Ron Harris and everybody else? One round after the next until both 9 mm pistols were empty and the sounds of gunfire finally dissipated into the night.

Matt waited for the echoes to fade, clouds of spent gunpowder hanging in the air around his head and seeping into his lungs through his flared nostrils. When the quiet returned he realized that the two cops from Metro had stopped calling for help. He tossed their pistols on the lawn and looked at Plank's corpse. His face was blown away. The sneer was gone and he no longer had any skin issues. He wondered if Plank had a wife and children, but only briefly.

He didn't really care.

Plank's karma had caught up to him tonight. Yin met yang and the big wheel turned.

CHAPTER 47

Matt watched Laura exit off the freeway.

If he died tonight, he'd die a murderer. A cop killer. There were two eyewitnesses handcuffed to each other and locked up in a black Chevy Suburban outside Laura's house. Two eyewitnesses who had seen everything but, like most eyewitnesses, understood nothing, in spite of their seats in the front row. If he died tonight, he would be remembered as a lowlife. A traitor to the cause.

All Matt knew was that the exertion had cost him.

Laura stopped at the light and hit the left-turn signal. Matt was leaning against the seat and door and thinking about being kissed by his best friend's wife. He was looking at her body and trying to replay the kiss in his head, but the image kept fading in and out, until all he could see was Plank's bullet-riddled corpse laid out in the grass.

He turned and glanced out the passenger window as a silver Nissan pulled up beside them and hesitated before making a right turn. The driver had been looking at him, staring at him. For reasons Matt couldn't fathom, both the car and the driver had a certain significance about them. A certain weight.

Was it something he couldn't remember? Did he know the man?

He wasn't sure, and it worried him.

"We're almost there," Laura said.

She made the turn onto Toluca Lake Avenue. Matt pointed at the doctor's house as he looked up and down the street. Grace and Orlando must have gone out to his place on the Westside. But the idea provided little comfort. Matt knew that it was only a matter of time before they figured out what was going on and doubled back.

"Park in front of the neighbor's house," he said. "It might buy us a little time."

She pulled over to the curb, then ran around the SUV and helped him step down onto the sidewalk. They didn't have to wait very long at the gate. Baylor heard his voice over the intercom and hit the buzzer. Within seconds the doctor was rushing down the walkway and helping Laura guide Matt into the house.

"It's the bleeding," she said. "It won't stop."

Baylor introduced himself as he shut the door. "This way, please," he said. "Let's get him downstairs."

They passed the den and made it down the steps through a hallway, until they reached a long, narrow room in the back of the house. There was a large worktable here with a stainless steel top and gutter rails on both sides that fed into drains. Against the wall a wooden counter with cabinets and drawers ran the entire length of the room. Through the French doors at the very end, Matt could see the terrace and backyard, the lights from the country club on the other side of the lake shimmering off the smooth water.

The doctor helped him onto the table, pulling away the gauze pads and examining the wound. Matt felt the ice-cold steel beneath his body and stared at the glass ceiling overhead, wondering if he'd died and this was his autopsy. After a while he lowered his gaze and noticed all the plants—orchids mostly—in full bloom. It occurred to him finally that he was laid out on a worktable in

Baylor's greenhouse. It occurred to him that Baylor hadn't asked a single question, seemed to have some idea of what had happened tonight, and was willing to help.

Matt looked him over. His brown, spiked hair bleached out from the sun. His tanned skin and meticulous grooming. The cobalt-blue eyes and chiseled face. The shallow lines etched into his forehead. The energy radiating from the man's being.

"How much time has passed since you were shot?" Baylor said in a gentle but excited voice.

Matt didn't know and shrugged. "An hour. Maybe a little more."

Baylor nodded, hurrying into the hallway and opening a closet door that appeared to be filled with medical supplies, canned food, bottled water, and anything else he might need to survive the next earthquake. He was scanning through the shelves and tossing things into a canvas tote bag. When he returned, Matt watched him give Laura a measured look.

"That bullet has to come out," he said to her. "I could use your help if you're willing. If you don't think you can handle it, that's okay, too."

She stepped closer, her top stained with Matt's blood. "Anything," she said. "I'll do anything to help."

He smiled and nodded and handed her a pair of surgical gloves and a pack of gauze. As she slipped on the gloves, he asked her to break open the gauze and apply pressure to the wound. Once she was ready, he turned back to Matt and examined him more carefully. He felt his forehead and neck, then ran his hands down the sides of his chest.

"Are you having any difficulty breathing?" he asked.

"No, I'm fine."

"What about chills?"

Matt nodded, watching Baylor take his wrist and check his pulse against his watch.

"I'll bet that you can feel your heart beating in your chest."

"Things happened tonight, Doctor."

"Yes, they did," he said. "But the chills and rapid heartbeat are from the loss of blood. You're still conscious, so I'm gonna guess that you've lost somewhere in the neighborhood of fifteen to thirty percent."

Laura broke open a second pack of gauze. "He needs more, right? He needs a transfusion?"

Baylor shook his head as he pulled another pair of surgical gloves from his bag and slipped them on. "All he needs is saline, and I've got plenty of that here."

Matt watched them hovering over him. While Baylor's voice remained firm and reassuring, he could tell that the doctor was worried. He could see it in his eyes, and by the way he was working at such a feverish pace. Not a single wasted motion, Matt thought—tying a rubber tourniquet above his right elbow and searching his arm for a decent vein, scrubbing the area with something he called ChloraPrep and inserting a needle, then taping down the catheter and applying a dressing until it was fixed to his skin. All this while trying to keep Matt's mind occupied by chattering away about the case.

"Have you figured out the riddle, Matthew? Is that what happened tonight? Is that why they shot you?"

The riddle. Matt couldn't cut through the brain fog to make the connection. He didn't understand.

"The riddle, Matthew. Your riddle. The Glasgow smile. The Chelsea grin. Don't you remember coming to my office after you reread *The Divine Comedy*? Don't you remember your remarkable idea that the killings are somehow related to greed and the seven deadly sins? You said that's why they were bound like animals and laid facedown. You said that it was about greed and social standing and screwing anyone they could in order to get ahead. You said that it was about punishment."

The memory surfaced, however vague or even reliable. "And you asked me why the victims were so young. If it's about greed, you said, why kill a girl who's still in school?"

"You're with me, Matthew. That's good. And I'm still looking at the riddle and thinking the same thing I thought the other day. The victims are all innocents. Why would anyone want to hurt them?"

Matt looked over at Laura and could see her trying to think it through. Then he glanced back at Baylor and watched the doctor hang a bag of saline solution from an irrigation pipe and connect the line to the catheter. When he was finished, he hung a second IV bag beside the first.

"Are you allergic to any medications?" Baylor said.

"Maybe penicillin."

"Then we'll be fine. I have to go upstairs for the anesthetic. Stay with me, Matthew, we're almost there."

Matt nodded as Baylor hurried out of the room. He looked at the saline solution dripping into his body and turned to Laura. She was running her free hand through his hair. Her eyes were on his eyes, and for several moments it felt like she was looking all the way in. Like she was somehow able to see everything—his thoughts, his feelings, his past and present, his entire being and essence—and at a time like this, it felt so soothing. So clean and pure.

"He likes you," she whispered.

Matt looked back at her without responding, his mind absorbed in the touch of her gloved hand stroking his hair and forehead. He wished that she wasn't wearing the glove. He wished that he could feel her skin.

"He likes you as if you were his son," she went on. "I can tell. Everything's gonna be okay."

His cell started vibrating in his pocket. He didn't notice it at first. Two or three pulses came and went before he pulled it out, saw Cabrera's name and number blinking on the screen, and took the call.

"Yeah," he said.

"What's wrong with your voice, Jones?"

"Lots of things. How'd it go?"

"Where are you? McKensie's in. We're coming to get you."

Matt paused, struggling to focus. "Tell me what happened."

"Taladyne's alibi checks out, man. The manager at the Ford dealership has three daughters and remembered his face from the news. He asked to see his driver's license during the interview. Taladyne had given him a fake name and refused. When the guy threatened to call the cops, Taladyne ran out of the building and drove off the lot."

"What about the motel?"

"A deputy sheriff stopped by half an hour ago with Taladyne's picture. The woman behind the front desk remembers checking him in a couple weeks ago. People who pay cash stand out these days, so she looked him up. On the night Faith Novakoff was murdered, Taladyne wasn't in LA. He was in Mint Canyon, trying to get a fucking job."

A moment passed, dark and jagged and all ripped up. Matt could feel the dread, the ice-cold chill, rippling up and down his spine.

"Then that's it," he said. "Taladyne's not the killer."

He could feel the idea settling in, the weight of their new reality— the finality of it all—cutting to the bone.

"That's it," Cabrera said. "And Ron Harris wasn't good for Millie Brown. I can't believe this is happening. Everything's so fucked up, one plus one adds up to zero. Now tell me where you are, Jones."

"Baylor's," he said. "Laura drove me—"

Matt's gaze shifted. There was a long-lens camera sitting on the counter, but that wasn't what was bothering him. It was the vase of cut flowers by the sink. They were dying. He glanced at Laura, then pointed at the vase. He wasn't sure why the flowers stood out from any of the other plants in Baylor's greenhouse. He wasn't sure why they seemed so important.

"The flowers," he said. "What are they?"

She crossed the room and brought the vase over. "Poppies," she said, "in October. The doctor must have a green thumb."

An image flashed before Matt's eyes. The sea of flowers he'd found growing on the eastern face of the ridge overlooking Brooke Anderson's dead body below the Hollywood sign. The hiding spot the killer had picked out to watch them deal with her corpse and process the crime scene. The flowers meant for April but springing to life toward the end of fall.

"What is it?" Laura said. "What's wrong?"

"Put them back on the counter," he said under his breath. "Hurry."

He could hear Baylor coming down the stairs. He shut off his phone and slipped it into his pocket.

The dead flowers meant nothing, he tried telling himself. They meant nothing because in and of themselves they didn't contribute anything to solving the riddle. It was no longer about a teacher or a copycat. It was about chasing down the One. The *only* One.

And if it's really about greed, why would the One rape and murder three innocent girls?

Baylor hurried into the room with the anesthetic and hung the IV bag beside the saline solution and the antibiotic. Matt watched him connect the third tube to the main line feeding the catheter in his arm. He must have been showing what he was thinking on his face, because when he glanced over at Laura, she seemed frightened and anxious, like she knew that all of a sudden the plane they were riding on had lost power over an endless forest of tall trees.

He looked back at Baylor, studying him carefully. "Jamie Taladyne turned out to be innocent," he said in a worn-out voice that blistered and cracked. "We just cleared him."

Baylor paused a moment, considering what he'd heard. Matt glanced at Laura, then up at the IV bags, the anesthetic beginning to drip into the tube.

"Are you sure about that?" Baylor said finally.

"His alibi checked out, and the rape charge he did time for turned out to be bogus. He's never hurt anyone that we know of."

"What about this fourth coed? What's her name? Anna Marie Genet?"

"What about her?"

"She's still missing, right? You know it's curious, Matthew. Her father and your father probably know each other. He runs a brokerage firm in Chicago."

It's all about the riddle, Matt thought. *It's all about chasing down the One. And if it's all about greed, why would the maniac rape and murder innocent girls?*

"How do you know anything about the girl's father, Doctor?"

Baylor paused to consider the question, and Matt thought that he detected a slight smile before the doctor caught himself.

"I saw it somewhere," he said. "On TV, I think, or maybe the Internet. Her father is flying into LA tonight." Baylor seemed pleased by the idea, even amused, as he checked the flow of all three IV bags and tapped them with his fingers. "You'll be sedated, Matthew, but awake. You'll think that you fell asleep because you won't remember anything when it's over."

Why would Baylor be pleased that the girl's father was traveling to LA tonight? Why did the doctor care about the girl's father?

Matt looked him over as another memory surfaced. He could see Baylor trying to comfort Brooke Anderson's mother at the coroner's office. He could see the terror on the woman's face as she got her first look at what had been done to her daughter. The cuts between her ears and lips that had become so exaggerated, so distressing and hideous. He could hear the woman gasp the moment the sheet had been lifted away. He could see Baylor holding her from behind and watching her take it all in—her life and dreams transformed into a single nightmare that would chase her until the end of time. Her only daughter violated in every imaginable way. Her only daughter ruined.

But even more, Matt could remember the look on Baylor's face. He didn't see it at the time. He didn't understand it. But now, even through the heavy fog, he could see Baylor's face and knew with certainty that his read was true.

It had been the look of absolute joy. The look of ecstasy and rapture.

The look of absolute evil.

Baylor was savoring the woman's grief—getting off on it, feeding on it—while committing every detail to memory.

It took Matt's breath away.

"What did Brooke Anderson's mother do for a living, Doctor?"

"You're slurring your words. And why would you ask a question like that at a time like this?"

"You said something about an insurance company."

Baylor smiled. "She runs a health insurance company, Matthew. A company so big that most people would call it a monopoly. She paid herself more than ten million dollars last year. Then she canceled the policies of the most ill and needy, policies that the people were paying for, and tossed them into the street. When the government forced her to take them back, she doubled their premiums and spent twenty-five million dollars at various resorts on herself and her executive staff. She likes the good life, Matthew. She likes it a lot."

Their eyes met, and in an instant the world skidded a mile or two past grim. Like all riddles, there had to be an answer, and for this one, now there finally was.

If it's all about greed, why would he rape and murder innocent girls?

Baylor's smile broadened, his madness burgeoning, and Matt guessed that the doctor had just figured out what he was thinking. Just figured out that he *knew*. Matt had reached the end point, the place where all the loose ends get tied into square knots. He was staring into the abyss. He gave Laura a last look and glanced back at Baylor. But then the anesthetic hit, and in the presence of a monster, he felt himself being pulled deeper into the chasm. He could feel his .45 being lifted away from his holster. He could see Baylor placing the pistol on the far counter beside the camera with the zoom lens. His eyes rose to that third IV bag filled with the anesthetic, drop after drop trickling down the line until they reached the catheter in his arm and began swarming his heart and mind.

He couldn't hold on any longer. He couldn't fight it. The angels were coming. They were in the air and all around, and he couldn't help it. He let go.

CHAPTER 48

Matt opened his eyes, overwhelmed and in complete awe. He hadn't thought that he would ever have the opportunity again.

He blinked several times, the world coming into focus.

Baylor's greenhouse. The doctor's operating room. The house of death on Toluca Lake Avenue.

He was alone. All he could hear was the sound of a small fan whirring in the background and water dripping in the sink. After a moment he became aware of something moving in the hallway and looked toward the door.

Baylor was wearing a lab coat and dragging a woman into the greenhouse.

Her eyes were closed, her naked body as limp and lifeless as a rag doll's. When Baylor started down the aisle, Matt got a look at her round face and dark hair and recognized her as the missing eighteen-year-old from the flyer he'd seen in McKensie's office. It was Anna Marie Genet, the girl who had seemed so familiar to him that he imagined her sitting across the dinner table at Thanksgiving, like a sister or cousin.

Baylor lifted her up and set her down on the other end of the long worktable. Matt noticed a body bag on the counter halfway down. His first thought was that the doctor would stuff the girl inside the bag and be done with her. Instead, Baylor gave her a shampoo and bath, then hosed her down, like an animal at the zoo. After toweling her dry and smearing her underarms with deodorant, he spent ten minutes styling her hair with a brush and blow-dryer. Once he was satisfied with her hair, he glanced at her face, pulled a stool over, and opened a makeup kit.

Matt couldn't believe the depravity.

He couldn't believe what he was seeing and wondered if he was even awake. A thought surfaced. The seven Ps carved into Virgil's forehead, each one removed by an angel as he passed through the seven terraces of the seven deadly sins. And then something else came to mind. The girl's father was traveling from Chicago to LA tonight. For whatever reason, the doctor, the grief collector, was planning to take another human being's soul and break it open like an egg.

"What the hell did your parents do to you, man?"

Baylor looked up, surprised. "You're back. How are you feeling?"

"What did they do to you?"

The doctor smiled as he considered the question. "I've never been one to think that Freud had much to say, Matthew. Sorry if that's a disappointment. My parents were two loving, nurturing, gentle souls who did their best to raise me and my three sisters in a tranquil, educated, and cultured environment."

"Then what happened to you? You're obviously out of your mind."

He laughed. "Who isn't these days? When was the last time you turned on a television?"

"Where's Laura?"

"Tied up, I'm afraid."

"Where is she?"

"In the sunroom," he said. "Sleeping."

"Then you didn't hurt her. She's alive."

The doctor nodded. "I haven't quite decided what to do with the two of you yet. I thought we might talk it over if there's time."

Baylor turned back to the girl and started applying makeup to her face. Matt took a moment to get his bearings. He thought that he remembered seeing the sunroom at the other end of the hallway as he was helped downstairs, but he couldn't be sure. Even worse, how could he take the word of a man who had murdered so many people? So many young women?

He thought about Laura being dead, then used all of his strength to block the image and push it out of his mind.

He filled his lungs with air and exhaled. He could see his gun on the far counter by the camera. On the rack above the vase of dead flowers, he noted the shears hanging beside a variety of other gardening tools. He gazed down at his chest. The blood had been washed away, the wound bandaged. Two of the three IV bags were still hanging from the irrigation pipe and connected to the catheter in his arm. While his arms and legs weren't bound, they didn't need to be. The weakness was so overwhelming, he felt like an insect that had been glued down and placed inside a picture frame.

"I can't move," he said.

"I'm guessing it'll be a while. I pulled the anesthetic, but all good things take time."

Several moments passed with Matt watching the plastic surgeon hover over the girl with his makeup kit. When she began to stir ever so slightly, Baylor produced a syringe from his coat pocket and injected something into her thigh, as if the moment had been expected and planned for.

But all Matt could feel right now was an overpowering wave of fear. He searched for his voice. Something steady that wouldn't reveal his thoughts or emotions.

"I don't believe the things you said, Doctor. Something happened to you when you were a child. Something horrible. Your life was anything but tranquil. Your parents, anything but loving."

"And you called your father what, Matthew? Dear old Dad? He walked out on you and your mother. He left you high and dry when you were only a boy."

Matt grimaced at the memory. "How would you know that?"

"I recognized you the moment you walked into my office. I told you that. You have your father's face, you have his name, but you don't even get a mention in his biography." The doctor took a moment to think it over, then spoke in a voice that seemed softer and more gentle. "Let's just say that it was a safe guess, Matthew. And that while you were under the anesthetic, I asked a few questions, and you answered back. I know about your mother's death from breast cancer. I know that your father, M. Trevor Jones— chairman of the board, president, and CEO of PSF Bank of New York, one of the five largest banks in the United States—M. Trevor Jones, the reigning King of Wall Street, refused to recognize your existence. I know that in the end you were raised by your aunt in a modest home and that you loved her very much. As you said yourself, she was a woman of uncommon grace and intelligence, a woman who loved the arts as much as she loved taking care of you."

Matt tried to ignore the feelings welling up inside his gut and clenched his teeth. "Was Millie Brown your first, or are there others, Doctor?"

Baylor noticed the shift in subject matter and seemed amused by it, maybe even saddened, then cheered up as he got back to work on the girl's face.

"Millie Brown was her daddy's pride and joy," he said. "And Congressman Jack Brown was a righteous daddy—a used-to-be fringe politician who switched parties every time his district was redrawn. Now he's been radicalized. He's a full-blown fanatic. You know how it is with liars, Matthew. They won't meet you halfway, because even when they're wrong they're always right."

"Okay, so he's a piece of shit. I know who he is. He was a piece of shit the day he was born. But his daughter didn't do anything. She was completely innocent."

"He's more than a piece of shit, Matthew. He influences people. He shapes the world we live in. He infects it with his ignorance and his lack of decency and taste. Pull away the veil and Jack Brown is pure white trash. And that's why I became so curious. How did Jack come into all that money? Just like you, he and his wife came from humble backgrounds. Their only income is from a congressman's salary, yet they live in a multimillion-dollar home in Los Angeles. How is that possible?"

"Why do you care? It must be part of your illness. You're broken."

"Easy, Matthew. Mind your manners. You want to know what happened, and I'm willing to talk about it while I get Anna Marie ready for her dance with the fates."

Matt tried to lift his head, but the room started spinning. Baylor noticed and laughed.

"Dizzy, huh?"

He didn't respond. The anger coursing through his veins was impossible to manage. A torrent of fire and rage, but also a sense of overwhelming despair. Matt tried not to let his mind linger too long on the girl's *dance with the fates* and looked back at the doctor.

"Okay," he said. "Okay. How did the shithead congressman get so rich?"

"It took me a while to figure it out. I watched the man for almost a year. I went to fund-raisers and listened to his perverted ideas. I made him my mission until one day, when I was sifting through his desk at the house, it became clear. I found out his secret."

"What secret?"

Baylor paused a moment, then turned to meet Matt's eyes. "As you might expect, it's not very creative. It's not even very new. In fact, it's quite ordinary. If I had been born a cynic, which I'm not, I'd say it went with the job."

"What is it? What's his secret?"

Baylor shrugged. "He's taking money under the table," he said. "And it's a lot of money. He's taking kickbacks for writing a bill that passed in his second term. Here's Jack's logic. If you give billions of dollars to a corporation that's already making billions of dollars, that's not welfare, that's a subsidy. Even better, that's a contribution to his campaign from every executive in that corporation. But if you pay for a lunch program for kids in school who can't focus or learn because they're starving to death, if you're standing on a hill with a loaf of bread and manage to feed the crowd, that's called *what*? Tell me, Matthew. What do the stupid people in this world call that? What words do they use to express their ignorance and hatred?"

The doctor's eyes flared up like a bonfire. He was seething. Matt remained quiet, watching the surgeon wrestle with his demons, his madness.

"I wanted to punish him," Baylor said, still pulling himself together. "I wanted to punish him when I discovered that he was taking food out of hungry people's mouths and had been doing it for almost sixteen years. I wanted to punish him for living a life that he'd stolen while masquerading as someone who was honest and forthright. A life built on the backs of others—the poor, the weak, the least able to speak up for themselves—anything it takes for Jack and his cunt wife to claw their way to the top of the shit pile. I wanted to hurt him in some fundamental way for living a life that he didn't earn. A life that hadn't even been handed down to him by his loved ones, his family, but instead was a crime. A felony. An outrageous lie. I wanted to deliver a mortal blow, Matthew, but I didn't know how to go about it. You see, one of the problems with people like Jack is that they have no real sense of the difference between right and wrong. They have no conscience, no manners, no feeling of guilt, no understanding of what's true or what's false, no ability to feel anything at all, no matter what they've done or who they've hurt. They're manipulators. They're sociopaths living in a place where everything has been dumbed down and facts have no meaning anymore. They're narcissistic. They think that the world spins around them and only them. And unfortunately people like this, people like Jack, are *everywhere* right now. So trying to come up with a punishment, something bold enough that he would actually notice, was a difficult process. But then a few weeks later I saw that his house was being remodeled. This time I went in through the front door. I pretended to be a building inspector from the county and walked in with a clipboard for a quick look around. And that's when I saw her. That's when I saw Millie. She was with Jamie Taladyne, whom I recognized from his rape trial. She was trying to seduce Taladyne in her bedroom. She was holding her blouse open and giving him a good, long look at those tits of hers—that is, until her dirty daddy came home."

"That's how you got the idea to commit multiple murders, Doctor? Watching Millie Brown try to seduce Taladyne? Watching a teenage girl interact with her father?"

Baylor seemed to relish the memory. "All the pieces were right there, Matthew. The victim, the fall guy, and the sacrificial lamb. All three of them were standing right in front of me. Like I said, Millie Brown was her daddy's pride and joy. And if there's any truth to the saying that in every great woman there's a bit of whore, she was on her way to becoming one of the best."

"Then you knew about Ron Harris?"

"Her science teacher? No, I didn't. Harris came as a complete surprise. I was talking about my time alone with her. We spent several days together before the freshness wore off and I became bored."

The thought of Baylor spending several days with his victim made Matt's blood curdle, particularly because he doubted that any of the doctor's victims were ever conscious. He wasn't sure if he could continue to listen to a maniac talk about right and wrong or what it means to be a sociopath in the modern world. He wasn't sure if he could keep all these bad thoughts in his head. He tried balling his hands up into fists but didn't have the strength. He tried to feed off the image of Baylor posing as a building inspector and walking into the Browns' home. He could picture the congressman loosening his tie as he headed upstairs to change. He could see the doctor eyeing him as if he were prey. Millie Brown had been murdered eighteen months ago. Matt hadn't seen her father's name in the news lately and wondered why.

"Her father," he said. "How did he take the loss of his daughter?"

"You don't keep up with current events, do you?"

Matt didn't respond. He read the paper as often as he could, in print and online. Still, there were days and even weeks and months when he had worked narcotics that life became too grueling, too harsh, and he needed distance between himself and the world.

"How did he handle it?" Matt repeated.

Baylor flashed a thoughtful smile. "It took a month or two, but Jack Brown eventually stopped showing up for work. He lost the fortune that he'd stolen in a divorce settlement that became so ugly, so perfect, I'm disappointed that you didn't hear about it. He lost everything—his money, his home, his wife, his seat in the House, and yes, he lost his not-so-innocent daughter, Millie. He lost it all, Matthew. They both did. Their lawyers took everything. I can't say that I've paid much attention to his wife since the divorce, though I've heard rumors that when she hit bottom it wasn't a soft landing. As for Jack, let's just say that he's become something of a professional drinker these days. Jack's a regular at a dive bar in the Valley called the Lucky Star. I go there for a cocktail from time to time because I'm still monitoring his progress. Last week Jack fell down on the sidewalk. I sat with him and smoked a cigar, but the man never came to. He just laid there, mumbling to himself and pissing himself in his pants. After a while the smell of urine got to me, so I left."

A moment passed—the weight of the horror settling into the greenhouse like an infection that had gone global and had no cure. Matt remained quiet while he gathered his thoughts. The doctor's insanity. His will to punish and hurt. The severity of it all.

"And what about Faith Novakoff?" he said finally. "Was it her mother or her father? What did they do to deserve your wrath?"

The doctor became quiet and seemed put off. Matt figured that it was his use of the word *wrath*, another one of the seven deadly sins, that slowed him down. As he watched Baylor return to the girl's makeup, Matt remembered Dante's description of vengeance as a love for justice where only revenge and spite remained. A love for justice that had become wicked and depraved.

Matt cleared his throat. "It is what it is, Doctor. What did Faith Novakoff's parents do to deserve your wrath?"

"It was her father," he said quietly. "Maybe you'll read about him someday."

"Is he another politician?"

Baylor looked up at the glass ceiling, as if struck by an idea. "No, of course not," he said, breaking into a Southern drawl. "And he doesn't run a health insurance company either. He's a TV evangelist from Kentucky. He wears a .45 on his belt and strokes the barrel like it's his cock during sermons. He performs miracles on country folk and likes to dress up in odd clothing. You've probably seen his show a hundred times."

"Never once, Doctor. What's his name?"

Baylor got up and sauntered over to the French doors. Matt couldn't tell for sure, but it looked like he was gazing at the lights shimmering off the lake. His face was awash in a fiery mix of orange and red hues, and it seemed like he was in some sort of trance.

"David Novakoff," the doctor whispered. "Davy . . . Novakoff. His show is called *A Sunday Sermon: I Can Hear God's Voice.*" Baylor looked over his shoulder, his eyes sparkling in the red light. "And if you send him a check, Matthew, you can hear God, too. You've got Davy's pledge. His personal guarantee."

Matt noted the doctor's smile, took in another deep breath, and exhaled. "I still don't understand why you care about these people," he said. "None of them make any difference. They're background noise. They're clowns. They're crackpots and knuckle draggers swimming in a small pond. These girls couldn't help who their parents were."

Baylor turned and gave him an odd look, almost as if he were seeing through him from a hundred miles away. After a few moments, he walked back to the stool and reached for something in his makeup kit.

"You're right about that, Matthew. They couldn't help who their parents were, and I never would've even known Davy Novakoff existed. Unfortunately, the preacher has expensive tastes. He likes to vacation on the Riviera. He likes to throw his money around, sort of the quintessential ugly American. He's rude and crude and he stood out. Naturally, once I found out what he did for a living I saw the hypocrisy and took an interest in him, just as I did with Brooke Anderson's mother. Over time my interest grew, along with my personal commitment. The preacher's got a horse ranch outside Louisville on one hundred of the most beautiful acres I've ever seen. He breeds racehorses and holds an annual summer camp for wayward boys. But his church only has one real charity. If you call the number at the bottom of the TV screen and send in a check, everything goes to the ranch. Everything goes to Davy."

"You were there?"

Baylor nodded and appeared saddened by the thought.

"What about here at the coroner's office?" Matt said. "Did you watch him identify his daughter's body?"

Baylor shook his head. "The connection to Millie Brown hadn't been made yet. I wasn't invited. But I managed to see him walk out of the building. I was sitting on the steps next door."

"Was it worth it, Doctor? Did you see what you wanted to see?"

"I did, Matthew. I did. Even better, I followed him back to Kentucky. By chance we sat across the aisle from each other on a red-eye flight to Louisville. Two first-class seats, with the cabin to ourselves. The preacher wasn't very talkative. Apparently, his daughter, Faith, was the only thing he really loved in this world, and now she was gone. I'm sure you missed it, because you've been busy this week, but his Sunday sermon has been dropped by the cable network. Davy got caught smoking crack cocaine and sod-omizing one of his boys from the ranch. A fifteen-year-old with a pretty face and a skinny ass in the backseat of his Mercedes. According to the newspaper, the child required medical attention that included a small surgical procedure. They don't go for that kind of thing in Kentucky. It's still a bit early, and I'm not sure Davy has the courage, but it'll be fascinating to see what he does with that gun of his, don't you think?"

Baylor had slipped into a Southern drawl again as he described the preacher's disastrous fall. Even worse, he seemed absolutely delighted with himself. Matt remained quiet, watching the beast finish the girl's makeup and open a tube of dark red lipstick. It seemed clear that the doctor had no respect for anyone or any liv-ing thing. It seemed more than clear that he was lost in a world of darkness and that the killing would never end, because no matter what reasons he might conjure up, no matter what societal icons caught his eye, it was the killing that turned him on. The idea that he had the power to save a life cut against the idea that he had the power to take one, too. Matt could see Genet's impending *dance with the fates*, her rape and murder, going down as if he had become part of the nightmare. The doctor had a location in mind. A place that he'd scouted over the days he'd held her. She was obviously sedated. After packing her up in the body bag and making the drive, he'd turn her naked body facedown, stake her to the ground, and butcher her face. Matt imagined that the big moment came just as consciousness returned, no doubt by something injected into her body at exactly the right moment. And that's when he'd violate her. That's when he'd show her what he'd done to her face. It seemed inescapable at this point. That's why the mirror was there. The doctor didn't need to beat or kick any of his victims in order to get them to scream.

All he needed to do was show them.

All he needed was a flashlight and a mirror to ignite the terror. Once they cried out into the night, once they began to wail in the moonlight, their wounds would burst open like a dam break. And then their blood would spill over the mirror and into the ground until their bodies were completely drained.

The Glasgow smile. The Chelsea grin.

It was a crime like no other crime. An atrocity so horrific in scope, so mean and cruel, that he wondered if Dr. Baylor wasn't more of a fiend than Jeffrey Dahmer, the Milwaukee Cannibal, who during a period of more than a decade raped, murdered, and ate seventeen boys and men.

Matt looked back at Baylor and watched him color the girl's lips. "What about this girl, Doctor? Anna Marie. You're punishing her father because he runs a brokerage house. What did he do to deserve this? Why do you want to hurt him?"

Baylor laughed but shrugged and remained quiet.

Still, the thought settled in Matt's mind. What crime could the girl's father have committed that singled him out? Particularly when he worked in a profession where all but a few held sacred the words uttered by the fictional character Gordon Gekko in the movie *Wall Street*.

"*Greed is good,*" Gekko chanted. "*Greed is good.*"

What moral crime could Genet's father have committed that caught the doctor's eye when this was their universal prayer? Even more, why did the doctor choose a man who ran a brokerage firm in Chicago? Why not New York? Why not the eye of the storm? Why not the place where his own father worked? Dear old Dad. Why not some prick on Wall Street?

Matt tried to make another fist as he chewed it over. The anesthetic's grip had loosened some. He couldn't lift his arm, but he could move his fingers.

"What about you?" he said. "Look at your house, Doctor, your address. If it's all about money and greed, why don't you do the world a favor and take yourself out?"

Baylor shook his head, painting over the lipstick with a cherry-red gloss. "Now you're disappointing me again," he said in a quiet voice. "Nothing we've spoken about has had anything to do with how much any of these people have or don't have. And I couldn't care less about their political affiliations, or even who or what they pray to. It isn't the *what* that stands out here, Matthew. It's the method. You're smart enough to understand that, aren't you? You couldn't be your father's son and not be bright enough to see the hypocrisy. To see the way things really are."

The way things really are . . .

Matt let it go. His body was coming back to life. He could bend his knees. He could unfold his arms and feel his back lift away from the stainless steel table as he stretched. Unfortunately, Baylor looked over and noticed. He crossed the room, snatched Matt's pistol, and slipped it behind his belt.

"Easy, Matthew," he said. "Relax."

Matt gave the doctor a long look. The brain fog was lifting. He could feel the rush of energy surging through his arms and legs and flowing into his mind.

He moved his hand over the catheter and began pulling away the dressing as he watched the doctor lift Genet up and lower

her into the body bag. He kept his eyes on the doctor's eyes. The
surgeon was distracted by his victim. He was studying her face
through the plastic, examining her hair and makeup, evaluating
the job he'd done, until his preparations were just right. When he
reached inside to make an adjustment, Matt ripped the catheter
out of his arm and wrenched his body up and off the table.

But he wasn't quick enough. Not even close. Baylor took a step
forward, pointing the .45 at his chest.

"Don't make me do it, Matthew. I will if I have to. There's not
much time left."

"What are you talking about?"

The doctor jabbed the muzzle of the gun toward him. "Time's
running out," he said.

That odd, penetrating look was back. Matt could see it in the
doctor's eyes. Something was going on. Something Matt didn't
understand. Something hidden from view. Baylor took a step
closer, still training the gun on him.

"Your arm's bleeding," he said. "You can't afford to lose another
drop. At least not for a day or two. Pull the dressing over the wound
and it'll stop."

A beat went by, and then another. Matt glanced down at the
spot where he'd ripped out the catheter, then back at Baylor with
the .45.

"Why did you help me?" he said.

"I'm a surgeon."

Matt shook his head. "That's not it. You saved my life. Why?"

"I did what any surgeon would do. I saw a wound and I mended
it. Simple as that."

From the look on the doctor's face, it was anything but simple.
Matt watched him hurry back to the worktable, part open the bag,
and check the girl's body. Then he turned to Matt with the gun in
his hand. He seemed jumpy, unusually nervous, his eyes flicking
around the room.

"We're running out of time," he said. "We're running out of—"

A shot rang out. A loud blast.

Matt flinched as blood sprayed across his face, then recoiled and tried to focus. Baylor's knees were buckling. The doctor had been shot and was going down hard. Matt saw the .45 skid across the floor and turned to the doorway. Grace and Orlando were rushing into the greenhouse with their pistols out. Matt noted the smoke venting from Grace's gun and lunged for the .45 still sliding across the floor. But just as he reached for the handle, Orlando pushed him out of the way and got to it first.

CHAPTER 49

We're running out of time. We're running out of—

Orlando smashed Matt in the face, then knocked him onto the floor and tucked the .45 behind his belt. When he started kicking Matt's stomach and ribs, Grace pistol-whipped the big man and pushed him out of the way.

"Knock it off, Joey," he shouted. "There's no time for your bullshit right now. Jesus Christ."

Something about Grace's voice was way over the edge, and Orlando backed away and became quiet. All Matt could hear was the sound of that fan whirring in the background, the water still dripping in the sink, and Lieutenant Bob Grace, of the Los Angeles Police Department, struggling to catch his breath. Grace stepped around the table, turned over the body with his foot, and stared at the doctor's face for what seemed like a long time. While he may have been bewildered by the true identity of the killer, he looked more distressed than that. More like a man who knew that he was cornered. Matt could see the anxiety showing in Grace's eyes, the panic.

Baylor had been shot in the back. A plume of blood from the exit wound was spreading across his upper chest. As Matt gazed at the wound, he couldn't help thinking about what had just happened and why. Baylor kept saying that they were running out of time. Was he expecting Grace and Orlando to show up this soon? And if he was, then why did he take the time to remove the bullet from Matt's chest? Why did he save his life? There was a moment when the doctor looked up at the glass ceiling, as if he'd just been struck by an idea. But now Matt wondered. Was it an idea, or had he heard something? Is that why he walked over to the French doors and looked outside? Did he know that someone was in the house? And what about those last few moments? Matt could remember the doctor checking the girl, then turning back with the gun. He seemed so agitated, so frightened. Did he know that he was about to be shot? Was there a place in the back of the doctor's demented mind, a place in the darkness, where there still might have been a bit of light? A place where a single candle burned, a small corner where his conscience remained intact and he understood who and what he had become? Was it possible that Dr. Baylor wanted to stop the murders but couldn't?

Was it possible that the monster wanted to be killed?

Matt let the questions subside and looked at Grace, wondering how much he and Orlando may have heard. The lieutenant was holding his head, like he had a migraine and was still trying to catch his breath. His suit, like his gray hair, was soaked through with sweat, his gaunt face dripping as if he'd just stepped inside from a hard rain. He holstered his pistol, then knelt down beside the corpse. Matt noticed that Grace had begun to tremble. He was looking the doctor's body over. He was examining the corpse, measuring it in every detail, inspecting the exit wound. And then the tremors quaking through his body appeared to reach some sort of fever pitch—his eyelids fluttered—and he slapped the doctor across the face.

"You piece of shit," he said in a low, dark voice.

He slapped him again. "You piece of human shit."

Matt thought that Grace might be weeping but couldn't really tell with all the sweat still dripping off his cheeks and forehead. It crossed his mind that Grace was on the verge of a meltdown. And even in death, Baylor wasn't offering the lieutenant a helping hand. Although his eyes were closed, the expression on the doctor's face was one of peace and serenity, and Matt imagined that for Grace it amplified his anger and fury beyond any possible calculation.

Grace seized the doctor by his shirt collar and started shaking him. "You died too easy, Baylor. Too fast. Look at what you've made me do, Doctor. Look at what you've turned me into. A killer, a murderer, just like you. You're the devil, Doctor. Lucifer and Satan—you're an evil spirit. Do you hear me? Open your eyes and tell me that you can hear me, Baylor. Open them, you sick son of a bitch. Open them."

A long moment passed with Grace holding the doctor's limp body close to his face. No one made a sound, and no one moved. And then, finally, the lieutenant lowered the corpse to the floor, grabbed the worktable, and pulled himself to his feet.

It was almost as if he'd aged twenty years in the last five minutes. There was a certain madness about this man.

It was out in the open, and Matt could see it taking over his entire being. His posture had changed. The way he was carrying himself. The glint in his eye that seemed so twisted now. As Grace moved slowly down the aisle toward the girl inside the plastic bag, his body rocked and swayed, as if he were a machine pieced together with old parts. He stopped and turned and looked through the opening at the naked girl. His head pivoted back and forth, then froze as he rubbed his hand over his whiskers.

It was in that look, the way the lieutenant's glazed eyes were fixed on the girl's face, that Matt knew he wasn't seeing her anymore. He wasn't even in the same room.

Look at what you've made me do, Doctor. Look at what you've turned me into. A killer, a murderer, just like you.

A memory surfaced. Something Matt remembered Nietzsche had written more than a hundred years ago, in *Beyond Good and Evil*. He had read passages from the book in his sophomore English class with Mr. Peterson. When his aunt saw the book on the kitchen table, she mentioned something about it as a possible explanation for what his father had become, and why he'd abandoned his wife and son. Now, as Matt gave Grace a long, hard look, he could remember the passage as if he had just read it with his aunt two minutes ago. It was all about fighting monsters and making sure that during the struggle the fighter didn't become a monster himself.

If you gaze into the abyss for too long, the abyss is bound to gaze back into you.

The thought lingered. Matt looked back at Grace and could see his vision turned inward as he stood over the girl, the sweat dripping from his chin onto her soft breasts. He could see the expression on Grace's face and guessed that he was staring into the looking glass, sifting through his memories, feeling the wrath as the abyss had its way with him.

He was putting it together, Matt thought. He was wrestling with all that had happened—the way things seemed and, in a split second, the way things really were. He was wrestling with the blowback—who he used to be and what he had become.

"You finally got your man, Grace."

A beat went by. Then the lieutenant's head swiveled to the left, until his zombie eyes came to rest on Matt. He spoke in a low, dangerous voice—a monster seething; a monster who would do anything to claw his way out of the hole and into the light.

"If you say one more word, Jones, I'm gonna put a bullet in your head."

"And how would that look? How are you gonna sell any of this without admitting that you planted the box cutter in Ron Harris's garage? How are you gonna get past the fact that there was no way Harris killed Millie Brown?"

Grace's face swiveled back to the girl. Matt watched his eyes shut down. He looked like a dead man. A ghost with a spent soul—half here, half gone.

"You killed your partner to keep that secret, Grace. You pushed Leo off that parking garage and murdered him. It's just like you said to Baylor's corpse. You've murdered a lot of people to keep that secret. My best friend. His partner, Frankie Lane. A lot of innocent people. And what about Jamie Taladyne, the man you and Joey murdered tonight? I've got bad news for you, Grace. I called it in, and his alibi checked out. He was telling you the truth. He didn't murder Faith Novakoff. He was in Mint Canyon at the time. There was never a copycat. Taladyne's in the clear."

"Yeah, he's in the clear all right," Orlando shouted. "Now shut the fuck up."

Matt turned, expecting to block a kick. Instead, Orlando had his cell phone out and was making a call. After a few seconds he shut down the phone and flashed a worried look at Grace.

"He's not picking up," he said. "A night like this, and he's not picking up. What the fuck's his problem?"

Grace didn't respond, still way too deep inside himself to care about a phone call. It suddenly occurred to Matt that Orlando had been trying to reach Plank. That they hadn't been to Laura's house, and Orlando didn't know that his partner was dead. It made sense if they were coming from Matt's house on the Westside. Laura's place was east of Toluca Lake, while Baylor's would have been on the way.

They had no idea that Plank's story was over, his bullet-riddled body either still on the lawn or pulled into the brush by the coyotes.

Matt glanced at the .45 Orlando had stuffed behind his belt and the 9 mm Glock he was holding in his right hand. Then he turned back to Grace, whose pistol was holstered on the other side of his body. He wondered if he could make a move without being shot. He wondered if he could get to Orlando and strip the pistol out of his hand. By any measure, Orlando was a big man. All the same, Matt had a certain level of strength back and could feel the tide of adrenaline still rising.

He looked at the tools hanging from the rack over the counter. The shears were too far away. On the counter below, several sizes of plastic cable ties were stored in glass jars, along with a spool of heavy twine. When he checked beneath the worktable, he spotted what he needed on the shelf just six feet away. Beside the rows of empty clay pots, beside the bags of fertilizer and potting soil, the doctor kept his shovel.

He looked up at Grace, the lieutenant's blank eyes still fixed on the girl. Then he began inching across the floor. Slowly. Imperceptibly.

"Just in case you're interested, Grace. That's Anna Marie Genet. She's not dead, and she's not dying. Baylor drugged her."

Grace clenched his teeth. When he spoke, his voice was just above a whisper and still dangerous.

"Joey?"

"Yeah."

"I want you to tie his wrists to the leg of that table."

Orlando walked over to the counter and picked out the jar with the longest cable ties.

"Don't use the ties," Grace said. "They'll leave a residue. Use the twine."

Joey reached for the twine, then spotted the gardening shears and grabbed them, too. Matt looked at the shovel, just five feet away but now completely out of reach. Grace had drawn his pistol and was pointing it at him as he moved down the aisle and stopped at his feet. Then Orlando knelt down, grabbed Matt's wrists with his mitt-sized hands, and started lashing them to the leg of the worktable.

Matt pushed him away, but all Orlando did was laugh at him, pull his hands back into position, and continue wrapping his wrists in twine. Matt turned to Grace.

"What are you trying to pull, Grace? Cabrera's on his way. McKensie's with him."

Grace knelt down and went through Matt's pockets. Tossing his keys and wallet aside, he scooped up his cigarettes and lighter. What struck Matt most was the change in Grace's composure. He still had that wooden look and feel of a zombie. The glint in his eye was still dark and twisted. But the tremors were gone, and he had stopped sweating. When he lit the cigarette, his hand was rock steady. So was the hand holding the pistol.

"Did you hear me, Grace?" Matt repeated. "Cabrera and McKensie are on their way."

"Stop fighting it, Jones. There's no way out of this for you. Hughes's wife? I assume that's who we found tied up in the sun-room—she's not gonna make it either. If Cabrera and McKensie wanna die, that's okay with me, too. Dying's easier when you're not alone."

Orlando tightened the knot, pinching Matt's arm.

"What about ligature marks, Grace?"

The lieutenant took a hit on the smoke and exhaled. "There aren't gonna be any ligature marks. I'm burning the place down tonight."

Orlando traded looks with Grace, then tied his last knot and cut the twine with the shears. After tossing the shears on the counter, he gave Matt another brutal kick in the ribs.

"See you on the other side, Jones. Nice working with you."

Matt tried to pull himself together. Grace had just given Orlando another knowing look and nod, sending Joey out of the greenhouse and upstairs. From the smirk on Grace's face, Matt guessed that it had something to do with the gas jets he'd seen feeding the fireplace in the den and probably a stove in the kitchen. He thought about Grace's plan and followed it through. His way out that would never work.

"You know what, Grace?" he said. "You can blame Baylor for everything you've done, but it's a farce. You made the decisions. You crossed the line on your own. I think that you like killing, and that's why you can't stop. Look at you. It's not what you've become. It's who you are. It's who Baylor was. Kindred spirits, rotten to the core."

Grace looked in his direction, but Matt couldn't tell if he was seeing him. "It's the only way," he whispered. "The only way, Jones."

"What about Baylor? Even if he burns, they'll figure out that he was shot in the autopsy. SID will find the bullet. They'll match it to your gun."

"Depends on how hot the fire burns. Don't worry about it, Jones. I'll file a report. You keep forgetting that you murdered Taladyne tonight, and that it's your word against mine. You executed the guy for killing Hughes and Lane. You were wounded in a firefight with your supervising officer and two LAPD detectives. You were on the run. Me and Joey found you here, and I took a shot but hit Baylor by accident. It's a shame, a real blow to the department and the investigation. Dr. Baylor was a good man, a man with a heart of gold, and an expert witness. I'll always remember him that way. I'll always think of him as someone I considered to be a true friend."

Matt shook his head, then rolled onto his side to get a better look at Grace. "If Baylor was everything you're gonna say he was, why did he help me?"

That sneer was back, Grace's voice barely audible. "Because you had a gun, Jones. You forced him."

"And what about Laura?"

"She was in it because she thought you got the guy who killed her husband. You were wounded. She drove you over here and held the gun on Baylor while he operated on you. He wanted to live. He had no choice."

Matt chewed it over. Grace thought that he had figured a way to talk himself out of the maze. A way to survive an official review in spite of the flaws.

"It won't work," Matt said.

"But it has to."

"Don't you understand, Grace? Are you that far gone? Taladyne has been cleared. It's not a secret between you and me. Everybody knows. The Sheriff's Department cleared him over an hour ago. There's no one left to blame except Baylor. There's no reason to keep killing, Grace. You'll never get away with it. No one will believe you. It'll never work."

"But it has to work," he whispered. "And you have to die to make it work."

Grace noticed Baylor's closet in the hall, stepped on his cigarette, and walked out of the greenhouse. As he rifled through the shelves, Matt pulled his wrists against the leg of the table and tried sawing through the twine.

"It's not over, Grace. Have you even thought about the girl in the body bag? She's still alive."

The lieutenant ripped open a carton that looked like it contained a dozen bottles of isopropyl alcohol. "Yes, she is, Jones. She's still alive. I'll have to come up with a way to change that." He pulled out a bottle and vanished down the hall. "She can't be found here, she can't be allowed to talk—or, like you said, everyone will know. It's no worry, really. No worry at all. I've always loved nighttime drives through the desert. Everything cools down and you're far enough away from the city that the sky turns into a sea of stars."

Grace was talking more to himself now, chattering away in circles. He came back into view, tossing the empty bottle onto the floor and grabbing two more. Matt could smell the alcohol in the air and guessed that he was dousing the carpet on the stairs.

He thought about Laura. If Grace and Orlando had seen her, then the sunroom really was at the base of the stairs. He kept trying to saw through the twine, but the edge of the leg was too smooth and dull. He looked around, the dread closing in on him. The shovel was out of reach. His eyes flicked into the hall as Grace dropped the empty bottles and grabbed two more, the smell of isopropyl alcohol heavier now. Matt gave the twine another try, then lowered his gaze and noticed that the screws securing the table to the tiled floor appeared rusty. After checking the hallway, he took a deep breath, reared back on his knees, and plowed his shoulder into the leg. It didn't budge. The stainless steel table was locked down and too heavy. He tried again, this time thinking about Laura burning in the fire. Nothing happened, nothing moved—nothing would ever move. He could see Grace coming back for the rest of the alcohol. He could hear Orlando starting down the stairs. Sweat was dripping into his eyes, and he couldn't see through the burn.

CHAPTER 50

The power shut down, the entire house went dark.

Matt could hear Orlando rushing down the stairs and shouting at Grace.

"We really need to get out of here," he was saying. "Now, Grace. Now. I counted three fireplaces and the stove. The whole fucking place is gonna blow."

"Grab the girl, Joey. I'm right behind you."

Matt tried not to panic, wiping his eyes against his arm and letting them adjust to the darkness. The lights glimmering off the lake, along with a small patch of moonlight, were providing enough illumination that he could make out the shape of the table, Baylor's corpse, and the French doors at the other end of the room.

Orlando hurried into the greenhouse, stepping over the doctor's body and racing down to the girl. After giving Genet a good look, he picked up the body bag and tossed the girl over his shoulder. Matt turned back as Grace struck the lighter, took a deep pull on a cigarette, then tossed the butt onto the floor. As the alcohol ignited there was a whooshing sound, and the hallway bloomed in an eerie blue light. Then Grace ran into the greenhouse, down the aisle, and behind Orlando outside onto the terrace.

Matt checked the fire, his mind reeling in chaos—thoughts of Laura all mixed up with the sounds and images of gas jets hissing away until the house exploded into a fireball in the dark sky. He tried sawing through the twine—short, frantic strokes, the kind made in futility and desperation. Strand after strand of heavy twine rubbing against the leg of a table that had no real edge.

He turned and watched Grace and Orlando fleeing across the lawn and around a row of bushes into the side yard. They were getting away with it. They were getting away.

And then he heard the first gunshot.

He ripped at the twine—yanked at it—his eyes locked on the view through the open French doors. One gunshot after the next—deep, loud blasts—and muzzles flashing in the darkness. He could see Grace and Orlando hiding behind the wall as they returned fire. Cabrera and McKensie had found the death house on Toluca Lake Avenue, and from the number of gunshots and the sweet, thunderous sounds of rifles, they had brought help.

The twine snapped free.

Matt's body sprung back onto the floor. He turned and stared at his wrists in disbelief, then jumped to his feet and ran for the door. The stairs were completely engulfed in flames, the fire turning yellow and red and beginning to climb up the walls. He could feel a breeze from the greenhouse behind his back, the smoke venting up to the second floor, the heat overwhelming.

Without a moment lost, he filled his lungs with air and held his breath, then raced through the flames to the end of the hall and the doorway he believed would lead him into the sunroom.

He found her here.

She was lying on a couch in the fetal position, the room filled with smoke. Her eyes were closed. Baylor had used tape to cover her mouth and bind her arms and legs behind her back. Matt couldn't be sure but thought that her blouse looked as if it had been disturbed. Images began to surface, brief glimpses whizzing by. The break-in at Laura's house, the footprints he found on the carpet leading to her bedroom, the night he caught Orlando hiding in the darkness, peeping at Laura through the kitchen window.

Matt picked Laura up in his arms, her body limp and lifeless. He tried to keep himself together, and rushed for the bank of glass doors opening to a small pool and the backyard. But when he tried to turn the handle, the door wouldn't budge. None of them would. He tried each one. He could see the dead bolts, the kind of locks often found on glass doors that required keys from inside and out. The glass looked as though it might be an inch thick, and he didn't see anything in the smoke-filled room that he could use to break it.

His eyes darted through the doorway into the hall, the stairway consumed by the blaze. He could feel time racing by, and he could see and hear those gas jets hissing away in his mind again.

He pulled Laura's face against his chest and bolted through the flames. The hallway seemed endless. By the time he reached the greenhouse, Laura's hair was on fire, his jeans were burning, and Grace and Orlando were still huddled behind the wall, shooting their pistols into the front yard.

Matt lowered Laura onto the worktable, frantically hosing her down and finally himself. Her eyes were opening. He could see the confusion on her face, then fear as she heard the gunshots and seemed to remember where she was. Matt removed the tape from her mouth, freed her arms and legs, and held her face in his hands.

"Are you okay?" he said to her. "Are you okay?"

She nodded. "I think so."

He turned and checked the yard. The body bag had been dumped on the lawn, and Grace and Orlando were pinned down and backstepping their way toward the greenhouse.

He met Laura's eyes. "You need to get underneath the table," he said. "You need to hide. If you see a way to make it outside, take it. · They've turned on the gas upstairs, do you understand?"

She nodded again, still groggy.

Matt helped her slide beneath the table, saw Grace and Orlando making a run for the greenhouse, and slipped into the shadows, where he hoped that he would be invisible.

He watched them carefully. Orlando ejecting a mag and drawing another from his pocket; Grace with that twisted look in his eyes but now overwhelmed by the moment and whimpering— both of them together, both of them cornered.

Orlando entered the greenhouse first, firing three deafening shots into the darkness. Grace made it halfway in before he stumbled and fell on the floor.

And that's when Matt swung the shovel and smashed Orlando in the face.

It was a hard, crushing blow, and the big man collapsed on impact.

Matt worked quickly, stripping him of his pistol, rolling him over, and lifting the .45 out from beneath the detective's belly. When he looked back at Grace, he saw the lieutenant sitting on the floor staring at his gun. His face was bathed in rays of moonlight. He had a sparkle in his eyes, that lost, spooky glint, as if he were all alone in a world far, far away. And he was sweating again, the shakes had returned. Even more, he was weeping. After a moment he stuffed the Glock into his mouth and clamped his eyes shut.

Gunshots sprayed into the greenhouse, the shattered glass raining down on them like jagged shards of hail, but Grace didn't seem to notice.

Matt looked through the French doors toward the lawn and saw Cabrera and McKensie moving in behind five members of a SWAT team, dressed in black uniforms and helmets with their rifles raised.

"Hold your fire," he shouted. "Hold your fire."

He turned back to Grace. His eyes remained shut, the gun wobbling in his mouth, like he couldn't find enough courage to pull the trigger. Diving across the aisle, Matt grabbed hold of the lieutenant's hand and struggled to pull the pistol away.

"Do you really think that I'm gonna let you take the easy way out, Grace? Give me the fucking gun. Give it to me. You're gonna own up to what you did. You're going national. You're going public. You're gonna burn."

Grace moaned, the muzzle banging against his teeth. Matt was surprised by the man's strength as they wrestled for control of the weapon nose to nose. When Grace opened his hollow gray eyes, Matt took the shock and couldn't help thinking that he had pulled the last veil away and could look all the way in. He could see the disease, the insanity, the final break. As he gazed past the glint, he could see the chasm.

The man who had lost his soul. The man who thought that murdering an eighteen-year-old girl and burying her body in the desert was the final answer, the ultimate solution. A righteous act that would bring him back into the light.

LAPD lieutenant Bob Grace.

The man who had already been responsible for the deaths of six people and murdered five of them to keep his secret. Ron Harris, Leo Rodriguez, Kevin Hughes, Frankie Lane, Jamie Taladyne, and Dr. George Baylor.

Matt wrenched the gun out of Grace's mouth just as the lieutenant pulled the trigger. Three rounds burst over their heads, through the glass and into the sky. Then he slammed the back of Grace's head into the wall and spoke in a low, dark voice that had heat to it.

"Fuck you, Grace. Is it cutting through, you sick son of a bitch? Fuck you."

He smashed the lieutenant's head against the wall a second time, then turned as he noticed the flashlights. The SWAT team officers were rushing into the greenhouse with their rifles still raised. His eyes flicked past them until he spotted Cabrera and McKensie with their pistols drawn. Cabrera hurried over and knelt down, taking in his shoulder, the bandage and wound. As the SWAT team's flashlights swept over the makeshift operating table, Cabrera appeared to zero in on the surgical instruments and the two IV bags, still hanging from the irrigation pipes. When he turned back, he spoke in a quiet voice filled with new concern.

"Did Baylor do this to you, Matt? Are you okay?"

Matt met his partner's eyes. "Orlando turned on the gas," he said. "The place is gonna blow."

Cabrera nodded and helped him up, then turned as Laura crawled out from beneath the table. Matt watched his partner take her hand and guide her through the French doors. When McKensie handcuffed Grace and dragged him away, Matt couldn't help but notice the satisfaction showing on his face. The SWAT team leader was giving the fire a last look, his men backing out ahead of him. Matt started to follow them but stopped when he remembered Orlando. Searching through the darkness, he found him on the other side of the table. He was just starting to move, just coming to. He helped the man get to his feet, pushed him outside, and made a run for the wall by the lake. But then his eyes danced across the lawn and landed on the body bag. He rushed over and grabbed it, dragging the girl across the grass until he reached the others.

The sunroom was fully engulfed in flames, and the windows were beginning to shatter and drop from the second floor. Several moments passed before Matt heard what he thought might be a scream from inside the house. He looked over at Cabrera. Then McKensie broke in with his gravelly voice.

"What the hell was that?"

Matt turned back to the house, staring at the fire. At first he wasn't sure if what he'd heard had been human. From the pitch and tone, it could have been a dog trapped inside somewhere. Perhaps Baylor had a pet after all.

But then he heard it again. A shriek. A human being.

It sounded like Joey Orlando, but how could it be? Matt had helped him up, or at least thought he had. He could remember pushing him through the doorway from behind. He could remember becoming distracted when he saw the body bag on the lawn.

His eyes swept over the faces of everyone huddled behind the wall. Orlando wasn't here. He wasn't with them. And then a thought surfaced. Something horrible. Something worse than horrible. He looked at the twine still wrapped around his wrists. He studied it closely and suddenly felt the ice-cold hand of death grab his spine and shake it.

There were no ragged edges. There was no way that the twine had been pulled apart in the heat of the moment. Instead, it had been a clean cut. The kind of cut a pair of gardening shears would have made.

Laura grasped his arm. "What is it, Matt? What's happened?"

He shook his head back and forth, still trying to comprehend. "Baylor," he whispered.

"What's happened?"

"He's alive."

He heard Orlando let out another horrific shriek and watched as the fire moved through the greenhouse. He could feel the churning in his gut as he gazed at the gruesome sight and waited for Orlando to stop howling in agony.

And then the gas finally ignited. The air cracked, and as Matt reached for Laura and ducked below the wall, he could hear a sharp clapping sound and feel the concussion. It seemed like the fireball was consuming the entire yard, eating into the homes on both sides of the property and rising all the way up to the stars. Matt traded another look with Cabrera and McKensie, then turned back to Laura and shielded her with his body. The inferno had burned away the night, and all of a sudden it was as bright as lunchtime on a hot summer day. He could feel the fire scorching the top of his head and rolling over his back into the lake. He could hear the sighs of relief as the flames ebbed away from the wall. And as he caught his breath, as he felt Laura rub her thumb over his palm, he could see the girl in the body bag waking up and beginning to move.

CHAPTER 51

The drive from the hospital to Laura's house didn't really register. It was after 9:00 p.m., and Matt sat in the passenger seat looking at her face and thinking about the five days he'd just spent laid up in bed with another handful of IVs in his arm. The examinations of his body and the bullet wound appeared endless. At a certain point he began to believe that the doctors were less interested in his well-being than their own standing. It seemed clear by the way they were acting that the procedure Dr. Baylor had performed in his greenhouse was the work of a very gifted surgeon. It seemed clear to Matt that the doctors examining him were looking for a way to find fault with the operation but couldn't, and now were taking it out on him with a barrage of senseless tests.

There had been only one break. A break taken in spite of his doctor's protest.

A two-hour stretch a couple of days ago when he left the medical center to attend the funerals of Kevin Hughes and his partner, Frankie Lane. They were buried side by side, under the watchful eyes of pretty much every law enforcement officer from every agency in the region who wasn't on duty. The fire department had shown up with a long line of fire engines and emergency vehicles. The mayor, along with every member of the city council, three members of the House, a US senator, and hundreds of onlookers were at the cemetery as well.

Matt and Cabrera had joined Lieutenant McKensie, Deputy Chief Albert Ramsey, and LAPD chief Richard S. Logan to stand by Laura's side, while the archbishop of Los Angeles, Francis Joseph Anastasio, led the ceremony. Now, as he sat in the passenger seat watching her exit off the 134 Freeway and make the climb into the hills above Glendale, Matt couldn't believe how well she had handled herself. What he imagined would have been the most personal and private of moments—a funeral service for her husband—had become a media event open to the public and recorded by a sea of cameras. But even beyond Laura's inner strength, beyond the archbishop's heartfelt words about peace and love, beyond the loss and sadness, the pain and finality, what struck Matt most about the service was the look he saw on almost everyone's face.

The shock that three police officers—Grace, Orlando, and Plank—three decorated officers had strayed so far off the mark. The disbelief Matt had overheard in one conversation after the next that they were here in this cemetery to pay their respects and bury two men who had been betrayed and murdered by three of their own.

As Matt read accounts of their crimes in the newspaper from his hospital room, as he watched the story unfold on TV, including an interview with Sally Rodriguez, the wife of Grace's partner, who'd taken the news of his betrayal particularly hard, he'd had the same feeling. It was almost as if the air had been sucked out of the city and for five long days everyone was still holding their breath.

Laura pulled into the drive. The house was dark, and they walked around the garage to the kitchen. After unlocking the door, she switched on the lights and then, as if on automatic pilot, began to pour a glass of wine.

"You want something?" she said.

Matt shook her off. "I'm okay."

He could tell that she had something she wanted to talk about. He could see the worry in her eyes, the same worry he'd noticed as they left the medical center at USC.

"When are they gonna know?" she said finally.

"Know what?"

"Who was in the house. The man who screamed."

"They already know. It was Joey Orlando. I heard his voice. You're safe, Laura. He's gone. I promise."

She sipped her wine, her eyes still on him. "I know," she said. "But when will they have proof?"

"Maybe tomorrow. Maybe the day after."

Matt understood why she needed a definitive answer—Orlando's fixation on her and his odd behavior were more than obvious—but the fire had burned so hot that investigators couldn't get in until late last night. As he'd been told during his initial debriefing by a Lieutenant Clyde Rayburn from Internal Affairs, the case had been taken downtown and split between the Robbery-Homicide Division and IA. While answers would probably begin filtering in tomorrow, Matt knew that he and Cabrera were on leave and out of the loop. It was only a guess, but he imagined that processing the crime scene in a high-profile case like this one could go on for another week or two.

He turned and caught Laura staring at him with those eyes of hers.

"Why do you think Baylor did it?" she said. "Why do you think he saved your life?"

He shook his head. He didn't know.

She set down her glass and moved closer, wrapping her arms around him and resting her head on his chest. When she spoke, her voice was just above a whisper.

"He did it twice, you know. He saved you twice. There's gotta be a reason."

The question had been dogging him since he looked at the twine wrapped around his wrists and realized that it had been cut. Still, at this moment and on this night, Baylor's motives for saving his life, even the doctor's whereabouts and physical condition, seemed to fade into the background. He could feel Laura pressing her body against him. He could feel her thighs pushing into his thighs. Her hips pinned against his hips. Her arms pulling him closer.

"I'm glad you're here," she whispered.

"I am, too."

"We need a break from all this, Matt. A couple of good days."

He nodded without saying anything, the smell of her skin intoxicating. Moments passed. Glimpses of heaven as she started rubbing her breasts against his chest—pure bliss, pure elation, pure ecstasy. He ran his thumb over her chin and met her eyes, their lips hovering through the air in a lazy, magnetic arc.

And then he kissed her—his best friend's wife—lightly at first, gently, once, twice, both of them testing the waters before they stepped in.

He couldn't help it. He couldn't wait. He'd fallen for her, and both of them were alive.

CHAPTER 52

Matt followed Cabrera through the last security gate and down the hall at Men's Central Jail. Lieutenant McKensie was sitting at a table in one of the visiting rooms when they entered.

"They're bringing him down now," he said in a scratchy voice. "He's not gonna say anything, but I wanted to take another look at the son of a bitch, and I thought you guys might want one, too. It'll make the bad dreams go away faster. You'll sleep better."

McKensie pounded the table with his fist, the heat and fire in his emerald-green eyes flaring up then easing some as he brushed back his white hair. Matt had been surprised by his telephone call this morning. Apparently, Grace had shut down. He'd only spoken once since his arrest, and that was a week ago during his initial interrogation. He understood his rights, he'd said, and refused any form of legal representation. Detectives from the Homicide Special Section saw their opening and had spent days trying to break the lieutenant down, but to no avail.

No matter what the evidence, no matter how many hours he had been deprived of sleep, Lieutenant Bob Grace was not going to admit that he had committed multiple murders.

Matt turned to the door. He could hear the sound of leg irons dragging across the tiled floor in the hall. The pace had a rhythm to it. A weary shuffle moving closer. After several moments, Grace appeared in the doorway, flanked by two guards. Matt watched the men guide his former supervisor into the room and over to the table. Once they shackled him to a chair directly across from McKensie and walked out, his eyes flicked back to Grace.

He couldn't stop looking at him, staring at him. And in a single instant, he understood the meaning behind McKensie's words and why he wanted to meet here.

It was more than just seeing Grace in this setting. More than the steel bars, more than the layers of meaningless graffiti that had been scratched into the table over the past fifty years by an endless line of losers. More than the fact that this visiting room wasn't a visiting room at all but a cage.

Grace had changed over the past week.

He was dressed in a bright orange jumpsuit and seemed small and frail, even withered. Whatever battle he had been waging over his own sanity had obviously been settled and lost. Even the mad glint was gone. All that remained was the shell of the man—the ghost, the empty vessel—sitting before them and staring straight ahead, like a mannequin waiting for a spot in a department store window.

Matt glanced over at Cabrera and could tell that he was seeing the same thing. Then he turned to McKensie, who had been watching him and quietly weighing his reaction.

"He won't eat," McKensie said. "And he's still on suicide watch."

Cabrera sat down at the table, clearly amazed. "Is there any way he could be faking it, Lieutenant?"

"You mean like that asshole in Colorado?"

Cabrera nodded, his wide-open eyes still on Grace. "Yeah."

McKensie leaned over the table and slapped Grace across the face. "The shrinks don't think so," he said.

Matt moved closer. In spite of the hard slap, there had been no movement, no reaction—just that wooden look in the man's eyes.

"What if they're wrong?" he said. "What if he wakes up out of this just the way Baylor did after he was shot?"

McKensie shrugged, then tapped his mouth with two fingers. "His family finally hired an attorney. We'll see what happens. You got a smoke?"

Matt shook his head, digging a pack of nicotine gum out of his pocket. The lieutenant didn't seem interested. As Matt pushed a piece through the foil wrapper and slid it against his cheek, he thought about the gun used to murder Hughes in the parking lot behind the restaurant in Hollywood. The finishing gun. The Glock 20.

He took a seat at the table. "What about his house, Lieutenant? Are you in the loop with Robbery-Homicide?"

McKensie nodded. "Everything's coming from the chief's office. They're still at it. Same with Orlando's apartment and Plank's house out in the Valley."

"What about the gun?"

"The Glock? It hasn't turned up yet."

Cabrera thumped the table with his fingers. "That piece is worth a lot of money."

"It is," McKensie said. "It's worth a lot of fucking money." He paused briefly, taking another look at Grace and sizing the man up. "I always thought this guy was a pussy. I always thought he was a piece of shit. Look at him. He's blown his wad and doesn't even know we're sitting in the same fucking room. But it almost worked, didn't it? If that deputy sheriff from West Hollywood hadn't lucked out, you'd still be looking for the three-piece bandit."

An image surfaced. Matt could see Hughes laid out on the front seat of that black SUV, his body coated in blood and shattered glass.

It seemed so long ago. So far away, yet still so vivid.

"Okay," McKensie said. "Okay. I need to run through a couple of things with you guys. We need to do some business. Cabrera, you're on leave for two more weeks. Internal Affairs wants another talk, so does Robbery-Homicide, then you're back in Hollywood, reporting to me." McKensie stopped and gazed at both of them for a moment. "That's right," he said finally. "I've been transferred to Hollywood. Jones, you're going down to Chinatown. You're off until the shrinks clear you—and before you say anything, let me give you some advice. Don't turn this into something it isn't. Don't make it ugly. It's just routine."

Matt shot McKensie a look, then got up from the table and started pacing. Nothing about letting the shrinks in the Behavioral Science Section in Chinatown play with his mind would be routine.

"Why?" he asked. "Why me?"

McKensie stared back at him. "You've been through a lot, Detective. More than most. Like I said, it's just routine."

"I don't think so. I think there's more to it than that."

A long moment passed. When McKensie finally spoke, his voice barely rose above the sounds of the jail drifting in through the open door.

"It's the way you killed Plank, Jones. The protection detail from Metro Division. The two guys you locked up in the car. They witnessed the shooting. They've given their statements. The chief thinks that you need some time to sort things out. Not a lot of time. Four, maybe five weeks. Enough of a break to settle down and think things through. Look at it like you're on vacation."

Matt glanced back at his partner, then took a deep breath and exhaled. He could remember the rage he'd felt when he saw Plank crossing the lawn with the shotgun. He could still feel the adrenaline rush, still feel the blood dripping down his chest from the gunshot wound in his shoulder, still smell the gunpowder wafting in the air as he emptied both Berettas into Plank's face and chest.

Plank got off lucky.

He died before the pain would have had time to overtake the shock that he was hit and it was over. Eddie Plank was a piece of shit. He'd reached the finish line. He'd run out of tomorrows. He wasn't invisible and had no chance.

The memory blanked out. Matt checked his watch and glanced back at Grace.

All of a sudden he wanted to get out of here. His visits to Chinatown, the things he said, the way he acted would become a matter of record and could follow him around for the rest of his career.

He liked being a homicide detective. He needed it.

He tried to push away the fear and paranoia, and turned to McKensie. "What about Baylor's house?"

McKensie gave him another look. "Why are you so pissed off, Jones? You'll be okay. Nothing's gonna happen. No one's taking your badge away from you. No one's taking your gun. The police commission has already nominated both you guys for the Medal of Valor."

Matt shook it off. "What about the doctor's house?" he repeated.

"The dental records match up to Joey Orlando, just like we thought they would. Dr. Baylor's loose and on the run, and the FBI took over the case about an hour ago."

"Why didn't you call? Why didn't you say anything?"

The lieutenant sat back in his chair and smiled at him, his voice warm and easy. "But I did, Matt, as soon as I got the news. That's why we're here."

A beat went by. Then another.

"Is there anything else?" Matt asked.

McKensie smiled at him again, but something had changed in his eyes. It was the look of open curiosity. An inquisitive expression that was working its way across his entire face.

"They're not sure," he said in an odd voice. "But the lab guys found a stain on the floor by Joey's body. They think that it might be residue from a cable tie. They think that the doctor may have strapped Orlando to the table so he couldn't get out of the house. They think that he wanted Joey to burn up in the fire. The FBI wants to talk to you, Jones. They want to know more about what the doctor said to you, and maybe more about what you said to him. They want to know why he killed Orlando but didn't kill you."

Matt remained quiet. He didn't have any answers, just this vague sense that something was beyond his reach. Something didn't feel right. Something was out of order or incomplete or just plain wrong. He checked his watch again. All he wanted to do was bolt. All he wanted to do was get out of the visiting room, the cage, the darkness, and catch his breath in the bright sunlight.

CHAPTER 53

Cabrera got behind the wheel of the Crown Vic, started the engine, then flipped open the glove box and fished out a pack of Marlboros.

Matt gave him a look. "What the hell are you doing?"

His partner shrugged. "I'm addicted. I'm hooked."

Matt laughed. "You're *hooked*? Since when did you get hooked?"

"I don't know. It just happened."

"You smoked your first cigarette a couple of weeks ago, Cabrera. How many have you had since? Three, four, maybe five?"

"This shit's mean, man. You see those ads on TV?"

Matt watched Cabrera light up then start coughing through his first drag. He didn't even know *how* to smoke.

"Take that thing out of your mouth and throw it out the window, or I'm gonna do it for you."

Cabrera shook his head back and forth, shielding his face with his arm as he took a second hit. Matt backed off and tried to get a read on his partner, his smile fading. Cabrera looked tired. Maybe worse than tired, like the nightmares had caught up to him and were gnawing at him in the dark. Matt had seen it overseas just as he'd seen it working as a patrol officer here in Los Angeles. Trauma had a way of playing with its victims. What might seem small enough to roll off one person's back had the power to decimate another.

He watched Cabrera crack open the window and toss the pack of cigarettes on the console. After a brief moment, and without even thinking about it, Matt got rid of the nicotine gum in his mouth and lit up as well.

He already knew he was hooked.

"Where to now?" Cabrera said. "If it's gonna be another two weeks, I need to grab some things out of my desk."

Matt nodded. He hadn't been working out of Hollywood long enough to have anything in his desk. Just his car in the rear lot. When they had gotten the call from McKensie, they decided to meet at the station and drive downtown together.

"It's fucked up what they're doing to you, Matt. About Plank, I mean. He killed cops, for Christ's sake."

"Yes, he did."

"He was there to kill you, too," Cabrera said. "Any one of us would've done the same thing. Even McKensie."

"Maybe."

Cabrera pulled out of the parking garage, passed the delivery entrance to the jail, and headed for the 101 Freeway. Matt sat back in the passenger seat, gazing out the window at the seemingly endless line of bail bond agencies lining the street.

Big Al's Got D'Keys. Abracadabra's Magic Carpet Ride. Freddy's Freedom Village.

He stopped looking at them. He stopped seeing them.

Traffic was light, and once they broke through the surface streets downtown, it only took fifteen minutes before they reached the Hollywood station and pulled into the rear lot. Not much had been said along the way. Matt had spent most of the time thinking about what it would take to satisfy a psychiatrist and get back to the homicide table. For the rest of way, he thought about the gun-shot wound in his shoulder. He didn't want to dwell on it, but there was something new going on. A deep, burning sensation that he'd never felt before. He noticed it just before Grace had been ushered into the visiting room and shackled to the chair. It seemed to go away, but now it was back.

He climbed out of the car, gazing at Orlando and Plank's Crown Vic parked by itself against the fence and thinking that it looked a lot like a ghost ship. After a few moments he followed Cabrera into the station through the rear entrance, past the hold-ing cells, and onto the squad room floor. As Cabrera headed for his cubicle, Matt looked through the glass into Grace's office and could tell at a glance that the two men using the computer and talking on their cell phones were feds. They spotted him just as quickly, waving him down the hall and into the office. As Matt walked in, the man wearing glasses with the light-colored hair and mustache switched off his phone and seemed glad to see him.

"I'm Jeff Kaplin," he said. "This is my partner, Steve Vega."

Matt shook their hands. "You guys out of Westwood?"

"No," Vega said. "DC."

"Lieutenant McKensie said you wanted to talk."

Kaplin nodded. "We do, but not just yet, Jones. We think that Dr. Baylor may have committed another murder two nights ago."

"Who?"

"Kim Bachman. She was twenty years old. She weighed less than a hundred pounds."

"In Hollywood or the Valley?"

Vega shook his head. "New Orleans," he said.

The idea had its own way of settling in. Dr. Baylor on the move.

Matt took a step back, measuring the two FBI agents as he thought it over. Both of them were in their midforties and seemed confident and at ease. But even more, both of them appeared to share an expression of being in a perpetual state of curiosity and wonder. Kaplin's curly blond hair had started to turn gray. He looked like he was in decent shape—a walker, Matt guessed, not a runner, who came off like a university professor. His partner, Steve Vega, had black hair and dark eyes and a physical presence that would have to be considered Kaplin's opposite. He was half a foot shorter and a good fifty pounds heavier but built like a powerhouse.

Matt leaned against the desk and turned back to Kaplin. "If you think it's Baylor and it's been two days, why didn't the murder turn up in the news?"

"We needed confirmation that the body found in the doctor's house was Joey Orlando. We didn't get that until this morning."

"Tell me about the girl."

Kaplin brushed his thumb and forefinger over his mustache. "She was a college student. She was found like the others, but that's all over the Internet now. Depending on how you look at it, the murder could have been committed by anybody—but we don't think so."

Matt kept his thoughts to himself. It all seemed too neat and too quick. New Orleans would have been a new setting for Baylor. A new city. And the doctor had been wounded. How could it even be possible? How could he have been able to select his next victim with so little time?

"What about the girl's parents?" he asked.

Vega opened a file folder and pulled out an e-mail from the New Orleans Police Department that included several crime-scene photos of the girl's nude body staked to the ground, along with before and after shots of her face. Until two days ago Kim Bachman had been an innocent-looking young brunette with light brown eyes. Now her face was mutilated, the moment of her death frozen in a grotesque smile that stretched from ear to ear. Matt stared at the photograph, still unable to comprehend how anyone, no matter what their psychological issues, no matter what their past, could do this to another human being, or any living thing.

It almost seemed as if the killer intentionally picked out the most pure, the most gentle, in order to underline their transformation from all that was beautiful in this world to all that was hideous.

Matt checked the first page. According to the time and date stamp on the header, the e-mail had been sent in the last hour and must have been printed here at the station. He thought about that pack of nicotine gum in his pocket, nixed the idea, then looked over at Kaplin and Vega, who seemed to have quieted down.

Both of them were staring at the before and after snapshots of the girl's face. And their expressions had changed. That perpetual state of curiosity and wonder no longer seemed so enduring. Matt didn't need to ask why.

"Tell me about her parents," he repeated in a quiet voice.

Vega nodded like he was trapped in a state of delirium. Once he managed to raise his eyes, Matt collected the e-mail printouts and returned them to the file.

"She has a mother," Vega said. "Heidi Bachman. Her father died in his sleep five years ago from a heart attack."

"What does the mother do?"

"She's a caregiver. A hospice nurse living in Baltimore."

"Did you guys get a copy of my statement?"

Kaplin and Vega nodded.

"Then you know the doctor's motive," Matt said. "It's more about the parent than the actual victim. It sounds like Heidi Bachman committed herself to helping others. There's no way that a hospice nurse would make Baylor's list."

Kaplin gave him a look, then sat down at the desk and pulled the computer closer. "This one might," he said. "She made headlines a couple of years after her husband died. The local media in Baltimore wouldn't give up on it and kept the story going for most of the following year. If Baylor was in the hunt, there's a better than fifty-fifty chance that he knew about her."

Matt joined Vega, huddling behind Kaplin's back as the agent opened an article from the *Baltimore Sun*'s archives dated twenty-four months ago. As he began reading, he realized that the article was a summary of the entire case. Apparently, Heidi Bachman had taken on a new patient, a woman in her sixties dying of cancer. After her first visit to the house, Bachman learned that the woman was married, that she and her husband were extremely wealthy, and that they had no children or family. No heirs.

Matt looked at the photograph of Bachman's patient, Janet Cameron, standing in front of her home with her husband, Bill. They were holding each other and showing smiles that seemed quiet and genuine. Still, Matt's pulse quickened as he looked at their house in the background. It was set in the countryside, and he could see horses in the fields on both sides of what could only be called an estate and mansion.

Kaplin pointed to the first paragraph on the following page. "The wife only lasted five or six weeks. But in that time, Bachman cozied up to the husband real nice and they got tight. We don't think that it was a sexual relationship. Cameron had lost his wife and was distressed and vulnerable. Bachman was young enough to be his daughter, had his trust, and held his hand."

Matt nodded. "And she had no plans of letting go of that hand. No plans of walking away from the treasure chest."

"Funny you should put it that way," Vega said. "But yes, she became his crutch. His most valuable asset, the daughter he never had. The old man's friends said that she forced herself into his world. She had his ear and started managing his life—pushing his friends away and isolating him. Anything she could do to make it look and feel like the two of them were family, she did."

Kaplin turned to Matt. "Everybody could tell that something was wrong. But if they said anything to Cameron, it worked in Bachman's favor. He dropped them, and they never heard from him again. When the old man died, no one was surprised that she had become the sole beneficiary of his estate."

"How did he die?" Matt asked, even though he could feel the answer stirring in his gut.

Vega smiled. "The same way her husband did. He had a heart attack in his sleep."

It clicked, the three them staring at the possibilities. When Kaplin spoke up, his voice was quieter, more matter-of-fact.

"The coincidence didn't sit well with anybody," he said. "Detectives from Baltimore PD took statements and tried to sort things out. An autopsy was performed. According to the medical examiner, the old man's pipes were clean. There was no sign of heart disease."

"How much did she collect from her husband's death?"

"Half a million off a life insurance policy," Kaplin said. "She claims she dumped his ashes into the Chesapeake but doesn't remember exactly where."

Matt had guessed right. "So you think she's good for both of them."

"We do," Kaplin said. "But Cameron's tox screen came back just as clean as his arteries. The detectives had no choice."

"She walked," Matt said. "They set her free."

Vega smiled again. "They cut her loose and gave her the key to the vault with all of the old man's money. He was worth more than fifty million dollars. And that's why we think it works, Jones. That's why we think the killer might be Baylor, on the move through the South and looking for a way out of the country. Heidi Bachman's profile fits every one of the doctor's victims like a glove. She's a piece of shit, just like all the rest. A greedy black widow who he'd say deserves to be punished. That's what this is about, right? Taking the one thing away from them that they can't live without? The one thing they can't buy back or replace? The one thing they love?"

Matt nodded, his mind racing. "Where was her daughter's body found? What part of New Orleans?"

Vega gave him a strange look and hesitated. "What you were just talking about a few minutes ago," he said finally. "The words you used—treasure chest."

"What about it?"

"A security guard found her in the middle of the night. She was staked to the ground by one of the levees near Treasure Chest Casino. It's a riverboat down there."

A moment passed, and then another. Long and dark and all ripped up. Matt felt the tingle rising up his spine. It was a sign from the doctor, a note, a message, another strike against greed by a madman.

Treasure Chest Casino.

It had to be him.

Baylor could have known about Heidi Bachman before he even got started in Los Angeles. For all Matt knew, she could have been the one who inspired him. The first victim to make his wish list. But even more, Heidi Bachman would have been considered the prize, the gold ring, because unlike all the others who had lied and cheated to steal their way to the top of the shit pile, only Bachman had committed one, possibly two murders in order to get her hands on the money.

It had to be him. It had to be Baylor.

Matt turned and spotted Cabrera staring at them through the glass. He waved him into the office and, after everyone was introduced, looked back at Vega.

"Has Bachman identified her daughter yet?"

"Last night."

"In person?"

Vega nodded. "Yeah."

"Any chance that the media covered it?"

Kaplin sat back in the desk chair and laughed. "Are you kidding? When they figured out who the girl's mother was, everybody showed up. It was a circus."

"We need to see that videotape," Matt said.

CHAPTER 54

Matt figured that the waitress knew something was up the moment she got a look at their faces and grabbed a couple of menus. Now, as she set down their plates and topped off their coffees, her eyes went straight to Cabrera's tablet computer and stayed there.

They were sitting by a window at Denny's in the strip mall across the street from the movie studios at Sunset and Gower. The same table they had shared on the way to Hughes's autopsy. The same middle-aged waitress with the same dyed red hair. Matt doubted that she could see an image on the tablet with all the glare. And even if she could, he didn't think it would mean anything to her.

Still, as they got started on their bacon and eggs French-toast specials, neither he nor Cabrera could take their eyes off the screen.

It was him, dressed in pale blue scrubs with an ID pinned to his chest pocket.

Dr. George Baylor helping Heidi Bachman as she struggled through the press line from the front entrance of the coroner's office to a black limousine idling in the darkness on the other side of the parking lot.

The NBC affiliate in New Orleans had posted the clip on its website as part of the station's coverage of the murder investigation. The camera appeared to be directly in front of Bachman, backing up as she marched forward, the handheld image rock steady. From the ruined look on her face, Matt guessed that the doctor had achieved all that he could have hoped for. From the look on Baylor's face, the sparkle in his eyes, and the dimples on his cheeks, the experience had been pure bliss.

Somehow he had found a way in. He had shepherded Bachman through the identification process and stood by her side as the sheet was lifted away and the woman's memories of her daughter were forever changed.

Forever mangled. Forever tattooed to her being and her mind.

A title graphic had been laid over the images at the top of the screen. Beside a photo of the twenty-year-old murder victim laughing with her friends at a bar in the French Quarter were the words *Special Report: Murdered Coed Identified. Who Killed Kim Bachman?*

Matt looked back at the victim's mother. Although Cabrera had turned the sound down on the tablet, he could hear the faint voice of a reporter asking the woman how she was feeling right now. When she didn't answer, someone shouted from the crowd, "Did you murder Bill Cameron? And what about your husband? Did you kill him, too?" Bachman remained silent, clenching her teeth and pressing forward through the gloom. She was dressed like nouveau riche, cheap and tasteless and adorned with designer labels, on a body that appeared bent but strong and noticeably dreary. As Matt watched her push a reporter out of the way with her fists, he thought that he detected something more than grief showing on her face.

Something more than even Grace or the doctor possessed.

He thought that he could break through her grim mask and see who she really was. Someone cold and calculating and devoid of human emotions. A conniving bitch, a complete blank who had probably earned a good living on her own but murdered two men because she thought that she deserved more and more, and even more than that.

The treasure chest.

Matt watched her climb into the limo, bark instructions at the driver, then snap the door shut. As the car eased through the press line and started to move off, the strobe lights switched to full auto, and night became day in a series of rapid-fire bursts. The light was blinding, and Matt could see Dr. Baylor shielding his eyes as he slipped into the shadows and disappeared into the crowd. While Kaplin and Vega were headed to New Orleans on a late tip that the doctor might have stayed at Le Pavillon Hotel, Matt guessed that they would find the room clean and the trail ice cold.

The shot on Cabrera's tablet ended and switched to real time, cutting to a female news anchor as she interviewed a senior investigator from the FBI's Behavioral Science Unit. A close-up photograph of Dr. Baylor's face had been placed over a map of the United States with the cities lining the Gulf of Mexico highlighted as possible escape routes.

Matt turned away and gazed out the window at the people on the corner waiting for the light to change in the oppressive heat.

It didn't matter. He already knew that they were too late. He also knew that Baylor would never set foot in any of the cities that were being discussed as *the most probable*. Baylor didn't do *probable*. Worse, he was a plastic surgeon whom the *Los Angeles Times* had deemed brilliant in their coverage of the story last week. One article included testimonials from his patients, most of whom remained grateful to him for his talent and refused to believe that he was anything but the best and brightest. No doubt he had colleagues across the country who felt the same way.

Even if the FBI got lucky and managed to find the doctor, odds were that they wouldn't know that they had found him.

In a few days, a few weeks or months, Matt guessed that the madman would become undetectable, his chance of capture requiring a new set of victims, another murder spree, and another pair of detectives who could see the pattern, put together the crimes, and identify the new face.

The new man.

In a few days, a few weeks or months, the doctor, the grief collector, would become invisible. So inconspicuous that Matt wondered if he would leave the country at all. After the smallest of procedures—a chin or a nose, the color of his hair, or the addition of a mustache to break the plane of his face—he could live anywhere, even here in Los Angeles. He could walk down any street, round any corner and, with his talent, rework his identity and start building a new medical practice.

And wouldn't it be just like the doctor to want to remain close and watch from a seat in the front row as the investigation in LA sputtered and eventually went cold? Wouldn't it be amusing to live in the one city where no one would be searching for him? Wouldn't it be thrilling to settle down in a place where no one would ever guess?

But even more, wouldn't it be frightening to live in a city where the doctor could be anywhere and everywhere at any time? A man who couldn't help himself. A man who killed because he got off on killing and the horrific wake it left behind for those who survived. A brutal, sharklike man who was smart enough to know that he needed a new methodology, a new way, to feed his addictions so that he could keep moving and keep living.

What would life be like knowing that the doctor was here?

Matt thought it over, pushing his plate away and finishing off his coffee. As he set down his mug, the waitress walked over with their check.

"You guys sure don't talk much, do you? It's like you've been married for thirty years."

Matt glanced at Cabrera as they got up from the table, then gave the waitress a long look. She was staring back at him with furrowed brows and a crooked smile. She was shaking her head at him the same way his aunt might have when her intuition told her that something was up, something was going on. He tried to smile back at her but only made it halfway. He was thinking about how they had failed. He was thinking about the death of Kim Bachman and that strange feeling he never acknowledged when either Kaplin or Vega mentioned that the twenty-year-old weighed less than a hundred pounds. It had a certain bite to it. It made the darkness darker—the pit deeper. It made everything worse.

CHAPTER 55

He didn't pick up on the silver Nissan until the sun spiked his rearview mirror at the bottom of the hill on Los Feliz Boulevard. He had just eased onto the entrance ramp to the 5 Freeway, heading for Laura's house in Glendale and the only place that he felt comfortable right now. The truth was that he hadn't been looking for the Nissan since his release from the hospital. He thought that the man had gone away. With everything that had happened, with everything that Matt had learned, even in the past few hours, the man in the silver Nissan seemed like the least of his worries.

Yet he was still here. Two cars back and tailing him.

For what possible reason?

In another hour it would be dark, and Matt had planned to spend what was left of the afternoon reviewing preliminary files on Dr. Baylor's background that the FBI had made available to him on the Internet. He had been given a password by Kaplin, and they had exchanged cell phone numbers. At least for now, it seemed as if both Kaplin and Vega wanted him in the loop.

But even more, he needed to be with Laura.

He needed to see her and touch her. He needed to hold her body close to his body. He needed to bask in her presence and live beneath her spell.

He checked the mirror as he slid into the first lane and picked up speed. The piece of shit was still on him. Still there.

Why?

Matt dug into his pocket for the pack of nicotine gum, pushing a piece through the foil and pressing it between his cheek and gum. He had been strong. As he and Cabrera were leaving the restaurant, his feelings for the victim in New Orleans and his own sense of personal failure had boiled up into a full-blown rage. He could have easily followed his partner into the minimarket and bought a pack of cigarettes. Instead, he found a way past the moment and drove off.

But now that moment was over, his strength beaten back by someone he didn't even know. An intruder violating his space, his privacy, his being and time.

He took a deep breath and exhaled. He tried to settle down and let the nicotine wash through his bloodstream. It didn't take long. Within a minute or two he could feel his mind beginning to clear and sharpen, his senses awakening.

He looked up and down the freeway, then across the lanes. There was too much traffic to outrun the Nissan. Too many chances that someone innocent might get hurt. As he passed beneath Colorado Boulevard and saw the signs for the 134 Freeway just ahead, it occurred to him that there weren't too many people left that the man in the silver Nissan could be working for. Grace wasn't in a position to even talk, much less hire a pair of shoes to keep watch for him. Orlando and Plank had hit the finish line and would never bother anyone again. The idea that McKensie might somehow be involved seemed ludicrous, off the charts, not worth wasting time over. And while it could be some sort of vendetta by a friend or relative of someone for the way things played out, it seemed more likely that the man following him had something to do with Dr. Baylor.

It had never occurred to him before, and he tossed it over—the doctor keeping watch on him from the beginning.

Why had the doctor saved his life? The question still plagued him, still made him feel uneasy. Why had the doctor taken the time to treat Matt's gunshot wound when he could have easily walked away and made his escape? Was the man in the silver Nissan a threat? Or was the situation benign and just an attempt by the doctor to keep an eye on him even now? Matt might have found the idea intriguing a half hour ago at the restaurant, but could it be possible that the doctor really was planning a return to Los Angeles?

Matt remembered walking up to the car when the man was watching his house that night in the fog. He could still see the .38 revolver resting on the console between the bucket seats. But he could also remember thinking that nothing about this guy or the car he was sitting in felt like any version of law enforcement, either public or private. It was something else. Something he couldn't put his finger on. The man was in his late thirties or early forties, on the chunky side, with a receding hairline. A white male with brown hair and a face so soft and plain that it would have been difficult to pick him out of a lineup. He remembered the striped tie, the glow of a cigarette burning between the man's fat fingers, the lack of any visible wear or tear on his hands or forehead or even around his eyes.

Matt slowed the car down enough to match the speed of traffic in the next lane. When he reached the 134 Freeway, he passed the eastbound entrance to Glendale and headed west. After finding the Nissan in his rearview mirror, he used his turn signal and exited onto Lankershim Boulevard.

He'd come to a decision. Probably a bad decision, but a decision nonetheless.

He would work his way through surface streets, heading for North Hollywood Park and the spot where Faith Novakoff's body had been found. He would take his time and act as if he had no idea that he had company. He wanted to lure the man out of his car. He wanted to confront him, but he knew that he needed privacy to do it. The park offered the cover of tall trees and dense brush. Even more, the steady sound of traffic from the freeway on the other side of the woods would mask the kind of conversation he had in mind.

Matt spotted the park, made a left on Tujunga Avenue, and after a block pulled over. He didn't see anyone on the lawns and guessed that with the sun beginning to set, few people if any would venture off the sidewalks or away from the overhead streetlights. After all, there had been a murder here. The story remained above the fold on page one of the *Los Angeles Times*, with no end in sight. The girl's death still had to be on everybody's mind.

Matt checked his rearview mirror and saw the man in the silver Nissan waiting at the corner. Digging his cell phone out of his pocket, Matt pretended to make a call and started across the lawn, hoping that he looked preoccupied and distracted. He couldn't afford to check his back. But once he disappeared behind the tree line, he shoved the phone into his pocket and began running toward the girl's memorial as fast as he could. A full sprint all the way down the long row of trees. He stopped to catch his breath, glancing at the fresh flowers and battery-powered candles, all the notes and photographs. He thought about the girl's father, the preacher with the gun who ended up in the backseat of his Mercedes with a crack pipe and a fifteen-year-old boy—but only for a moment or two. Then he slipped into the bushes behind the trunk of a large oak tree, drew his .45, and waited to see if the man in the silver Nissan was curious enough to get out of his car.

Five or six minutes passed before Matt thought he heard something. He knelt down and peered beneath the branches. And then he flashed a grim smile. He could see the man's chubby legs in the distance. He was moving quickly, taking a few steps, then slowing down, then bursting forward again.

The man in the silver Nissan had picked the wrong day to get out of his car.

Matt parted the leaves slightly and watched as his follower appeared at the other end of the aisle and started up the row of trees. The guy seemed nervous. Jumpy. He kept checking his back. He kept slowing down, his eyes flicking left and right, and finally spotting the memorial just ahead. Matt quieted his breathing and became very still. They were less than six feet away from each other. He noted the gun in the man's right hand, the .38. He could see the man turning his back to get a better look at the girl's memorial. He could hear the man trying to catch his breath over the din from the freeway on the other side of the trees.

He'd picked the wrong day.

Matt raised his .45, took two steps forward, and pressed the muzzle into the back of the man's head. The man yelped and nearly jumped out of his skin. Then Matt double-checked the lawn. It was starting to get dark. They were alone.

"Nice and easy," he said. "Drop the fucking piece."

The man tossed his .38 on the grass. Matt picked it up and slid it behind his belt.

"Now get down on your knees."

"Please," the man said in a shaky voice. "Please don't hurt me. Why do I have to get down on my knees? What are you gonna do to me?"

Matt pushed him over, and he rolled onto his back. The man raised his hands, his entire body trembling in the grass. His eyes kept flicking between the .45 and Matt's face.

"Who are you?" Matt said. "Why have you been following me?"

The man shook his head back and forth, like he didn't want to talk about it. Like he couldn't.

Matt prodded him with his foot. "Who are you?" he repeated.

The man shrieked and gasped for air. "I can't," he said quickly. "I made a mistake. If you let me go, I'll never bother you again. I swear I won't. Just don't hurt me."

Matt stood over the man as he chewed it over, his pistol aimed at the guy's chest. He didn't know what to make of the situation. He couldn't get a decent read on the guy and wondered if he should just call McKensie and have him picked up and taken in.

"Are you working for Baylor?" he said.

"Just let me go. I'll never bother you again. Please. You're a cop. Do the right thing."

Matt narrowed his eyes. "How did you know that I'm a cop? You're working for Baylor. What does he want?"

The man remained quiet, refusing to speak.

Matt realized that no matter what secrets his follower might hold, no matter what answers, he didn't like him. He took a step closer. He was losing his patience. As his left hand swept around his belt, he remembered that he had been put on leave. His hand-cuffs were on the chest of drawers in Laura's bedroom.

"Okay," he said. "Okay. Here's what's gonna happen next. You listening, pal?"

The guy nodded.

"Good," he said. "Because I'll only say it once. I'm gonna search you, mister. While I'm searching you, my .45 will be pointed at your chest. And that's why you're gonna lay back in the grass and pretend you're dead. One move, one *anything*, and I'll blow your heart out of your chest. Got it?"

The man must have been visualizing the gunshot. His eyes snapped wide open, and he nodded again, fast and nervous and scared shitless.

Matt held his gaze as he moved closer. "Be good, mister. Be smart. Play dead and live to see another day. Get stupid, and it's the last thing you'll ever fucking do."

He knelt down and worked quickly. A one-handed search from top to bottom. He tossed the keys to the silver Nissan in the grass, the man's wallet and his cell phone, his cigarettes and lighter and a pocketful of spare change, then checked his waist and legs for another weapon. When he felt satisfied that the man was unarmed, he grabbed the wallet, stood up, and backed twenty feet away.

The headlights from the cars and trucks on the freeway were bouncing off the trees and flickering through the canopy of leaves. After glancing back at the man on the ground, he opened the wallet and turned it into the light.

His name was Billy Casper, like the ghost, and according to his driver's license he was from out of town.

San Francisco.

It seemed odd.

Matt went through his cards but didn't find a license for the gun or anything that might identify Casper as a private investigator. Just twenty-three bucks, two credit cards, and an ATM card issued from Wells Fargo Bank. But it was the wallet itself that Matt found the most telling. The leather was cracked and worn out. Most people would have replaced it a long time ago. Billy Casper hadn't.

"How's business, Billy?"

Casper didn't say anything, his big eyes still locked on Matt and the .45 pointed at his chest.

Matt tossed the wallet in the grass and stepped closer. He looked at the clothes Casper was wearing: the frayed shirt collar, the wrinkled slacks, the same striped tie that he'd seen before. As he looked back at the big man's face, he noted the two-day beard and the hint of body odor wafting in the air. When he checked his hands, his fingers, he didn't see a wedding band.

And then a pair of images surfaced in Matt's mind, uninvited and ill timed—the before and after shots of Heidi Bachman's daughter, Kim. He could see each photograph so clearly. He tried to concentrate on what the girl looked like before her murder. He tried to think of her drinking that beer at the bar in the French Quarter and laughing with her friends. He tried to push away the second photograph, the close-up of her face that had been taken at the coroner's office. He tried with all his might but knew that like the victim's mother, he too would never be able to see the girl any other way again.

He looked at Casper. Just the sight of the man brought on a torrent of anger. He tried to settle down. He turned away, then turned back. He could hear those words playing in his head again.

She weighed less than a hundred pounds.

When he finally spoke, he saw Casper flinch and knew that something about his own voice and demeanor had changed. It was the mainspring inside his gut, he figured. The main wheel. Something about the way it turned had changed enough to frighten Casper. The safety switch was off.

Matt filled his lungs with air and exhaled. "You're not a private investigator, Billy. You're obviously not law enforcement. You're just a guy with a gun who keeps winding up in my rearview mirror."

Casper pricked up his ears and froze, then began stammering. "Please, Jones. You'll never see me again. I swear."

Matt laughed, then knelt down beside Casper and lowered his voice as he thought it through. "Why would Baylor pull you out of San Francisco? You must have a history. You and the doctor must go way back. I'll bet you know everything. I'll bet that you're a part of everything. You know what he did because you were there. It makes sense that he would have needed help."

"Jesus Christ, Jones. Please. I don't know anything. Put the fucking gun away."

A moment passed, the light churning through the tree branches, the candles set on the ground glowing like a campfire. The wind had picked up—a dry, unforgiving wind—and Matt listened to the rushing sound of the leaves as he turned and gazed at the memorial to Faith Novakoff. Her picture had been stapled to the trunk of the tree where she lost her life.

Hallowed ground, he kept thinking. Hallowed ground. She seemed so innocent. So young and pretty.

He turned back to Billy Casper, who had been watching him. "Where is he, Casper?" he said in a dark voice. "Where's Dr. Baylor?"

Sweat had begun to drip from the big man's forehead, and his shirt was stained across his belly and underneath his arms. He couldn't stop trembling, shivering in the heat.

Matt pointed the .45 at his chest and slapped him across the face. "How does he pay you? How do you communicate? When was the last time you talked?"

Casper shook his head back and forth. Matt slapped him again, harder this time. Then again and again.

"Where is he, Casper? What does he want with me?"

The big man shook his head one more time, still refusing to say anything. Matt felt himself losing control, thought about that safety switch, and decided to roll with it. He traded the .45 for Casper's .38 revolver, left a single round in the cylinder, and gave it a spin. Then he cocked the hammer with his thumb and moved in.

"It's not your night," Matt said. "It's not gonna work out for you, Billy. You're not gonna make it."

Casper panicked, his eyes glassy. "No, no, no."

Matt jammed the muzzle into his mouth. "Where is he?"

Casper clamped his eyes shut and started weeping, mumbling, writhing on the grass. "No, no, no."

Matt pulled the trigger.

It felt like the air had been sucked out of the entire park in a single instant. A long moment passed. Just silence, just stillness, and that din from the freeway on the other side of the trees that seemed to have faded into nowhere—into utter silence.

Casper opened his eyes, batting his lids as he gazed up at the light in the trees. Matt grabbed his chin, turning his head back and staring at him face to face.

"Where's Baylor, Casper?"

The weeping came back like rain, and Casper couldn't seem to catch his breath or swallow. "Please, Jones. Please."

"Fuck you, Casper."

Matt gave the cylinder another spin, pulled back the hammer, and jammed the muzzle into the man's mouth.

"Where is he?"

Casper's body wriggled in terror. "No, no, no."

Matt pinned him to the ground and pulled the trigger. His heart almost stopped, and he grimaced. He watched Casper's body freeze up, then start squirming beneath him when he didn't hear the sound of a gunshot.

Matt didn't care anymore. Casper was in on it. Things were in motion. It was too late to stop.

"Where is he?" Matt said. "What does he want with me?"

"I'll go away, Jones. Jesus Christ, I'll go away."

Matt gave the cylinder a third spin and jammed the muzzle into Casper's mouth. "Where is he?"

When he pulled back the hammer, Casper's eyes spun out like a slot machine, and he soiled himself. Tears streamed down his cheeks, his words garbled.

"Okay, okay, okay. I'll talk, Jones, I'll talk. Just don't pull the trigger."

Matt eased the gun out of Casper's mouth and watched as the big man tried to pull himself together. His chest was heaving, and it looked like he was taking a leak in his pants.

"Where is he, Casper?"

Casper wiped the tears off his cheeks, his hands quivering. He rolled onto his side and leaned on an elbow. When he spotted his cigarettes and lighter in the grass, he looked at Matt for permission, then grabbed them and tried to light up through the jitters. It took several tries. Once he managed to touch the flame to the end of the cigarette, he took a deep drag and exhaled. His eyes were wagging back and forth across the grass, his wheels turning. When he spoke, his voice sounded weak and tired and drenched in hopelessness.

"I have no fucking idea where he is, Jones."

"That's not good enough, Casper. Not tonight it isn't. It won't even buy you another five minutes."

Casper looked at him as he took a second long pull on the smoke and exhaled. "It's not my job to know where Baylor is. It's not in my job description."

"Then how do you get paid?"

Casper paused again, taking another quick drag. "You don't get it yet, that's all."

"Get what, Casper?"

"Who I'm working for."

"The doctor."

Casper shook his head, staring back at Matt with an odd glint in his eye. "Nope, it's not Baylor. I've never met the man in my life."

Casper crossed himself, as if not meeting the doctor had been a blessing.

Matt gave him a long look. "Okay," he said. "Okay. So if you're not working for Baylor, who's signing your checks?"

"That's the hard part. You're not gonna like it."

Matt pointed the .38 at Casper's head and pulled back the hammer. "Who is it, Casper? Who's signing the checks?"

"Life isn't easy, Jones."

"It sure beats dying. Now tell me who you're working for. And don't say it's McKensie."

Casper turned, met his eyes, and held the gaze. "I don't know who McKensie is," he said finally. "I'm working for your father. Your old man. M. Trevor Jones, the King of Wall Street."

Time stopped.

And everything about the night turned wretched, even the dappled light from the trees and that swirling wind that seemed to choke up in midair.

If Casper had mentioned anybody else, any other human being, it could have been a play. If he had, it could have been a play.

But not now.

Matt released the hammer and lowered the gun. He wasn't sure how long he sat there before Casper lit another cigarette and finally started talking again. He couldn't feel anything. The blow had hit him too hard and too deep. Everything about the moment seemed too close and too real.

Casper cleared his throat. "It was the security cameras," he said in a low voice. "The cameras picked you up at your old man's place in Connecticut the last time you were there, Jones. I was given your name and a photograph and some idea of where you were. But the truth is, I didn't really put it together until I saw you, until I did my own research. You look just like him. Now everything makes sense."

"Everything makes sense?"

Casper nodded slowly. "Your father wants to know that his reputation will be kept safe. He wants you to stay away from him and his family. He wants some assurance that you'll never come back to his house again. That you won't make any more phone calls to his office, or attempt to reach him in any way."

"That was a long time ago, Casper."

"Yes, it was. You'd just come back from Afghanistan. But things have changed over the past five years. You're starting to make a name for yourself. Pictures of your face have been printed in every newspaper from here to New York City. Your name and image are all over TV and the Internet, and have been ever since you took your first case. What was the kid's name? The three-piece bandit? The kid who was out of work for so long and had a wife and newborn son?"

"Sean Hudson."

"That's it—Hudson. That story's still running, Jones. And now we've got an LAPD lieutenant and two detectives out of Hollywood who gunned down your best friend and murdered his partner. Even worse, we've got a nationwide manhunt underway for a doctor, a madman, who likes to rape and kill college girls. You see where I'm going, right? Your father would like you to consider changing jobs to something with a smaller profile, or better yet, something with no profile at all. You need to cut the guy a break and see it the way he does. You need to put yourself in your father's shoes. Like I said, I did my research—enough to know what's what and who's who, and after that, I'm pretty sure I can fill in most of the blanks. Your father's a brand name, a VIP, Jones. It would embarrass him if you were to come forward now. It would hurt his reputation if anyone knew that he abandoned his wife and son. It would damage the brand if anyone found out that your mother died of cancer, and your father didn't care enough to help either one of you out. It's an old story. It's easy enough to understand. His second wife came from money. She didn't have the looks your mother had and probably couldn't match her personality or intelligence. But her father was in the business, had connections, and made things happen for him. Your old man did exactly what a lot of people who are smarter than everybody else do every day. He saw an opportunity and he took it. And look what happened. Jesus Christ, look how it paid off. According to *Money* magazine, he's worth more than a billion dollars."

It hung there, twisting from the tree in the dark of night.

The words. The pain. His mother's angelic face. Matt could feel her arms around him as he sat on her lap. He could hear her voice, so gentle and soothing, as he snuggled in and laid his head on her soft breast. But he could also feel the jolt he'd taken as he watched his father walk out the door with his suitcase. He could still see the man getting into his car and driving off without even looking back. He could still remember the sound of his mother's tears as he woke up in the middle of the night and heard her weeping through the wall.

Matt looked at Casper, lying on the grass in his soiled clothing. The man seemed relieved. Deeply shaken and a night or two past being burned out, but relieved.

"It's simple," Casper went on. "Your father wants to know what it will take to keep your silence."

"What it will take?"

"It's all about money, Jones. It's always about money. Your old man needs to know how much you want."

"How much I want?"

"Look at it like this," Casper said. "You've just won the lotto. It's your lucky day, kid."

Matt shook his head, thinking that he might vomit. That he needed a shower. That his father, dear old Dad, was every bit as vile as he had always thought he was. He looked back at Billy Casper, the man his father had chosen to deliver the message. Somehow it made him feel better—the idea that regardless of social standing, deadbeats work with deadbeats, because they share some sort of perverted attraction for each other. The idea that the doctor, no matter how irrational or insane, had been right when talking about the parents of his victims. It was never about how much they had. Instead, it was all about who they were.

Matt gathered up the five bullets in the grass, got to his feet with the .38 in his hand, popped open the cylinder, and tossed all six rounds into the woods. He was thinking things over, the words he wanted to use.

"Tell him," he said finally. "Tell him that you made a mistake, and I turned out to be the wrong guy. He has no worries, Casper. I have no intention of ever trying to communicate with him again. As far as I'm concerned, my father died with my mother a long time ago."

"Give me a break, Jones. You'll be rich. All the man wants is your word that you'll keep your mouth shut about where you came from. His reputation's at stake. He wants your help, and he's willing to pay for it."

He wants your help, and he's willing to pay for it.

Matt almost laughed. His father's request seemed so absurd and tainted, so dark and mean. The man had given him nothing, and now he wanted everything. Did his father, the King of Wall Street, really think that he would succeed? Was he so out of touch and full of himself, so rich and powerful that he thought he could buy his own son's soul?

It took Matt's breath away. The various shades of evil that he'd been forced to witness and confront over such a short time. One monster after the next, until he'd reached three in a row.

Grace and Baylor, and now his own blood, M. Trevor Jones.

He shot Casper a hard look, then pitched the .38 into the brush ten to twenty feet away from the six bullets.

"Okay," he said in a low voice. "Okay. If that's not good enough, Casper, then tell him the truth. Tell him that nobody's safe and all bets are off. Tell him that it's a dangerous world out there. He should know all about it. He's one of the shitheads who helped fuck everything up."

CHAPTER 56

She was wearing that raspberry-colored bra he'd seen hanging on the chair a few weeks ago. Something about the color brought out the smoke in those dark blue eyes of hers.

He gave her another long look.

Even in the places where the candlelight couldn't reach, her face seemed to radiate a certain warmth that he had never seen or experienced before. They were already so comfortable with each other—they had been through so much and managed to survive—that there were times when he didn't feel the need to say anything to her. It worked like magic. Whatever might be on his mind, she already seemed to know.

He kissed her as he unhooked her bra and pulled it away from her breasts, swaying in the air. Then he gazed down at her hands, her long, elegant fingers, and watched as she unzipped his jeans, slid them over his legs and feet, and tossed them on the floor. After she pulled away his boxer shorts, she rolled over onto her back, her tangled blond hair cascading off the pillow. And then she smiled at him. It was a gentle smile. The kind of smile that felt like it was emanating from her entire being. When they embraced, when his chest met hers, when he filled his lungs with the scent of her body, when their stomachs and legs rubbed against each other—skin on skin—all wounds were healed and he reached that special place he'd been looking for but had never found.

Pure joy. Pure ecstasy.

The next half hour rushed by in a wondrous blur, the electricity playing with his senses and singeing them. And then there was a different kind of joy. A different kind of ecstasy—quiet and still, with everything in the world at rest.

Matt looked up and watched the light from the candle dancing across the ceiling. He wondered if what they had together wasn't heaven-sent. He wondered about his own beliefs and whether or not there could be an afterlife. With all of the cruelty in this world, the senseless violence, the will to power and money, the sheer ignorance of the few and of the many, the existence of an afterlife didn't seem very likely. Yet there were times when Matt couldn't help thinking that Kevin was with them. That somehow his lost friend had found a way through the void to give them his blessing, particularly after they made love.

Matt concentrated on his breathing and exhaled slowly. In spite of the good feeling, his mind had already started going again. The things he'd seen over the course of his life, and that long list of certainties that still didn't feel all that certain. He looked over at Laura and realized that she had been studying his face. She smiled at him, visibly curious.

"Something's wrong," she said.

Matt shook his head. "Everything's good. Better than good."

"No, it isn't. I can tell it isn't. I was watching you."

He rolled over and looked up at the light on the ceiling again. The flickering shapes moving back and forth seemed to quiet his mind, almost as if he had begun a new meditation. But then Laura threw her leg over his thigh and brushed her fingers through his hair—face to face, eye to eye.

"You're thinking about the girl you told me about," she whispered. "The one who died in New Orleans."

"Kim Bachman," he said.

"It's not your fault, Matt. You're not responsible for her murder."

Matt glanced at her and nodded. "I know."

"There's nothing you could have done any differently. By the time you found out who Baylor was, you were bleeding to death, and he was feeding you an anesthetic."

"You mean *we*, don't you? We found out together."

She lowered her head to the pillow, her eyes losing their focus. "There's nothing more we could have done. We were lucky we survived. And now, after everything, we're together and not alone. We have a chance to get through this. I don't know how long it'll take to forget what's happened, but we have a chance to make something out of our lives and move on."

He kissed her. "You're right," he said. "We have a chance to forget. A chance to move on. It's just the idea that he was right beside me the whole time. That if I'd known I could have stopped him, and Kim Bachman would still be alive."

"Maybe," she whispered. "But think of who you're talking about. It's still only a maybe."

She closed her eyes. Matt could feel her body beginning to let go and started smoothing his hand over her back and easing her into sleep. When her breathing slowed, he sat up and reached for what was left of a glass of bourbon on the bedside table. Laura had been through enough, and he didn't want to worry her. He didn't want her to see his face or read his mind. What was keeping him up tonight didn't have much to do with Baylor, or even the girl the doctor had murdered in New Orleans.

It was his shadow, his follower. The man with the gun who kept showing up in his rearview mirror.

Billy Casper.

The man with the dull face who wore shabby clothing, needed a new wallet, and had the ability to melt into the crowd. A man with a gun who wasn't a private investigator or a cop but understood how to become invisible and practiced the art, albeit with mixed results.

Matt took a sip from the glass, savoring the bourbon as it lit up his throat and warmed his stomach.

Something about what happened in the park tonight was off. Matt could feel it in his bones. Something about what happened tonight was way off.

A memory surfaced, an old one—words of advice from his sergeant on the last night he spent in the States before his flight to Germany, and then Afghanistan. His sergeant had always shown a special interest in him. That night he asked him into the office but didn't give a reason. It turned out that he wanted to show Matt a scene from a movie directed by Stanley Kubrick called *Full Metal Jacket*. The clip his sergeant wanted him to see was a joyride in a chopper over Vietnam in which a soldier fires his machine gun at anything and everything he sees moving on the ground. At first glance, Matt took it as a typical Hollywood exaggeration. But when the scene ended, his sergeant switched off the movie and had other ideas. He said that most fatalities in Afghanistan were occurring in the first few months of a soldier's tour of duty, because it takes that much time to figure out what he called *the golden rule*: when in combat with an enemy who isn't wearing a uniform, no matter where you are in the world, shoot first and think later. Don't use your fucking brain, Jones. Use your eyes and ears and pull the goddamn trigger.

His sergeant's advice had saved his life many times, including the night he'd emptied two mags into Edward Plank here on the lawn by Laura's garage. Still, he wondered why the memory surfaced and seemed so vivid tonight.

He found his boxer shorts and got out of bed, then walked over to the window and took another sip of bourbon as he gazed outside. That dry wind was still up, the trees bending and creaking, the night clear enough that he could see the Library Tower standing tall over downtown Los Angeles.

No doubt about it, his father's messenger, his father's hire, was a lowlife in need of money. So why had Casper waited so long to deliver the message? That was the catch, right? That was the warning beacon, the glitch that sent the train off the tracks. Why did the big man wait so long? Matt had been mulling it over ever since he left the park and still couldn't come up with an answer that made any sense.

Why did Casper risk losing his life while Matt stuffed that .38 into his mouth and pulled the trigger? He took it twice. He took it hard. Why did Casper refuse to talk under that kind of pressure? Why would he have gone through any of what happened out there when just a few minutes later he was admitting that he worked for Matt's father? That he was acting as his agent and trying to broker a deal to keep Matt quiet and out of the way?

The cadence was off. Everything about it was off.

As Matt thought it through, he realized that the ruse began the moment he pulled over to the side of the road. He may have wanted to lure Casper out of his car, but the fact that the man actually followed Matt into the park just as the sun was setting—

Matt took another sip of bourbon.

Casper wouldn't have done it. If he had been trying to buy Matt's silence, if his story had been genuine, he would have picked another time and place. He wouldn't have followed him into the park at night.

No one would.

Matt had wanted to confront Casper and thought that he needed privacy to do it. He had picked North Hollywood Park because of the trees and brush, the sounds of the freeway, and a hunch that few people had the stones to wander off the sidewalks in a place where a girl's murder was still on everybody's mind.

A beat went by, and then another.

It dawned on Matt that Casper could have wanted the same things—the trees and brush and the din of freeway traffic to mask the sound. It dawned on him that the big man had a legitimate reason for getting out of his car. That following Matt into the woods at night wasn't a mistake after all.

Matt could feel the hair on the back of his neck beginning to stand on end. He could see it now. He could see it.

Casper wasn't there to cut a deal between dear old Dad and his long-lost son. The slob had taken the risk of eating his own gun because there had never been a deal, and M. Trevor Jones couldn't afford to be connected with what was supposed to transpire tonight in any way.

Casper had botched it. He'd taken all that he could take, two pulls of the trigger, then spilled out who he was working for to save his own skin. He'd taken all that he could take, then made the mistake of letting Matt know who was really signing his paycheck.

Matt took a heavier swig from the glass as another uncertainty finally became certain. He could remember Casper saying that his father wanted Matt to take a job with a lower profile or, even better, no profile at all.

No profile at all.

It had been a hit, and Casper had blown it. Matt had taken him from behind at gunpoint, ordering Casper to drop his .38 before he could use it.

Moments passed. Matt shook his head as he thought it through a second time and realized that this was the only explanation that filled in all the blanks. His father had paid Billy Casper to kill him in order to preserve his reputation on Wall Street. His father wanted him dead in order to prevent anyone from finding out that he had abandoned his wife and son.

His father wanted him dead.

It hung there, all of it, in the candlelight and in the shadows, and on a night in late October when the dry wind howled. His father wanted him dead. His father wanted him—

Matt finally noticed his cell phone vibrating in the background. He found his jeans on the floor and fished the phone out of his pocket. It was McKensie, calling after midnight. His father wanted him—

"Bob Grace is dead," McKensie said in a raspy voice.

Matt checked on Laura. In spite of the phone knocking against the floor, she was still sleeping. He moved back to the window, unable to slow down his mind.

"How?" he said.

"The same way Ron Harris died, Jones. He tied a sheet around his neck and pushed himself off the bed. I always thought he was a coward."

Matt didn't say anything for a long time. He was thinking about his father, his father wanting him dead.

"Are you there, Jones? Are you there?"

"Yeah," Matt said. "Did he leave a note?"

"We didn't find one."

"Are you sure he did it himself?"

"You know, I thought the same thing. For what he ended up doing to the department, I'd guess plenty of guys on our side would have offered to tie the knot for him."

"But we'll never know, will we, Lieutenant? We'll never know, because there's no note."

McKensie paused, as if taking a hit on a cigarette. When he finally spoke, Matt could hear the sarcasm in his voice.

"That's right, Jones. We never will. I'm just glad that the motherfucker's dead. I figured you would be, too."

McKensie hung up. Matt listened to the digital hum for several moments before switching off his cell. He could see the irony in the way Grace had followed his first victim, an innocent Ron Harris, dying in the same place, perhaps even the same cell, by his own hand. If he let the thought continue, he could see the possibility that Grace was murdered and had nothing to do with his own death at all. Still, nothing about the news of Grace's passing was strong enough to wipe out what had happened in the park tonight with Billy Casper.

Matt sat down on the bed, glanced over at Laura, and knocked back the last of his bourbon. He wondered if he should go downstairs and pour another. It was just a guess, but he didn't think he'd sleep much tonight. His father wanted him dead.

CHAPTER 57

He stood up and looked out the window from Kevin's study on the second floor of the house. He could see Laura in the backyard by the pool cleaning up the fallen branches and leaves from last night's windstorm. He was checking on her. It probably wasn't necessary. Still, he needed some assurance that everything was okay.

After a long, sleepless night, Matt had come to a single conclusion: in spite of the risks, in spite of the fact that Casper had mentioned Matt's father by name and revealed his motive, in spite of everything, Casper's obvious need for cash would override his ability to reason, and he would make another attempt on Matt's life.

Matt was certain of it. That's why that memory had surfaced last night, the lesson his sergeant had passed on to him, *the golden rule*. That's why the memory had seemed so vivid.

He'd made a mistake and broken the rule.

The context and setting might have provided a certain degree of cover, but Casper's purpose had been palpable enough that Matt should have caught on from the very beginning. He'd realized about twelve hours too late that he should have reloaded the

.38 and pulled the trigger one more time. He should have sent his father a message. One crude enough that he might understand, especially if it came directly to his office in an overnight FedEx box.

He should have sent him Casper's head.

But now the water was muddy. Because of the way he'd shot Plank he couldn't tell McKensie what had happened—he couldn't tell anyone, even Laura—without raising more doubts about his own frame of mind. Who would believe his story? Who would believe that his father, a man he hadn't spoken to since childhood, a man of wealth, power, and prestige, had hired a lowlife like Billy Casper and was trying to kill him? Would anyone even believe that M. Trevor Jones was his father at all? They shared the same name, and no one could deny the obvious likeness—sure, it could be proven with a blood test—but how many lawyers and PR firms and doctors on the take would be standing in the way? How many years and how much money had his father already spent in deleting their history and writing a new one?

Even more important, what would the LAPD psychiatrists in Chinatown think? What would be their first impression of him? Their first take? That he was a head case? That what went down over the past few weeks triggered delusions and a serious bout with post-traumatic stress disorder? If he became tagged with PTSD, wouldn't that follow him around for the rest of his career? Wouldn't his work, his being, always be shrouded in doubt and riddled with asterisks? Wouldn't his return to the homicide table be delayed? Couldn't his story and the rumors that would go with it snowball into something where he never worked another homicide case again?

Worse still, wouldn't that be his father's goal? A goal worth fighting for. A goal worth *paying* for.

Matt let the bottom line settle in for a while. He needed to pull himself together and stay focused. He needed to keep his mind free of distractions. He needed to keep an eye out for Billy Casper, and if they ever met again, put him in the ground.

A moment passed.

He couldn't believe what he was thinking and tried to shake it off. What he'd done to Plank might have been overkill, but it was righteous. What he'd just been thinking of doing to Casper was something else.

What was happening to him? What was he becoming? Was it really true that we become what we hate most?

He gave Laura another look, then took a sip of coffee and returned to the worktable, where he had set up his laptop beside Kevin's. The preliminary reports the FBI had put together on Dr. Baylor's background were further along than he expected. To his delight, the link he had been given opened a file that was essentially live and had the same feel as the chronological record in a murder book. When any member of the team learned something new or had a thought or question that seemed relevant, it was added to the file, then stamped with the agent's electronic signature, along with the time and date. For all intents and purposes, the file worked like every other blog on the Internet. Everything about it was fluid, everything current, except in this case everything was validated and a matter of record.

Matt skimmed through the entries and counted more than twenty agents working the case along with Kaplin and Vega. While Los Angeles and New Orleans remained hot spots, the investigation had expanded into the Midwest and East Coast. Just after midnight, evidence had been uncovered that seemed to suggest that the doctor had stolen his name and identity from a man who had been killed in a hit-and-run accident while jogging some fifteen years ago. The man lived in Chicago and had graduated from medical school. Six months before his death, he'd completed his internship and residency at the University of Chicago Medical Center.

Two photographs of the original Dr. George Baylor had been posted on the blog, along with a physical description provided by his last driver's license. Even though fifteen years had passed, Matt could see it clearly enough. And when he continued reading, he realized that the FBI did, too. Nothing about the original Dr. Baylor's death could have been accidental. Unless he believed in coincidence, the man had been singled out and hunted down for his name and background. By all accounts he was the perfect host for a man trying to hide his true identity and showing early signs of his predatory nature. The original Dr. Baylor had no siblings or wife, his parents were dead, and no one was left to look after his name. The two men were about the same age, their eyes and hair about the same color. Matt paged down to a photograph of the new and especially lethal Dr. Baylor. If he squinted, the two men looked like brothers.

The match was so close that the feds believed the two men might have known each other or crossed paths in some legitimate way. Because of their age, they might have even attended the same medical school, sat in the same classroom, or worked in the same lab.

Matt took another sip of coffee and looked at the rays of sunlight spilling through the window onto the carpet. Something about the idea that the doctor had stolen his name and identity fascinated him. According to the blog, three years passed before the new Dr. Baylor finally surfaced. Chicago was long gone by then, the doctor having moved to Los Angeles to begin his medical practice.

So what was the new Dr. Baylor hiding? What was he running from?

It had to be something horrific. Something he needed to get rid of; something that occurred in the first thirty years of his life that needed to be erased; something so devastating that he saw killing his own identity, and another person, as his only way out.

Matt pulled the computer closer and continued reading. An agent working out of Washington was trying to piece together a profile of the new Dr. Baylor by examining his bills and credit card receipts. The process would take time to complete but had already shown promise and seemed to indicate that once a year the new Dr. Baylor spent two weeks on the East Coast. Using the Ritz-Carlton in New York City as his base, he spent three days in Princeton, New Jersey, and another three days in Greenwich, Connecticut. Because the trips were identical and occurred annually over fifteen years, the agent believed that the locations might point to the doctor's original identity.

Matt wondered if their paths had ever crossed. Princeton was only fifteen minutes north of Pennington, the town where he had lived with his aunt. They did their grocery shopping in Princeton. His doctor and dentist were located in Princeton. Matt used the library at the university on a regular basis for years. He sifted through his memory and began to feel uneasy. When he read the following post, his concern only intensified.

The doctor had managed to escape from a burning house and vanish before their eyes but hadn't made a single attempt to withdraw money from his bank or even borrow against a credit card. An examination of his accounts, a lack of assets or any investments at all, only seemed to raise more questions. His home on Toluca Lake Avenue had been worth millions of dollars. Baylor had paid for the property in cash, then applied for a loan equal to the value of the house. It seemed clear that he preferred living off the bank's money rather than his own. But even more, no one could tell where the money from the loan went after the first year. No one could even say what happened to the funds he earned from his practice each month. Once the money was deposited into his checking account and his bills were paid, anything over twenty-five-thousand dollars was withdrawn in a wire transfer. Every single dollar over a balance of twenty-five grand disappeared.

Matt didn't understand why the agent who posted the information was confused. It seemed so obvious. It was an insurance policy, his life as Dr. George Baylor a shell. Either the doctor had a second false identity, or his real identity remained active and was clean enough that he could still bank his money there and feel safe about it.

His real identity.

Why had the doctor taken the time to save his life? What was he doing so close to home in New Jersey? And what about Greenwich, Connecticut?

Matt closed his eyes. He could feel the bullet wound in his shoulder beginning to burn again. He could feel the churning in his stomach.

Why had the doctor risked his own life to save him?

Kevin's computer beeped as an e-mail was delivered to the in-box. Matt knew that Laura had been using the laptop ever since it was returned by the crime lab. But when he glanced over at the screen, he noticed that the message had been sent to Kevin and that it didn't look like spam. Even more, Matt thought that he recognized the sender's address. Seeing his lost friend's name printed on the header felt so eerie and unsettling. He stared at the screen for a moment. The e-mail address was Laura's. The words on the subject line were more than vague.

It's me, were all they said. *It's me.*

Matt wheeled the chair over for a closer look. He could remember reading an e-mail thread between her and Kevin just after his murder. They were love letters that dated back to when he and Kevin were overseas. Matt hesitated for a moment, absorbing any pangs of guilt as best he could, then pushed through it and opened the new e-mail. It was another love letter from Laura. As he read the words, feelings of confusion were overtaken by waves of sadness and a profound loss. He thought about the things Laura had said last night after they made love. The idea that they had the opportunity to forget what had happened to them, but it would take time. As he continued reading her heartfelt words, he wondered if this was part of the grieving process. He could see her writing an e-mail on her tablet, then sending it to Kevin's laptop as a way of keeping the connection open and his memory alive. He knew that many people who lose a family member keep their cell phone accounts open so that they can listen to their loved one's voice in the outgoing message and leave a new message of their own.

Matt finished reading the e-mail and settled back in the chair. He could remember the pregnancy test kit he'd seen on the windowsill in the kitchen the night he'd told Laura that Hughes was dead. He could still see her sitting at the table in her pajamas. The anguish in her eyes. The tears streaming down her cheeks. All the heartache that had risen in an instant and, in the end, would never really go away.

He looked back at the e-mail and reread the last sentence, then noticed that Laura had included an attachment. He clicked it open and realized that it was a partial view of a nude photograph. After maximizing the window, he sat back and stared at the image. He sat back and took the hit head on.

It wasn't Laura.

It was another woman.

Matt opened the thread and began skimming through the e-mails. The messages went back and forth, the last twenty-five dated *after* Kevin's death. He had been having an affair, a long-term affair, and Laura had found out about it and—

His heart skipped a beat.

The e-mails that he'd read a few weeks ago had been written to and from this woman, and she had no idea that Kevin was dead. Laura had been posing as Hughes ever since he was murdered. Laura had been pretending to be—

His cell phone started vibrating. He dug it out of his pocket and glanced at the caller's name on the screen. It was Henry Rollins, the forensic analyst from the Photographic Unit at the crime lab. Matt had sent him video images recorded by a security camera that picked up Hughes's murder from half a block away. Things had been moving so quickly, he never had the chance to follow up on it. Besides, Grace, Orlando, and Plank were all dead.

Matt switched on the phone, still skimming through the e-mails. There were hundreds of them. He'd just assumed that they'd come from Laura. If he hadn't seen the nude snapshot, he never would have guessed.

"What's up, Henry?" he said in a low voice.

"Did you think I forgot about you, Jones?"

"Are you talking about the video?"

"Yeah, I'm talking about the video."

"What's the point?" he said. "Everybody's dead."

"We've got a problem, Jones. Actually, it's more than a problem."

Matt already knew what the problem was. Hughes was having an affair, and Laura had found out about it. Fate made its move and caught up with them, and everything about what happened next cut to the bone.

"Tell me what you've got, Henry."

"I just sent you a link. Are you anywhere near your computer?"

Matt rolled the chair over to his laptop, saw the e-mail from the analyst, and clicked the link. A few seconds later the video of Hughes being robbed and shot in the parking lot behind the restaurant started playing on his screen. The images seemed clearer than he remembered. Everything appeared brighter.

"I'm on it," he said. "And you've made progress."

"I still can't identify the shooter, Jones. But I can tell you who we're ruling out."

Matt couldn't move. It felt like he was sinking into a void, a black hole, his entire world crashing into the ground and skidding

into a deep ocean. He glanced at the love letters on Hughes's laptop.
He didn't need Rollins. He didn't need anyone. He already knew.

"Well, it's not the three-piece bandit," he said quietly.

Rollins cleared his throat. "It never was the bandit. We found
that out a long time ago."

Matt shook his head, his eyes glued to the screen. "And it
doesn't look like it's Grace, Orlando, or even Eddie Plank."

"It can't be. That's why I called."

Matt shut his eyes and opened them again. He could see the
shooter aiming the Glock 20 at the black SUV and firing round
after round into Hughes's body. When the muzzle flash finally
ended, the shooter began running across the parking lot toward
the camera. Rollins had slowed the speed down to a crawl here.
Matt wondered why they had never even considered that Hughes's
murder could have been a crime of passion. That the number of
holes the coroner counted in Hughes's body added up to a lover
wronged.

"So let me have it," Matt said in a quiet voice.

"It's all about body type," Rollins said. "The picture's bright
enough that we can see it now."

"Tell me what I'm seeing."

Rollins cleared his throat again. A long moment passed.

"The shooter's a female, Jones. Look at her hips, her arms.
Look at the way she's running. The shooter's definitely a woman."

It didn't really need to settle in, but it did. Hideous and devoid
of any light or any hope. Matt switched off his phone and looked
away from the screen, still drowning in that ocean at the end of
the way. Still unable to tell the difference between up and down
or where the surface might be. He could hear words playing in his
head. A single string.

How much time would it take to forget?

As much as he had. As much as he would ever get. As much as
there was or ever would be.

A picture came to mind. Driving through the heat of the desert on a road that had no end. And then another. Kevin Hughes's unrecognizable body lying on the front seat of that black SUV, his entire corpse covered in blood and slivers of shattered glass. He could still smell the blood, the meat.

He looked out the window. Laura wasn't in the backyard anymore. He moved closer and didn't see her by the pool. When he turned, he found her standing in the doorway. Her eyes were locked on the video playing on the laptop, then all over his face.

CHAPTER 58

"You did it," he said in a quiet voice. "You shot Kevin. You murdered him."

Laura couldn't look him in the eye any longer. She lowered her head and started weeping, pleading.

"I didn't, Matt. You have to believe me. I didn't."

Matt shrugged it off and kept going. "You found out that he was doing this woman, and you killed him for it. Now tell me the truth, Laura. Tell me that you shot Kevin."

"But I didn't shoot him. I wouldn't. I couldn't."

She fell onto the couch, still weeping and trembling and struggling to catch her breath. Matt fished through his briefcase, dug out the pack of cigarettes he'd bought after his confrontation with Casper, and lit up.

"You have to believe me," she whispered. "I didn't kill anyone. I couldn't kill anyone. I'm not that kind of person."

Matt gave her a hard look. "Yes, you are," he said. "You could, and you did. You shot Kevin. It doesn't matter what he did. You murdered him. That's all that counts right now."

"No," she said, burying her face into the pillow. "Please, Matt, stop it. I loved him. He's all I ever wanted."

Matt took a pull on the cigarette and moved closer. "What's her name?"

Laura shook her head into the pillow but didn't say anything.

"Come on, Laura. You've been writing to her and pretending to be Kevin. What's her name?"

She lifted her head up and looked at him, her eyes wet and glassy. "Nicole," she said finally.

"What's her last name?"

"Jennings. She never uses her name in her e-mails."

"So who is she?"

"An old girlfriend from high school. She's in his yearbook."

"And you got her to send you a nude picture. Why?"

"I wanted to see what she looked like now."

Matt nodded. "You mean, Kevin's lover."

Laura straightened her back, her eyes turning inward, as if in a trance. "His lover," she managed. "Oh, God, Matt. I loved him so much."

"You did it, Laura. Tell me that you did it."

"Oh, God."

He shook his head at her in complete dismay. "You don't get it yet, but you will," he said. "The clock's already ticking, and we don't have time for all this back and forth. They know that Kevin was killed by a woman. They have proof that it was a woman. That means you're at the top of the list. That means you're the only one on the list. And don't think that you've got what it takes to bluff your way out of it. The case will go to a couple of bulls in Robbery-Homicide. Bulls that have seen everything from every angle ten times over. They'll see through your little act the minute you walk into the room. Even if they play by the rules, you won't stand a chance. You're still too close to it. You still can't admit to yourself what you did. And that's why it's gonna be so easy to break you,

Laura. They're gonna break you down, and they're gonna hurt you. You'll be lucky if you get life without parole. Kevin was LAPD blue. He was one of their own. The way you shot him, the way you left him, I'll bet the district attorney asks for the death penalty. And I'll bet he gets it."

She closed her eyes for a moment—fear and agony showing on her face, as if she were visualizing her own execution. Then she looked up at Matt standing over her. When she finally spoke, her voice was barely audible and she seemed panic-stricken.

"Oh, God, Matt. I did it. I shot him. I killed Kevin."

He grimaced. Hearing her say it felt like she had just taken a sharp knife and ripped open his soul. Matt took another pull on his smoke, then flicked the ash into the wastepaper basket and sat down beside her to think. He was lost in a world of bitter disappointments. Lost in a world of fear and anguish. He wasn't looking at her, just listening to her shaky voice, her hoarse whisper.

"I loved him, Matt. You've got to believe me. I loved him more than I ever loved anything or anyone. I wanted to have a child with him. A family. I wanted us to grow old together. I can't tell you what it was like when you guys were overseas. How many nights I lost sleep because I was worried that Kevin wouldn't come home. The dreams I had, the nightmares. The house felt so empty, so quiet and still. I couldn't imagine living without him. If he died over there, if he did—well, I wasn't sure I'd be able to go on. When he finally did come home, it was like a gift, a sign that everything would be the way I wanted it to be. The way I dreamed it to be. And then one afternoon I found those letters on his computer. I found out that he was cheating on me. That he was writing to this woman. That she lived in Austin, and that they were seeing each other and meeting on weekends every once in a while. That they were loving each other. That all of my worries, all of my hopes and dreams, all of my prayers had been a complete waste of time. He was doing this other woman and making a fool out of me. He was humiliating me."

"He betrayed you," Matt whispered.

She wiped her cheeks, still looking back, still in the trance.

"He humiliated me," she repeated in a firm voice. "He cheated on me and made a fool out of me. Not for a week or a month but for a long time. A real long time. I sat there and watched as everything we had together was swept away. Everything we shared turned to dust. When he touched me, when he fucked me, it didn't feel good anymore. It felt dirty. Everything about him hurt. And so I killed him. I shot him with his own gun. I'd seen the news about the three-piece bandit. I knew what it needed to look like. And so I did it. I pulled the trigger over and over again because he deserved it over and over again. And when the blame switched from the bandit to those three dirty cops in Hollywood, I took it as another gift, another sign that everything would be the way I wanted it to be. The way I dreamed it would be."

A moment passed. The way Laura dreamed it would be.

Matt took a last pull on his smoke, got to his feet, and doused the butt in his coffee mug. Then he turned back to Laura without saying anything. He was still chewing it over, still thinking it through. For several moments he tried to look at her without loving her but couldn't seem to get the ball to go over the plate.

"What did you do with the gun?" he said.

Laura didn't answer, studying his face as she mulled it over.

He shrugged. "Where is it?"

"I buried it under some flowers."

"Which flowers? Where?"

"Under the oak tree out back."

Matt glanced through the window at the oak tree, then sat down on the arm of the chair beside the worktable. "What about the things you took?"

"What things?"

"His wedding band was missing. His badge and watch and the gun he wore on his belt."

She batted her eyes, no longer showing so much gloom on her face. "Why are you asking me these questions? What does it matter now?"

Matt tried to look at her without loving her again. The exercise seemed futile, so he stopped trying.

"You shouldn't have written to that woman," he said. "Not after Kevin's death. It was a mistake. A big one. When she finds out that he's dead, she'll come forward, and they'll put it together. They'll have copies of what she wrote to him and what he wrote back. They'll have proof that you knew."

She was trying to get a read on him and seemed confused. "What are you saying, Matt?"

He paused for several moments, sizing her up. "If we're gonna make a run for it," he said finally, "if we're gonna get away with it, we need to get rid of everything you took that night."

"Oh, God, Matt. Are you saying . . . ?"

His voice hardened with determination. "You need to give me everything," he said. "Then you need to pack a small bag, one or two days' worth of clothing. Some of your makeup, but not all of it. And leave your toothbrush. If they think we're still here, it might give us an extra day or two. While you're packing, I'll dig up the gun."

He could see the joy showing on her face. The surprise and relief, the glimmer of hope. She ran across the room and threw her arms around him. She was still trembling. She still seemed overwhelmed by it all. He looked into her glazed eyes and smiled at her. And then he kissed her, gently at first, then deeper and deeper still.

"Do you mean it, Matt? Do you really mean it? Do you love me?"

He pulled her into his arms and kissed her again, but he was really thinking about Hughes. He was doing what Hughes would have wanted him to do. What a friend expects from a friend in a time of crisis.

"I'll go get the gun," he said. "You need to hurry."

Matt watched her run down the hall into her bedroom, then packed up both laptops and carried them downstairs into the kitchen. The plastic bags were in the top drawer by the fridge, and he pulled two out of the box and headed outside. As he hurried down the steps, he became overwhelmed by a feeling that someone was chasing him, that he was watching himself from a great distance. Everything before him seemed so far away. He could see himself grabbing a trowel from Laura's garden caddy. He could see the image flickering as he rushed over to the oak tree and started digging up the flowers.

The soil was fresh and loose. He found the Glock 20 about six inches down. As he stared at the pistol lying in the dirt, the oversized semiautomatic that had killed Hughes, he knew that it was yet another image he would never be able to shake. Another image just as hideous as seeing the sheet being pulled away from Brooke Anderson's ruined face at the morgue.

He pulled himself together, digging the Glock out of the earth with his hand inside the first plastic bag and dropping the weapon into the second.

He shivered and turned. A gardener was watching him from the property next door. Matt guessed that he hadn't seen the gun yet and stared at the man until he turned away. Then he replanted the flowers and rushed back to the kitchen, shielding the gun from view with his body.

Laura was just entering the room. She was carrying a knapsack and Kevin's shaving kit, which she handed over to Matt.

"It's all there," she said. "Everything."

Her eyes went to the Glock 20 inside the plastic bag, and she looked uncomfortable and anxious. Matt unzipped the kit and found the pistol Kevin carried on his belt, his watch, and his badge.

"Where's his wedding band?"

She looked back at him but didn't answer.

"Where is it, Laura?"

She took a deep breath and exhaled. Then she reached around her neck, unfastened a chain, and handed it over. Matt dropped the chain and wedding band into the shaving kit and zipped it up.

"I'll grab the laptops," he said. "Now let's get out of here."

CHAPTER 59

Matt raced down the hill on Pacific Avenue, then slowed some as he passed Glenoaks Boulevard and another cop hiding in the lot at the Jack in the Box. Once he reached the entrance to the 134 Freeway, he gunned the Honda up the hill and slid into heavy traffic. The entrance to the Golden State Freeway was just ahead, and as he steered into the curve, he glanced down at what was left of the Los Angeles River. It wasn't much to look at even before the heat wave dug in and the wind picked up. But now it seemed more like a dry creek bed walled in with concrete that had been scarred by layer after layer of graffiti.

He looked back at the road. He thought that he could hear Laura saying something, but he couldn't make out the words. He couldn't seem to focus. In spite of the clear blue sky, it seemed like he was rolling through a thick patch of fog. Everything felt like it was upside down. He was still drowning in that ocean at the end of the way. Still watching himself from a distance. Still thinking about what it meant to be a decent friend when everything he knew and wanted had burned up before his eyes.

Laura touched his arm. "Where will we go?" she said. "What will we do?"

"I know a place," he said.

"Will we be safe?"

He nodded. "It's a special place."

"Where?"

"You'll see when we get there."

"Is it in Mexico?"

"No," he said. "That's the first place they'd look."

"Then we're going to Canada?"

He shook his head. He felt dizzy.

"It's here in California. If we're smart, if we take it easy, it'll all work out."

Matt exited off the Golden State onto Los Feliz Boulevard and started up the hill toward Hollywood.

Laura seemed concerned. "Why did you get off the freeway? Why here?"

"My bank," he said. "I have a safe-deposit box. We're gonna need cash. At least in the beginning."

Laura sat back in her seat and appeared to relax. Matt wheeled the car up and around and down again, until he reached Sunset Boulevard and made a right off Western Avenue. He was cruising. He was on autopilot.

They drove past the movie studios on Gower, then Denny's restaurant on the corner. As the street sign to Wilcox Avenue came into view, he heard Laura crying softly and turned to her. She was staring at him and appeared hurt and wounded and extremely nervous. He could see tears beginning to drip down her cheeks.

"Please, Matt, don't do this," she said.

"Don't do what?"

"What you're doing. Where you're taking me. Please don't do it."

Matt didn't say anything. He made a left on Wilcox and another left into the rear lot at the station. Then he pulled up to the building.

"You said you loved me. You said it, Matt."

"I said a lot of things."

He pushed the gearshift into Park but left the engine running. He looked around the lot, then at the rear entrance to the building. No one was around. Unfastening his seat belt, he dug his cell phone out of his pocket and sent his partner a short text message. Laura's eyes rose to his face.

"There's still time," she said. "We could get away. We could go to that place. That special place."

Matt could see that place in his head. He could see himself holding her and loving her until the end of time.

"You don't understand," he whispered to her.

"We've been through a lot, Matthew. I know that. But eventually we'd get over it. It could all work out. We could love each other and be happy."

He looked at those blue eyes of hers. Her dirty blond hair, her full lips, the near-perfect cut of her cheeks and chin. He could see himself making love to her on the stairs, on the kitchen floor, or on a blanket on the lawn by the pool.

"He was my friend," he said quietly. "And you killed him, Laura."

"But he wasn't a good man."

"Maybe he wasn't, but somebody has to pay for his death. And since you did it, it may as well be you."

"Please, Matt. I know that you love me."

"That's true, too," he said. "I love you. But at the end of the day, when everything's said and done, all I'll have left is who I am and what I want to become. At the end of the day it won't matter that I love you, that I want you, or even that I need you. At the end of the day it'll come down to this: Kevin and I were brothers in arms. We fought the good fight and somehow both of us were lucky enough to come home. He had my back, and now I've got his."

The station door opened and Cabrera started down the walkway with Lieutenant McKensie.

Laura looked at them, her hands trembling, then turned back to Matt with tears still streaming down her cheeks.

"Please, Matthew. Don't do this. Tell them that you made a mistake. I'm in love with you. I can't live without you."

A moment passed with Matt staring at the fork in the road. Everything swimming in his chest, his guts. Everything ripped out.

"I'm not sure I can live without you either," he said. "But our timing was off. It's just the way it is. It's just the way things turned out. Now let's go."

He met Cabrera's eyes through the window and nodded. Then his partner opened the passenger door, unbuckled Laura's seat belt, and helped her get to her feet. Matt popped open the trunk and grabbed the shaving kit, the Glock 20, and Hughes's laptop computer.

"Here's the murder weapon, Lieutenant. Inside the shaving kit you'll find everything Hughes was carrying on the night she killed him."

In spite of the fact that Matt had given both Cabrera and McKensie a quick heads-up text message more than half an hour ago from the bathroom off the kitchen, they were staring at him and still appeared to be deeply shaken by the new reality. The new way. When Matt handed over the computer, his lieutenant's voice was low and imbued with emotion.

"What did you find on the laptop?"

Matt paused a moment, pulling himself together. "Hughes was cheating on her," he said. "Check his e-mail. An old girlfriend from Austin. Sounds like it was going on for a long time. Sounds like he deserved some of what he got, but not all of it. I've gotta get out of here. I've gotta go."

Cabrera grasped him by the shoulder and met his eyes. "Are you okay to drive, Matt? Anything you want or need, it's done, man. Just say it."

Matt still felt like he was in a vacuum, a tin can with no air, but lied. "I'm good," he said. "Thanks."

He turned and looked back at Laura one last time, hoping that if he ever did manage to forget the things that had happened, her face wouldn't be one of them. The scent and feel of her skin. The sound of her voice. All of the things on that list of could-have-beens.

He'd fallen for her. He was all the way in with her.

He walked around the car and climbed in behind the wheel. Then he turned and watched her being taken away. When they finally vanished inside the station, he waited until the door snapped shut before rolling down the window and lighting a cigarette. Moments passed, the engine idling.

Where would he go? Who would he be with? How would he get through the night?

He took a hard pull on the cigarette. He was no longer able to think or feel. His body and mind had shut down and everything was gone. Everything was lost.

CHAPTER 60

He knew a guy.

A small-time dealer who only sold high-grade weed. Victor Colon claimed his stuff was grown about fifty miles north of the Golden Gate Bridge outside Santa Rosa. Colon worked at a café in downtown LA called the Blackbird and sold his reefer on the side. The situation was perfect. The café was hidden in the middle of a narrow alley and catered to artists and musicians who wanted to relax without being hassled. Matt had discovered the place through Colon when he worked narcotics. He liked the mood of the Blackbird, the art on the walls, the books on the shelves, the view of downtown, and the fact that almost everyone sitting at the tables whispered as if they were in a library. There was a certain reverence for the place. A certain level of comfort that he couldn't get anywhere else.

But even more than that, Matt liked the coffee. The Blackbird Café brewed the best cup of coffee he had ever tasted. And he really needed a decent cup of coffee right now. He needed to relax without being hassled. He needed everything to slow down.

He walked in but didn't see Colon behind the counter. After ordering a medium French roast with two sugars, he passed through the café and stepped out onto the terrace, where he could look at the city and smoke. Unfortunately, he wasn't alone. A woman was sitting three tables away. Even worse, the minute their eyes met, he sensed some degree of recognition on her face.

He sat down and tried to ignore her as best he could. The coffee was piping hot, and he took a first sip through the steam. Once he settled back in his seat, he turned to check on the woman again and found her staring at him.

He tried not to react and took another sip of coffee. As he pretended to gaze at the city, he wondered if he knew her. He guessed that she was about thirty. Her hair was light brown with blond streaks from the sun, her eyes a dusky blue, her face angular and refined. Mulling it over, he didn't think she seemed like the kind of woman anyone would forget. Even at a glance, even in this state of complete turmoil, he could tell that she had too much going on.

He tried to steal another quick look at her, but her eyes were still pinned on him. Even more troubling, he thought that she might be carrying a piece underneath her jacket.

He tried ignoring her again. He tried to imagine that she wasn't there. That she wasn't fixated on him. That she wasn't measuring him. He didn't need this. He heard her clear her throat.

"Are you okay, Jones?" she said.

A long moment passed before he finally turned and gazed at her. No doubt about it, she had a semiautomatic underneath her jacket big enough to be a .45.

"How do you know my name?" he said quietly.

She parted her jacket to reveal an LAPD badge clipped to her belt and black jeans. "Everybody knows your name. The word's out that you're the best and brightest."

He shook his head. "But I failed."

"It sure doesn't seem like it."

"Baylor's loose," he whispered in a voice riddled with despair. "He's free."

"But it's not over, Jones."

Matt lowered his gaze and turned away. He couldn't remember how the day got started. There seemed to be huge gaps in his memory. Did he make love to Laura before they got out of bed this morning or not? Did he really hear her admit to shooting Hughes? Didn't he just turn her in to his partner? Before he'd read that e-mail on Hughes's computer, before he'd read that love letter and *knew*, wasn't he a man filled with hopes and dreams and a future worth fighting for?

"You don't look so good, Jones."

Matt's eyes were wagging back and forth across the ground. "Leave me alone, lady. Please, just keep it to yourself, okay?"

He got up and staggered out, knocking over his coffee cup and spilling the hot liquid all over the table. He sensed that she had followed him out of the café. And even now, as he ran down the alley toward his car, he could feel her behind him. He needed everything to slow down. He needed everything to stop so that he could sort things out.

Who was he going to be with? Who would he talk to? Who was left?

He blinked his eyes and looked through the windshield at the traffic on the Hollywood Freeway. He wasn't sure how he'd gotten here, and the gap in time frightened him. He couldn't tell if his memory had been damaged from all the stress and anxiety, or if he might not be experiencing short blackouts while driving.

He switched on the radio. A woman had just begun introducing the next cut, "Comfortably Numb"—not from a Pink Floyd album, but from a live concert David Gilmour recorded at the Gdańsk Shipyard to commemorate the twentieth anniversary of the revolution in Poland. The concert had been videotaped, and

Matt had watched the clip on the Internet more than a handful of times.

He settled back in the seat and let Gilmour's voice sweep him away just as it always seemed to sweep him away, along with his remarkable guitar, that black Stratocaster. He listened until the music stopped, then found himself gliding into the parking lot at Griffith Observatory. He tried to pull himself together. He got out of the car and started walking up the fire road. His mouth became dry, but he could see Dante's View at the top of Mount Hollywood. He wasn't sure how much time it had taken to reach the peak, but when he spotted a bench, he sat down and gazed at the city. He could see the entire basin, from the tall buildings downtown all the way to Venice Beach.

He thought that the view from the top of the mountain would ease his pain, or at the very least give him some breathing room.

But the heat was unbearable, and he could feel the sweat evaporating as it dripped down his spine. He turned and gazed at the Hollywood sign across the way. In spite of the distance, he could see a small group of people praying over the spot where Brooke Anderson had been murdered. They were dressed in black and appeared strange.

The sight triggered a series of grim memories that made him feel even more anxious. He wondered if he wasn't in the middle of something he couldn't get out of on his own. Maybe he should drive down to Chinatown and check himself in. Maybe he should talk to somebody and get some rest. But what if they saw him this way? What would they think?

He heard something and his mind floated to the surface. It was a popping sound, and he saw a man running down the fire road. As his brain fog lifted, Matt realized that it was Billy Casper, the man in his rearview mirror, rushing toward him with his .38 still hot and smoking in his right hand.

Matt swept his fingers across his shirt, then looked down at the blood splashing onto his jeans. He'd been hit twice in the gut. He tried to get to his feet, but his legs wouldn't move. When he reached for his .45, Casper beat him to it and tossed the pistol on the ground. His eyes rose to Casper's face. The big man had an even bigger grin, stretching from ear to ear, as he grabbed Matt by the shoulders and threw him off the bench.

"Your father sends his best," he said. "Fuck you, you piece of shit."

Casper aimed the .38 at Matt's chest and pulled the trigger. Matt felt his entire body shudder as he took the bullet and groaned. Casper was laughing at him and hurrying off.

He turned and searched for his pistol. It was just out of reach, a foot or two ahead, but he couldn't move his legs. He rolled onto his stomach, digging his elbows into the dirt road and dragging his lame body forward. When the pain rocked through him from deep inside, he screamed out in agony. He gritted his teeth, glancing back at Casper. Then he dug his elbows into the ground and pulled his body another half foot forward.

That feeling was back. He was watching himself from a distance again. He could see himself grasping his .45 and rolling onto his side. He could see Casper's sweat-stained shirt just beyond the muzzle. He watched himself pulling the trigger and clicking through the mag until all the noise stopped. Until all eight rounds had found their home in the big man's back. And then it was over. Casper's body went limp and started tumbling down the steep hill.

Matt watched the corpse hit the rocks and settle in a patch of thorns.

The pistol fell out of his hand, and he rolled onto his back. He could feel himself hyperventilating. When the pain came back even harder, he took it this time. He ate it and winced.

He glanced at the three wounds in his chest, all the blood gushing out, and knew that his father would be pleased. He wondered where he'd be when he received news of his first son's death. Maybe aboard his yacht, the *Greedy Bastard*, out of Greenwich, Connecticut. Or maybe on the terrace sipping wine with his cheap-looking wife and their twisted sons.

A shadow moved across his face. Someone was standing over him. He wondered if he had already died. He wondered if it wasn't the undertaker, preparing to drain his body of what little blood he might have left. He blinked his eyes again. He couldn't be dead. Death wasn't supposed to hurt like this.

The figure stepped closer, then knelt down beside him. After a while he realized that it was the woman from the Blackbird Café. She had blood all over her hands and blouse, and she seemed upset. She was on her cell phone. Every few moments she would look into Matt's eyes and say, "Hold on, Jones. Hold on and everything will be okay."

Matt looked her over when it suddenly dawned on him that he knew her. He'd met her once in the elevator at the crime lab. Her name was Lena Gamble, a detective out of the Robbery-Homicide Division. She'd closed a big case last year—two prosecutors in the district attorney's office had turned, and she put one of them down. The case made headlines for six months.

He knew her. He'd met her.

He gave her a long look.

She seemed so far away. He could barely see her. He could barely hear her. He felt his head drop back. Images began flashing through his mind. The moments he had spent sitting on his mother's lap before she died. The relief he had felt when his aunt welcomed him into her home. A day he spent with Hughes in Afghanistan when they didn't hear a single gunshot. Just the sounds of the people, the stillness of the mountains and plains. The last time he and Laura kissed—the good-bye kiss he had given her in the study when he realized what had to happen and why.

He tried to swallow but couldn't.

He guessed that he was losing it. He could feel a hard wind churning up all the dust from the dirt road. He could see Gamble shielding her eyes and face, the dust cloud so dense that she almost disappeared. Even more, there was this roaring noise, this rushing noise, the sound of rotors—all of it becoming louder and louder, until he couldn't hear Gamble's voice anymore.

He looked up at the sky. A bird flew by. The sun seemed so bright.

ACKNOWLEDGMENTS

Many thanks go to my editors, Kjersti Egerdahl, Charlotte Herscher, and Marcus Trower, and to the entire team at Thomas & Mercer and Amazon. I'd also like to thank my agent, Scott Miller, for his advice and support. This novel wouldn't feel authentic and true without the help of many good friends. Much thanks go to LAPD detectives Mitzi Roberts and Rick Jackson (retired) from the Robbery-Homicide Division, Cold Case Special Section. And to Charlotte Conway, Peter Ellis, Neil Oxman, Mark Moskowitz, and "Wild" Bill Carey. In the end, this is a work of fiction. Any technical deviation from facts or procedures is my responsibility alone.

ABOUT THE AUTHOR

Photo © 2015 Charlotte Conway

Robert Ellis is the international bestselling author of *Access to Power*, *The Dead Room*, and the critically acclaimed Lena Gamble Novels. His books have been translated into more than ten languages and selected as top reads by *Booklist*, *Publishers Weekly*, National Public Radio, the *Chicago Tribune*, the *Toronto Sun*, the *Guardian* (UK), the *Evening Telegraph* (UK), *People* magazine, *USA Today*, and the *New York Times*. Born in Philadelphia, Ellis moved to Los Angeles to work as a writer, producer, and director in film, television, and advertising.

For more information about Robert Ellis, visit him online at www.robertellis.net.